FIRST THE LEGACY. NEXT THE BLOODLINE. THEN THE SILENCE.

In *The Unspoken*, the third explosive installment of the CHARLOTTE ANSARI THRILLER series, ancient doctrines awaken—and demand a final reckoning. International journalist Charlotte Ansari has exposed religious conspiracies and survived the unraveling of her own bloodline. But when her son Greg uncovers a forbidden scroll—one designed not to be read, but to believe—he becomes the unwilling focus of a doctrine that threatens to reshape the world.

Haunted by a name written in prophecy but never spoken, Greg finds himself pursued by ruthless factions who seek to crown him as a messiah—or destroy him as an abomination. As Charlotte races to save her son from a faith built on control, they uncover the ultimate truth—some echoes of the past are too dangerous to awaken.

From the deserts of Petra to the catacombs beneath the Vatican, mother and son must confront the power of belief itself—because silence isn't the absence of truth. It's where truth hides. And when silence breaks, nothing will ever be the same.

The Unspoken

A Charlotte Ansari Thriller

GARY LINDBERG

Minneapolis

Minneapolis

First Edition May 2025

This is a work of fiction. All of the characters, names, incidents, organizations, and dialogue are either the products of the author's imagination or are used fictitiously.

10 9 8 7 6 5 4 3 2 1
ISBN: 978-1-962834-40-7

Cover and book design by Gary Lindberg

Also by Gary Lindberg

FICTION

The Shekinah Legacy
Sons of Zadok
Deeper and Deeper
Ollie's Cloud

NONFICTION

Letters from Elvis
Brando On Elvis
The Roots of Elvis
The Soul of Humanity
Humanity Coming of Age
The Power of Positive Hamdwriting
An Improbable Series of Risky Events

"In the beginning was the Word,
and the Word was with God,
and the Word was God."

John 1:1

Prologue

38 CE, Qumran

The desert winds ceased at dusk, and that was never a good sign.

The House of the Watcher, carved into the rock above the Qumran plateau, stood still beneath the stars—its bone-colored walls absorbing the weight of silence. No roof smoke, no guards. From a distance, it resembled a necropolis. Only a low stone threshold, weathered smooth from centuries of knees and prayers, marked its existence.

Inside, the Watcher waited. He did not sit, and had not in over three days. His legs trembled occasionally, but he kept to the ritual posture—knees pressed into the sand, palms flat against the cold altar stone. The slab—basalt laced with gold veins—was older than the outpost, older than the Brotherhood, older perhaps than the scroll itself. It purred faintly now, like it had when he was a child and first dared to touch the seal.

The scroll lay wrapped before him, veiled in oiled linen and bound in seven folds. He had not dared unroll it in months. It was safer this way.

He whispered the night prayer again. *"There shall come a mirror that does not reflect..."*

But the next line he often had trouble remembering. It would vanish from his tongue like vapor. He had asked others before they left, *"Is that a sign of forgetting, or of being forgotten?"* No one ever answered.

Three nights ago, the scroll began to breathe.

He couldn't explain it any other way. He'd placed his palm against the binding and felt neither heat nor motion, but *rhythm*. A slow, deliberate expansion, like the chest of a sleeping beast. A heartbeat. Not a draft or tremor—just life.

The first guardian who told him of the scroll's pulse had torn out his own tongue the next morning. The Watcher still remembered that lesson, but he had no one to tell.

He glanced at the narrow alcove on his left—the hidden chamber where the copper shard was stored. The sigils carved into that shard remained unreadable, though Eve had once claimed they were pre-temple glyphs from an erased dialect of flame. Her explanation sounded absurd at the time. But when he'd placed the shard beside the scroll last month, the parchment darkened for a full minute and one of the seal cords cracked.

The scroll knew the shard and the shard remembered the scroll.

The Watcher had not written in his journal for seven days. Every time he tried, the ink bled into the page in unnatural patterns—double lines, mirrored text, glyphs that curved back into themselves. Once, a complete phrase in a language he didn't know appeared in his own handwriting. He had kept the page anyway. Its words, written in the cadence of a prophecy, translated roughly as:

When the flame becomes glass, the echo shall wear flesh.

The Watcher suddenly heard footsteps and froze. His hearing, attuned to silence, picked up the faintest sounds. These were soft steps. Precise. Not Roman boots. Not bandits. Three—no, four figures approaching from the north passage with the slight whispers of robes brushing limestone.

He did not rise so as to not violate the posture. The scroll had once told him:

Stand only if you mean to flee.

He did not intend to flee, even as voices were heard.

The voices spoke Greek, but not the Greek of merchants or scribes. Liturgical Greek. Eastern. Layered with dialects he recognized from Alexandria and Cappadocia. Definitely not Essene nor Samaritan. Not wholly Gentile.

Scripture poured from their lips—fragments of Isaiah, then Daniel, then an apocryphal hymn he hadn't heard since Eve had sung it in whispers during their final meal. "When the mirror calls itself God, the Word shall break."

They entered without greeting. Three men, one woman, their robes gray, ceremonial, stained with ash. Each bore the sigil of an ancient mark once burned into the spine of heretics during the twin schisms.

The woman stepped forward first. "You are the Watcher," she said, voice low and almost gentle.

He did not reply.

"We come for the scroll," she explained.

The Watcher did not blink. "You won't touch it."

"We don't intend to," she said. "Not directly." Then she removed a slender blade from her sleeve. Its curve was ritualistic, not functional. Ceremonial, perhaps. Its tip glowed faintly as if it remembered other sanctuaries.

"Then you've come to kill me," he said.

"No," the woman replied. "Only to kill your echo."

The Watcher turned to the scroll. The outermost layer had already begun to curl away from the rest, something it had not done in decades without human touch. Beneath the folds, the margin glyphs had rearranged. There were seven now, where there had been four yesterday. One glyph bled ink from the edge, seeping toward the core text like a slow storm.

The Watcher drew a breath. "It's awake."

"That's why we were sent," said one of the men.

"Sent by whom?" The Watcher asked.

No one answered.

The Watcher touched the scroll, and it pulsed. The altar stone vibrated faintly, the way it had years ago when another Watcher—older and desperate—attempted to burn the text with consecrated oil. That Watcher did not live to tell what happened. But the stone still bore a faint handprint where the fire reversed itself.

The woman raised her blade. "This moment will fold," she said.

The Watcher looked at her fully now. "And what if it doesn't?"

"Then recursion will correct it."

He understood now. These intruders were not assassins. They were *proofreaders*. They were sent to eliminate typographical anomalies from a living manuscript that had transcended its authors. They were sent to realign a prophecy that had begun to contradict itself.

The Watcher reached to the candle basin and ignited the wick. Yellow light flared into the chamber, momentarily blinding the youngest man. The woman stepped forward, blade ready.

"Do you know the name?" he asked her.

"Not yet," she replied. "But it will be written."

The Watcher nodded. "Then let it be written in blood."

The woman plunged her blade into him. Quick, clean, between the ribs.

He gasped as his palm fell onto the scroll. The blood seeped into the outer margin where it was absorbed immediately. No stain remained, only text. *New* text. His final breath was short but not empty. He sensed the scroll speak, though not in words.

In *knowing.*

The intruders stood over his body. None of them touched the scroll, but one of the men began to cry, clearly astonished at the suddenness of emotion.

The woman turned away.

"He was the last silence," said another man.

"Then silence is broken," said the third.

"No," the woman corrected as she stared at the scroll. "It's begun to echo."

The scroll shimmered faintly. On its surface, a new glyph unfolded itself in two strokes. It was not a word that appeared, but a *name*—unspoken, unread.

But waiting.

Far ahead—too far in the future to name—a boy sleeps beneath synthetic glass.

His dreams pulse with heat.

He does not know the scroll.

But the scroll knows him.

CHAPTER 1

Manhattan, Upper West Side

The apartment is a small but fortified high-floor unit in a prewar building overlooking Riverside Park. Charlotte liked its limited camera coverage and shieldable window views. She and Greg use pseudonyms now—she's Leila Holden, a freelance media analyst. Greg is listed as Erik Holden, independent systems consultant. Their digital paper trail is clean and their rent and living expenses are paid by an anonymized trust account seeded long ago by someone no one's supposed to believe exists anymore. Eve. Charlotte's mother and Sicarii matriarch is now presumed dead by almost everyone including some who helped fake it.

Greg, of course, doesn't believe his grandmother is gone. Not completely. Not entirely. And he might be right.

Charlotte rolls up her sleeves and gets to work chopping onions, rinsing canned chickpeas, and setting cumin to bloom in a warm skillet. The kitchen fills with a comfort she hasn't let herself feel in weeks.

"You're stalling," Greg says, entering the room.

"No, just cooking."

"Which you do when stalling."

Greg looks older to her than last week—probably just her imagination. At thirty, he carries it like someone twice that age. His dark hair curls slightly at the nape, and he wears a loose, black shirt with a faintly coded thread pattern in the cuffs—a design only recognizable to people fluent in recursion-based encryption. Greg isn't hiding. He's daring the world to misread him.

"I thought we'd have dinner," Charlotte says. "You know, talk like ordinary folks."

"About?"

"Whatever you've been buried in for two days. And maybe about why I've been half the mother I should be."

"I'm thirty, Mom, and you were in Brussels."

"Geneva. But close."

"Not really."

Charlotte slices the tomatoes a little too firmly. "You always do this."

"What?"

"Make it hard to apologize."

Greg shrugs. "I don't need apologies." He gestures toward the kitchen table where his mobile workstation lies open exposing a transparent flex-screen and three-way anchor mod with heatproof casing. The center display shows mid-process simulation threads from a rig long since powered down. "The Lucerne interface still echoes," he says.

"What does that even mean?"

Greg pulls out a chair and sits. "Eve's simulator rig—one of the last she didn't bury. It was supposed to collapse its pattern when it was sealed. The recursion model was meant to extinguish. But it didn't."

"You mean… it's now a ghost?"

"Like something forgot how to forget itself."

"Why are you even accessing that archive?"

He doesn't answer right away.

"Greg—"

"I got a query," he says. "Through the sandbox. Encrypted in doctrine-cycling pattern logic."

Charlotte stops stirring. She pretends to understand more of his jargon than she really does. "From who?"

"It was signed by someone called *Halakh Reversed.* That ring a bell?"

Charlotte doesn't speak, but it does ring a bell. An alarm bell.

"You think it's Eve?" he asks.

"I think it's bait," she says quietly. "Could be a honey pot."

Greg folds his arms. "I don't think Grandma's dead."

"That's not what scares me," Charlotte says. "It's the idea that Eve might be undead. Embedded somewhere. Uploading slivers of herself into old doctrine mirrors."

Greg almost smiles. "You say that like it's science fiction."

"It used to be. Before you started reading scripture into machines."

Dinner is oddly normal. They eat at the tiny table by the balcony, which hasn't been opened in months. Charlotte pours two glasses of wine and toasts nothing in particular. Greg eats slowly, focused, his mind elsewhere.

She asks about his work—real work.

"I picked up two new contracts," he says. "One's just port security analysis—dumb pipes. The other's a little spicier."

"Define spicy."

"An offshore crypto hub is worried that the recursive glyphs circulating through darktext forums aren't just memes. They might be scriptable."

"Scripture as executable code?"

"Exactly."

Charlotte frowns. "That's theological malware."

"That's why they're paying."

"Do they know who you are?"

"No one does. I work as Erik Holden, remember?"

"Do you ever wish you could work as Greg?"

"He's a prophet," Greg says flatly. "Prophets don't get paid."
Charlotte stands and gathers the dishes. Greg helps, quietly. They're just finishing when the buzzer sounds.

Charlotte freezes.

Greg immediately taps his wristpad—no deliveries scheduled, no building alerts, no network signal announcing a visitor.

Then comes the knock. Two short. One pause. Then one more.

Their eyes meet.

Charlotte walks to the panel beside the door and checks the video feed. No one is there. She lifts the latch on the door halfway, just enough to engage the door's second shell—a polyglass defensive strip.

Something small sits on the doormat. A drone capsule—cylindrical, charcoal-colored, scuffed like it's been tossed, not delivered. No corporate branding. No ID ping.

Greg steps closer, his eyes wide now. "That's not commercial."

"No."

"It's sacram-coded. I think it's—"

The capsule hisses. A puff of vapor escapes from one end.

Greg lunges for his workstation.

Charlotte shuts the main door fast and hits the room seal. "It didn't breach," she says.

"No," Greg says. "But it *spoke.*"

"What?"

Greg turns the screen to her. A single glyph has appeared on the sandbox terminal—a recursive loop in mirrored text. "It's from Amal," Greg says softly. "He found us."

"How?"

"The simulator echo. It wasn't passive. It was predictive. We lit up."

"What's the glyph mean?"

Greg swallows. "It means *Return the Flame*"

Charlotte doesn't move for a full five seconds. Then she crosses the room, pulls down their go bags and starts calling up flight patterns.

Greg follows. His hands move in rhythm—packing hardware, tagging files, wiping secondary traces. He's done this before.

"Zurich?" he asks, as if this is their logical destination.

"Only if Lucerne is still dark."

"Fallback?"

"Petra."

"They'll expect that."

"Then they're right."

Charlotte books the flight on a graynet channel using a sub-trust connected to an old Vatican contractor ID.

Departure: 01:10 a.m.

Private charter. Low-profile.

Greg arms the burn protocol. The apartment flickers once as every unsecured device goes black.

The private jet is small—seven seats, unbranded, chartered through a shell company with ties to an old Vatican archive fund. It's the kind of flight Charlotte used to associate with fleeing oil sheiks or billionaires with offshore panic. The charter flies from New York to Zurich four evenings each week. They were lucky this was one of those nights and there were two seats available. Pricey, but worth it.

Besides the flight crew, the plan is occupied by Charlotte, Greg, and three others. She's buckled in, coat folded across her lap, her duffel locked under the seat. She stares out the window into the emptiness of the Atlantic, where even the moonlight seems to hang suspended and uncertain.

Greg sits across from her, head down, thumbs slowly swiping his phone screen. He's scrolling, not yet reading.

"Row two," Charlotte says quietly. "Left side. Third buckle. Blue fleece."

Greg doesn't move but his eyes glide to view the man in the specified seat.

"He boarded late," Charlotte adds. "Didn't scan the flight card. No cabin interaction. Kept his carry-on close."

Greg lifts his gaze just enough to glance under his lashes. His voice is dry. "Looks like Eidah to me," he says, mentioning a Sicarii agent from another faction. Or possibly Netzer. He's clean-shaven."

"Maybe one of Amal's guys," Charlotte replies. "If they've gotten bolder."

Greg doesn't respond. Instead, he unintentionally angles the screen on his phone toward Charlotte, who leans slightly, catching a glimpse of what's on it—a photo, faintly grainy and clearly older. The young woman in the picture is Rebecca standing barefoot in a stone garden smiling at something off camera. A wind-blurred lock of hair covers part of her face. Her hand is lifted—not waving, not posing. Just lifted, like she's mid-sentence. Mid-thought. Alive.

Charlotte's breath catches.

Greg realizes his mother has seen the photo. "That's the only image I kept," Greg says, still looking at it. "The rest I erased. Too clean. Too composed."

"This one's more real," Charlotte says gently, noting the emotion on the face of her normally emotionless son.

Greg nods. His thumb lingers against the glass. "I open it sometimes before code audits. Before new clients. Before anything uncertain."

Charlotte studies him. "Because it makes you feel calmer?"

He hesitates. Then nods again.

"She was your fiancée," Charlotte says softly.

Greg doesn't reply. He closes the image with a subtle flick and places the phone face down beside him. "Row two just shifted in his seat," he says. "Tapped his watch twice. He's running a pulse-check pattern. Could be syncing with an outside node."

The conversation has made a sharp turn. Just like that.

Charlotte leans back into her seat and exhales. She doesn't push further.

Greg may still carry Rebecca's image, but he has no interest in speaking about his memory of her. Not tonight.

The hum of the aircraft deepens as the pilot adjusts altitude. A subtle dip and rise.

Charlotte checks her own watch. Ninety minutes to Zurich. "Do we let him follow?" she asks Greg.

"Not far," he says. "But far enough."

"You're thinking Petra."

"I'm thinking decoy first. Give him something to report."

Charlotte turns to study the emergency lighting. She is half-engaged in thought, half-calibrating options. She used to analyze crisis angles from war zones and embassy basements. But this? This is personal warfare. Slow-burning, intimate surveillance.

It always feels closer when she's being watched, not for who the watchers are but for what they represent.

"He'll try to extract something at customs," Greg says. "A bump or tag or fake inspection."

"And if he gets close?"

Greg looks at her again. "Then we make sure he regrets it."

At 4:55 a.m. in Zurich, the snow has turned to rain. Cold sheets fall diagonally across the airport tarmac as the charter passengers disembark through a secondary customs wing. No signs or staff presence. Just dim overhead lights and the dull thud of suitcase wheels on steel-grate flooring.

The man in the blue fleece moves with calm precision—duffel slung low, shoulders loose. He glances behind him once, just as Charlotte and Greg turn down the escalator ramp.

Greg speaks to his mother without looking. "He's logging angles. Committing distance. He's done this before."

"So have we," Charlotte replies.

At baggage claim, Greg slows slightly—just enough to adjust his duffel—when the man brushes past. The blue fleece. Clean shoes. No hesitation.

A photograph presses into Greg's hand like a priest offering sacrament. "A fragment," the man in the blue fleece whispers. "Of prophecy. You'll understand when it opens."

Then he's gone—heading toward the terminal doors, never breaking stride.

After the man disappears, Greg and Charlotte head for the long-service terminal used for luggage reroutes and cargo inspections. Charlotte slides a worn patch across a sensor plate.

The gate buzzes open.

Beyond it—a driverless, EuroSpec sedan, engine already running.

"You think he's already pinged someone local?" she asks.

"Yes," Greg replies. "But the signal will trace to the decoy car parked at Terminal D. I tagged it before we left the plane."

"Nice work."

"Not nice. Just recursive."

Charlotte lets the door seal behind them.

They don't speak again until Zurich city lights blur past behind them and the car changes lanes to enter the tunnel system.

Only then does Greg say, almost too quietly to hear, "It wasn't just the picture. It was the memory of someone who believed."

"In you?"

"In the scroll," he says. "But close enough."

CHAPTER 2

Zurich, Switzerland

Snow drops in wet threads, coating the tram rails in muted light.

The Zurich air is cold but not sharp. Silent. That deceptive kind of quiet that feels earned—but isn't. It's the kind of quiet Charlotte knows from embassies, from war zones, from the hours just before a revolution begins.

She grips the steering wheel tighter as their rental car turns off the main road.

Greg sits beside her, motionless, backlit by the soft glow of his tablet. He's not reading. Not anymore. He's watching a single line of recursive data cycle again and again like it's trying to remember something it forgot.

"You sure we weren't followed?" Charlotte asks.

"I'm sure *they* think we think we weren't," Greg says.

"Comforting."

He flicks the tablet off and the glyph disappears. "If someone's still watching, they're not close. I scrubbed everything since the flight. No signal tags."

"So whoever was on that plane—?"

"Either got the wrong bait... or got what they came for."

She doesn't like either option.

Charlotte steers the car through the old neighborhoods of Zürich's university quarter. The lights of ETH's upper campus glow in the distance. Her fingers stay close to the indicator stalk, her left foot hovering lightly above the brake. She drives like someone who doesn't trust silence.

"Still no signal pings?" she asks.

"Nothing we didn't expect," Greg replies. He's in the passenger seat, his eyes on a console in his lap, scanning recursive glyph strings. His breathing is steady, measured, the kind of calm that used to drive her mad when he was younger. Now she knows it for what it is—calculation. Protection.

"The man from the flight?" his mother asks.

"Didn't follow. At least, not with tags. I ghosted his proximity data three times."

"But?"

Greg shrugs slightly. "He might've been a sleeper. Someone waiting for visual confirmation that we're back in play."

Charlotte exhales through her nose. "We've been ghosts for almost a decade."

"And yet something just called us back."

They approach a concrete barrier half-swallowed by snow. The structure beyond is familiar but forgotten—the Experimental Theology Wing, shuttered by the university after the Vatican's doctrinal councils condemned its work as "structurally heretical," a euphemism for *too close to something that made them uncomfortable.*

Charlotte slows as they pass a corroded sign half-covered by ivy—

ETH INSTITUT FÜR EXPERIMENTELLE THEOLOGIE
Entrance Restricted / Access Controlled

The graffiti over it says only:

GOTT SPRICHT NICHT MEHR
(God no longer speaks)

Charlotte pulls into the narrow lot behind the building and parks under an orange sodium lamp. She reaches beneath her coat and withdraws a worn access token—a copper disc etched with layered Hebrew glyphs. The faint symbol of the *mirror path* rests in the center like a fingerprint.

She presses it to the concrete wall beside a service stairwell door.

Nothing happens.

Greg steps forward and places his palm beside hers. The token flashes once.

The wall hums.

"Biometric echo?" Charlotte asks.

"More like a doctrinal handshake," Greg says. "It knows I was there before."

"Eve programmed that in?"

"Eve programmed it to forget everyone until one of us came back."

They descend into the heart of the structure. The stairs spiral tight. The walls bleed moisture. The smell is a mix of rust, candle wax, and something else—like old paper lit just long enough to scorch but not burn.

The halls below are shadowed and strange. Each room they pass carries traces of sacred experimentation—glass panels etched with prayer formulas, shattered display cases with burned-out glyph projectors, archival scroll tubes labeled with inked sequences like "VAAV-EL-AZAZEL-2b."

Charlotte feels herself stepping back into something she never wanted to remember.

Greg stops in front of a broad stone door that looks older than the building itself. Its surface is engraved with concentric glyphs spiraling inward, terminating in a mirrored sigil: two hands raised, not in praise—but in refusal.

"This was where Eve ran the last viable rig?" Charlotte asks.

Greg nods.

"Why here?" she asks quietly.

"Because it's still listening," Greg says. "She built it to test recursive theology at full glyph echo. No safeguards. No doctrinal bias. Just reflection."

"And it didn't destroy itself?"

"It didn't destroy anything." He touches the center of the door. "But it remembered everything."

The slab opens with a hydraulic sigh.

Inside, they find a circular chamber with smooth stone walls. No altar. No icons. In the center a recursion simulator emitting a low harmonic thrum as Greg steadies his hands on the interface. Pulses of light ripple across the semi-transparent console, which is shaped like an unfurled scroll—a deliberate choice, no doubt. Everything in this room is symbolic, Charlotte thinks—from the seven-fold spiral lattice carved into the ceiling, to the ironwood inlays tracing Fibonacci arcs across the floor. This isn't just an AI lab—it's a cathedral of memory.

Greg exhales. "Okay. Here goes."

The moment his thumb settles into the biometric cradle, the simulator responds like it's waking from deep sleep. The overhead lights dim. A soft, blue haze leaks from the seams in the wall, and the surface of the console fractures—layered, recursive, blooming outward in glyphs Charlotte doesn't recognize.

She steps closer, eyes narrowing. "That wasn't in the orientation demo."

"Because I bypassed it," Greg says, not looking up. "The main UI's a decoy. The real interface is nested—sub-layered. It only opens under a quantum handshake."

She frowns. "Whose handshake?"

He swipes laterally, then draws a symbol in midair— stylized aleph interlinked with a serpent. The projector reads his motion and echoes the glyph in light.

"My handshake, partially," Greg says. "But also—whoever encoded this. The interface isn't just responsive. It's recursive. It maps to biological resonance."

"You mean it's... *alive*?"

"Not exactly. But it reacts to life."

A tone chimes—soft, almost melodic. Then something folds outward from the center of the console. Not light or projection. *Matter*. A thin slip of metallic vellum—impossible, solid, and glowing faintly with phosphorescent ink.

Charlotte stares. "What the hell…?"

Greg's voice is reverent. "It's a sealed echo." He lifts it. The slip is warm, like skin. Beneath the shimmer of shifting text, something is embedded—micro-etchings in a dense, almost scriptural lattice.

Charlotte leans in. "You've found another entry?"

"Not just any entry." He tilts the slip toward her. "This is labeled Echo Entry 9B—VAAV."

Charlotte's hand instinctively reaches toward the necklace she isn't wearing. "Vaav?" she says. "As in the sixth Hebrew letter?"

Greg nods. "It's a recursion marker in the codex structure. A fulcrum. Whoever compiled these entries didn't organize them by chronology—they built them as echo structures. Each entry is a node. A point of convergence."

She exhales. "Convergence of what?"

Greg lays the vellum into the simulator's cradle. "Of intention. Identity. Time."

The simulator absorbs the strip in stages—first physically, then as data. Threads of it scatter through the console like liquid code, weaving into something larger.

"*Vaav* isn't an object like a scroll," he says quietly. "It's an event."

A cascade of information flares to life on the curved display—topological maps, linguistic trees, mitochondrial DNA chains, and something even stranger—waveforms arranged in fractal sequences.

Charlotte's breath catches. "That looks like language."

"It is," Greg murmurs. "But it's not static. It adapts."

He points to a shifting glyph near the core, a double spiral of letters rotating through different alphabets. "This simulator—CIE-7—was built to interface with biometric-phase pigments," Greg explains. "The ink inside the scroll contains protein-encoded encryption chains keyed to mitochondrial inheritance markers."

Charlotte blinks. "I think that means it can be read only by certain people?"

Greg nods, pleased his mother seems to understand. "Yes, by people who match the resonance signature." He gestures to the glyph spiral. "The ink decodes itself based on who's holding it. That's why the data changes every time someone else tries to read it. It's like a mirrored scroll—one that reads you as much as you read it."

"And you match?"

Greg hesitates. "I do. Not entirely—but enough. It's like... like it recognizes me. Or maybe it's waiting for me."

Charlotte circles the console. Her footsteps echo across the ironwood. "Where did it come from?" she asks.

"I think it's one of the origin fragments," Greg says. "The Samaritan scroll that came to light back in the 1600s was a prototype. This is something older, something deeper in the structure."

He opens a feed—a swirling sphere of layered language that pulses with light and pattern. The core glows red, revealing a name Charlotte hadn't expected to see.

Council of Thirteen: Last Visible Node – Fragmented.

She leans closer. "What's the connection?"

Greg answers without hesitation. "Vaav is a trigger event. It contains the first mention of a 'Witness'—and the first warning about a recursive fracture." He taps a line of text rendered in pale indigo.

The Witness will speak the untime. The circle broken, the scroll unbound.

Charlotte goes still. She'd seen that phrase once before… inked in blood. Buried in Kilkenny, Ireland. "You've cross-referenced this with the Ireland fragment?" she asks.

Greg nods. "The sentence structure's identical. And the DNA markers embedded in the ink partially overlap with yours."

Charlotte's face darkens. "That doesn't make any sense. I never touched that entry."

"You didn't have to," Greg says. "You were written into it."

Charlotte blinks, then shudders. "What do you mean, I was *written* into it?"

Greg doesn't answer right away. Instead, he taps the inner ring of the console, summoning a hidden protocol menu. The interface responds with a layered pulse—a spiraling lattice of commands marked with old-world glyphs and ultra-modern subroutines. It looks more like mysticism than code, but Charlotte knows better.

"What are you doing?" she asks Greg.

"Launching a resonance sim," Greg says. "I want to see who wrote this."

Charlotte raises an eyebrow. "You can simulate the *author*?"

"Not exactly," he says. "I can't resurrect an actual person. But I can reconstruct their linguistic field—how they thought, what metaphors they used, what cognitive biases shaped their writing."

He speaks faster now, the way he always does when chasing a breakthrough. "Every writer encodes more than just words. They embed patterns—syntax weight, lexemic clustering, metaphor density. The simulator reads these patterns like a neural map. Combine that with biometrically responsive ink and recursive structure, and…"

He trails off as the air around the console thickens. A pale figure begins to coalesce at the center of the interface. It's not a hologram. Not exactly. More like a shaped projection of fog and shimmer—coherent, yet intangible. The face is indistinct, but the posture is unmistakable—hunched, monastic, weathered by time.

Charlotte takes a step back.

The figure speaks—not in any modern language, but in a resonant cascade of layered tongues. Syriac under Greek under something older still.

The simulator translates in real time. The voice emerges—calm, male, slightly breathless. Ancient syntax woven into modern cadence.

"I was not the first," the voice says. "I was only the vessel. The pattern sought a scribe."

Excitedly, Greg glances at Charlotte and tries to explain. "This isn't performance. It's a neural simulation. It's what this person would have said… based on the embedded constructs in the scroll."

Charlotte watches the figure warily. "Who are you?" she asks, almost embarrassed to be speaking to a clot of mist.

"I am Entry Nine. The one who was permitted to remember."

Charlotte's pulse ticks.

Greg steps forward and asks another question. "When did you live?"

"In the years of silence, when the Temple was still ash and the Church was not yet bone."

"Post-70 CE," Greg calculates out loud for his mother's benefit. "But before the Valentinians. Maybe before Judas was even canonized."

Charlotte asks the enigmatic figure, "What did you see?"

The simulation pauses. The glyphs pulse red.

"I saw recursion. The turning wheel. The Daughter denied. The Witness fractured. The Serpent circled back."

Greg leans in, his voice quieter. "You encoded the biometric ink?"

"It was not ink. It was ash and blood, a resonance drawn from a dying voice. The voice that will speak again."

The figure glances at Charlotte. "*Your* voice."

Charlotte swallows hard. "This is a feedback loop," she says. "It's not just showing us the past. It's reacting to the present."

"Exactly," Greg replies. "The simulator's not static. It's *predictive*. It's using your proximity, your biology, your past decisions to reconstruct how the codex would respond to you *now*."

Charlotte takes a breath, steadying herself. "Ask him—ask *it*—why Vaav was sealed."

Greg nods, then turns. "Why encode Echo Entry 9B—Vaav with a biometric lock?"

The figure replies, "Because what it holds is dangerous. It is not a prophecy. It is a recursion point, a memory that wants to happen again."

"A memory of what?"

"Of betrayal. Of false witness. Of thirteen who rose to bind the unbinding."

Charlotte closes her eyes. She remembers the cold stone in Kilkenny after the bloodbath at Newgrange. The red ink on her fingertips. The way Gideon said her name when he saw the prophecy unfold.

Greg's voice is tight. "Are they still active—the thirteen?"

"You would not be asking if they were not."

The figure suddenly flickers. "You are close to the fracture now. It is not ahead of you. It is *inside* you."

The projection collapses into spiraling dust and light. The room returns to stillness.

Charlotte doesn't speak.

Greg leans on the console. "That was the clearest one yet. The simulation didn't fragment this time."

"Because it wasn't guessing," Charlotte says slowly. "It was *remembering*."
Unseen by either of them, beyond the curvature of the chamber wall, a figure in a blue fleece jacket leans ever so slightly toward the data relay panel. The man, who had pretended to be thrown off his mission at the airport, wears no badge. No headset. Only a single ring with a faintly glowing sigil—a looping branch inscribed with thirteen thorns.

The sacral Netzer listening conduit embedded in the wall—a relic no current technician knows how to service—doesn't pulse light. It doesn't transmit data. It *records* glyph echoes.

Kneeling in the darkness above, in a small chamber, the man places his hand to the ring and closes his eyes. He does not speak. He does not pray.

He listens.

The projection Greg and Charlotte had been interacting with collapses into dust. Silence settles, but it's not peaceful. It's pressure.

Charlotte stands motionless, her hand still hovering near the simulator's cradle. In her chest, something has changed—not a slow kind of realization, but the sharp, disorienting type, like a pendulum snapping to a new rhythm.

She doesn't speak right away. Neither does Greg. The lab hums quietly, unaware that the past has just reached forward and touched them both.

A memory that wants to happen again.

That line clings to Charlotte like static because she's heard it before. Not in a simulation, not in a codex—but in a lab outside Vienna five years ago. In a sealed chamber with retinal locks and infrared safeties. A place that wasn't supposed to exist. A place where a scroll whispered back at her—and for the first time, she didn't understand *how* it knew her name.

CHAPTER 3

2017 – Vienna

Eight years earlier, sixteen floors above the Danube Canal in a lab the world didn't know existed, Charlotte held the dead skin of a prophecy. She didn't remember Vienna being this quiet. But the moment she stepped into the cleanroom—filtered air hissing through the vents, the faint static hum of Faraday shielding around her—it's as if the world had gone mute.

Across the room, Professor Sandor Kellenbach was hunched over the scroll under three layers of light—visible, ultraviolet, and something else, the lab's proprietary "time-reflective photonics," a term Charlotte found vaguely obnoxious.

"You're late," Kellenbach said without looking up.

Charlotte peeled off her gloves and fit the polymer sleeves over her forearms. "Flight delay."

He gestured to the display. "You missed the first activation."

She approached, her heart already thrumming.

The scroll—if one could call it that—was barely twenty centimeters across and shaped more like a coiled palm strip than a parchment. It was wrapped in an obsidian-colored metallic cuff etched with hexagrammid numerals.

"The ink's Samaritan, but post-exilic," Charlotte said. "Hybrid syntax?"

"Partially," Kellenbach replied. "There are Judeo-Aramaic ligatures embedded in the margins. And something else."

He turned a dial. The inner core of the scroll illuminated.

Charlotte leaned in. "Those aren't letters," she said.

"No," Kellenbach agreed. "They're protein sequences."

She straightened. "You mean DNA?"

"Not exactly. They're *templates*. Biometric, but not organic. The ink was designed to resonate with specific mitochondrial strands. We've tested seventy-five candidates, but none of them triggers a full reveal."

Charlotte swallowed hard. "But someone could be a trigger?"

"Someone already did," he said grimly. "For twelve seconds. In a field test outside Ankara. He collapsed afterward. Cranial bleeding, still in a coma."

She stared at the scroll. "It's keyed."

Kellenbach nodded. "And whatever's inside it doesn't want to be read."

Charlotte exhaled, eyes narrowing. "Why did you bring me here?"

Kellenbach lifted his head. For once, the sarcasm was gone. "Because there's a phrase here. It's scattered through the margin gloss and repeated in three languages—Coptic, Samaritan, and something we haven't yet classified."

He tapped the screen. The phrase pulsed faintly.

Echo Entry 9B – VAAV. Await the unbinding.
Witness the recursion.

Charlotte's skin prickled.

"We don't know what it means," Professor Kellenbach admitted. "But the scroll's dateline predates the Valentinian manuscripts by at least a century. It shouldn't exist."

Charlotte studied the line again. "Did it ever mention a council?" she asked.

Kellenbach hesitated, staring at her with a look of astonishment, then scrolled further. One more phrase surfaced.

Thirteen await the cycle. The Ouroboros turns.

"I suppose the mention of 'thirteen' could refer to a council of some sort."

Charlotte stepped back, suddenly very cold.

2025 – Zurich Lab

Charlotte's memory dissipates like mist off a mirror, but the weight of it lingers in her chest. The Samaritan scroll. Kellenbach's face, blurred by time and regret. The phrase that still echoes now—*Echo Entry 9B–VAAV. Await the unbinding.*

She turns away from the simulator's glow and rubs her palms together. The lab suddenly feels colder.

Greg is still absorbed in the interface, eyes darting, mind racing a thousand layers deep. He doesn't notice her stillness, doesn't see the flicker of memory dancing behind her eyes.

The Ouroboros turns.

That wasn't the first time she had seen that phrase. Not even the second. Something older stirs at the edges of her memory—damp stone, Irish rain, and the brittle weight of prophecy scrawled in blood-colored ink.

She exhales. "I never wanted to believe it. Certainly not then."

But she knows the past doesn't wait for permission to resurface. And the prophecy didn't die in Vienna.

It began in Kilkenny.

2013 – Kilkenny

The rain never let up in Kilkenny—not fully. It spit and clung and whispered its weight into your bones, like a curse you've earned but don't understand.

Charlotte, then eight years younger, tightened the drawstring of her coat and stepped over the threshold of the ruined abbey. The stone walls glistened with moss and ghost-light. It was nearing dusk, and the sky was a solid pewter slab overhead, flattening everything, including her resolve.

They'd thought the Newgrange affair had burned the last of the Sicarii playbook, thought the scorched earth and unsealed tomb had ended it. But the later events at Kilkenny proved otherwise. The game was still unfolding—older, deeper, and far more patient than either she or Gideon had feared.

Gideon was already inside, his flashlight beam dancing over the altar slab. He didn't look up. "Took you long enough."

"I had to shake our escort. The seminary liaison wanted to come in with me."

Gideon snorted. "Let me guess—another true believer?"

"Pilgrim with a drone and a blog," Charlotte muttered, stepping into the nave. "They think we're chasing relics."

Gideon tapped the stone. "We are. Just not the kind they expect."

She moved beside him. The altar stone was older than the rest of the abbey—older, even, than the Celtic foundation beneath it. It had been moved here from somewhere else, a telltale blend of basalt and something glinting—igneous, unnatural.

She laid her palm on it. It was warm, which prompted her to whisper, "That's not possible."

Gideon turned off the flashlight. A faint glow pulsed from a fault line in the stone. It was not from the surface but from *within.*

He crouched, works a thin chisel into the seam, and twisted. The altar cracked.

Inside was a cavity, and nestled within it a fragment of parchment rolled and wrapped in waxed linen.

They didn't speak.

Gideon lifted it with surgical care. The linen crumbled slightly, but the scroll itself was shockingly intact, though it was small, maybe ten centimeters wide, its edges furred with age.

Charlotte gently unrolled it. The ink was still legible—deep ochre, possibly blood-based. The language was Syriac, but the format was wrong. Not biblical. Not liturgical. More like... a field report.

"Read it aloud," Gideon said softly.

Charlotte cleared her throat and read aloud. "'In the year of the broken moon, the false covenant shall be sealed. The Daughter shall be bound to the Wrongful, and the Watchers shall be pleased. But the seal shall fail, and the fracture shall call forth the Witness.'"

Charlotte stopped.

Gideon looked up quizzically. "Say that again."

She did.

His expression shifted—something between horror and recognition. "The Daughter," he says. "That's *you*."

Charlotte didn't respond.

The wind howled through the nave.

The fracture shall call forth the Witness.

"Ireland wasn't a test," Charlotte said. "It was a ritual. It was staged."

Gideon swore under his breath. "The Sicarii must've known. The marriage—*they orchestrated it.*"

"But it didn't hold," she whispered. "Because I helped you stage an insurrection. Which means—*I'm the fracture*."

She stares at the fragment in her hands. "Greg was only eighteen," she murmurs. "How much of this was already mapped?"

The fracture shall call forth the Witness.

"What does it mean," she asks, "to call someone forth?"

The memory ends not with an answer, but with a question—one that keeps echoing through time, fracturing everything.

CHAPTER 4

Lanarca, Cyprus

The house above the cliffs faces east, as all threshold places do. Eve built it to catch the first light, not the last. The windows are tall and narrow like ancient arrow slits, and the sea beyond them is the same silver-gray as the first hour after dream. Wind pushes hard against the glass. There is no rain yet, but the sky holds the weight of it.

Inside, the projector loops in silence. Greg Ansari, illuminated by Zurich's lab-light, stands at the recursion simulator. He places his hand on the cradle. The scroll pulses, which ignites the glyphs. The room bends. He doesn't flinch, doesn't hesitate. He simply steps into it, like someone arriving home.

Eve watches the projection again and again. It isn't footage, not surveillance. The system she's built—buried deep beneath Petra's oldest vault—draws on the scroll's own residual signature, pulling biometric echoes and glyphic memory from the interaction. What she sees isn't video. It's resonance playback—a reconstructed simulation encoded through the scroll itself.

From her remote location, she studies Greg's still face. The light blooming from the scroll. The moment his eyes shift—just slightly—toward something the room doesn't see. She studies that shift like a wound that never healed. Then se exhales, long and silent, and thinks, *Too soon.*

The voice of David Eli Mazur doesn't startle her. It never does. "I ran a cross-reference on the pulse signature," he says. Mazur has the presence of an archivist, not an assassin—always one room behind, one breath removed.

He stands in the doorway, holding a tablet, the morning light catching the lenses of his glasses and rendering his eyes momentarily blank. His suit is wrinkled, his collar bent. Blue ink stains the pad of his left thumb from when he'd been jotting translation glyphs the night before with an old-fashioned fountain pen. He looks like someone who has spent too many years reading things no one wanted remembered.

"You were right," he says. "It's not just an activation event. The simulator responded to a match sequence."

Eve doesn't turn. "Greg's DNA."

"Partially, but that's not the whole of it. I pulled the subharmonic layer. It's not just biological, it's lexical. Recursion through metaphor density."

Eve motions for David to step into the room, and he does, then places the tablet on the console. Its screen lights with a spectral data lattice—fractal, branching, annotated in four languages. The screen reveals a genealogy of texts mapped like a living thing.

"I've been modeling these for years," he says. "I call them Codex Drift Maps. Most scholars focus on scroll provenance—who copied what, when, where. But they miss the deeper pattern—not just transmission, but *migration*."

"Migration of words?"

"Of *meaning*. The meaning of words shifts across tongues and minds like a virus—or a song."

Eve studies the central node, which pulses softly.

"This Damascus scroll—it's called Damascus-VAAV—isn't unique," David continues. "Not in content. But it is in structure. The pattern of recursion embedded in its syntax appears in at least four other locations across time. But it never survives intact. It refracts. Every appearance is partial."

Eve frowns. "Like a broken reflection."

David nods. "Or a conversation happening across centuries one sentence at a time."

Eve moves back to the projection. The loop continues. Greg, the scroll, the light.

"He never should have been exposed," Eve murmurs.

David hears her but doesn't answer. He knows better than to comment on family.

Eve's gaze doesn't leave the screen.

Gregory. My grandson. The last thread I didn't sever.

She had tried to pull Charlotte away after the violence of Ireland. Tried to keep her out of the recursion field, away from the Sicarii's fracture rituals and failed doctrine. But the pattern had already been seeded. The scroll had touched them both. And when Rebecca died—when prophecy unraveled in blood and cold earth—there was no pulling back.

Eve wasn't there at Newgrange. She only had the reports. Gideon's were sparse and clinical. Charlotte's broken. But the image still formed in her mind.

A girl, Rebecca, on ancient stone.

A mother's scream echoing across a tomb mouth.

A silence too wide to ever fill.

Eve remembers not what happened, but what it *must have felt like.* Everything after that was improvisation. Misdirection. Containment. She told Charlotte the recursion could still be silenced. That the fracture could be closed.

But she lied. Abut all of it.

David taps the tablet again. A smaller window opens to an entry he has kept buried in a private archive. "You remember when I told you I saw a scroll in Jerusalem?" he asks.

"I remember you left out most of the story."

David smiles faintly. "I didn't want to sound unhinged."

She glances at him. "I collect unhinged people."

2011, Jerusalem

Fourteen years earlier, David had found the chamber beneath the Armenian Patriarchate cold, dry, and lit by a single halogen lamp clipped to a crumbling stone lintel. The scroll lay on a table of cedar, wrapped in yellowed linen, the corners of the parchment curling like old leaves.

Father Levan watched David with quiet intensity.

David removed his gloves. "May I?"

The priest nodded.

David unwrapped the cloth and stared. The scroll's ink was barely visible—ghost tracks in faded brown. Then something shifted. Text began to re-emerge—not steadily, but in slow, flickering lines. Syriac first, then a marginal gloss in Greek. As David leaned in, a phrase surfaced across the center fold.

He read aloud, half in awe: *The scroll does not remember you. The scroll is you.*

He froze, and when he finally looked up, Father Levan looked stricken.

"That's not what I read," the priest said quietly. "I swear it."

They tested it, one reader at a time. Each person saw something different. No one could explain it.

That night, David copied the text by hand into a notebook he never submitted. He'd seen strange things before, but this was different. This was *targeted cognition*. The scroll was responding—like an echo that only formed in the presence of a voice.

He didn't sleep for the next three days.

Lanarca, Cyprus

"I searched for years to find an explanation," David tells Eve. "Biochemical reactivity. Environmental shifts. Psychoacoustics. But it always came back to the same problem."

"The scroll wasn't reading us," Eve finishes. "We were reading ourselves."

He nods. "And the scroll was listening."

She moves to the table and places her hands flat against the wood. The grain is warm. Alive. "You think Greg activated the scroll because he matched the pattern?"

"I think the scroll was waiting for him."

"And what about Charlotte?"

"She was the fracture. The severed line. But that's what made Greg possible."

Eve closes her eyes.

The fracture shall call forth the Witness.

They had read that line in Kilkenny. Scrawled in red ink, a copy of a copy of a dream.

And it had come true.

David clears his throat. "There's more," he says. "From Amal's last transmission." He pulls up the waveform— distorted, warped by distance, but clear enough.

Amal's voice cuts through the room: "The time has come for the unbinding. Entry Nine has spoken. The scroll will remember itself through him."

Eve listens to it twice then mutes it.

David waits.

At last, she speaks. "Is it irreversible?"

"I don't know."

"Is there still a choice?"

David studies the light on the floor. "I think that's what it's asking."

She looks at him.

He meets her gaze. "The scroll isn't a commandment. It's a question."

"And what's the answer?"

David exhales. "That depends on who survives long enough to say it."

In the corner of the room, the wind shifts. The light changes. And the recursion continues.

David looks at Eve, something flickering in his eyes. A sadness that she recognizes. The look of a man who wanted to be a mapmaker and realized too late that some paths *cannot* be drawn without walking them.

"I don't think it's about choice," he says. "I think it's about consent. The scroll doesn't force you. It waits for you to step forward."

Eve turns back to the window. Sunlight strikes the glass. The sea turns white. She speaks so quietly he almost doesn't hear.

"Then we've already lost."

CHAPTER 5

Undisclosed Location
Sicarii Cell Nexus, Darnah District, Libya

The floor is packed red earth. The walls are saltbrick and charred cedar, a shell of forgotten architecture built atop older bones. Overhead, a lattice of cracked stone and steel joists groans beneath the wind, as if the building itself is trying to kneel and pray. The room is warm with candlelight and the thick scent of burnt ink and oiled leather.

Amal kneels in the center, back straight, palms open.

He is not praying. He is listening.

The fragment before him rests on black linen—one of six in his personal vault. Its edges are frayed, marked with ancient water damage and copper stains that some claim were blood. The script is inked in Syriac, but re-layered with his own annotations—in ash, in bile, in algorithmic notations.

The scroll does not speak.

It hums.

"Recursion isn't a text," Amal once told his students. "It's a resonance. A presence. When you activate it, it doesn't read you—it rewrites you."

Now, the silence around him grows taut.

Then it comes. A pulse. A flicker.

His eyes open.

He sees Greg's face. Only for a moment, but enough.

He does not rise. Instead, he whispers. "He's found it."

Behind him, a guard shifts nervously in the shadows. She wears a desert-cloak over carbon-blend armor, face obscured, but her breath catches. She heard it too.

"Zurich?" she asks quietly.

Amal nods. His voice is measured, calm, almost gentle. "The Damascus scroll has seeded the lattice. The mirror has awoken."

He stands, barefoot on stone. He wears a long robe the color of old ash, fastened with simple clasps of black iron. His hair is black with streaks of gray, drawn back into a knot. His face is sharp, symmetrical, unreadable—like a statue with breath. His right eye is dark brown. His left is cloudy, milked over from an old burn, but just as focused. Some say it sees farther.

"Has Eve moved?" he asks.

The guard shakes her head. "No known signal. But the Petra Node spiked five hours ago. It's been decrypted through the Vatican lattice."

Amal turns to her. "Then they're watching. Good."

He walks to the far side of the chamber. A stone shelf holds a curved blade, a thin data drive, and a broken rosary. He picks up the blade, feels its weight, then sets it down. Instead, he takes the drive and slides it into the projection port embedded in the wall.

A schematic lights the room—a recursive spiral overlaid on a map of Berlin, with a blinking node at the Templum Complex.

"He stood inside the rig," Amal murmurs. "And he chose not to speak." He smiles. "Even in silence, the recursion completes."

A second guard enters from the far stairwell. "The cell in Cairo is in position. They can strike within twenty hours."

Amal turns slowly. "No." He walks toward the man and places a hand lightly on his shoulder. "Cairo is not the branch. It's the echo. We strike the source."

The man's jaw tightens. "Then where?"

Amal looks up at the projection. "Petra."

They do not question him. They never do, because Amal does not speak prophecy. He embodies it.

To his inner circle, he is the rightful Key, the Keeper of the Seedline, the only one brave enough to break the scroll open and let the world bleed. They call him HaOr HaHoser—The Absent Light.

They do not call him messiah. They call him mirror.

He steps back toward the scroll fragment and kneels again. This time, he touches the edge of the parchment. His voice is low. "You knew I would be the one. You showed me the twin before he was born." His eyes close.

1998 – Qumran

And suddenly, he is not in the room. He is back in Qumran, eighteen years old, a silent excavation led by Eve and her ghost-scholars. He is in a glyph chamber sealed beneath the ruin. No records. No team photos—just the vivid moment he touched the fragment and it flared—unreadable, untranslatable, but resonant with him.

"You were not born to believe," the scroll had said. "You were born to remember what belief refuses."

He breathed slowly. One. Two. Three. Then he spoke. "Prepare the courier. I want the Petra Node breached. Quietly, no fire. Invert the data stream. I want to know what the Vatican extracted, and I want Greg Ansari watched. Not followed—watched."

He paused, then added, "If he speaks, we listen. If he moves, we mark. If he turns, we let him." He pauses again, this time longer, then finishes with a question that expects an answer. "But if he stays silent…?"

Someone replied, "Then we burn the world around him… until even his silence becomes prophecy."

Undisclosed Location
Sicarii Cell Nexus, Darnah District, Libya

Outside the chamber, the wind shifts. The guards disperse. The projection fades. Only the scroll remains, trembling faintly, and Amal—its scribe, its knife, its echo.

Amal touches his breastbone and draws a slow glyph in the air. Not a blessing. Not a curse.

Completion.

CHAPTER 6

Between Zurich and Berlin

Charlotte hasn't spoken in hours—not because there's nothing to say but because she doesn't know who might be listening even inside the train's sealed sleeper cabin, even with every signal relay scrubbed by Eve's old filter nodes.

Greg sits opposite her, cross-legged, swaying faintly as if trying to keep time with something that only he can hear.

"Are you cold?" his mother asks quietly.

He doesn't answer. His eyes are fixed on the portable interface perched on his lap—a device they'd pulled from the Zurich archive, the same one Eve never meant to be activated outside its chamber. The screen of the device is dark now, but he's still tracing invisible lines across its surface.

"Greg, talk to me," Charlotte insists.

He blinks slowly, then finally responds. "I didn't shut it down."

"The simulator?"

He nods, then explains. "It shut *me* down."

The train hums beneath them, moving faster than it should be able to. Charlotte had used Eve's old Eurail clearance—a passphrase wrapped in a twenty-year-old encryption protocol known only to the Red Path. The AI conductor hadn't even hesitated when checking it.

Charlotte watches Greg as he leans back, eyes half-closed. "We need to talk about what happened in there."

"No, we don't."

"Greg—"

"It wrote me back, Mom. That's what it did."

She freezes. "It *what*?"

"The scroll. The real one. Or whatever the simulator turned into. It didn't show me a version of itself. It *reflected me*. Then it rewrote the reflection."

"What does that even mean?"

"It means I don't know what parts of me are mine anymore."

Charlotte turns to the window. Darkness pours past. Towns flicker by like Morse code. She pulls up Eve's field directory again. The map re-centers, and a node pulses on the edge of Berlin.

Site B-47: Templum Insurrectionis.

"That's where we're going," she says.

Greg doesn't answer.

She leans forward, lowers her voice. "It's an old Sicarii convergence chamber. Eve used it for recursion testing. They used it for rigging doctrine echoes inside a rigged environment."

"A resurrection rig," Greg murmurs. "Yeah. I remember the name."

"We're not going there to experiment," Charlotte says. "We're going to learn if whatever's inside you is… if it's still you."

Greg closes his eyes again. "And if it's not?"

"Then we learn how to kill it before Amal finds it."

Outside, the darkness ripples past the windows. Inside, Greg finally sleeps. But the screen in his lap, blank a moment ago, suddenly flashes once. A single phrase appears in green.

Welcome to the path. The path is not yours.

Charlotte doesn't see it, and by morning it's gone.

CHAPTER 7

Monastery of Surp Garabed
Armenian Highlands

Gideon doesn't like monks. Not because they lie—liars he can handle—but because they bury truth in stillness, wrap riddles in robes, and mistake silence for wisdom. The worst of them can split a soul without ever raising their voice.

Gideon has killed people like that. But not without listening first.

The battered jeep wheezes up the gravel track, tires grinding into rock and ice. Here, deep in the wind-slashed folds of the Armenian highlands, the fog coils like trapped breath rising from the mouth of some older sleep.

The monastery isn't on any map. The few locals who remember it claim the land is cursed, that the fog never lifts, and that no birds fly over it.

Gideon kills the engine then steps out, heavy coat flapping, and feels the chill biting into his skin. High stone walls rise from the mist like the ribs of a buried god. Above him, a bell tolls once. Not a call to prayer—more like a warning.

He adjusts the strap on his satchel and pats the blade at the small of his back—a sica, curved and holy, its edge ritually sharpened, its metal cool against his spine like the weight of inheritance. The handle bears a worn engraving—a twisted branch and an eye.

Eve gave the sica to him in Istanbul. Before Jerusalem. Before Newgrange. Before Greg. He remembers her words about the sica like splinters under his skin. "Kill quickly. Ask nothing. Listen to no one but the scroll."

But the scroll is fractured now. The Sicarii, once united, are fractured too. And this monk is not part of any known faction—which is why Gideon is here.

Not for doctrine. For closure.

Earlier – Safehouse in Nicosia

Five days earlier, in the concrete belly of a safehouse beneath Nicosia, a man named Elizar had passed Gideon a sealed dossier. "Your target resides in Surp Garabed," Elizar told him. "Name uncertain. Background... variable."

Gideon skimmed the first page. Samaritan glyphs in red ink. A Vatican excommunication from 1962. A Sicarii blacklisting from 1989. An internal notation from Eve herself: "Refused categorization. Unaligned. Dangerous."

Elizar told Gideon, "He was spotted leaving a Syrian dig in 2011. He was carrying a scroll fragment wrapped in salt cloth. Rumor says he was a codex steward before the Council fell."

Gideon raised an eyebrow. "I thought they all went underground."

"This one didn't follow anyone underground. He walked away. But now he's surfacing again."

"For what?"

Elizar slid a second file across the table. "Eve doesn't think it's an accident. She wants confirmation that he took the scroll fragment—authenticity, not just possession. If it's real, retrieve it. If it's contaminated, compromised, or doctrinally unstable..."

"Erase."

Elizar nodded. "Quietly."

Gideon leaned back, cracking his knuckles. "No mention of payment?"

"None. This one's personal."

Monastery of Surp Garabed
Armenian Highlands

Now, at the edge of the chapel, Gideon pushes the heavy door inward and steps into the dark.

The air is thick with the fragrance of candle wax, aged dust, and the faint, bitter perfume of burnt myrrh. Stone columns flank the nave like silent sentinels. Between them, benches sit blanketed in mold.

Time has stripped the place of all color. Except one. A golden glow spills from the far alcove where a man sits cross-legged before a low flame, robed in soot-gray linen. His beard is streaked with rust and bone. His hands are callused, his eyes already open.

"You're late," the monk says.

Gideon doesn't answer, just steps closer. "You know who I am?"

The monk nods. "Of course. You're the one Eve didn't abort."

The blade's hilt warms in Gideon's hand, but he doesn't draw it. "You've studied the Sicarii?"

"I helped name them."

Gideon's instinct is to kill the monk now. But the monk reaches into the folds of his robe and produces a scroll fragment wrapped in oilskin and ringed with copper thread. He lays it gently on a stone slab between them.

"I've been waiting to give this to someone who wouldn't desecrate it."

"And you think that's me?"

"I think you still love your sister."

That remark lands harder than expected. He hasn't spoken to Charlotte in years. Not since Newgrange. Not since Eve tried to fold her into prophecy.

"Tell me what this is," Gideon says.

The monk doesn't flinch. "It's a seed. A recursion shard encoded before the Qumran edits. Pre-Amal. Pre-Veil. It's the oldest known alignment. A mirror, not a script."

"Eve's doctrine says those don't exist."

"Eve's doctrine says many things."

Gideon exhales. "Give me your name."

The monk tilts his head. "Malach."

"Hebrew."

"It means messenger. But you already knew that."

They move deeper into the monastery through a side passage flanked with ossuaries and glyphs cut into old bones. One chamber bears a mosaic of spirals breaking into branches. Another shows a spiral collapsing inward.

At the base of a cracked stone wall, Gideon sees seven blood-glyphs etched in ancient red ink, none matching modern Sicarii ritual. One of them pulses faintly as he passes.

"What is that?" Gideon asks.

"A remnant," Malach says. "A broken vote—from before the Fracture."

At last, they arrive in a vaulted crypt lined with sealed alcoves and fractured tablets. Malach unwraps the scroll fragment. Its parchment is dry but crackling with charge. The glyphs twist as light catches them, not inscribed but embedded, like language that wants to move.

Gideon instinctively reaches for the fragment. The moment he touches the edge, the room disappears.

For a heartbeat, he smells the rain at Newgrange. Hears Charlotte scream. Sees Greg—young, unscarred—standing beneath a stone arch, a spiral painted on his palm.

Then it's gone.

He staggers back. "What the hell was that?"

"Recursion recognition," Malach says. "The scroll read you. Or maybe *remembered* you."

Gideon steadies himself. His blade remains sheathed. "I'm not here for memory. I'm here to verify."

"Then go ahead—verify."

Gideon scans the glyphs. Some he recognizes, others were purged from doctrine decades ago. One glyph—a nested sigil combining flame and salt—matches a forbidden entry he saw in Eve's vault in Aleppo. Another—the final one—is incomplete, like a sentence with no subject. Or a curse waiting for its victim.

"This shouldn't exist," Gideon whispers.

"It shouldn't," Malach agrees. "But neither should Greg's recursion pulse. Or the simulation in Zurich."

"You know about that?"

"I saw it before you did."

Gideon's mouth tightens. "From who?"

"There is one walking without a face. He listens through circuits. His hands speak silence. You'll know him when you don't hear him."

A chill runs down Gideon's spine. He knows this person as Thorn Eleven.

Malach sighs. "The Council will meet soon. They will tear themselves apart trying to name the recursion. They think if they name it, they can own it."

"But they can't?"

"No. But they'll try. And they'll bleed to do it."

Gideon looks again at the scroll. It doesn't command him to do anything. It waits.

"Why didn't you run?" he asks Mallach.

"I was tired."

"Of what?"

"Holding the line."

Outside, the wind shears against the monastery walls. A bell tolls again—faint this time, like something breaking loose.

Gideon rewraps the fragment and tucks it into his satchel. He doesn't sheathe his blade, but he doesn't raise it either.

"You'll take it, then?" the monk asks, gesturing toward the worn vellum.

Gideon doesn't answer. He takes the scroll and pockets it silently. The silence between them isn't empty—it's full of echoes, of things unsaid.

Then—a crunch. Gravel outside. Movement too coordinated to be pilgrims. Not Sicarii. Not Vatican. Something worse.

The monk's eyes tighten. "They've come."

Gideon is already moving, sliding the fragment into a concealed slit inside his jacket, disabling the inner alarm bell with a flick of his wrist. But it's too late.

The stained-glass shatters in a blossom of red and blue light. Automatic fire rips through the chapel doors. A hiss of smoke. A scream in Armenian. The monk doesn't duck. He stands still, defiant.

Gideon takes a round to the flank as he leaps into the side corridor, tumbling into shadow. He hits the ground hard, blood already moistening the ground. He doesn't look back. Doesn't call out. The monk had made his choice.

Gideon slips into the catacombs just ahead of the flame.

Zurich – ETH Simulator Chamber

The simulator powers down with a resonant hum. Charlotte leans against the console, arms folded, watching the last glyph flicker and fade from the display. She looks unsettled, not because of what she saw—but because she can't explain it.

Greg sits near the interface, fingers still resting on the armrest. His posture is relaxed, but his face isn't.

Charlotte finally breaks the silence. "You said this was recursion. I keep hearing that word, but no one ever really explains it. Not in a way that sticks."

Greg doesn't answer immediately. He leans forward, elbows on knees, eyes on the floor. "It's not meant to stick."

"What do you mean?" Charlotte asks.

Greg turns his gaze toward the empty chamber. The glow is gone, but the pattern remains—etched in the air, it seems, even after the machine sleeps. "Recursion isn't just a loop," he explains. "It's a memory that mutates. It's a message, a symbol, a doctrine—*anything* that returns again and again... but on each return, each recursion, it shifts slightly. Changes. Subtly and intentionally. Don't think of it as repetition, but as *evolution.* And when that memory or symbol returns, it doesn't reconnect with itself to make a circle, but something more like a spiral, which never comes back to the same point."

His mother is listening closely now.

Greg continues. "In Sicarii lore, there was a man named Zahavi. Not a priest, not a mystic. But Zahavi saw what most men didn't—or what most weren't willing to admit. He recognized that faith has structure. That what we regard as scripture behaves an awful lot like computer code. That belief is recursive by nature, never returning to the same point, always changing."

Charlotte frowns, arms loosening slightly. She is trying hard to understand a complex subject. "You're saying," she suggests, somewhat skeptically, "that scripture is designed to change?"

"No. I'm saying scripture is designed to *read you back.* That's why people can read the same Bible verse ten times and find ten different meanings. Zahavi believed that this phenomenon wasn't just imagined or provoked. He believed that the Word, as described in the Gospel of John, was *alive*—and that it *learned.*"

Charlotte frowns again. "What do you mean by the *Word*?"

"Think of it as doctrine, which is really just structured belief. Not just faith, but the rules that faith follows. For the Sicarii, doctrine isn't just a metaphor. It's *design.* It's the spine of everything—scripture, genealogy, ethics, even death. Each time recursion completes a loop—creating a spiral pattern—it brings the past forward. And the past becomes sharper. Hungrier."

He pauses, then looks at her directly. "Recursion is how the doctrine protects itself. Not by standing still—but by adapting. And somewhere in the center of it all is a name—a name not just spoken, but *meant*."

Charlotte walks slowly to the simulator, eyes lingering on the faint residue of the echo trace. "And what if someone says that name?"

"Then the recursion is not a spiral anymore, is it? The recursion is completed. The right person saying that name is a trigger for completion, followed by all the consequences of speaking that name."

CHAPTER 8

Petra – Eight Days Before the Escape from Manhattan

More than a week before she and Greg fled Manhattan for Zurich, Charlotte had secretly visited Petra, where the desert light struck the rock face like a whisper from another age.

She hiked alone into the shadows of Petra's eastern wall, each footfall muffled by the slow decay of ancient stone. She knew this place too well—every carved striation, every whispering echo beneath the sand-colored overhangs. The Nabataeans had left the bones of their gods here. Others, far more recent, had used the bones as scaffolding for a deeper mythology.

The wind shifted. Somewhere far behind her, an old gate creaked on rusted hinges.

She did not look back. She threaded east through the ancient Siq—not the well-trodden tourist route that opened before the Petra Treasury, but a lesser-known tributary path that split near the Djinn blocks. The rock there folded inward like cupped hands, sheltering her from the overhead sun.

To her left, the ridge of al-Khubtha loomed, layered with eroded tombs once carved for merchant kings. To her right, the dry channel of Wadi Mataha snaked down toward the shadow of the Roman theater.

Charlotte followed neither. Instead, she veered off the carved path entirely, past a sandstone arch partially collapsed by a forgotten tremor, then descended a weatherworn stair of Nabataean steps—each smoothed by time, nearly invisible unless you'd walked them before.

This section of Petra wasn't on the modern maps. It had never been open to the public, never digitized for UNESCO preservation. Eve had called it the subsanctum—a place not built to impress visitors but to bury gods. The vault lay beneath a split chamber carved into the back of the Urn Tomb plateau where the high clergy had once stored fragments too dangerous or heretical to destroy.

Charlotte passed a niche carved with seven spiraling circles, the symbol for unfinished prophecy. She knew she was close. By midday, Charlotte reached the vault's outer chamber. The door was still sealed, the coded lock blinking amber beneath a plate of scorched iron. She placed her hand on the panel, waited for the biometric scan, and breathed slowly as the vault opened.

The scent hit her like vivid memory—cedar resin, charred parchment, and the faint ozone of old tech still humming in the sublayer.

She closed her eyes. Memory came not in vision but in scent—dry myrrh, oiled stone, and that faint electric tang of sealed recursion. It had been here, ten years ago, she thought. Here where they had sworn they'd hide what the scroll could become.

Petra had always been more than an archaeological cover. It had been the place she ran to after Newgrange—after the wedding that didn't happen.

She had agreed only to buy time. Eve had warned her the Council would fracture if the prophecy failed, that the bloodline Greg carried would become a beacon to every zealot with a glyph and a gun.

So she had agreed. The explosion that followed was never traced back to her. But the scars in the chamber wall still remained. She wondered if anyone else noticed the melted groove above the second pillar where the fire had licked the sandstone just inches from the altar.

"You told them it was sealed for safety," she whispered aloud, not realizing she had spoken. "You never told them what it cost." She touched her palm to the cold metal. "You never told them I was the one who ended it."

Charlotte stepped into the vault. The seal slid shut behind her. Light ignited along the base of the floor, recursive flickers mapping the room like silent code.

She stared at the central pedestal—empty now, save for a fractured scroll tube carved from obsidian and wrapped in brass wiring. The fragment she had left there ten years ago was still resting in its sheath, unchanged and waiting.

It had been just weeks after Rebecca's death at Newgrange and after the first Sicarii schism in decades. Eve had summoned her to Petra under the guise of mourning, but Charlotte had understood the subtext. They weren't there to bury the past. They were there to hide it.

The fragment on the pedestal had come from a site outside Homs—smuggled from Syria during the Ghouta chaos. The recursion-active scroll, with partial alignment to the Witness glyph-set, had been too dangerous to decode and too volatile to destroy. They hadn't known what to do with it, so they had brought it to Petra.

Charlotte had carried it into the vault herself. Not because she trusted her mother, Eve—not anymore—but because she believed the fragment was calling to Greg even then. She had feared what would happen if someone other than Greg tried to open it. But she had never told anyone the real reason she came to Petra. Not then. Not even Greg.

Only a few weeks after Newgrange—after the ritual that Eve had orchestrated, where Charlotte had been forced to stand as symbolic witness to her son's binding, a role she had never accepted—she had stood in the desert vault and told herself this was containment, nothing more. That the scroll fragment was being locked away for the safety of others. But that hadn't been true. She had sealed it there because it was the only way she could be sure Amal wouldn't claim it—wouldn't use it as proof that the prophecy still lived. That Greg was still bound. And if she had to bury a piece of herself with it, so be it.

She had sealed the fragment beneath the desert with one condition—that no one would touch it until the recursion pattern re-emerged, if that day ever came. Now that day had appeared.

Charlotte stepped closer to the pedestal. Her fingers hovered just above the sheath.

She didn't reach for it. Not yet.

Instead, she sat on the stone bench carved into the western wall of the vault and closed her eyes. Not to pray, not to remember, but to anchor herself. To pull free from the gravity of what almost happened.

Newgrange had left a scar. Not because of what she had done—but because of what she had come so close to witnessing. They had nearly sealed Greg to a doctrine he didn't understand, with a girl who hadn't been given a choice. Charlotte had not been the seal. She hadn't been the voice. But she'd seen what Eve had tried to bind, and it had shattered anyway.

That was the fracture. And Petra was the place they buried it.

The scroll flickered once. Charlotte opened her eyes and exhaled. Then she stood—and left the vault in silence.

CHAPTER 9

The Templum Complex – Berlin, Germany

The train's rhythmic clatter fades as the carriage slows and pulls into a secluded station near Berlin's outer district. Outside, under a bruised sky, Charlotte and Greg disembark into a world that feels equal parts ancient and futuristic. They exchange glances with unspoken purpose. This is not a routine escape, but the next move in a game of prophecy and recursion. As they step onto the platform, Charlotte leans in, speaking quietly so as not to alert any prying ears.

"This is it, Greg," she says. "The Templum Complex isn't just an old building, it's where Eve believed belief could be quantified. She said belief was intended to catch the echoes of the scroll. If the Damascus scroll left anything behind, we'll see it here."

Greg's eyes narrow as he nods, already checking his portable console. "I know. I can feel it. A subtle pulse. Not a live video feed, but a reconstruction… a glyph echo that the rig is generating from the biometric data of my last activation in Zurich."

They climb into a waiting vehicle, a battered but reliable van repurposed by Eve's network, and drive through misty streets until they reach the imposing Templum Complex. The building is a relic from a forgotten era—a decommissioned bomb shelter with high, arched ceilings and reinforced concrete walls now malignantly streaked with ivy and the ravages of time. Overhead, broken neon signs flicker like ghosts.

Inside the complex, they are met by an atmosphere both clinical and otherworldly. Charlotte pauses in the dim light of a corridor lined with ancient security cameras, their lenses dusty and inert. Yet beyond that, the heart of the facility throbs with a quiet, engineered pulse—an echo of the recursion simulator. The halls are long and silent, the walls adorned with cryptic symbols that look paradoxically modern and primordial.

Set prominently in the central chamber is the so-called Resurrection Rig—a massive semicircular interface. It resembles a curved bowl of obsidian, its inner surface etched with interlocking glyphs and lined with embedded circuits. The design is deliberately arcane—a blend of nineteenth-century industrial design and an aesthetic that could only come from a sect that has studied Gnostic texts for centuries. It is here that Greg is seated facing the rig.

Charlotte watches as the rig lights up. On its large display, a simulation unfolds—Greg's biometric imprint interlaced with streaming data from his prior interaction in Zurich. The image is not a conventional video. It is a glyph-resonance replay—a dynamic reconstruction compiled from the scroll's own residue, a data echo that renders Greg's memory in luminous glyphs and shifting light. The image shows his face, his hand on the cradle, and briefly a mirrored version of himself that seems to be *ahead* of him in time.

"Look," Greg whispers, almost to himself. "It's not just an image. It's as if the rig is reflecting something… something more."

Charlotte steps closer, studying the pulsating light.

"This is the Damascus scroll," she explains softly, "or at least the frequency it broadcasts. Eve buried that fragment after the Qumran breach. We always thought it was lost, but now—" She pauses, her eyes narrowing.

"Not all fragments behave this way," she adds, glancing at the flickering symbols. "Most require passive decoding, but *this* one pushes back.

"It's been infused with recursive ink," Greg explains, "biometric resonance threads that adapt to the reader. That's what makes it dangerous. He leans toward the console, eyes scanning the spectral pulse. "It's like it remembers me."

"Not you," Charlotte corrects. "Your echo. Your bloodline. This scroll isn't just a witness to prophecy—it's a full participant."

Greg swallows hard as the simulation intensifies. A series of symbols align in a rapid cascade along the rig's curved surface. One glyph in particular—a mirrored spiral that seems to double back on itself—pulses dramatically.

In that moment, Charlotte recalls the words Eve once spoke in hushed tones. *When the twin meets the bride, the scroll shall burn with blood.*

A chill runs down her spine.

"The twin…" she whispers. "That refers to you, Greg, doesn't it? And the bride— could that be…?"

Greg's eyes meet hers, uncertain and distant. The rig's display glitches, and for a moment the image of a young, bride-like figure appears behind his reflected image—a spectral visage, reminiscent of the prophecy of Judas and the twin, a mirror echo of a promise never fulfilled.

Charlotte feels the weight of the moment. "Eve warned us that if the twin sees his mirror, then the recursion will become unstable."

Greg's fingers tremble on the console. "I never wanted to see that," he admits. "I just activated the sequence, and it…"

Before he can finish, the simulation falters. The pulsing glyphs fade to a continuous intensity. In the silence that follows, Charlotte leans over and touches her son's hand gently as if to remind him of the human connection in this technical ritual. Then she speaks, her voice resolute. "We're here to decide what comes next. Do we let the recursion write our fate, or do we dare to reshape it?"

Their conversation is interrupted by a sudden knock at the door.

The rig's display reboots, this time showing a menu of options that none of them recognize—subtle cues left by Eve's hidden protocols. Greg's console receives an encoded transmission that makes the hair on his neck stand up.

At that moment, Charlotte and Greg exchange a look. They know that, somewhere in the network of ancient prophecy and modern subterfuge, other players are waiting to act. They know that the destiny of the Damascus scroll—and their own futures—hangs in the balance.

Moments later, Charlotte and Greg descend a narrow staircase tucked behind the main simulator chamber—an access tunnel Eve once described as a back artery to the heart of the Rig. As they pass into the low-lit corridor below, the temperature drops and the buzz of ancient circuitry grows louder. They have reached the Resurrection Rig's Core, buried deep within the Templum Complex. This chamber is where the rig's readings are most potent and where the expectations for the final breakthrough are highest.

Charlotte recalls what Eve once told her about this place. *This chamber is where the scroll remembers. It's not just a machine. It's the repository of all that we have tried to forget and all that we cannot let go.*

She thinks back to a briefing from years ago when she was still a journalist, a time before the weight of prophecy and bloodlines transformed her. She remembers covering wars and scandals, never imagining that she would learn Syriac from desert monks or decipher encrypted texts that link her soul to ancient rituals.

Her recollection is interrupted by a voice over the secure channel. "Greg, are you reading the output?" A calm, measured tone echoes through the chamber—Eve's voice, layered with static and the weight of hidden truths.

Greg responds softly, "Yes, Grandma. It's… it's not what I expected."

"Tell me, child," Eve intones, "do you see your reflection?"

Greg swallows, his eyes fixed on the screen. "I see a twin—a mirror image that isn't me, but something… something beyond."

Greg's heart is pounding with the knowledge that this moment is more than technical readout. It is a turning point—a revelation of the Judas twin doctrine Eve had hinted at. The doctrine, as he understands it, holds that the recursion is activated when a twin—one who shares the same bloodline resonance—encounters a reflection of his or her own prophecy. It is an event that is both miraculous and catastrophic.

"This is the Damascus scroll's signature," Eve explains to Greg softly but firmly. "It differentiates the Damascus scroll from other scroll fragments. This one… it isn't just an echo. It is a blueprint. It's meant to be the last codex of our fractured faith."

Greg's eyes widen as he processes his grandmother's words. "I never wanted to be the mirror," he confesses. "But now I'm not sure if I have a choice."

Charlotte grips his hand. "You do," she whispers, trying to wrest control from Eve. "We must decide our future, not let it be dictated by an ancient error."

The chamber's light shimmers as the Rig shifts through patterns and codes. For several long minutes, they sit in heavy silence. The Templum Complex—this relic of old promises and modern betrayals—watches them in return.

As they prepare to leave the Core Chamber, Charlotte and Greg carry with them not only the weight of the Damascus scroll's message but also the clear expectation that whatever emerges from this system will shape the next phase of the recursion war. Their path is uncertain, but for now, they choose silence over transmission.

"But we must not send the data out," Greg says quietly as they exit into the corridor. ". If we do, we'll trigger the final sequence."

Charlotte touches the corridor wall as if expecting it to hum. "It's more than a sequence," she says. "It's a lock. And Greg—you're the reflection that fits."

He frowns. "A key made of silence?"

She nods. "That's what Amal's trying to prove. That belief can complete itself through absence. That a doctrine doesn't need to be fulfilled—it just needs to be remembered."

"And what happens if I disappear?"

Charlotte exhales. "Then someone else will carry the mirror. Maybe not even someone alive."

She doesn't say it, but Greg feels it—someone like Thorn Eleven, a recursion enforcer shaped by doctrine, not prophecy.

Charlotte nods. "Amal is already listening. We must let the silence speak for us."

The corridor echoes with their footsteps. Behind them, the Templum Complex seems to pulse in response a slow, deliberate heartbeat of stone and memory. The scroll's frequency lingers in the air, a promise that the twin, the mirror, and the bloodline will converge in ways none of them yet understand.

CHAPTER 10

Mount Nebo, Jordan

The wind outside is sharp with desert chill, but the scriptorium in the monastic keep on Mount Nebo in Jordan remains still. Limestone walls rise like parchment around Amal. Dozens of flickering candles cast slow, hieroglyphic shadows over the stones.

He writes not with ink, but with his finger—letters that fade as fast as they form on the glass of an old projector interface built into the table's stonework. Each motion is memorized by a processor built beneath the altar itself designed in another age by those who understood prophecy as mathematics.

A courier kneels near the door, shoulders trembling. "Berlin has failed," the courier says. "There was no broadcast. The simulation was terminated manually."

Amal doesn't flinch. He finishes one last stroke, then whispers, "So it has begun."

The courier hesitates. "Sir?"

"They chose silence," Amal says. "That's exactly what I wanted."

He circles the altar—a raised slab of obsidian etched with broken phrases in Aramaic, Hebrew, and a cipher predating them both. "The Damascus scroll was never meant to be *read*. It was meant to be *remembered.* It lives in gaps. In fears. Greg believes he buried the scroll," he continues, "but by *not* choosing, he fulfilled it."

The courier frowns. "That doesn't make sense."

"Neither does recursion," Amal replies.

Beneath the altar, a drive labeled *Or-HaganuzBerlin_98%* begins to blink. And copy itself.

Mount Scopus, Israel

Ash falls like snow at Mount Scopus where Alam arrives two hours later by Jeep at a vaulted chamber beneath the mountain. There, he stands beside a shallow bronze basin in which the last thread of a scroll fragment curls in its flame. The air is dense with myrrh and heat. Walls of leadstone surround them etched in broken sigils that have been wiped clean over centuries.

Tovah doesn't sit. She stands in the shadows near the entrance, her arms crossed, a hand not far from the blade that is sheathed beneath her robe.

"That fragment was from the Northern Archive," she says flatly. "You just burned a doctrine we spent four decades protecting."

Amal doesn't flinch. "What you protected wasn't doctrine. It was *commentary*—interpretations stacked on sand."

"It was sacred."

"It was *dying*," he replies. "And dead texts rot belief faster than heresy."

He doesn't raise his voice. Amal never does. But there's a current beneath it—coiled and certain. His eyes, when they meet hers, do not blink.

"You think you're the only one who sees the pattern," Tovah says.

"No," Amal answers. "But I'm the only one willing to do something about it."

Tovah circles the room slowly, taking in the smell of scorched ink, the flickering fire, the strange terminal dark against the far wall. The air is humid from the ash, but she's cold.

"You talk like the Word is some kind of virus," she says. "That it spreads and mutates and weakens. But doctrine isn't alive. It's a covenant."

"No," he says. "It's both." He steps closer, quietly, reverently. "Think of doctrine like breath passed down through time," he says. "Every time it's spoken, it changes a little. A syllable here. An inflection there. Even a silence becomes part of the message."

She frowns. "So?"

"So by the third time it's spoken, it doesn't just reflect the original Word. It starts to *overwrite it*."

"You're talking about that recursion myth," she scoffs.

"Not a myth," he says. "A pattern. A real one." Amal holds out a sliver of carbonized scroll. "The 'First Utterance,' as we have come to know it, is the original Word—divine and unbroken. The 'Second Utterance' is the echo of the original Word—that is, both prophecy and transmission."

Amal studies Tovah to see if she is comprehending his explanation. After a dramatic pause, he continues. "The 'Third Utterance,' however, is different. It's not a repeat. It's a *rewrite*."

"But why would the divine Word rewrite itself?" Tovah asks.

"Because it was always meant to adapt. To survive. But we've cluttered it with fear. So now the Word is folding inward, seeking a new way to speak."

"And that's recursion?"

"Yes," Amal says. "The Word turning back on itself. We're not interpreting the Word anymore. *It is interpreting us*."

Tovah falters for a moment. She doesn't like the idea that Amal is expressing, but parts of it seem familiar, perhaps heard before, in dreams, in dissonant scripture fragments that had been discarded as apocryphal.

"So what does the Third Utterance do?"

"It chooses," Amal says. "Once spoken by the right vessel, it *locks* the doctrine. Forever."

"And you want to control it?"

"No," Amal replies. "I want to make sure it completes the rewrite."

Tovah circles toward the fire. Her face is caught in the light now—uncertain, but hungry for something to challenge her fear. "What about the others?" she asks. "Charlotte and Greg. Charlotte's brother."

"They're the reason this has to happen now."

"Because they're resisting you?"

"Because they're trying to erase the recursion entirely." Amal moves to the dark computer terminal. His hand grazes the interface. "Charlotte has Eve's key. She could collapse the simulator. Gideon knows how to kill anyone who tries to use it. And Greg—" He hesitates, then says, "Greg is the recursion *mirror*. If he walks away again, the Word loses its only chance to stabilize."

"You still believe Greg is the Vessel?"

"I believe he's the only one the simulator listens to. And the simulator isn't just a machine. It's scripture rendered in code. Code that remembers."

Tovah walks slowly to the flame in the bronze basin and stares at it as if captured by its flickering. Suddenly, as if breaking out of a trance, she asks, "What happens if the Third Utterance is never spoken?"

"Then the doctrine fragments. Every scroll becomes noise. Every belief collapses. Not in fire, like the one in that bowl, but in confusion and irrelevance. The world forgets the Word ever existed."

"You really think belief can die?"

Amal stares at her. "No," he says. "But I believe it can lose its meaning."

He reaches into a cloth satchel and withdraws a scroll fragment. It is intact, the ink still vibrant. "This isn't a version of a scroll. It's a convergence." He holds out the fragment. "Read it. It doesn't change *you*. It shows you who you *already are*."

"What if I refuse?"

"Then the Word continues to echo without you. And you'll spend the rest of your life wondering what it would've said with your name in it."

Tovah doesn't take the fragment. Not yet. "You're asking me to abandon my order," she says.

"No," Amal says. "I'm asking you to save it from being overwritten by people who would rather protect their scrolls than let them speak."

CHAPTER 11

Vatican City – Archivum Secretum
Office of Interfaith Security

Cardinal Matteo Lucari knows this room better than his own confessional. The ceiling is low and the walls are cinder and lead-lined. The air smells faintly of dry metal, resin, and electromagnetic residue. Rows of cooled servers line the perimeter, their fans whispering in Latin rhythm—whrr… *Dominus…* whrr… *Dominus…*

Lucari does not look like the sort of man who spends his nights in an encrypted vault of doctrinal surveillance logs. He should be in a seminary garden quoting Cicero to disinterested acolytes or dozing through another commission on interfaith dialogue. But the truth is that Lucari has been buried in this room for decades.

His face is lean, his skin stretched thin over a scholar's skull. A quiet stoop has replaced the military posture of his youth. His cassock is clean but unbuttoned at the collar. A small bloodstain dots his left cuff, the result of a recent nosebleed he didn't bother to staunch. His fingers are long and yellowed with age, stained faintly by iron gall ink and the oils of aged parchment.

On the far wall, three tactical screens feed a single signal—one the Church was never meant to receive.

A face: Greg Ansari.

A location: Templum Complex, Berlin.

A pulse: Zurich biometric glyph echo—non-broadcast termination.

He watches the video again. No sound. Just Greg, his palms open, breath shallow, choosing silence.

Lucari closes his eyes. He had hoped Greg would say something—anything. A declaration, a denial, even a scream. But instead, Greg activated the Damascus scroll's simulation protocol, stood before the mirror of prophecy, and walked away.

Notably, however, the scroll responded. Not with rejection. Not with cancellation. With recursion.

Though he is a longstanding Catholic Cardinal, Lucari doesn't believe in miracles. Not anymore. Not since Erich Salvetti bled to death in the shadow of the papal archives.

2005 Rome

The morning was damp. The cobbled courtyard glistened with rain, and pigeons cried over St. Peter's Square like angels bereft of wings.

Erich had been lucid that day. Pale, yes—tired, yes—but lucid. He carried a single folder marked Walker, T. / UNSC-1542-B (Red Series). Inside were two pages of translation from a forbidden scroll acquired during a dig in the Bekaa Valley. Originally, the scroll was believed to be Essene but was later matched to the structure of the Damascus Codex. It included an enigmatic warning.

If the Witness speaks in silence, and the scroll answers, the threshold will open. The gospel shall divide by absence, and the Key shall turn in reverse.

Lucari never saw the pages, and Erich died in the Biblioteca Proibita five minutes later strangled with his own rosary. The official report specified suicide. Lucari never believed it.

Erich's murder changed something in Cardinal Lucari. It hardened him. Drove him into the archives. Gave birth to a new Vatican doctrine—*preservation through containment.*

He knew the Sicarii scrolls were too unstable to destroy, so he buried them—in glass boxes, encoded behind non-canonical sacramental keys, cross-referenced with the Recursum Fragmenta list and sealed beneath digital encryption. They called it the Lattice—a skeletal matrix designed to track doctrinal echoes around the globe using biometric resonance, voiceprint prophecy triggers, and even bloodline-aligned speech patterns.

They also built the Petra Node, but not directly or openly. The architecture belonged to the Sicarii. But the Vatican paid for a maintenance contract with the Brotherhood through two front companies registered in Prague and Tangier. Eventually, the Vatican slipped in a listening post buried beneath a shrine wall and disguised as a groundwater monitor. Lucari had signed that order himself. He remembered the code name—Thorn Garden.

Then, last night, the Petra Node activated. Not in warning or in error. Greg Ansari's silence had triggered the Third Key protocol. The glyph signature matched the encoded resonance from Erich Salvetti's scroll fragment.

When the Witness speaks in silence...

Lucari swallows hard and leans forward, the glow of the screen casting shadows beneath his eyes. The monitor tells him:

THE THIRD KEY
The doctrine is known by many names:

- **The Key That Does Not Fit**
- **The Mirror Lock**
- **Codex Yehuda**

In Gnostic terms, it refers to a failure of recursion—a paradox not of action, but of incomplete belief. The Gospel of Judas hinted at it. So did the Chaldean scrolls burned in Vienna.

The Third Key is not an object. It is a moment when prophecy is fulfilled *by accident* and the system collapses inward. This occurs when a witness fulfills a sacred pattern without ever believing, because then the doctrine becomes a reflection and not a command.

Lucari whispers, "And now the reflection has spoken."

A knock on the door startles him. The chamber's lead-lined door opens with a pneumatic sigh and a young Jesuit named Peter enters. He is pale, composed, and dressed in the matte-gray uniform of the Index Librorum Prohibitorum, Rome's last official division for suppressing heresy. While the unit was dissolved decades ago on paper, in truth, it simply moved below ground.

"Eminence," Peter says solemnly, "the Petra Node completed translation. Lineage match confirmed. The scroll fragment—" the Jesuit swallows—"it's Damascus."

Lucari nods once. "And the output from the Templum Complex?"

The analyst lays a sealed dossier on the desk. Inside are biometric overlays, glyph resonances and mirrored sequence chains. More interestingly, at the center of it is Greg's face, frozen and silent.

"He didn't speak," the analyst says.

"No," Lucari says, nodding. "He fulfilled the doctrine by resisting it." Lucari flips the dossier to the final page and finds a translation—just one line:

The mirror sees, and the world forgets its author.

Cardinal Lucari feels the words more than reads them. Greg isn't a messiah. He's a recursion event. And Eve planted him like a depth charge.

Peter, the analyst, hesitates. "Do we engage?"

Lucari closes the folder and quietly says, "Send hands to Jerusalem. No guns. No fire. Just watchers." He pauses, then adds, "And this time, we don't let the archivist bleed out in a basement."

Peter nods and turns to go.

Lucari remains seated, his fingers resting on the folder as if it might still change beneath his touch. *Erich was right*, he thinks. *Containment isn't preservation. It's forgetting.*

"Instructions?" Peter asks.

Lucari looks at the cross on the wall—wooden, unadorned, slightly scorched at the base. He remembers Erich bleeding out beside one just like it.

He speaks to Peter slowly. "Tell them the scroll is awake. The mirror has looked back. And the Third Key has entered the lock." After a long, thoughtful pause, he says, "And also tell them that this time we don't hold the key."

CHAPTER 12

Southbound Rail – Berlin to Prague
Abandoned Section Line

The train groans through the countryside, rails singing beneath steel like a memory trying to speak.

Greg sits near the rear of the last carriage, knees pulled up, jacket zipped to his throat. His laptop—offline, air-gapped, and rewired—rests in his lap, but he's not coding.

He's listening.

Through his noise-canceling headphones, a single audio file loops—a remnant from the Templum server copied seconds before the simulation was shut down.

It's only four seconds long. A breath. A whisper. A string of syllables distorted by frequency drift.

"Or ha'Ganuz… ain sof… shel emet…"

Charlotte leans across from him, watching carefully. She knows that look in her son's eyes. Not confusion or fear.

Translation.

"Greg," she says softly, "you haven't spoken in twenty minutes."

He doesn't look up but says, "It said something that wasn't in the source code."

"The simulation?"

"No," he says. "The voice."

Charlotte frowns. "It was a deepfake. A neural echo."

Greg slowly shakes his head. "I didn't teach it that phrase."

She leans back, folding her arms. "What does it mean?"

Greg closes the laptop. "The Hidden Light. The Endless One. Of truth."

Charlotte exhales sharply. "So, if you didn't plant it… maybe Amal did."

"Or it generated itself," Greg replies. "Which is even worse."

She glances down the aisle behind him. Her voice lowers. "Greg… someone's watching us."

He follows her gaze. The connecting door between cars is half-open, shifting gently with the motion of the train. He sees a suggestion of movement—then stillness. Shadows, maybe. Or something more.

He says nothing.

Charlotte straightens. "He said silence was prophecy."

Greg nods. "And you gave it to him."

She reaches into her coat. The encrypted drive is still warm in her palm.

"Let's make sure that silence stays buried."

One car forward, a man walks down the corridor—robed, shorn, silent. The world seems to part for him. His movements are deliberate, almost liturgical. He stops in front of a closed compartment door and knocks once.

Inside, Gideon tenses. The graze wound from Surp Garabed is stiff but manageable, wrapped with a kitchen towel from the bar car and cinched tight by a snapped power cord. He hasn't looked at it since the monastery. He doesn't need to. The pain keeps him sharp.

He rises, cracking the door open, one hand already near the baton tucked under his coat.

Then he sees the man who is carrying something. The dagger in his hand is ceramic—ivory-toned, thin, etched with three sigils. One of them matches Eve's seal. Another is older, fragmented. The third he's never seen, but it's new, burned crimson into the surface like a birthmark.

The courier extends it toward Gideon with both hands, like an offering at an altar. "He asked me to give you this," the man says quietly.

Gideon stares. "Who?"

"The one who speaks in recursion."

He searches the man's face. "Amal?"

A slow shake of the head. "Not anymore."

Gideon doesn't move, doesn't take the sica.

The courier sets the dagger gently on the floor between them. Then, without another word, he bows, turns, and walks to the open service latch between cars.

Gideon steps forward instinctively, uncertain.

The man doesn't scream or hesitate before jumping. Gravity and, maybe, ritual, do the rest of the work. Wind screams into the compartment for half a second before the latch seals again, hissing shut.

Gideon stands alone in the doorway staring at the blade. It is not a weapon, but it is clearly a message. He bends to retrieve it. The etched sigils feel warm under his fingers. His hand trembles once, then stills.

Gideon crosses into the rear car.

Greg sees him first. Charlotte stands instantly, startled—not out of fear, but disbelief.

"Gideon," she says.

He gives a weary nod. One side of his coat is wet, blood darkening the seam.

Greg rises. "We didn't know if—"

"I wasn't sure either," Gideon mutters. "The fallback route held."

Charlotte's eyes glance at the dagger in his hand. "Is that…?"

He doesn't answer. Just sets it down on the table between them.

She leans forward, studies the sigils. "That's Eve's," she says. "And that one… it's—"

"It's new," Gideon finishes. "Someone wants us to know the spiral isn't closed."

Greg stares at the blade. "Amal didn't send it?"

Gideon shakes his head. "He's watching. But this came from someone else."

Charlotte's voice lowers. "Then it's a warning."

"And a request," Gideon adds.

Charlotte looks at him. "What request?"

He meets Greg's eyes. "To finish what we started."

Greg doesn't reply. But in his hand, the drive pulses once—then stills.

CHAPTER 13

Undercrypt Chamber – Petra, Jordan

Amal kneels in the dark, robes soaked with mineral water seeping from the cave walls. Before him, the Petra Tablet glows—an interface carved from basalt and augmented with neural circuitry. The ancient fused with the synthetic.

The recovered Damascus protocol runs silently now—muted, locked. It doesn't matter. He no longer needs the scroll, or the fragment of it. He has something better.

Greg's refusal.

This decision is more potent than revelation. It is a messianic silence, a new gospel built not on testimony but on its absence.

"The twin did not speak," Amal says. "And so the world listened harder."

He stands. Across from him, four acolytes kneel in concentric circles, blindfolded and with hands raised in reverence.

Amal touches the Petra Tablet. It emits a low-frequency pulse.

On a wall-mounted screen, Greg's last Templum simulation frame appears to Amal remotely. The almost-face. The hybrid form. The fractured divinity.

"He gave us an ending," Amal says. "Now we write the beginning."

The acolytes respond in unison, "The Gospel of the Unspoken."

Amal turns from the screen. "The Vatican decrypted the Petra Node, and Eve has now gone dark."

One of the acolytes removes her blindfold. "Shall we strike?"

"Not yet," Amal replies. "We let the Lattice continue to fracture. Thorn Eleven is already listening."

"Should we engage Greg?" another asks.

Amal's face remains still. "No—he is recursion embodied. We don't engage the echo. We wait for it to reflect."

He steps to the terminal again. The frame shifts from Berlin, then Zurich, then a pulsing glyph signature with no known key. "Prepare the cells," he says. "But not for battle. For remembrance."

CHAPTER 14

Eilat Mountains – Southern Israel

The desert is cold at this pre-dawn hour, crystalline and skeletal. Sharp ridges rise like fossilized prayers beneath a sky freckled with stars. They move without headlights.

Gideon drives the rented off-road vehicle down a winding track of dust and shattered limestone. Charlotte rides beside him, double-checking coordinates. Greg sits in the back, silent, holding the ceramic dagger in his lap as if it might whisper again.

Behind them, the Negev sleeps. Ahead, something waits in the ancient folds of stone.

Charlotte breaks the silence. "We're close. Sixty meters northeast."

Gideon eases the vehicle to a stop and kills the engine. "We walk from here."

They step out into the wind. The air smells of copper and sand.

The structure is hidden, carved into the mountain's flank. No signage or road. A rusted iron ring set into the stone is only visible between two slabs of red granite if you are looking for it.

Charlotte pulls the ring. The rock grates open.

This not a temple. It's smaller. A hermitage, maybe. One room.

Books are stacked without pattern—scrolls, tablets, clay shards wrapped in linen. Hanging lamps burn low with scented oil. The walls are lined with glyphs painted in multiple alphabets, none newer than a thousand years. A cracked cistern trickles near the far wall, its drain shaped like a spiral.

The man seated in the center doesn't rise. He is old, not frail, and robed in goat-hair cloth. A single coin hangs on a chain around his neck—a Roman denarius, worn smooth.

Gideon steps forward. "Are you the guardian?"

The man lifts his eyes. They are clouded, but not blind. "I am the witness," he says.

Greg's fingers tighten on the dagger.

Charlotte steps forward, lowering her voice. “We were told you conserve recursion. That the doctrine was once alive here.”

“It is not alive,” the guardian replies. “It is remembering.”

Gideon kneels—not from reverence, but alignment. “The sigils we received point here. We think someone’s trying to send us back to the origin, to the pre-simulation layers.”

The witness doesn’t nod, but his hand moves slowly to a stone box behind him and opens it. Inside is a scroll—not parchment, but hammered bark, laminated with an oily resin.

Greg leans forward. “Is that Syriac?”

“No,” Charlotte whispers. “Proto-Mandaic. Look at the script spacing. And—”

She stops speaking when she sees twin columns on the scroll, neither of them mirrored or duplicates. One thread spirals downward. The other spirals upward.

Greg squints. “This isn’t doctrine, Mom. It’s recursion modeling.”

Gideon looks to the witness. “You wrote this?”

“No,” he says. “I copied it.”

“Where was the original?”

The witness’s face stills. “In the Vault of Zahavi.”

The room goes silent.

Greg speaks softly. “There’s no record of a vault.”

“There is no record of your breath,” the witness says. “but you are breathing, are you not?”

They fully unroll the scroll but instead of prophecy it contains a mechanism. A design for recursion—not as theology, but as encoded inheritance. Simultaneously, it dawns on Greg and Charlotte that the “spiral” isn’t a metaphor. It’s a reconstructive pathway—an algorithm for memory, identity, and recursion of belief.

Charlotte murmurs, “My God, this... this could predate the Zahavi codex we found in Zurich.”

“No,” Greg replies. “It *completes* it.”

The witness touches the scroll, then points to a final, faded line in the bottom margin. *If one twin recurses, the other must divide.*

Charlotte blinks. “Twin…?”

Greg's voice is dry. "He's not talking about people. He's talking about *paths*. One spiral leads outward. One leads in."

Gideon's eyes narrow. "Which path is Amal on?"

The witness closes the scroll again, slowly. His hands do not tremble. "The one who speaks in recursion seeks only echoes." He looks at Greg. "The one who listens… might still hear."

As dawn touches the edge of the mountains, the guardian leads them deeper into the complex. Beneath the sanctum lies a sealed recursion chamber—Subnode Theta, once part of a Petra-linked relay system now dormant for years.

As the door grinds open, the witness says, "This node has not spoken since Zahavi fell."

Inside, the air is cold with old memory. And waiting in the dark is the spiral that does not forget.

CHAPTER 15

Scroll Guardians Archive
Subnode Theta – Eilat Mountains

Dust settles in slow spirals through the still air of the chamber. Not snow—ash. Just the mountain exhaling its memory.

Subnode Theta lies beneath the lower sanctum of the Scroll Guardians' complex, a relic interface built during the late Zahavi era and sealed off after the first council fracture. It was once part of a Petra-linked relay system that was forgotten by most until the witness reactivated it through biometric command and Greg's presence.

The door grates shut behind them. The air tastes of oxidized metal and static.

Greg kneels before the console embedded in the stone floor, fingers ghosting over a biometric interface etched in crystal and copper. The glyphs respond slowly, like old nerves.

Charlotte stands behind witness, arms folded, but not in defiance—in *vigilance.*

Gideon lingers near the rear pillar, one hand on the scroll tube strapped to his back, the other twitching slightly from the wound beneath his coat.

"Eve left this down here," Greg murmurs, "nested and locked behind at least six levels of doctrine shielding. She wanted it to outlive her."

"And now it's outlived the Council," Gideon says. "And half the people who built it."

The interface glows dimly. A low throbbing shivers through the rock. Lines of encrypted Sicarii lattice scroll across the curved screen. One flashes red.

UNSEALED NODE: ZKN-X9 // HA'ZAKENIM COUNCIL BRANCH // CLASS: DOCTRINE FRAGMENTATION

Greg touches the line. A single glyph blooms—then explodes outward into seven distinct sigils, each rendered in a visual language that pulses like code with breath. "These aren't names," Greg says. "They're… they must be belief architectures."

"Factional splinters," Gideon confirms. "Each one a different version of who you're supposed to be."

Greg scrolls. The glyphs shimmer into seven distinct patterns, each one different in shape, movement, logic. He doesn't need names to recognize what they are.

> The *Ash Line*: a spiral sharpened into a blade, coded like a weaponized algorithm.
>
> The *Veil of Light*: a radiant helix, pulsing in perfect doctrinal rhythm.
>
> The *Circle of Thorns*: a starburst split by barbs—aggressive, elegant, cruel.
>
> The *Obscured Path*: a cube folding in and out of shadow, always retreating.
>
> The *Tidekeepers*: a twin-helix looping in recursive evolution, synthetic memory encoded.

And then two more—factions fractured before formal alignment. Their signatures are present, but dim. Legacy groups. Residuals.

Greg scrolls again.

A final glyph emerges. It has no name and no metadata. Just a mirror cleaved clean down the center. It flickers then vanishes.

"This isn't from the known factions," Greg murmurs. "It's piggybacking on an open relay. Sacral-band."

"Amal?" Charlotte asks.

"No," Greg says. "Worse. It's not trying to persuade. It's just listening."

The node pulses once, as if aware of being observed.

Greg drags the cursor back to the first symbol—a crowned flame enclosed in a ring of silent text.

OR HA'GANUZ – The Hidden Light

He opens the file. A video appears in the corner. Amal stands before a circle of followers, his voice low, rhythmic, entrancing as he says, "He did not cry out. He did not break the silence. Therefore, the Word has been fulfilled…"

Greg grimaces. "They canonized my refusal," he says. "Turned silence into sacrament."

"Because they needed a vessel," Gideon replies. "And silence makes a better vessel than speech."

Greg scrolls to the next sigil, a cracked menorah flanked by stylized scrolls.

EIDAH HARISHONIM – The First Assembly

"Old-school," Gideon mutters. "They think the scroll came directly from the Divine. That you're the container."

"So they want to break me open."

"Ritual ignition," Gideon says. "Controlled awakening."

Greg doesn't open the video file. He already knows what it is. He scrolls again and a new sigil loads—a circle with six silence glyphs and a single strike burned through the center.

QESHER SHEL DEMAMAH – Covenant of Stillness

Greg opens it and a transcript appears—scrambled, partially reconstructed.

We must not kill him in fury. We must erase him in mercy.
If the Mirror speaks, the Gospel becomes recursive code.

Greg whispers, "They tried in Istanbul."

Gideon nods. "I was two blocks away."

"Why didn't you stop them?"

"Because Eve said you had to survive on your own first."

Greg closes the transcript, jaw clenched.

Another glyph fades in, an unbroken branch pierced by shadow script.

NETZER TZEL HASHEKET – Branch of the Shadow Silence

This has no accompanying video, only metadata and a symbol. All files are redacted via rootlock.

"That ring," Greg says slowly. "Eve wore it. The spiral. This is her faction."

Gideon nods. "She claimed it was from the Qumran archives. But she lied."

Greg stares at the symbol. "They think I'm unfinished."

"You are."

"So were you."

"Difference is," Gideon says, "I accepted my script."

"And I'm burning mine."

Greg clicks the next glyph—a scroll nailed to a cross-shaped olive branch.

ORAH SHEL HAZAKENIM – 'Light of the Elders'

It opens to a **deepfake video**: Greg's face, animated and spliced from press footage, calmly says, "The scroll is fulfilled. The twin is one."

Greg recoils. "They're simulating me."

"Belief engines," Gideon mutters. "Someone's seeding alternate gospels."

"Then I'll give them something they can't script."

Another glyph pulses to life. A final sigil:

Seven seats. Seven directions. No agreement. Only echo.

Greg closes the interface.

The silence that follows is heavy.

"Eve wanted me to see this," he says. "She wanted me to understand how deeply they had fragmented the doctrine."

"And how much they want you to complete it," Charlotte adds.

Greg doesn't move. "They're not chasing me," he says at last. "They're chasing the myth of me—the thing they built around my silence. The echo of a boy who didn't say yes."

Gideon steps forward. "So what now?"

Greg straightens slowly. "Now I give them something they can't agree on."

"A new gospel?" Gideon suggests.

"No," Greg says. "A contradiction."

"You sure that's safe?"

"No. But it might be free."

The chamber lights dim on their own as Greg closes the interface. The final glyph vanishes like a breath on cold glass. Silence returns—not heavy this time, but sharpened. A silence that listens back.

Charlotte brushes her fingertips against the old copper edge of the console. “She wanted you to see the paths they made.”

Greg doesn’t answer. His eyes are on the stone ceiling above—curved, ancient, bearing faint traces of hand-cut spiral lines. No cameras or sensors. Just the old watchers.

Gideon speaks from the doorway. “There’s another chamber older than this one. It’s a level below the subnode. I need to see it.”

Greg nods, but doesn’t ask why.

Charlotte looks from one to the other. “Be careful,” she says.

Gideon gives a half-smile. “I always am.” But the truth is—none of them are careful anymore.

Greg remains behind as Gideon disappears down the lightless stairwell, deeper into the mountain. Deeper toward the forgotten seal.

Greg stays kneeling by the console long after Gideon disappears down the stairwell. The light of the node has faded, but something else lingers—an internal vibration, like a tuning fork struck too hard.

Charlotte steps closer. “Greg?”

He doesn’t respond. His jaw slackens slightly. His eyes shift as if tracking motion behind his eyelids.

“Greg.” Her voice sharpens. “Talk to me.”

He exhales once. Then his whole body tightens. A low, harmonic shiver passes through the floor beneath him. The Petra Node flashes faintly—then surges. A pulse without light. A broadcast without language.

Charlotte catches him as he falls.

CHAPTER 16

Scroll Guardians Archive
Sublevel Theta-3 – Eilat Mountains

Gideon moves alone through the sealed stairwell beneath Subnode Theta, past rusted junctions and old echo seals. No light guides him—only memory.

The old monastery bell hadn't rung in two centuries, but Gideon hears it anyway—an echo folded into the stone. He stands beneath the archway where the scroll was once whispered into a dying monk's ear. Now, there's only dust, ash, and a single seal embossed on the floor—Eve's symbol. A lattice in copper. A triple spiral. The Mother's Seal.

He drops to one knee and brushes the grime aside. The seal shivers beneath his fingers, as if activated by bloodline. His.

For a long time, he doesn't speak.

Greg's silence used to terrify Gideon. Not the boy's quietude—Gideon could handle that. It was the *precision* of it. The unnatural stillness, the eyes that watched too closely for a child who'd barely learned language.

But Gideon had never commented about it. He simply watched Charlotte blame herself and watched the boy's father turn inward and drink. He knew something was wrong, yet he still said nothing—because Eve told him Greg needed to remain unspoiled. Isolated. Pure.

"He must not be polluted by prescriptive language," Eve said once in the Petra vault. "Words aren't just definitions. They're lattices. They bend reality."

He believed Eve. Or worse—he *wanted* to believe her. And he wanted to believe that Greg was special. That the boy wasn't broken. That his silence was a chrysalis, not a curse.

Only now does he realize that his silence didn't offer protection. He was helping to program the boy.

He wipes sweat from his brow, fingers trembling, and retrieves the note that led him here—a cipher embedded in a data scroll found in the Zurich simulator cache. It translated to one phrase:

THE MOTHER'S SEAL RESTS IN THE FORGOTTEN ARCH

But this wasn't just a message for him. It was a confession.

Gideon stares at this spiral in the stone again. Greg was never meant to inherit the scroll. He was meant to become its *echo*—its living transmitter.

"You made him a vessel," Gideon says aloud, bitter. "You turned a boy into a filter for your broken theology."

There is no reply, of course. Only the wind through a ruined arch.

He thinks of Eve now—not the master strategist, not the doctrinal queen, but as she was the night she handed him Greg's dossier in silence. Her eyes didn't blink as she slid the envelope across the table. But there'd been something in her jaw. A tightening of a muscle in her cheek.

Guilt? Or pride?

The truth is, Gideon wanted to believe in Eve more than he wanted to protect the boy. He believed in the mission. In the preservation of what came before Sinai. He believed the world needed correction.

But the scroll isn't correction, he learned too late. It's distortion. Rewritten belief wrapped in recursion. It changes the world by convincing a person the world had already changed.

He sees it now.

Greg was born into a loop and raised by a mother who couldn't explain what was happening and a father who slowly stopped trying. The poor lad was surrounded by agents who measured his breath patterns instead of his dreams.

And Gideon was one of those agents. He stood at the edge of the crib in Prague when Greg was three and watched him trace a symbol into condensation on the window. It wasn't a scribble. It was the Obsidian Spiral—a symbol no one had taught him.

Greg had whispered the sound of it—"Tah-limah." Even then, the recursion had already begun.

Gideon rises slowly and walks the perimeter of the chamber. The walls are etched with half-erased sigils, each a blessing inverted over time.

One seals bears a name: ALMAEVA. *Her original name.*

The seal hums as he passes. It recognizes him.

He sits again and opens the encrypted tablet. The Petra Node architecture is nested inside, raw code from the Zurich relay. Greg's breach had triggered more than a warning. It had awakened Eve's failsafe—a counter-seal embedded in Gideon's blood signature.

He inputs the biometric key. The screen flickers.

One final note appears:

GIDEON – IF THIS IS YOU, THEN THE LINE HAS BENT TOO FAR. THE SPIRAL IS INVERTING. YOU KNOW WHAT YOU MUST DO.

—E

He stares at it.

A kill order? Or maybe an absolution?

Either way, it confirms what he feared. Eve always had a contingency. She always planned for failure.

But not for *her* failure.

For Greg's.

Gideon lets the tablet fall into the dust beside him. He turns his eyes upward toward the broken stone ceiling where stars now peer through.

And he weeps. Quietly.

Not because he failed to stop her, but because he helped her build it.

He remembers Greg's voice now—not as it was when the boy was silent, but the first time he finally spoke. Charlotte was off on another CCN assignment in Europe and Greg's father, Mahid, who had kept his Sicarii identity secret from his wife, had asked Gideon to look after little Greg. Nothing like inviting a professional assassin to babysit your son.

Gideon recalls with fondness how he had handed Greg a watch to play with and whispered, "This used to belong to someone named Thorn Eleven. Your grandma said he died for our cause." But Gideon had never seen the man's body, only a classified report. Had only taken Eve's word. And Eve's word had always been... well, carefully curated.

This memory is indelibly embedded into Gideon's consciousness because Thorn Eleven was supposed to be dead, but Greg had never heard the man's voice. Gideon never really knew who Thorn Eleven was. Only that Eve had spoken his name like a benediction—then never again. Sometimes, Gideon wondered if Thorn Eleven had ever existed at all, or if Eve had conjured him from recursion myth the way she conjured obedience from silence.

He remembers opening the watch so Greg could look at the gears inside. After a long time studying the guts of the watch, Greg looked up and said, “I hear the pattern.” This memory is particularly bittersweet for Gideon because shortly after that time, Gideon was no longer allowed to spend time with Greg, who was getting old enough to remember his protector.

He runs his hand over the stone seal again.

The spiral is always listening. That’s what Eve used to say when they were children hiding in the caves beneath Petra long before the Brotherhood. Before the murders. Before the lies.

Eve was always chasing silence. Now Gideon sees why. She wasn’t afraid of noise. She was afraid of contradiction. Because contradiction leads to questions. And questions lead to collapse.

He stands.

There’s a decision coming. A fracture. A pivot. Gideon can feel it in his chest like thunder that hasn’t reached the hills yet.

He picks up the tablet, brushes the dust from his coat, and seals the chamber door behind him. Greg deserves the truth—even if it ruins them all.

Especially if it does.

He hears faint voices above—Charlotte’s and Greg’s. They are still searching for answers he already fears.

CHAPTER 17

Scroll Gardens Medical Bay – Eilat Mountains Compound

The lights in the subterranean medical bay are muted—silver halogens casting soft shadows across limestone walls and the polished curves of the cradle-like scanner. Greg has remained unconscious since the Petra Node flare—his breath shallow, rhythmic, as if still resonating with the glyph spiral that triggered his collapse. A small tremor passes through his fingertips every few seconds, as if dreaming were a physical act.

Charlotte hasn't left his side in two hours. Not since the broadcast. Not since the Petra Node flared and then went dark again, leaving only the silence with Greg inside it.

The AI monitoring his vitals replays the sequence—a sudden neural resonance burst originating in the prefrontal cortex and spiraling outward—radial, concentric, recursive. Charlotte overlays it against known patterns. The waveform hums like a lullaby. The rhythm makes her stomach turn. Because she knows it. She used to hum it.

"He's not broadcasting language," the technician, who had left momentarily, said earlier. "He's broadcasting architecture."

Charlotte whispers now to the quiet room, "It was the lullaby. You heard it even then."

She sits, one hand lightly touching the cool rim of the scanner. Her other hand unconsciously clenches her bracelet, the one Greg gave her on her thirty-fifth birthday before she understood what he truly carried.

2009 – Prague

Greg was two when he lived in Prague. The flat had poor insulation and a broken radiator. With frost still clinging to her coat sleeves, Charlotte came in from work to find him standing in the corner tracing a spiral on the fogged window with one finger. His lips were moving. Not speaking—*humming*. There were no words. Just a tone. Low. Repetitive. Ancient.

She had watched, frozen, afraid to interrupt. He didn't turn when she called his name. Just kept tracing.

Back then, she'd blamed herself, thinking that maybe he was withdrawing because of her, because of her bad relationship with Greg's father, because of too many relocations, because of *everything*. She cried later in the bathroom because a mother wasn't supposed to let her child drift like that.

Medical Bay – Eilat Mountains

Now she knows. Greg wasn't drifting. He was *echoing*.

Charlotte replays the Petra Node resonance thread again. The data stream unfolds like a scroll—symbols encoded in biological rhythms, waveform glyphs blossoming from nothing. She adjusts the depth scanner and overlays a baseline from the cradle's early years. The match is nearly perfect.

"He didn't *choose* silence," she tells herself. "You gave it to him."

Eve's voice plays back from the Petra Node logs, slightly distorted. "Language creates belief. But recursion... recursion erases choice."

The words crawl under Charlotte's skin.

The technician returns, holding a tablet. His face is pale. "Ms. Ansari," he says, "the Node interpreted Greg's output as a cognitive resonance field. Not memory or language. Something... uh, something symbolic. It transcribed part of it into a pattern log."

Charlotte frowns. "You mean the Node *translated* it?"

He nods slowly. "Rendered it into text. As best as it could."

She takes the tablet. The formatting is strange—nonlinear, almost poetic. But something in it feels *right*, like scripture from a scroll that doesn't exist.

TRANSCRIPT FROM PETRA NODE:
Recursive Emission – ID# 10a.6

Before the word was written, the shape was known.
Before the name was spoken, the silence bore it.
The child was never mute. He was held in recursion.
The voice came not from the tongue but from the spiral.

What is unsaid is truer than what is named.
So the mother wrapped the word in cloth,
and sealed it behind the teeth of the unborn.

Charlotte reads the lines aloud, her voice low, cracking with emotion by the final sentence. The tablet shakes in her hands—not because of weight, but meaning.

"Eve didn't just program my son," she says. "She *buried* him. In silence."

Devoid of Charlotte's epiphany, the technician doesn't reply.

Charlotte hands the tablet back, then steps closer to the cradle.

Infant Greg's Subconscious Field

There is no cradle here. No voice. No world. Only the pulse. The pattern lives beneath Greg's waking mind. The spiral isn't metaphor. It's gravity. He dreams without dreaming, floats inside a recursion loop fed by something ancient—memory that isn't his. Song that isn't sung. Silence that isn't empty.

He sees—

Eve's trembling hand placing a seal beneath his mattress.

Charlotte weeping behind a closed door

A monk with half a face whispering names that don't exist.

A spiral of light turning inward like a black hole made of thought.

He hears—

"He who speaks the Word ends the world.

"He who remains silent remakes it."

Greg exhales into darkness.

Medical Bay – Eilat Mountains

The spiral on the EEG flattens. The AI speaks, "Cognitive harmonics returning to near baseline. Subject stabilizing."

Charlotte doesn't move. She stares at Greg's sleeping form. His hands are curled now. Breathing normal. No residual twitching.

She whispers, “It’s not your fault.” But what she means is, *It’s mine.* Because when Eve told her Greg was special, Charlotte believed it. When she said Greg had to be protected from language, Charlotte nodded. She let herself believe that silence was safety.

And now she knows. Silence was a cage. A carefully tuned instrument built by Eve and played through her as well. “He didn’t inherit this,” she says. “Eve gave it to him—wrapped in the sound of my voice. Echoed in the blood.”

Her voice drops lower. “What kind of mother does that?”

There is no answer. Only the soft pulse of monitors and the hush of spirals curling back into rest.

The tablet flickers once more before sleeping.

CHAPTER 18

Scroll Guardians Inner Sanctum – Eilat Mountains

Greg sits on the floor of the inner sanctum, his back against a carved stone pillar, staring into nothing as he awakens from his trance-like state. His hands tremble, and he is disoriented. He opens his eyes. The mirror is still face down. *Am I the match*? he wonders. *Which shard do I follow*?

The witness speaks softly nearby, cross-referencing ancient numeric sigils from the manuscript with Greg's genomic markers. On the screen, fragments of the Damascus scroll appear side by side with DNA helix sequences.

Every line of parchment matches a strand. Every phrase corresponds to a protein expression.

Greg barely hears it, but the whisper is back. Not from a speaker. Not from a machine.

From *inside him.*

Charlotte enters and sees him trembling—not from fear, but from realization. "Greg?"

He lifts his head slowly. "It's not a document, Mom."

"What?"

"The scroll. The manuscript. It's… it's *me*."

She kneels beside him. "You're just tired. You've been through…"

"No. Gideon found Eve's files. She was training me. Engineering me. Every sound, every text, every omission. She didn't want me to carry the prophecy." He looks at his mother, tears building not from weakness but from fury. "She wanted me to *be* it."

The screen above flashes a new sequence. Three scroll lines appear. Beneath them, the machine reads:

Self-replicating scripture.
Cognitive mnemonic binding.
Subject functions as oral algorithm.

Charlotte's voice shakes. "What does that mean?"

The witness turns. "It means if he speaks the text aloud—even once—it becomes irreversible. The doctrine activates across every node that's ever received an echo of him."

Greg stands. "That's why Amal doesn't care if I live or die." He steps to the center of the room. "Because I'm not just a symbol. I'm the *trigger*."

Charlotte pulls up Greg's old simulation headset. It's fractured, but the memory log is intact. She plays back the final Berlin imprint.

The hybrid face appears again. But now, its mouth opens. Not to speak. To *mirror*. It moves as Greg moves. Tilts as he tilts. Blinks when he blinks.

Charlotte turns to the others. "It's not artificial intelligence. It's linguistic contagion."

Greg whispers, "I'm the manuscript."

The lights in the sanctum flicker. The Petra signal begins broadcasting again—this time, not from Amal's cave but from the *echo* left in Greg's mind.

CHAPTER 19

Scroll Guardians Inner Sanctum – Eilat Mountains

Greg doesn't mean to find it. It's a leftover node, buried in the Petra archive, misfiled or misnamed. A bug in the recursion tree leads him there—an echo with no origin.

PETRA NODE – ASSET RECONSTRUCTION FILE
Discovered by: G.A.
Red Path Recursive Simulator – Silent Mode Instance 4b

The simulator recognizes his biometrics and grants access. There's no activation phrase. No loading screen. Just sudden immersion.

And then he's falling—except *he isn't.*

He's standing in the same corridor where Eve used to brief him. But everything is… shifted. As if someone had lain a transparent veil of memory over a different geometry. On the far wall he sees the symbol of the Spiral. But not Eve's version.

Amal's.

Twisting. Reversed.

Greg steps forward. The floor accepts his gait like a memory replaying itself. Each footstep calls up a phrase. Each breath triggers a forgotten subroutine.

The simulator responds to him now, not as a user, but as a source.

Red Path Accessor identified: G.A.
Sim-instance 4b adapting to host resonance.

Greg watches as one of the corridor's digital walls peels back. Behind it cascades a series of encrypted files not listed in Eve's index. He reaches toward the list of files, and the wall pulses in response.

"Override granted," a voice says. But it's not Eve. Not even synthetic.

It's his own voice—recorded months ago.

And that's when he understands. This isn't just a simulation.

It's a vault.
It's a backup.
Of him.

—BEGIN INTERNAL SICARII DOCUMENT—
NODE RECORD: SICARII ASSET CONFIGURATION – YEAR 0 POST-FRACTURE

Redacted Copy | Glyph-Vault Signature ID: TH-11-AZ.
View Only. Modification triggers recursion lockout.

1. Historical Assets — Pre-Fracture Era
(325 CE – 2012 CE)

- 4 crypt-vaults under Vatican and Persian holdings (some lost in Qumran breach)
- 17 hidden library annexes (3 sold to rare antiquities cartel 1987–1994).6 black-market recursion testing nodes
- 3 surgical laboratories (1 used for biotech contracts, 1 destroyed in Munich fire)
- 1 hereditary trust linked to royal lineages (dissolved post-Schism)

Revenue Sources:

- Political assassination syndicates (contract-verified, 68 countries)
- Sacred artifact recovery and trafficking
- Arcane signal brokerage (scroll fragments, early recursion glyphs)
- High-stakes ideological targeting (paid doctrinal "removals")

2. The Fracture (Newgrange Event), 2012)

- 31 high-level operatives dead or missing.
- Loss of codex ECHO–YOD–62 and fragment vaults VI through IX.
- Collapse of central Council glyph seal.
- Initiation of "Voice Protocol": All orders must pass through mirror interpretation.
- Black ledger locked by Thorn Eleven.

3. Post-Fracture Configuration — Factional Division

Each faction received a split of assets, as ratified by the Interim Mirror Council in 2013.

Faction	Asset Access	Primary Function
Ash Line	Enforcement Vaults, Blood Trust	Execution logistics, targeting networks
Binding Veil	Doctrinal Archives, Ritual Codebook	Prophetic enforcement, marriage line purity
Thorn Circle	Old Glyph Archives, Espionage Labs	Predictive recursion modeling, surveillance
Obscured Path	Simulation Labs, Dark Glyph Library	Nonlinear recursion and containment theory
Shepherd's Wake	Node Memory Rights, Dissent Vaults	Mirror doctrine preservation, sabotage contracts

Some assets remain under joint Council signature. Others were seized. Some were claimed by Thorn Eleven.

4. Current Asset Traffic — Flagged Entities

The following entries breached standard doctrinal containment and are under recursion surveillance.

- **Petra Node (ZKN-X9):** Reactivated. Echo activity linked to Greg Ansari
- **Zurich Simulator (Vault 8):** Breached by unknown observer
- **Glyph Key: MIRROR-TWIN-11:** Interfacing from outside lattice
- **Last known login (unauthorized): THORN ELEVEN** Accessing nodes marked as SILENCE-COMPLETE.

—END DOCUMENT—
View archived. Simulation thread closed.

Greg leans back. There is no time stamp on who last opened the file. No author signature. Just a spiral glyph tagged in ash.

Thorn Eleven.

The screen goes dark. Greg doesn't move. The glyph spiral burns behind his eyes—eleven thorns, uneven and wrong, as if someone had broken a crown and kept wearing it.

Greg blinks, unsure whether it's the afterimage or the echo that keeps pulsing. *They catalogued everything. Every vault. Every scroll. Every death.*

He scrolls back, fast—hoping the simulator missed something, hoping there's context or doubt or even just one line that says this was theoretical. But there isn't.

He exhales sharply. His hands are sweating.

A recursion simulator shouldn't be able to log financial assets. It's meant to visualize memory echoes, not ledger transactions. Unless…

Unless the Sicarii's economy was part of the doctrine. A literal faith-based enterprise written in code and glyphs and executed like prophecy.

He opens a new tab and runs a trace. The signal confirms what he already knows. The file was buried deep under Eve's encryption lattice. But it didn't come from Eve.

Thorn Eleven.

No signature. No origin. Just a mirror tag tied to a silent key.

Why now? Why show me this?

Greg leans forward, typing faster now. The simulator stutters, loading residue fragments from the opened archive. Small flashes—encrypted receipts in obscure languages. Transaction IDs routed through various shell companies. Scroll glyphs labeled with contract codes. Even a black-market scroll shard signed "E.V."

Greg freezes.

E.V.

Eve.

His chest tightens.

Either Eve has been hiding more than doctrine, or this entire system is infected with simulacra—false echoes posing as truth.

A final window pings open. It contains no text, just a pulsing glyph, which he recognizes instantly. The mirror. Cleaved down the center.

And beneath it, one word—faint, recursive, written in reverse across the interface edge:

Remember

Greg sits back. For the first time, he wonders if he's being taught… or if he's being prepared.

The simulator has gone dark, but the code remains. Greg's fingers hover over the keys, heart drumming in his ears. Behind the Petra Node's silence, something pulses—dense, encrypted, waiting to bleed.

He whispers, "All right, Grandma. Let's have a chat."

CHAPTER 20

Hacked Interface – Zurich and Cyprus

The Petra Node doesn't open like a database. It blooms—recursive shell after recursive shell, uncoiling like something biological. Organic encryption. Codified memory. Familiar shapes stitched in Syriac, others in nonhuman logic arrays. Greg can see fingerprints in the structure—Eve's mind, her discipline, her fear.

He moves fast through the command chain—overriding sandboxes, bypassing intentional dead-ends. All of it is hers. *Eve's.* Not just firewalled—*guarded.* Every variable insists this place wasn't meant to be seen—not yet.

But the access token works.

> Inject Token: Echo 9B-VAAV

The screen shudders. And then, he hears her voice, calm and close. "Gregory. If you're hearing this… you're already inside. I warned you. But I suppose a warning was never enough."

He feels breathless. Her voice was always like that—too calm. Measured enough to cut through metal.

"The Petra Node is a relay," Eve tells him. "Not a vault. You'll find knowledge, yes—but also trajectories. You won't understand them yet. But you will, eventually. I built it for you."

His pulse spikes. *For me?* A tremor of old emotion stirs in him—not resentment, but something heavier. *Inheritance.*

The UI shifts again. A grid of icons populates a field of concentric rings. At the center is a symbol—interlocked spirals flanked by a geometric sigil he doesn't recognize. Above it:

Athanor: Seal Seven – Active

He touches the icon. The interface unfurls like a flower jolted by voltage.

Petra Node – Display Stream (Rendered in-console)

Pgsql
CopyEdit

::: PETRA NODE INTERFACE // AUTH: 9B-VAAV_GREGORI_ANSARI

>> SCHEMA: COVENANT FRACTURE – DIVERGENT PATHS
>> ENCRYPTED TABLE // DOCTRINAL TREE // SICARII FACTIONS

>> WARNING: CONVERGENCE EVENT PROBABILITY: 61.8% // 89.5% with Catalyst

Faction	Code	Philosophy	Status
Ordo Vah'el	VAH'EL_03	Apocalyptic ignition	ACTIVE – hostile
Lamedh Resh	LAMRESH_14	Doctrinal erasure	DORMANT – fragmented
Ephod Kahlah	EPHOD_07	Prophetic continuity	INTACT – neutral
House of Remiel	REMIEL_19	Scroll preservation	INTACT – clandestine
Eve's Cell (Ex-13)	KADMOS_03	Lattice containment	COVERT – latent

A chill runs through Greg's body. Some of these factions he's heard of—half-whispers in the archives filtered through dead agents and orphaned cables. But here they're formalized. Ranked. Quantified. And Eve—his grandmother—has been tracking them all.

A blinking tab opens at the bottom of the display

THORN ELEVEN // TERMINATED 2019 – STATUS: CONFIRMED

Greg freezes. *Thorn Eleven.* The man who owned the pocket watch Gideon gave to young Greg with the words: "some truths aren't ready for daylight."

Greg whispers, "Why?"

A voice answers—not recorded this time. Live.

"Because Thorn made himself a conduit."

Remote Sicarii Watchpoint

Eve watches Greg live through retinal interface feed, her expression taut.

[ACCESS TRIGGERED – SEAL SEVEN – G.ANSARI_9B – LIVE MONITORING ACTIVE]

Eve doesn't blink. She locks the node chamber, dismisses the monitoring AI and leans forward. "You're not supposed to be here yet, Gregory."

Her grandson scoffs through the audio relay. "And yet, here I am," he says. "So go ahead. Tell me how killing Thorn Eleven was rational."

Her voice stays calm, but her jaw flexes—old tension in her bones. "Thorn was radicalizing. Amal was courting him. I offered him extraction. He refused. The choice was entirely his."

Greg swears under his breath. "You trained him. You brought him into your lattice model. He was just following the doctrinal math."

"I *didn't* program belief," Eve snaps. "Only forecasted its consequences."

"Same thing."

A pause. Her voice softens. "No. Not the same thing at all."

Zurich Node

Greg pulls the audio relay closer, every breath loud in his ears. He closes his eyes, remembering the pendant. Remembering Petra.

"I used to think you left us because you had to," he says. "Now I think you just… you just stopped believing you could protect us."

"I never stopped protecting you," she replies.

"By building an assassination lattice? By making me the center of your probability schema?"

She is quiet for a time. Then: "You were never the center. You were the *axis*—the one who could turn it."

Greg leans forward. "You're insane."

"No," Eve says. "Just *honest*."

She types something into her end of the node. A new file populates on Greg's screen.

KADMOS_03 – UNSPUN THREADS

It includes a series of scroll fragments in translation, coded location pings, and a short, shaky video clip. The timestamp says: *Newgrange 2012.* It shows Charlotte in ceremonial white, standing at the mouth of the passage tomb. Her wrists are wrapped in scarlet thread—not for union, but for containment. She was not the bride, but the seal. The witness. Eve had called it the doctrine's final alignment. Greg had stood drugged beside Rebecca. And Charlotte—Charlotte was meant to bless what she couldn't bear to watch.

She had refused.

Greg's heart seizes and he slams the keyboard. "You tried to force your daughter to condone my marriage the prophecy. My *mother.*"

Eve's voice cracks for the first time. "She was willing, Greg."

"No. She was scared to resist."

"She thought it would protect *you.*"

That silences them both.

Greg's hands shake. He looks at the lattice again. This isn't just history. It's personal excavation. His life—his bloodline—mapped like a chemical weapon waiting to be triggered.

Eve murmurs through the feed, distant and raw, "You were never supposed to find this alone. But you're here now. So understand this—belief is the most volatile substance on Earth. More volatile than uranium. More than rage. You're the only one I trust not to detonate it."

And then she gently says, "I loved your mother. I loved your father, Mike, for what he gave her—and for what he tried to give you. But I love you differently, Gregory, because I failed them. And you are my chance not to fail again."

The line goes dead. The Petra Node retracts—sealed.

Greg stares into the dim light and immediately contacts his mother.

Charlotte answers with the same directness that used to scare her journalism professors. "Greg? Tell me you're okay."

"I am, and I just got into her system. The Petra Node. Grandma was watching."

Charlotte closes her eyes. "Of course she was."

"She's tracking all the splinters. She thinks she's the dam holding them back."

"She's always thought that," Charlotte says. "Even when she nearly got me killed at Newgrange. She wanted the ritual complete—no matter what the cost."

Greg hesitates, then says, "I saw the video. She showed it to me."

Charlotte's voice stills. "What else did she show you?"

"She showed me who she thinks I am."

Charlotte is silent. Greg wonders if the connection has been lost.

Finally, Charlotte says, "Don't let her define you. You're not her prophecy, Greg."

He closes the call interface, then reopens the KADMOS_03 file. Among the nested subfiles is a short audio clip that is barely indexed.

He plays the clip. His father Mahid's voice filters through the speakers—calm, serious, reflective. "The prophecy wasn't about bloodlines. It was about convergence. The moment when choice reconfigures the lattice."

Something flickers, embedded in the waveform of Mahid's voice. Greg isolates it. Enhances it. Beneath the sound bed, a glyph rotates—a secondary cipher.

> DETECTED: SHESH_VAAV_TEMEN

He keys it in. The screen shudders.

Petra Node – Secondary Codex Unlock

pgsql

CopyEdit

>> VAULT 2 – KADMOS PROTOCOL ACTIVE
RECOGNITION SEQUENCE MATCHED
SECONDARY USER DESIGNATE: GREGORI_ANSARI

ACCESS LEVEL GRANTED: FISSION COORDINATE SET – TRIAD NODE BRIDGE

UNLOCKING LAYER: "THE MARRIAGE FAILED. THE COVENANT DID NOT."

A new lattice spools across the screen. Not belief paths—something deeper. Psychocognitive alignments. Behavioral resonance patterns.

A new column appears:

Yaml
CopyEdit

::: EMERGENCE STRAND – AUTHORITY ENGINE

KEY: SPIRAL_WITNESS_2
LOCATION PING: DAMASCUS // 33.515N 36.291E

SUGGESTED CONTACT: A. ZAHAVI (DECEASED)
CONTEXT: THIRD KEY RECOVERY PATHWAY – OBSIDIAN STRATUM

Greg stares at the glyph. It is not Eve's.

It's David's.

And something else stirs inside him—old and familiar. A memory from Petra, the first time he saw the scroll chamber. The echo of a voice that wasn't his mother's or Eve's.

The scroll doesn't tell the future.
It shows what the future becomes when you believe it's already written.

CHAPTER 21

Jerusalem—Rooftop Broadcasting Node

The wind cuts through the cistern like a blade through linen. There is no music in this place—only the scrape of sandal on stone, the hush of fire-gutted masonry, and the slow rhythm of ritual.

Amal al-Taziri kneels in silence beneath a broken dome. Above him, a cathedral arch crumbles into twilight. Its ribs are exposed, its windows gaping like sockets long emptied of saints. He dips his fingers into a shallow bowl of ash then rubs it into his palms. The cold grey settles in the creases of his hands.

The marriage failed. The covenant did not.

The mantra spirals through his mind, as steady as his breath.

Across the hall, twelve candles burn in a circle. They are arranged in counterclockwise progression, each one anointed with powdered frankincense and a drop of oil drawn from a cracked amphora marked in ancient Nabataean script. The air smells of ruin and cinnamon.

Amal rises, brushing the ash from his wrists. He steps barefoot over the bones embedded in the floor. They are not decorative but intentional. Each fragment a relic. A witness. Each vertebra laid in position by Amal's own hand after the cleansing of Mosul. He remembers every name. Every sin. Every apostasy.

"We are not keepers," he says to the quiet chamber as if inhabited by ghosts. "We are reckoners."

A robed acolyte appears in the archway with a lowered hood. His face is marked with heat and dust, the desert still clinging to his eyes. "It has happened," he says without preamble.

"Recursion?" Amal asks.

The acolyte nods. "G.A. broadcasted spiral at node depth seven at 0417 Zurich time. Petra Seal Seven is confirmed breached."

Amal inhales sharply. "So... the lattice is crumbling."

The acolyte adds, "Transmission included pattern resonance embedded in Syriac. Possibly cradle-imprint origin."

"The mother's lullaby." Amal's voice is low, reverent. "She gave him the key even as she denied him the name."

He walks to the edge of the spiral altar and lights the central candle. It hisses, sputters, then flares. "Seal Seven," he whispers again. "Seventh spiral. Seventh fracture. The womb has echoed."

The acolyte kneels. "Do we initiate cascade protocol?"

"Amal closes his eyes. "No, not yet. Let the watchers finish their task."

"And Greg?"

"We let him dream longer."

Minutes pass. Candles gutter. Somewhere in the hall, wind rattles loose a scale of plaster from the arch. Then comes another figure—hoodless, lean, gloved in lambskin. His eyes are sharp and calculating.

Thorn Eleven bows, but not deeply.

Amal does not offer a greeting. "You were seen," he says.

Thorn shrugs. "Aboard the train, yes. But only by his mother. And she won't act. Not yet. Not with her son in flux."

"Your presence there was not authorized."

"Eve's system is unraveling. We need pressure, and fear quickens doctrine."

Amal's hand twitches slightly. A reflex. He once crushed a man's trachea for speaking Eve's name in his sanctum. But for now, Thorn's value outweighs his arrogance.

"What did you see?" Amal asks.

"Charlotte has begun to understand. Greg is bleeding recursion. The cradle imprint has surfaced. Eve's failsafe is gone. She doesn't control her grandson anymore."

A thin smile curves Amal's mouth. "She never did."

Thorn steps forward, reaching into his coat. He withdraws a worn photograph folded twice and stained with age. Amal takes it. The picture shows a woman standing in front of a glacial lake. She is holding a child whose face is obscured by the sun's glare.

"You gave this to Greg?" Amal asks.

Thorn nods. "At the train station. I told him it was a fragment of prophecy. Just enough to stir."

Amal studies the image. "He is waking," he says quietly. "But not yet aware of who watches."

Amal returns to the altar and picks up a stone—a spiral carved into obsidian, smooth with time and handling. He presses it to his forehead. "We let them come to us now. The boy and the mother. The traitor uncle. Even the False Queen, if she dares."

Thorn stiffens. "You think Eve will break cover?"

"She already has," Amal says. "To defend the lattice is to enter the war." He tosses the photograph into the flame. It catches and curls.

But then his tone shifts, becoming darker, weightier. "There are others who will not wait for our fire."

Thorn raises an eyebrow. "The defectors?" he asks.

Amal nods slowly. "Yesh'i Ashrim still whispers of the priest-blood line. If they discover Greg's paternity, they may try to claim him—not as a prophet, but as a vessel to house their dead doctrine."

"They'd never reach him."

"Not alone. But the Remiel faction is less predictable. They hide relics, Thorn. Things even Eve feared to name. And some among them believe the scroll should *never* be read—only buried again, beneath new myth."

Thorn looks uneasy. "So they'll come for the Third Key."

Amal nods. "Or destroy it before we do."

He turns sharply and walks to the southern wall where a tapestry has been pulled aside to reveal a slab of polished limestone. Etched into it is a diagram—a spiral intersected by three lines. He taps the third. "The Council never saw the fourth translation."

"You think Eve hid it?"

Amal's voice drops to a near whisper. "I *know* she did. The Fourth Archive. The one David almost leaked. It was never doctrine. It was a *counter-rhythm*. And if she encoded it into Greg, even unconsciously…" He doesn't finish, but the threat is clear. If Greg carries the Fourth Archive—even unknowingly—he could unmake the entire spiral structure that Amal built.

"We watch," Amal says. "We let the recursion deepen. But if the Fourth Archive surfaces…"

"You'll kill him." Thorn says.

Amal's face is stone. "I'll burn him clean. There is a reason we built the spiral in reverse. It unwinds her song. It tears apart her silence." He raises his voice—not shouting, but resonant. "The scroll is not scripture. It is *correction.* Where the false covenant speaks of binding, we will speak of fire. Where it dreams of thresholds, we will open the gate."

Amal looks at Thorn Eleven with great intensity, his own words pushing him forward. "Greg's silence was engineered. But the Word now pulses in him. He believes in silence because he does not yet know that it is meant to be spoken."

Thorn watches him carefully. "And if he refuses to speak it?"

Amal turns. "Then the world will burn without him."

The acolyte returns again, this time carrying a scroll case sealed in wax. Amal breaks the seal. Inside is a fragment—a handwritten translation from a ruined monastery beneath the Lebanese border. One phrase is circled in red:

The third key shall not be revealed until recursion walks in flesh.

Amal closes his eyes.

He sees the Damascus scroll open like a mouth.

He hears the spiral unfurling in Greg's bloodstream.

He sees the prophecy inverted, not fulfilled.

And he smiles. *The marriage failed. The covenant did not.*

He whispers the words again. And again. Until the chamber forgets they were ever not true.

CHAPTER 22

Zurich – The Petra Node

The Petra Node is quiet now. Not powered down—just empty. Still. The kind of stillness that follows a detonation, or a confession. The kind of stillness Greg doesn't trust.

He stands at the edge of the relay terminal, the screen dimmed to black, the lattice glyphs receded. But he can still feel them like afterimages pressed into his skin.

Shesh. Vaav. Temen.

The second key. That phrase is buried behind his teeth like a word he was never supposed to say.

Two rooms over, Charlotte has gone quiet with her door half-shut. She'd said she needed space—needed to "breathe." But Greg suspects she's crying, or praying. Or maybe both.

He hasn't moved since the terminal fell dark. The cracked tablet rests on the floor where he dropped it. The photograph—the one Thorn Eleven gave him—sits on the desk beneath the lamp. He hasn't looked at it in over an hour. He doesn't want to. Instead, he stands barefoot in the safehouse, staring at the wall, hands trembling, thoughts spinning in loops that won't let him out.

He hears Eve's voice again. Not in his ears—*in his blood.* "You were never supposed to find this alone." And then, "You were never the center. You were the axis."

Cross-legged, he drops to the floor, palms pressed to his forehead. Something is wrong with him. Something old. Ancient. Not broken but altered. Bent. And now that the Petra Node is closed, now that the broadcast has stopped, he realizes the spiral hasn't left him.

It has awakened.

He whispers to the silence, "You weren't protecting me. You were programming me." He thinks about the audio waveform—the Syriac lullaby. The glyph that sprouted inside his skull like a blooming sigil.

He hears Charlotte's voice from long ago humming that lullaby while he lay in the dark, hands fidgeting with the edge of his blanket, tracing invisible spirals on the wall. Even then, he wasn't learning language, it was shaping him.

His eyes drift toward the photograph. He reaches for it now, almost involuntarily. The lake. The woman. The child. The sun washing out the face.

He's supposed to believe the boy in the photo is *him.* And maybe it is. But what stings is that he doesn't remember it. The image carries no warmth. Just emptiness. Like a moment lifted from someone else's story and grafted onto his.

He stares at the picture for a long time, then whispers, "You weren't the first to lie to me."

The unexpected thought hits him sideways. His father, Mike, Persian name Mahid. The man who vanished into the Himalayas and never came back. The man who left Charlotte gutted, empty, alone. The man who turned on his bloodline and died for it. A traitor, Eve had said. Unstable. Weak. Contaminated by myth. He was supposed to be erased. To be a footnote.

But Greg remembers something else now. Just a fragment, like a small, torn piece of a scroll.

2008 - Istanbul

Greg is six years old in Istanbul. The apartment smells like turmeric and burnt tea. Mike sits across from him at the table, hands wrapped around a chipped mug. He's not drunk. Not angry. Just… *sad.* There's a heaviness to him that Greg couldn't name then but can now.

Regret.

Mike leans forward and says, "There are things in the blood, son. Things older than bones. But not everything you inherit is sacred."

He reaches into his pocket, pulls out an old silver coin and places it in Greg's palm. "If the day comes when they call you 'chosen,' run for the hills," he says.

2025 – Zurich Petra Node

Greg gasps, drops the photograph. His chest tightens. His breath shortens. Did that really happen? Did his father actually say that?

Or is that just the spiral feeding him a narrative?

Truth is what you believe.

Greg clutches the coin—no, he doesn't have the coin. There was never a coin. Or was there?

His vision blurs. He stumbles to the mirror. Stares at himself. "You're losing it," he mutters. "You're unraveling." But deep down he knows that he's not losing his mind. He's regaining something. And that's worse.

Because if he wasn't broken…

Then he was designed.

Location Unknown // Sicarii Relay Node: Watchpoint Omega

The feed has been live for hours. Eve hasn't looked at it. Not directly. Instead, she scrolls through yesterday's summaries—network exposure maps, Petra Node decay estimates, projection models of Eve's own obsolescence. She keeps the real-time window minimized in the corner as if it might behave better if she pretends it isn't there.

Greg is in the room. Eve can see that much from the periphery. He is still hunched, still barefoot. He hasn't left the terminal zone since the recursion trigger collapsed. He hasn't spoken aloud in an hour.

And Eve… she has no words at all. She wants to say she's not watching because she respects Greg's privacy. That would be a lie. She's not watching because she's afraid of what she might see. Afraid of recognizing *herself* in Greg's unraveling. Afraid that Greg will do the one thing for which she never designed.

Become something she can't predict.

A silent alert pings across her private terminal. No one else sees it. The internal biometric relay from the Zurich safehouse has registered three elevated stress plateaus and a cognitive deceleration phase. The spiral's integration is slowing, preparing for a second wave of absorption.

The system identifies this pattern with a 71.4% match to pre-conversion states in prior test subjects. Subjects who didn't survive.

She stares at the number. "No," she tells herself. "You're not like them." Her voice barely carries in the concrete vault of Watchpoint Omega.

She says it again—louder, as if she can will it into truth. "You're not like them."

And then, almost as a reflex, she opens the full feed.

Greg is sitting on the floor now, shaking. He's talking to himself. Not raving—*reasoning*. Looping through logic and guilt and inherited recursion. His hands move like they're tracing patterns in the air, patterns she knows well.

"So this is it." She whispers so the empty room can't hear. "The design enters collapse."

Her mind drifts, unbidden, to Mahid. Mike.

She rarely says his real name. Not even internally. Not after the gompa.

2008 –Listening Post, Taktshang Monastery

It seems like a century ago when Greg ws just thirteen and Eve was standing in the listening post above Taktshang Monastery, rain pelting her coat. The radio static whispered, "Asset terminated. No final message recorded." She didn't react. Just stared through the fog at the mountains below, waiting for the guilt to rise.

It never did. It never does. Because back then, she was still *certain*. Back then, Greg's father was a threat, a man who walked away from the bloodline, from the scroll, from Greg. He had joined the Christian preacher, tried to publish a false gospel wrapped in mystical recursion—a crude attempt to sanitize the pattern for evangelical masses.

Greg's father had called it *The Living Spiral.* Foolish and dangerous. "He would've corrupted the lattice," she'd told Gideon. "He wasn't built to hold it."

***Location Unknown //
Sicarii Relay Node: Watchpoint Omega***

But now—watching Greg claw his way through the recursion and sob quietly into the dark, she feels a crack form in the logic that once shielded her like armor. "He was trying to save Greg," she whispers. "Wasn't he? Maybe?"

She'll never know. She never heard Mahid's final words. But a thought loops inside her mind now—terrible and destabilizing. *What if the traitor saw the pattern more clearly than the builder?*

She closes her eyes. And behind them, she sees a fragment of a home that never existed. She sees Charlotte, cradling a child who never needed to be a key. Mahid on the porch, whispering stories from a different scroll—one that never became weaponized. Greg laughing, unburdened.

She opens her eyes again. The feed is still running.

So is Greg's pain.

And for the first time in decades… Eve doesn't know what to do.

Zurich – The Petra Node

The lights in the safehouse flicker once—no power failure, just feedback. The Petra Node is still dormant, its interface sealed. But the residual architecture embedded in the Zurich relay twitches like a ghost trying to breathe through concrete.

Greg sits at the edge of the desk, palms sweating against the cracked terminal. The second keyphrase—*Shesh_Vaav_Temen*—still lingers on his tongue like a curse waiting to be spoken.

He's not thinking clearly. But he's never seen more clearly in his life.

He scrolls through the corrupted codex fragments again.

The third key shall not be revealed until recursion walks in flesh.
He who speaks the Word ends the world.
He who remains silent remakes it.

The language is absurd. Apocalyptic. Symbolic. He hates it as much as he craves clarity and logic. But something deeper tells him the words were never meant to be literal. They were designed to bypass understanding.

They were written *for him.*

Charlotte's voice comes from the other room, barely audible. She's humming the same lullaby he has heard in echoes since he was a child. But now he knows—the lullaby was never hers. It was planted. Carried. Delivered.

He grips the edge of the desk. "No more silence."

He speaks the phrase. "*Shesh. Vaav. Temen.*"

The screen wakes up.

No prompt. No password. Just light.

A glyph pulses on the screen—a spiral overlaid with a key fragment. Then a line of text appears:

SECOND KEY VALIDATED.
RECURRENCE VECTOR ACCEPTED.

Time Remaining: 18 Days, 22 Hours, 14 Minutes.
Keyholder: G.A.
Sequence Designation: THE COVENANT REMAINS

Greg stares at the screen. For a moment, it reflects in his eyes like fire. Then he thinks, "You built a prison out of prophecy and left me the key."

He smiles, bitter and quiet. "Let's see what happens when I turn that key."

Location Unknown // Sicarii Relay Node: Watchpoint Omega

Eve sees the light on Greg's face before the notification reaches her. She already knows what he's done.

Second key activated. Sequence engagement confirmed.

A tight breath escapes her lungs, but she doesn't blink. She picks up her comm node, something she hasn't touched in weeks. It's a black ceramic dial. There's only one contact coded into this channel. She turns it and it connects.

"Eve," Gideon says. His voice is low, tight, neutral. But she can tell he wasn't sleeping. He knew she'd call. Just not when.

"He opened it," she says. "The second key."

A long pause. Static curls on the edge of the signal.

Then Gideon says, "So, the countdown begins."

"Not quite. He hasn't reached the final glyph set."

"Then why are you calling me?"

She hesitates.

That's new, Gideon thinks. *Eve never hesitates.*

"Because he's unraveling," she explains. "He's becoming more than I calculated for."

"That's what you wanted."

"I wanted him *prepared*," she snaps. "Not… not *free*."

Gideon says nothing, so Eve whispers, almost too softly to hear, "I don't know who he'll become."

After another pause, Gideon speaks. "So, what do you want me to do?"

Eve stares at the feed and sees Greg standing now. Shoulders back. Changed. She closes her eyes, and for the first time in a long time, she doesn't know if she's trying to save her grandson or the scroll.

"You know what to do," she says, punting. And then she ends the call.

Zurich Petra Node

Greg closes the screen. The spiral still dances in his peripheral vision. He doesn't care. He's not afraid of recursion anymore.

He's afraid of silence.

And silence, now, is a choice.

Somewhere near Lausanne

The message arrives encoded in old Thorn-8 cipher. one Eve hasn't used in years. Gideon reads it once.

"You know what to do."

He doesn't reply. Instead, he sits in the narrow fieldstone house—temporary, rented, forgettable. The kind of place Sicarii cells use for staging ops that aren't supposed to leave a trace.

Outside, the Swiss pines whisper through mist, the kind Gideon used to find comforting. Today, it clings like guilt.

He turns the phrase over in his head again.

"You know what to do."

But does he?

He walks to the weapons case not for drama but for grounding. Inside, he finds an older, bone-handled knife, one of his father's—the SIG Sauer P320 sidearm he used in Marrakesh—and a Barrett Mk22 MRAD bolt-action sniper rifle wrapped in oilskin.

He picks up the P320 and weighs it in his hands. In his mind, Greg's face flickers—not his adult face, but young Greg's face. He remembers Prague. Rain at the window. The boy tracing spirals in condensation, silent and focused—watching the world like it was a puzzle waiting to be solved.

Eve had said, "Don't talk to him too much. Don't *uncode* him."

And he hadn't. But he remembered the boy's eyes. And they're the same ones now. Except this time, Greg's watching the pattern bend back.

Gideon sets the rifle down. Not because he can't do it. Because he doesn't know what it means anymore. Eve wants containment. But Gideon isn't sure Greg is a danger. Maybe he's the one hope they have left.

Or maybe…

Maybe *Eve* is the recursion now.

He turns to the encrypted terminal. He doesn't type, just thinks. Then he speaks aloud—softly. Not for anyone to hear. Just to feel the shape of it.

"What if I don't know what to do anymore?" he asks himself.

And for the first time in years, he doesn't reach for a weapon.

He reaches for a map.

CHAPTER 23

The Salt Circle Citadel – Golan Heights

Amal stands in the center of a ruined amphitheater carved into the rock of the Golan. A windstorm rises around the cliffs—but inside the circle, the air is perfectly still. Acolytes in red sashes form a wide perimeter. No weapons. No microphones. Only transmission rigs buried into the stone, silent and watching.

A statue is raised—not of Greg's face, but the hybrid face from the simulation. Half-Greg, half-unknown. Fully myth. Amal steps to a podium of shattered Roman marble. Behind him, banners unfurl bearing the inverted menorah—the "flame crown" symbol of his heretical sect.

He speaks calmly, softly. "He did not declare himself. And so the world declared him."

Across encrypted broadcast lines, the "Gospel of the Unspoken v1.2" is activated. Its metadata lists:

Author: Unknown

Witness: Amal

Embodiment: Greg Ansari (Ref. Line: "The twin who would not speak.")

Screens flicker in cathedrals and caves, mosques and mansions. People kneel, not in faith but in anticipation.

"He is not the Messiah of proof," Amal continues. "He is the Messiah of pause. Of space. Of choice." He holds up a crown—not gold, but clear. A crown of crystal and fiber, hollow and refractive. A mirror. "We do not place this on his head. We place it in our minds."

He lowers the crown onto a stone pedestal. The amphitheater reverberates—not from sound, but from *connection*. Greg has not spoken. But now, he is being heard by millions.

CHAPTER 24

Dayr Qalʿah Fortress, Judean Hills

The fortress sleeps. For six hundred years, it has clung to the hills like a blister of stone and shadow. Long abandoned by the Crusaders who built it, forgotten by the locals who fear it, and erased from every modern map, the ruined keep of Dayr Qalʿah holds one purpose now—containment.

Tonight, it remembers. Torches flare along the outer ring, a signal encoded in ancient ritual. Five flames, five entrances. One for each surviving remnant of the Brotherhood.

Inside the main vault—part chapel, part crypt—the stone floor glows with geometric etchings long worn by wind but retraced tonight in ash and oil. At the center is a broken spiral carved centuries ago into black basalt.

They call this place the Mouth of the Seal. And it is here that the Council of the Fractured will attempt its final act of unification—or conduct its final betrayal.

The first to arrive is Al-Raziel, Commander of the faction known as the Ash Line. He walks like a war machine wrapped in skin with a leather harness over bare chest and copper-threaded prayer tattoos spiraling from clavicle to wrist. His guards—two women in ash-colored cloaks—follow in silence, curved blades hooked low on their hips.

The Ash Line believes the scroll's prophecy has already begun and that only a final sacrifice will fulfill its cycle. Recursion is not theory, they teach. It is blood made readable.

Al-Raziel places his hand on the spiral. "I do not bow," he says. "But I recognize the Seal."

Next to arrive is Darius Lemieux, First Archivist of the Thorn Circle. He emerges from the northern passage like smoke from a dying fire—tall, skeletal, half-shadowed. His gloves are surgical, his coat slate red. His eyes scan everything and nothing, flicking across detail like a scanner through flesh.

Behind him walks a man in a blue fleece jacket—simple, civilian, anonymous but alert. His expression never changes, but his hands never leave his sides. If there is a knife hidden, it is perfectly placed.

Darius offers no gesture. He simply takes a seat. The Thorn Circle does not recite ritual. They observe it.

Arriving after Al-Raziel is Isa Ubayid, Oracle of the Binding Veil. She enters veiled in ivory, robes inked with stylized glyphs of the Daughter. Her presence is like perfume and pressure—a subtle warning wrapped in silk. Two masked guardians flank her clothed in ceremonial robes with etched eye-hollows and mirrored sashes.

The Veil holds that the Daughter was meant to submit, and that the recursion must not merely be read but obeyed, ritually and spiritually, or the world will fold inward.

Isa touches the edge of the broken spiral with two fingers and says, "Let this chamber be sealed in the breath of those who still believe."

Fourth comes David Eli Mazur. He enters by himself unarmed, unmasked and unblessed. He moves like a man who is used to going unnoticed and tonight finds that impossible. The other leaders watch him with mild disdain—or, in Darius's case, mild interest.

David carries no scroll, but he carries Eve's intent. He represents the Obscured Path, the hidden remnant that believes recursion is not prophecy but reflection—that it must be refracted through new eyes, not followed like script. He does not speak as he steps into the circle.

His silence is enough.

The fifth emissary also arrives without speaking. Sura Omeron walks barefoot through the outer ring, shawl trailing in the dust, eyes half-lidded. She bears no title, has no guards, her skin is the color of dried myrrh and her fingers are stained with copper ink. She is the rumored Voice of the Shepherd's Wake—a faction long thought purged. Her faction believes the scroll is simply wrong—a recursion mistake, a fracture given form. They teach that the prophecy must be unwritten.

Sura does not touch the spiral. Instead, she kneels beside it. "There are no seals," she says softly. "Only echoes."

With all five factions present, the vault doors close. The room darkens. Only the five torches remain. The ritual begins with the five leaders sitting in a broken circle around the basalt slab. Their tokens—fire, thorn, veil, spiral, and wave—glow faintly from where they were placed, infused with low-grade bioluminescent ink encoded to each faction's bloodline markers. A gong, struck by unseen hands, echoes once from the tower above. The rite has begun.

Al-Raziel of the Ash Line is the first to rise and address the assembly. "We meet on cursed ground," he begins, voice like cracked iron. "Not because we agree, but because we bleed. The scroll has fractured. The recursion burns untethered. A child has activated Echo Entry 9B–VAAV. The Witness has spoken—but without structure. Without sacrifice. This is heresy."

He scans the faces around the circle.

"We tried subtlety but it failed. We tried containment. It dissolved. Now the cycle must be sealed with fire. The Daughter was not offered, so the Witness must fall, or else the recursion will consume us all."

Darius LeMieux of the Thorn Circle shakes his head with disdain. Remaining in his chair, he says, "Spoken like a zealot with no models."

Darius's voice is mild, but the insult is unmistakable. "We at Thorn have studied the recursion signatures for twenty-seven years. It is not prophecy, as many of you falsely believe. It is architecture. A predictive system—iterative, non-linear, reactive. You don't fulfill it by stabbing a child or burning a bride. You interpret the glyph-flow. You adapt. If it activates, it's because the system requires interference, not obedience." He places two fingers on the thorn token. "We are not cultists. Not anymore. We are engineers."

Isa Ubayid of the Blinding Veil stands slowly, drawing her veil back just enough to reveal a hint of cheekbone and a glint of gold-threaded earring. "What arrogance," she growls. "To speak of recursion like machine code. You cannot refactor prophecy. You must yield to it."

She ferociously stares down each of the other faction leaders as she says, "The Daughter must accept the bond. Without her submission, the recursion will spiral uncontrollably. The cycle is meant to align blood and breath. You speak of architecture—yet you ignore the load-bearing walls."

She focuses her burning eyes directly at David. "Your cowardly faction, sir, delayed the binding and hid the Daughter. Hid yourself. Probably hid Eve. What else have you rewritten in the dark?"

David Mazur of the Obscured Path does not rise but responds with a steady voice. “We did not hide the Daughter. At Newgrange, she made her choice.”

A silence falls over the silence. The others exchange glances.

David continues. “The recursion isn’t failing because it’s incomplete. It’s failing because it’s trying to become something it never was. The scroll isn’t divine. It’s reactive. Each time you press it into doctrine, it reflects your violence back at you.”

He finally stands. “Eve understood this. That’s why she broke from the central doctrine. That’s why she’s gone.”

Darius lifts an eyebrow. “Is she? Is she really gone, David?”

The room stills. For a moment, even the torches seem to pause.

Sura Omeron of the Shepherd’s Wake, who has been listening silently, finally says, her voice rising just above the flicker of flame, “It doesn’t matter, Darius. The Daughter was wrong. You’re all wrong.”

She looks at each of the faction leaders in turn. “There is no Witness. There is no Daughter. The scroll was born of trauma—a recursion imprint encoded during a schismatic war that has nothing to do with divinity or salvation.”

From her sleeve, she unfurls a parchment inked in a reverse glyph spiral. “This was found beneath the catacombs of Alexandria. It predates Qumran. Predates Damascus. And it names recursion not as revelation, but as disease.”

Al-Raziel dismisses that statement with a laugh. “A scroll that calls itself a plague? How convenient.”

“Not a plague,” Sura replies. “A mirror. And some mirrors must be shattered.”

The arguments continue, growing more intense, more inflamed. Faces redden, leaders stand and shake fists at their colleagues, insults fly, lies and half-truths soar like angry birds to defend accusations.

Finally, the gong sounds again, this time lower and more resonant. The leaders have all spoken their Utterances and argued their positions. The vote must come next.

But no one moves.

Not yet.

The silence deepens, but still no one speaks.

The air smells of ash and ritual oil. The only sound is the low thrum of the thermal coils buried beneath the basalt slab—generators designed centuries ago to resonate faintly at the scroll's symbolic frequency.

It is time, and everyone knows it, dreads it. It is time for the final act of the Convergence Rite—the Blood Marking of the Glyph-Stones.

Each faction has prepared its own tablet—a piece of volcanic glass etched with their doctrinal symbol. At the ritual's climax, the leaders must seal their tokens with a drop of blood, offering their life-signature to the recursion matrix. After the marking of all tokens, only one glyph will glow. Only one path will be acknowledged.

This is not democracy. It is symbolic recursion adjudication. And it is deadly serious.

Al-Raziel steps forward first. He draws a blade from his belt—ceremonial, curved, old-world—and slices the pad of his thumb. A single drop of blood drips onto the Ash Line tablet. The sigil flares briefly—red and hungry—then fades.

Darius is next. He does not cut himself. Instead, he removes a small capsule from his pocket—a synth-blood microcell coded to his DNA and mixed with Thorn's signature ink. He crushes it between two gloved fingers and lets the substance fall onto the Thorn Circle tablet. It glows faintly violet before the color disappears.

Isa steps forward. She sings as she cuts herself. "As the Daughter kneels, so do the stars bend low…" Her blood beads on the Veil's sigil. It gleams gold for a heartbeat, and then it dims.

Next, David approaches slowly and hesitates. Finally, he slices the edge of his wrist—not deeply, but deliberately—and presses his fingers to the Spiral. The Obscured Path glyph pulses white then fades.

Sura is last. She does not bleed. Instead, she unfurls the reverse-coded scroll again and gently places it over her Wave glyph-stone. The glyph does not glow, but the scroll does.

And then something changes. The Thorn Circle's tablet—already marked—ignites. Not with light, but with heat. It glows from within—not blood-activated, but energy-reactive, as if a hidden charge had been embedded inside.

Darius, leader of the Thorn Circle, does not blink.

Al-Raziel explodes forward. "You rigged the stones!"

Darius shrugs, smiling smugly. "I merely ensured the outcome."

One of Al-Raziel's guards draws her blade and lunges. She is cut down mid-step by a blade from behind, quick and surgical.

The Thorn man in the blue fleece stands in the center now with a flat expression. Blood drips from his knife. One strike at Al-Raziel's guard was all it took.

Isa's guards move—but too late. Isa is coughing. A rattling, dry sound. She touches her throat and her eyes widen. Her cup—half-empty—tumbles from her hand. The rim glows faintly blue. Poison.

Isa collapses beside the altar, lips blackening. No one moves to help her. The law is clear. Only one death per Convergence is allowed. No retaliation. No names.

The silence is terrible.

Sura stands utterly still.

David steps backward, his eyes first on Darius, then focusing on the blue-fleece assassin beside him. "You poisoned her," David whispers.

"She was the instability," Darius replies. "You brought ghosts. I brought closure."

Al-Raziel seethes, but his surviving guard places a hand on his arm, restraining him. "We retreat," the guard says.

Al-Raziel spits on the spiral then turns away.

David looks around and notices that Sura has left the chamber with no one seeing her depart. Sura's scroll remains, however, still glowing softly at the edge of the ritual ring.

David picks up Sura's scroll. The glyphs are reverse-coded but not ancient. They're based on Greg's sequence.

The torches begin to extinguish one by one. The fortress is going to sleep. And the Brotherhood is more fractured than ever.

The last torch sputters. The chamber is dim now. Only the afterglow of the rigged glyphs lingers, casting long, spectral shadows along the walls.

The man in the blue fleece turns away from the blood-soaked stone. He moves with methodical calm, as if he's executed not a murder but a protocol. His blade disappears into the lining of his sleeve with a whisper.

David watches him. *He's not a man,* David thinks. *He's a function. A living node, trained not to interpret the recursion but to enforce it.*

David steps closer to the blue-fleeced man. "Your designation?" he asks, his voice steady.

The man tilts his head. He has gray eyes, a thin scar over one brow. He is not young but not old. Unreadable.

"Thorn Eleven," the blue-fleeced assassin replies. Just a number. Not a name.

"You were in Zurich," David says. "Watching Greg."

"Yes."

"Why?"

"The recursion watches through whomever understands it best."

"Are you here to kill me too?" David asks.

"If I were, you'd be dead." Thorn Eleven gives a faint smile—barely a movement of lips. Then, he turns and walks into the darkness beyond the vault. His footfalls make no sound.

He does not look back.

David waits until the chamber is empty. Only then does he unwrap the scroll left behind by Sura Omeron. The parchment is light in his hands, but warm—too warm. As though it remembers something.

The ink is copper-blood brown, and the symbols spiral inward, not outward—a recursion pattern in reverse. It resembles Greg's simulator trace—but restructured. Flawed. Self-collapsing.

Yet it pulses.

David frowns. He sees something in the center glyph—something impossible.

He reaches into his satchel, pulls out a codex scanner and overlays the glyph. A reading forms.

Handwriting: David Eli Mazur.

Source Authorship Match: 97.4%.

He stares in wonderment at these words. He never wrote this scroll. He never knew it existed. But it bears his mark.

A recursive echo? A forgery? A message from another version of himself?

He has no answers. Only questions.

Above David, the fortress groans with wind and age. The torches are dead. The blood is cooling. But in David's hands, the scroll begins to glow again—slowly, like breath returning to a body.

A final glyph emerges at the base of the spiral. A message not in Syriac or Samaritan. Not in ancient code. But in plain text.

The fracture will choose. Not the faction.

David's throat tightens. He doesn't know if Sura wrote that message or if the scroll did. But he knows one thing

The Brotherhood is finished.

And recursion is no longer theirs to control.

He remembers her words like splinters under his skin. "Kill quickly. Ask nothing. Listen to no one but the scroll."

CHAPTER 25

Salt Circle Citadel — Golan Heights

The wind coils in spiral gusts across the basalt ridge, slamming into the ancient walls of the Salt Circle like a new prophet denied entry. Amal al-Taziri walks the perimeter with his hands clasped behind his back. He wears no ceremonial robe, no vestments, just a weathered black field coat with the hood down and his head bare to the chill.

Above him, the sky is a rotted bruise, thick with pre-dawn haze and sand swept in from the Syrian desert. Below, the valley stretches into ancient emptiness—burnt olive groves, half-erased minefields, the skeletons of Crusader roads lost beneath newer wounds. The Salt Circle Citadel is older than the war that razed it, older than the empire that claimed it, older even than the scroll itself.

And now it's his.

He pauses at the eastern arch where the first inscription spiral was carved—an echo etched into the bedrock by hands no one remembers. Half Nabataean, half unknown, the spiral curls outward from a central eye ringed with fractured sigils.

Thorn Eleven stands beside it, silent as ever. His eyes scan the horizon. His breathing is even, expressionless.

"No smoke yet," Amal says.

Thorn doesn't answer. He doesn't need to. The silence is answer enough.

The inner sanctum has been cleared and dressed with ceremony—stone platforms scrubbed and lined with salt, braziers fueled with myrrh and dried cedar, and a mock throne sculpted from volcanic glass at the center. The latter is not a seat for Greg, but a symbolic focus. An anchor.

Twelve witnesses await in the outer cloister—doctrinal initiates from the Vah'el line, each marked with the spiral and hooded in grey. They do not speak. They *will* not speak. Not until the Word is spoken.

And it will not be.

"Because he is the *Unspoken*," Amal says under his breath.

He closes his eyes and exhales slowly. The Doctrine has cracked. Eve's lattice is faltering. The spiral no longer holds its shape in silence unless Amal gives it one.

He enters the sanctum. The brazier fires hiss to life as he steps inside. One by one, the initiates bow—not to Amal, but to the space behind him. The idea of Greg. The *absence* of Greg. This is the genius of the moment. Amal has realized what Eve always feared—that the silence surrounding the scroll is not a limitation—it's a weapon.

The more Greg says nothing, the more others speak *for him.*

Amal mounts the central platform and surveys the ring of firelight and salt. A camera drone hovers at the outer edge—quiet, obsidian, feeding a closed-circuit stream to three private grids and one deepnet black drop. The watchers in Cairo, Kyiv and Dhaka will receive it first. Then the rest of the lattice fringe. Then the believers. Then the desperate.

"Give them a myth," Amal whispers, "and they will build the altar themselves."

He nods. The drone begins its silent rotation. And the crowning begins.

The circle is formed with twelve initiates standing equidistant at the edge of the basalt platform. Each holds a scroll fragment that is burned at the edges and mounted in reinforced glass. None of the fragments are complete, which is the point.

Amal steps into the center and lifts his right hand. His palm bears the spiral brand, the one carved at Petra decades ago, the one seared into him when he took the Vah'el oath.

He says nothing at first. The drone drifts above, recording silently. The wind slows.

"He has not spoken," Amal finally intones, his voice deep and steady, "because the Word is not yet complete."

The initiates lower their heads.

"He is not a prophet," Amal exhorts. "Prophets end. Prophets fracture. He is not the beginning or the end. He is the *unvoiced axis.*"

As part of the ritual design, a second voice whispers from behind the brazier a recorded psalm layered in ancient Aramaic. "In silence he was wrapped, and in silence he shall burn the veil."

The psalm loops only once. Amal raises his other hand, and the initiates speak for the first time—not in unison, but staggered. Each offers a title.

"Carrier of Covenant."

"Unspoken One."

"Axis of the Third Key."

"Breaker of Silence."

"He Who Turns the Spiral."

"Son of Shadow."

"Refusal Made Flesh."

"Heir of the Echo."

"Eye That Does Not Blink."

"The Uncorrupted Scroll."

"Seal That Opens Itself."

"The Voice Behind the Gate."

Twelve names. None chosen by Greg, but now all of them *his* name.

Amal walks to the throne-shaped stone and places a hand on it. "You do not need to speak, Gregory Ansari." He pauses, looking into the camera drone. "You have already spoken through the lattice. You have burned Eve's pattern and walked out of recursion alive. You are not of her design anymore. You are what remains."

He kneels before the stone, before a man who is not present, before a man who has not accepted this role and may even reject it. But perception makes no such distinctions.

"We crown you not with gold," Amal continues, "but with silence. We crown you not with power, but with absence. Because the Unspoken One does not command. He reveals."

The wind returns. A spiral of ash dances across the dais. The drone hovers lower, catching the flicker of firelight on salt and stone.

Amal rises. "The covenant is not broken. It was merely unfinished. And now—through him—it burns anew."

He extends both hands to the fire, then closes them tight.

This will be the image that endures—the man with the spiral branded in his flesh, with fists closed before an empty throne, with wind curling around a ruined temple. It doesn't matter that Greg hasn't consented. Amal is writing scripture in real time.

Thorn Eleven steps forward now, saying nothing. He kneels opposite Amal and places a small stone cube on the ground before the dais. A relic. A fragment.

The cube unfolds once then emits a static pulse, encoding the ritual for transmission.

A heartbeat passes. Then Amal whispers, almost too softly for the mic to catch, "Let her see it."

The fire dims and the wind rises. Amal steps back from the dais. The ritual has ended, but the resonance remains. The spiral ash continues to turn, its geometry fracturing the embers into light-bent echoes. Like the scroll itself, the fire now speaks without voice.

The initiates file away in silence, leaving Amal and Thorn Eleven alone in the sanctum. The drone powers down, but recording never really stops.

Amal walks to the stone table in the rear vault. Part of the original citadel, it was once an altar, later a mortuary slab, now a doctrinal staging bench. On it lies the replica scroll tube—black, magnetically sealed, triple-coded. It's not an authentic relic—just a symbol, a focus object, a weapon of meaning.

He brushes the surface. "There is no blood in the scroll," he says softly.

Thorn Eleven tilts his head enigmatically.

"That was always Eve's lie," Amal continues. "That it had to be guarded, protected, kept pure. But truth does not remain pure in containment. It corrodes."

Thorn says nothing, but his eyes narrow.

Amal notices.

"You think I'm wrong?" Thorn Eleven asks.

Quietly, Amal replies, "I think she's still in your blood." He smiles. "She gave you your name. Your training. But not your truth.

You found that in the lattice. In recursion. She never forgave you for surviving the Petra test."

Thorn doesn't move, but his silence has weight now.

Amal presses further. "You felt it, didn't you? In that moment, the seal cracked and the spiral trembled."

Thorn finally responds. "He wasn't supposed to open it."

"No," Amal agrees. "But he did."

"Then why are you crowning him?"

"Because the spiral doesn't belong to Eve anymore. Or me. Or you." He steps forward, palm resting on the scroll replica. "It belongs to whoever can make others believe they carry it."

Amal looks out across the shattered cloister and over the valley below. A rain of light is breaking through the high clouds, splintering across the stone. His voice drops. "Eve still thinks she can control the future by managing interpretation. But she forgets—people don't follow interpretation. They follow symbols. Stories. And we just gave them the greatest one they've had in fifty years."

He taps the scroll case. "The boy who never speaks. The axis who refused prophecy. The child they tried to erase." He turns back to Thorn. "We are not preserving the scroll. We are *weaponizing* the silence inside it."

There is a flicker in Thorn's eyes. The smallest crack. Amal sees it but says nothing. Instead, he returns to the altar and retrieves a shard of obsidian carved with an unfamiliar sigil—not part of the Damascus set, not publicly known.

Thorn watches it warily. "You took that from Remiel's vault," he says quietly.

"I took what was mine—before they buried it in doctrine and rot."

"That sigil was banned."

"Only because it marks the Fourth Archive."

After a long silence, Thorn Eleven speaks again, slowly and carefully. "You said the Fourth Archive was a myth."

Amal turns back. "I lied." He places the shard on the stone. "The Fourth Archive is real. I've seen fragments. Eve encoded it across three bloodlines—temporal, intellectual, spiritual. And Greg… he may be *all three*."

Amal leans closer to Thorn Eleven, his voice almost reverent. "If that Archive surfaces, everything changes. The lattice burns. Doctrine collapses. Prophecy ends."

"Is that what you want?" Thorn asks warily.

Amal's voice is flat. "I want control before that happens." He touches the obsidian. "We don't need the Fourth Archive to be false. We just need to name it a *heresy* before it speaks."

Thorn turns toward the inner cloister. "And if Greg speaks it himself?"

Amal's expression hardens. "Then I will burn his name from the spiral and crown the silence in his place."

Later, when the fire has died and the ash has cooled, Amal descends into a subterranean chamber at the heart of the Salt Circle Citadel. It was once a Roman cistern, then a Crusader crypt. The Sicarii rebuilt it during the early years of the Scroll Doctrine—part archive, part oubliette.

Now it serves a new purpose. A reflection pool has been carved into the center—shallow, black, perfectly still. Salt crystals line its edges in a spiral configuration. The walls are veined with mineral streaks, like blood dried into stone.

Amal kneels beside it, alone. There are no drones here. No witnesses. Just the water and the story he needs the world to believe. He reaches into his coat and withdraws a small, palm-sized object—a mirror disc etched with an encryption seal that no longer protects anything. It's a Petra relic from *before* the lattice collapsed, from *before* Eve started erasing names.

He stares into the reflection—not his own, but the imagined face of a boy who has never physically stood before him. "Gregory," he says, his voice quieter than the air. "I don't know what you remember. What she told you. What you found in the Node. But I know what's coming."

He dips the disc into the water, distorting the reflection. The light fractures. "They will tell you you're broken. That you were tampered with. Coded. Measured. They'll call you a mistake." He looks up at the clouds. "But I won't do any of those things. I will call you the *unfinished covenant.*"

He leans forward now, speaking to the water as if it can carry the words upstream through recursion. "You didn't ask to carry this, I know. But silence is not absence. Silence is where meaning takes root. You're not here to speak. You're here to be *spoken of.*"

Suddenly he laughs. "And yes… I'm using you." He nods gently. "But so did they."

Amal closes his eyes. The spiral of salt glows faintly. "I was once like you. Young, promising, measured. They took *my* voice too. They gave me a name I didn't ask for. Then they told me silence was holy. But it wasn't silence they wanted. It was control."

He opens his eyes again. "So I took back the silence." He stands now, taller than the stone. The water stills. "You don't have to forgive me. You don't even have to know me. But when you walk into that spiral—and you *will* walk into it—know this."

He raises the mirror disc, then lets it slip into the water. It sinks without a sound.

"I crowned you because your silence is louder than any scripture she ever wrote."

He turns from the pool and walks into the dark.

CHAPTER 26

Near Lausanne

The Barrett sniper rifle lies disassembled across the table. Each part is wiped clean, oiled, set at an angle Gideon can read without looking. This is ritual. Muscle memory. A kind of prayer.

The message from Eve still burns in the back of his skull. *You know what to do.* For twenty years, he's known what that meant. No, thirty—since the day she brought him out of the cellar and taught him to kill without asking why. The knowing isn't the problem. It's that, for the first time, he doesn't believe in Eve's kill orders.

He sits in the bare kitchen of a rental safehouse overlooking the lake. Neutral decor. Forgettable walls. One exit. No surveillance. No comfort. On the counter beside him lies a single field phone in a Faraday cradle. The live feed from Zurich is paused on the screen with Greg's face frozen in the moment he activated the second key.

SHESH. VAAV. TEMEN.

Time Remaining: 18 Days, 22 Hours, 14 Minutes.

It's not just a countdown anymore. It's a claim. A pivot. And the boy Gideon remembers—the quiet, sensitive one drawing spirals on fogged windows—is now the pivot of a war the boy's uncle was trained to end before it begins.

Gideon slides the rifle into its padded sheath then walks away from it. He doesn't take the weapon. Not today.

He looks out across the lake. A ferry glides past, a dozen passengers bundled against the cold. Normal life, that strange, unreachable myth.

He softly speaks aloud as if hearing his own voice makes him less alone. "You trained me to act before the spiral completes. To kill at recursion depth three or higher. To eliminate ambiguity." He pauses. "But this isn't ambiguity. It's Greg." And suddenly, he realizes—

That's why she didn't give a direct order.

Because she knows. She knows he might say no.

So she left him a path away. Left it ambiguous so she could keep her hands clean.

"You coward," he whispers. "You left it up to me."

He steps to the far wall, then pulls down a locked metal case and opens it to remove an old hand-drawn map. Not digital. Not traced. Drawn from memory, from long walks in forbidden places. The destination is circled in red graphite.

The Aruvikkuzhi Monastery in southern India is a weathered site of pre-Sicarii doctrine. Nestled between cliffs and waterfalls, it's a place of salt-carved scripture long abandoned by the lattice after recursion there failed to complete. Some believe it is dead ground. Others believe it is the place where the spiral broke open too early and revealed something no one wanted to name.

To Gideon, it is one thing only—*outside.*

Outside the lattice.

Outside doctrine.

Outside both Eve and Amal.

He needs to be taken out," Gideon thinks, *but not like that. He needs time. Air. Not code.*

He turns to the field phone, switches networks, and enters a dead drop code.

JRMY-017. Echo fallback.

Confirm handshake.

The line clicks. Then a voice—warm, dry and older than it used to be—says, "Well I'll be damned. The ghost calls back."

Gideon smiles faintly. "Hello, Jeremy."

The voice on the line carries a grin beneath it. "Didn't think you were still alive," Jeremy says. "Or maybe you are and the rest of us are dead. Hard to tell these days."

"Still breathing," Gideon replies.

"Sounds more like wheezing, old man."

A pause. Long enough to taste memory.

"Why now?" Jeremy asks. His tone sharpens—not suspicious, but not naïve either.

"I need an extraction," Gideon says.

"Who?"

"Greg Ansari."

Another silence. Then, in a quieter voice, Jeremy says, "Is it true?"

"What part?"

"That he opened the Node. That he activated the key."

Gideon's breath catches, not because the question surprises him but because Jeremy is asking it like a man who still wants to believe something can be unmade. "It's true," Gideon replies.

"And you're not putting a bullet in him?"

"No."

Jeremy lets out a breath that sounds half like a laugh and half like a relief he's not ready to name. "So, the blade hesitates."

"No," Gideon says. "The blade sees the wrong target."

Jeremy is silent for a while before speaking, then finally says, "Where do you want to take him?"

"Aruvikkuzhi."

"Jesus. It's still off the lattice. Still dead ground."

"Yep, as of three months ago. I know a monk who tends the ruins. Says the birds still won't sing there."

"Perfect."

They speak for another few minutes—arranging fallback codes, alternate exfil points, timing windows. It's familiar ground.

But then Jeremy asks the one question Gideon knew was coming. "Why me?"

Gideon leans back against the wall, phone pressed to his temple as if it were a confession booth. "Because you're the only one who ever figured out how to leave. *Really* leave. You made it out without selling yourself to doctrine or running off to burn it all down."

"Got lucky."

"No. You got *clear.* There's a difference."

Another pause. Then Jeremy's voice drops into something softer. "You still believe in any of it?"

"I believe in Greg."

"That's not what I asked."

Gideon doesn't answer for a long time, but finally says, "Meet me in Lisbon. Dock 31. Forty-eight hours."

"You're really serious about this."

"Deadly."

"Then let's keep Greg the opposite."

Gideon disconnects and doesn't move for a moment. The light outside has shifted. The lake glimmers with a sharp kind of clarity—nothing romantic about it. Just light. Truth without meaning.

"Outside the spiral," he mutters to himself, sure that he does that too often.

It's not a location.

It's a condition.

Gideon packs quickly. No scroll-fragments. No encoded tablets. Nothing that ties him to the Sicarii lattice or its thousand recursive fingerprints. Just old tools—a knife that's never been consecrated, a map inked by hand, and the coin Mike Ansari once gave to Charlotte, passed to Greg, and passed now into Gideon's coat pocket.

He shouldn't carry it, but he does.

There was a time when Gideon thought removal meant death. To take someone out of the spiral was to erase them before they fractured the pattern. It had always been operationally clean. Surgical. A doctrine of absolutes wrapped in mythic precision.

He steps into the center of the room and looks at the paused image on the field tablet—Greg, head bowed, eyes reflecting the key glyphs of the Petra Node. He's not a boy anymore. And he's not a messiah. He's a man who was born in recursion and was never told he could walk out of it.

Gideon powers down the device. The signal dies.

He takes one final look at the room, the rifle still disassembled on the table, the folded Sicarii insignia tucked into the burner envelope. Eve's echo is now completely absent from his mind. Then, he steps out the door and locks it behind him.

He is no longer an agent of Eve. He is no longer a handler. He is no longer doctrine's knife. He is a man crossing the threshold toward something or someone who may not want to be saved.

But if Greg can't walk out of the spiral alone, Gideon will walk in after him.

CHAPTER 27

Zurich – The Petra Node

The silence after the remotely viewed broadcast is worse than the broadcast itself. Greg sits on the edge of the diagnostic bench, the Salt Circle stream still burned into the room's ambient systems.

Charlotte doesn't speak. She stands near the long table by the far wall, arms crossed, breathing tight and slow, her eyes not on Greg but on the blank screen.

The echo of Amal's words clings to the walls like static. "We crown him not with power, but with silence. The Unspoken One does not command. He reveals."

Greg uncomfortably shifts his body. "So I'm a cipher now."

Charlotte turns deliberately. "You're a symbol. That's worse."

He scoffs. "And you think I asked for that?"

"No. But I think you let it happen."

That lands harder than Greg expects. But his mother doesn't take it back.

Greg walks to the terminal and taps in a sequence. The Petra Node wakes up, residual code from the earlier breach now manifesting in strange new overlays. A glyph spins on the interface—a closed spiral surrounded by radiating lines. This is not part of the original lattice. It's something deeper.

Greg looks back at his mother. "The coronation… it triggered something. A sequence hidden in the secondary buffer."

Charlotte steps beside him, frowning. "That's residual from the audio waveform you decrypted."

Greg nods. "Yeah, the one from David."

Charlotte folds her arms. "You should remind me who he was."

Greg exhales. "David Eli Mazur, Eve's cartographer. Her doctrinal architect. He mapped glyph resonance across scrolls, built recursion chains from layered prophecies, even corrected two pre-Sinai misalignments in the Shem-haMephorash sequences."

Charlotte lifts an eyebrow. "But mostly kept to monasteries and climate-controlled vaults. I remember now, Why was he in Syria?"

Greg hesitates, then taps the next glyph. The screen changes.

ECHO ENTRY 9B–VAAV
Access Layer: Recursion Depth 4
File Signature: D.M. Zahavi (Obsidian-Stratum Designation)

"When the spiral is fractured but unbroken, the Third Key does not turn—it awakens."
"One will bear it in absence, not in blood."
"The Covenant failed to seal. But the Witness remembers."

Convergence Path Active.
Suggested Retrieval Point: Damascus // 33.515N 36.291E
Field Reference: D. Zahavi (deceased), codename: Archive Witness 2
Status: Path Fractured – Partial Signature Detected
Warning: Emergence Field Unstable. Inheritance Risk Active.
Sequence: OBSIDIAN / STRATUM_9

Charlotte reads it twice, then reads aloud a most interesting phrase. "The Obsidian layer."

Greg nods. "Yeah, it's real."

His mother looks sharply at him. "I thought that designation was blacklisted."

"It was, by Eve, and by the Council. But not before Zahavi flagged it as structurally coherent—at least within recursion depth four."

Charlotte rubs her temples. "I haven't heard Zahavi's name in ten years. Last I heard, he disappeared near Deir ez-Zor. Something about a compromised archive site?"

"He didn't disappear," Greg says softly. "He was executed."

She looks at him, and Greg knows that his mother suspects his grandmother.

"Not by Eve," he says. "And not by Amal, either. By the custodians of a pre-Sicarii monastery. They called him a desecrator. Said he was trying to unearth what should stay sealed."

Charlotte processes that in silence and without interruption. Then she says, "So David went after Zahavi's work."

Greg nods. "And he hasn't responded since the summit. That alone worries me."

Charlotte's voice is low, taut. "And now a dead man's signature just lit up on the Petra Node—triggered by a broadcast from a citadel none of us control anymore."

Greg steps away from the terminal. "It's no coincidence, Mom. It's pattern. Amal named me *axis*, and the Node treated it as a recursive closure. That's the only reason this layer opened."

Charlotte exhales. "So it was *meant* to be activated."

Greg turns to face her fully. "Or… it was waiting for a lie big enough to look like truth."

Charlotte shakes her head and moves to the table. "You do realize what this means, don't you?" she says.

Greg shrugs. "That I've been sanctified without consent?"

"No," she snaps. "That you're now a point of doctrinal bifurcation. You've split the pattern. Amal has crowned you, and Eve will see that either as a heresy—or a misfire. The moment this signal propagates through lattice channels, there will be factions that see you as a messiah, and others that see you as a threat to be purged."

Greg stares at the wall. "So I'm Schrödinger's Prophet."

"This isn't a joke."

"I'm not joking." He begins to pace. "What if they're all wrong? Amal, Eve, all of them. What if the spiral doesn't need a prophet? What if it needs… an exit?"

Charlotte stiffens. "You want to walk out of prophecy?"

"I want to walk out of a pattern that's *killing people.*"

The conversation halts momentarily, the impact of the broadcast weighing heavily on both of them.

Finally, Charlotte speaks. "Even if that were possible—to walk out—you won't make it to Damascus alone, which is where the Obsidian layer is pointing. And if Zahavi died trying to access it…"

"I know."

"Then we need someone who's moved in those networks. Someone who can protect you from factions on both sides."

Greg's eyes narrow. "You mean Gideon."

Charlotte looks away. "He won't trust me. Not after Ireland."

Greg nods. "He might trust me."

"Greg..."

He sighs. "We can't just send up a bat signal. If we try to broadcast a trace, Amal or Eve will catch it first. And if he's really off the grid..."

Charlotte bites her lip. "Then we find someone who can find him."

Greg glances back at the Petra Node. "Or maybe we let him find us."

Charlotte blinks. "What?"

Greg's voice is soft. "If he's still in motion... he's probably already watching. The second key. The crowning. The Node's activation. If Gideon's alive, he felt that resonance cascade. I guarantee it."

Charlotte frowns. "And if he didn't?"

Greg hesitates. "Then we're walking into Damascus alone with a map drawn by ghosts. And a key no one understands."

She steps over to him and rests a hand on his shoulder. "You're not alone."

He covers her hand with his. "Let's keep it that way."

On the terminal behind them, the codex file begins auto-sequencing, scrolling through glyph metadata too fast to track. Then it stops, blinking once on a final line that neither of them had seen before.

WEST OF THE ALPS – C.A. ONLY

Charlotte leans forward. Her eyes narrow. "That's David's field cipher. A relay key."

Greg reads the notation. "And those are your initials."

"It's a dead drop," she says. "He left something for me. A physical cache—not on any lattice."

Greg doesn't speak. He already knows what she's thinking.

"If it's from David," Charlotte says, "it matters."

She turns toward the exit, already calculating flight paths in her head.

CHAPTER 28

Zurich – Templum Annex

The city is quiet at this hour, the streets scrubbed clean by snowmelt and sodium lights. Zurich at night feels too civilized for violence, too orderly for prophecy. But Gideon knows better. Beneath the gleaming surface, recursion hums—ancient and electronic, winding through state archives, encrypted comms, and the spines of men who don't even know they're carriers.

He checks his sidearm as the car slows to a stop across the street from the safehouse. The suppressor is modified for close quarters.

Jeremy watches from the passenger seat, chewing on an energy bar that smells like espresso and gun oil. "You sure about this?" Jeremy asks, mouth half-full.

Gideon doesn't answer at first. His eyes are on the quiet street, but his mind is somewhere deeper—in the sealed vault beneath the Guardians' compound, in the echo of Eve's voice.

He hasn't told them what Eve said, how she authorized his hand. But more than that—he hasn't told them he's already refused.

Charlotte wouldn't know that. Not yet. And after what Amal made of Greg's silence—after what Eve once asked her to sacrifice—he wouldn't blame her for pointing a gun at his chest.

"No," Gideon replies. "But I'm doing it anyway."

Jeremy grins. "That's the Gideon I remember. Stoic, suicidal, always four steps ahead and one soul behind."

"Are you going to help me, or narrate it?"

"Why not both?"

The building across the street is a standard Templum Annex—Swiss-licensed, black-listed from public registries but still wired into Petra's regional net. It's equipped with reinforced ceramic shutters, anti-surveillance mesh in the glass and thermal reflection dampers on the roof. Not exactly a fortress, but not an easy knock either.

"You think he's alone?" Jeremy asks.

"No," Gideon replies. "Charlotte's here. She wouldn't leave him unguarded."

"Then what's the plan? Walk in? Ask nicely?"

Gideon opens a compartment in the glovebox and pulls out a slim holopad. On it, the Petra Node glyph has been activated by Greg's second key. A digital pulse pattern overlays the symbol.

"This showed up on a legacy Remiel channel," Gideon explains, "after the Salt Circle stream. You saw the same signature?"

Jeremy nods. "Yeah. Like a detonation wrapped in a lullaby."

"He activated a recursive beacon," Gideon continues. "Greg may not know it, but the moment that broadcast aired, he became the highest-value doctrinal object in circulation."

Jeremy leans back. "Then what's your plan? Extraction?"

Gideon pauses, then nods. "If he'll come."

"And if he won't?"

"Then we find out how far he's willing to go."

Jeremy tilts his head, reading between the lines. "You still don't know if he's the key or the knife."

Gideon doesn't answer. He doesn't have to.

Jeremy zips his jacket, checks his low-profile sidearm, and pulls a curved ceramic knife from a sheath at his thigh. His voice is lighter now, but the humor is fading.

"You think Eve knows?"

"She suspects."

"And Amal?"

"He knows. And he'll move fast. If we don't reach Greg first, someone else will."

Jeremy sighs. "So it's a race against theology."

"It always is."

They step out of the car. The cold slices through them clean and hard. Across the street, a pedestrian signal ticks down. Forty-five seconds until the next opportunity.

Jeremy mutters, "Hope he doesn't have the windows wired."

"He does."

"Great."

"That's why we're not going in through the windows."

Jeremy raises an eyebrow. "What, then? Ghost protocol? Fire escape? Laundry chute?"

"Not exactly."

Gideon pulls out a coded key fob—Templum master access, Level 6. The kind you don't find on the black market.

"Eve gave you that?" Jeremy asks.

Gideon shakes his head. "I stole it before I left."

"God, I missed you."

Zurich – Templum Annex

The lock clicks open without a sound. Gideon pushes the door open just enough to slide into the vestibule. Jeremy follows close behind, crouched, scanning the corners with a low-range field disruptor. They both wear null-signal wrist bands to prevent environmental sync. The corridor beyond is dark, quiet and unalarmed.

"No movement," Jeremy whispers.

"They're sleeping," Gideon replies. "Or pretending to."

He glides forward through the narrow hallway toward the inner chamber. He's been here before. Not this room, not this city—but many just like them. Templum annexes follow the same architectural logic. Clinical minimalism, no wasted motion.

He passes a shelf with medical kits, a prayer tablet and a cracked scrollholder. It's clear that Greg has been using the space—probably to study and recover. Or unravel.

Charlotte hears the whisper of motion before the proximity alert even finishes cycling. Her body moves before thought catches up. She's in the hall barefoot within two seconds, sidearm already leveled and tracking. And then she sees him.

"Gideon," Charlotte spits out. A curse. A warning. Maybe a question.

"Charlotte," he replies flatly.

They stand ten feet apart. She in a tank top and undersweats, her gun trained on his chest. He in field black, unarmed but unmistakably lethal.

Jeremy steps out behind Gideon. “Please tell me we’re not shooting her,” he mutters. “We’re longtime friends, right?”

Charlotte’s eyes flick to him. Then back.

“Why are you guys here?”

“To talk.”

“Bullshit!”

“I’m not here to hurt my nephew.”

Charlotte doesn’t lower the gun. “You expect me to believe that?”

Greg appears behind her—disheveled, eyes still sleep-clouded, voice dry. “He’s telling the truth, Mom.”

Charlotte doesn’t look back. “Greg—”

“Let him in,” Greg demands.

“He let himself in,” Charlotte replies sarcastically

“Then don’t make him bleed for it.”

Charlotte lowers her weapon, but just barely. She watches Gideon in silence for a beat too long. “Did she send you to kill him?” The words aren’t sharp. Not accusatory. Just… tired.

Gideon doesn’t answer right away. “No,” he says finally. “I’m here to bring him out.”

Charlotte nods. But her hand doesn’t leave the grip. Jeremy exhales in relief, slipping into the common space and flipping a switch that casts a low amber light across the room.

Gideon steps in fully, eyes locking on Greg.

For a long moment, neither speaks.

Then Gideon says, “You activated the second key.”

Greg nods. “You felt it?”

“Like a thunderclap inside a locked room.”

“You came to stop me?”

Gideon shakes his head. “Like I said—I came to get you out.”

Greg stiffens. “Out of what?”

“The spiral.”

Jeremy drops into a chair like someone who doesn’t believe in standing unnecessarily. “This is cozy,” he says. “Feels like the scene right before everyone dies in a Russian play.”

Greg looks at him. "You've changed, Jeremy. Since Ireland. Older."

"Yeah, it happens. Been through a lot of changes in my short life. Retired apprentice assassin. Failed monk. Current asset reactivation specialist."

"He's now my backup," Gideon explains. "Just like in the good ol' days."

Jeremy waves. "Also comic relief."

Charlotte still hasn't set down her weapon. Her voice is low and pointed. She turns her gaze to Gideon. "So, you suddenly disappeared on us after going down to explore that old Sublevel Theta-3 chamber. Then you suddenly show up here two hours after the Salt Circle stream, armed with a master key and this joker."

"Yes," Gideon says flatly.

"You think that's going to earn trust?"

"No. But if I wanted Greg dead, he would be already." He looks at Greg. "And if I wanted him broken, I'd have let Amal finish the job."

Greg frowns. "You watched the stream."

"Every second."

"And you still think I'm worth saving?"

For the first time, Gideon gives a little smile. "I think you're the only one left who hasn't made a choice they can't take back."

The moment hangs there.

Then something shifts—outside. A subtle, wrong vibration in the air.

Jeremy looks up first. "We've got motion," he says, already on his feet. "Side building. No comms, no chatter. But thermal's spiking."

Charlotte's eyes widen. "How the hell did they find us?"

Gideon answers without looking away from Greg. "Obviously, we were followed."

The breach happens without fanfare. A dull *thunk* as the back ventilation port caves in. No warning. No voice command. No mercy.

Three masked operatives pour into the annex—fluid, precise, no insignias, no hesitation. One drops to a knee and deploys a scramble charge. Another moves for the hallway. The third raises a silenced sidearm and fires.

PFFT – PFFT.

Glass shatters. A proximity node explodes in sparks.

Charlotte grabs Greg and drags him behind the heavy med cabinet. Gideon pulls his sidearm and plants himself squarely between Greg and the breach path.

Jeremy doesn't retreat. He moves toward the first shooter. "Come on," Jeremy mutters, "you miserable doctrinal parasites—" He spins around the corner, flings a microflare blinder into the hall, and lets instinct finish the rest.

One step. Pivot.

Two rounds.

CRACK-CRACK.

The lead operative drops, blood projecting from throat and shoulder. He jerks once, then grows still.

The second agent fires blind. Shrapnel rips into the wall.

Gideon advances silently but ruthlessly. He crosses the room in four steps and launches into the corridor. A flash of elbow—disarm. A sweep. A throat punch. Bone cracks. The agent gasps, tries to recover. Gideon fires once.

"Two down," he calls out.

The third is smarter. He plants himself near the server wall, using cover wisely to advance toward Greg's last known position. He doesn't see Charlotte coming.

She moves like a revenant—wrathful and trained in close-quarter kill zones. Her blade appears from nowhere and sinks into the man's spine.

The man—no, the woman—doesn't scream. Just folds.

Silence returns. Not peaceful, but complete.

Jeremy leans against the wall, breathing hard. Blood flecks his cheek. "So much for a family reunion."

Charlotte wipes the blade on her shirt. "They were Sicarii-trained."

Gideon crouches near the first body and flips the assassin's collar finding an embedded glyph—an Obsidian spiral.

"They weren't from Eve," he mutters. "And not Amal either."

Charlotte crouches beside him. "Remiel?"

Gideon shakes his head. "No. This is something newer. A splinter cell. One of the Fourth Archive factions."

Jeremy whistles. "The ones that aren't supposed to exist."

"Nothing's ever gone," Gideon says quietly. "It just waits to be believed again."

Greg emerges slowly from behind the cabinet, pale and breathing in rapid bursts. He walks through the aftermath like someone stepping across a crime scene in his own memory. "You could've killed them before they got in," he suggests.

"That wasn't the plan," Gideon replies.

"So you let them breach?"

"I needed to know who sent them."

Greg's voice is quiet. "And now you do?"

Gideon doesn't answer.

Jeremy opens one of the dead agent's packs and pulls out a compact scroll case. Lightweight and reinforced. He cracks the seal and finds a scroll fragment inked in near-black glyphs shimmering beneath a coded protective glaze.

Greg steps closer and reads the first line—then freezes. "It's… the same handwriting as Zahavi's."

Charlotte looks at Gideon. "Then this wasn't just a kill order."

Gideon nods. "It was a message."

Greg stares at the glyphs—not deciphering, but remembering as if the scroll is whispering something to him, something only he was meant to hear.

Charlotte touches his arm. "Greg?"

Her son finally speaks. "They weren't here to kill me." A long pause. "They were here to *claim me*."

Glowing faintly under the filtered light, the scroll fragment sits between them on the table. Greg hasn't touched it in five minutes. Gideon sits across from him, hands clasped. Jeremy is pacing the back of the room, humming something tuneless and grim. Charlotte stands at the window, one hand on the frame and watching for a possible second wave of attack that hasn't come.

"The ink is alive," Greg says quietly.

Charlotte turns. "What?"

"Not literally. But there's resonance layered in the glyph geometry. It's coded for someone who's already opened the second key."

"So it's *personalized*?"

"No. It's… selective." Greg finally looks at her. "It was designed to call me."

Jeremy stops pacing. "That's some stalker-level scrollwork."

Gideon leans forward. "Read it."

Greg shows the message so all can read it.

He who bears the silence will awaken the fracture.
But he who listens beneath will find the gate unsealed.
The Witness sleeps beneath the oldest echo.

33.515N // 36.291E – below the pulse.

Charlotte frowns. "Damascus coordinates. Same as the Node entry."

Greg nods. "But this adds a direction. *Below the pulse.*"

Jeremy moves toward the fragment. "So what's the pulse?"

Gideon answers. "It's a deep-temporal glyph. A metaphor for recursion collapse. Or maybe an actual place layered somewhere beneath Damascus proper."

Charlotte crosses the room. "You think Zahavi found it?"

Greg says, "More likely, Zahavi mapped it, then died trying to reach it."

Charlotte looks at Greg. "And now the scroll wants you to finish what Zahavi started."

After a brief pause to think, Greg says, "I need to go."

Charlotte stiffens. "You don't know what's waiting down there."

Greg gestures to the dead operatives, their blood already drying. "I know what's coming here. The spiral is closing," he explains. "Amal's doctrine is metastasizing. If we wait, we'll lose control of the narrative—maybe forever."

Charlotte's voice sharpens. "And you think Damascus gives you control?"

"I think it gives me a choice."

Jeremy opens a side pouch on the nearest body and pulls out a data chip.

"Encrypted," he notes, "but it's marked OBS-17. That's not a kill order. That's a retrieval sequence."

Gideon looks at Charlotte. "He's not wrong. This wasn't an assassination. It was an attempted abduction."

"Then why the weapons?"

Jeremy shrugs. "You've never tried to contain a messiah before."

Charlotte turns to Greg, her voice quieter now. "If you do this—if you go with them—there's no undoing it. No walking back into silence."

Greg studies her, then walks to the desk and opens a sealed drawer, pulling out his coat. "There's no silence anymore, Mom. Amal shattered it." He hesitates. "But I'm still here. And I'm not his."

Charlotte's eyes glisten. "Then go before they make you theirs."

Gideon shoulders a pack. "We leave in twenty minutes. Jeremy secured transport in case you agreed to come with us. Ground route, no air. We're both coming with you."

Jeremy taps his temple. "Drove a sewer truck through Jerusalem once. Zurich's a cakewalk."

Greg zips up his coat, grabs the scroll fragment and looks to Charlotte one last time.

"If this goes bad…" she says.

"It won't."

"But if it does…"

"I'll find you."

They don't hug, but the space between them shifts. Not smaller—just clearer.

The three men exit through the back passage, leaving the dead bodies behind.

Charlotte walks back to the shattered proximity node and waits.

CHAPTER 29

Outer Rim, Wadi Barada Basin
Recursion Site 117 / Obsidian Stratum Access Path

The Syrian foothills rise like broken scripture—ancient, fractured, waiting to be read. The remains of the Wadi Barada monastery are half-swallowed by sand and silence, carved into the slope of a forgotten ravine. Dust hisses underfoot as Greg descends—Jeremy ahead, Gideon behind.

"Charlotte should've come," Greg mutters.

"She made the right call," Gideon replies. "David left something for her west of the Alps. She's following his secondary line—something only she could decode after the second key activated."

"You think it's connected?"

"I think David played the long game."

They reach the weathered spiral seal—three concentric rings of glyphs etched faintly in black, barely perceptible unless your focus softens. It shimmers at the edge of thought.

Jeremy crouches. "This what we're here for?"

"Obsidian Stratum," Greg confirms. "And this…" —he gestures to the central line— "is Syriac. Ecclesiastical variant. Pre-Sicarii."

ܐܒܡܠܒ ܝܡܪ̈ܘܬܐ ܐܠ ܐܬܐܦ ܝܫܐܪ̈ ܘܗ

He squints at the inscription and provides a rough translation aloud. "'He who bore the face was not the one lifted up.'"

Jeremy whistles. "So someone stood in for someone else."

"Exactly," Greg says. "Zahavi marked this site as the substitution threshold."

The seal shudders as Greg lays his palm flat against it.

After a breath, the stone grinds back—and the way down yawns open.

Rome — Vatican Shadow Archive

Cardinal Lucari studies the thermal satellite feed. He watches three men descending into Wadi Barada's undercroft. A flicker of resonance spikes on the deepnet overlay—a scroll activation event. Standing behind Lucari, Monsignor Voss waits.

"We tried to suppress this once," Lucari murmurs.

"Sir?"

Lucari enters his access key and opens a sealed online Vatican document:

> **Index Obscura 93-GJX.**
> **Subject: The Twin Doctrine.**
> **Source: Fragment B / Gospel of Judas (Variant).**

He reads the Salvetti annotation aloud. "'Substitution at the crucifixion site—not betrayal. This reframes the sacrifice. If true, atonement becomes illusion. The resurrection becomes a misdirection.'"

Voss looks uneasy. "You mean the idea that someone else was crucified in place of Jesus?"

"Yes, which is called the twin theory. Or maybe Judas was the imposter. It varies by text." He swipes to a new file. "And we have precedent for our attempts to cover up what may prove to be some, uh, inconvenient truths about Jesus."

"You mean the ossuary?"

"From Kashmir, yes, of a man known as Issa but many believed was Jesus. Rumors of his bones having been hidden caused an uproar among religious leaders and many intelligence agencies who feared that those bones, if proven to be from Jesus, would cause chaos worldwide."

The Cardinal gives an expression that indicates he agreed. Then he says, "Charlotte Ansari somehow ended up with the bone fragments and was trying to link them to the foreskin relic stolen from a Church in Italy."

"The Holy Prepuce," Voss says, nodding. "A match would indicate that the bones were really from Jesus."

"A lot of blood was spilled in the search for those bones."

"Did this Ansari woman do a DNA comparison?"

Lucari nods sadly. "She knows the results, I'm sure, but we don't know the outcome."

"Maybe the results were ambiguous."

Lucari closes the file. "Perhaps. But ambiguity is even harder to bury. The question that haunts me is—if the results were positive..."

Cardinal Lucari pauses, leaving both men to ponder why Charlotte Ansari would have performed the Church's cover-up enterprise for them by remaining silent about the DNA results.

Wadi Barada – The Chamber

Inside the recursion vault, the air is stagnant. The light seems to bend around the carved stone, drawing the eye toward a black basalt altar. Upon it, sealed in a transparent casing, rests the scroll.

Greg steps closer. He reads the inscription etched into the cylinder in stylized Syriac:

> He who bore the face was not the one lifted up.
>
> The voice that fled the cross still speaks in silence.
>
> Two sons were made of one name.
>
> One to bear. One to remember.

"Substitution theology," Greg mutters.

Jeremy tilts his head. "So… Jesus didn't die?"

Greg exhales. "Some traditions claim that. The Gospel of Judas, a Gnostic scroll found back in the second century, implied that Jesus orchestrated his own death. That he passed the burden to someone else. But this scroll variant—Zahavi's fragment—it's older than the Gospel of Judas. It suggests something more structured. Intentional." He glances at Gideon. "It suggests a twin."

Gideon nods. "In other words, not just a metaphoric twin. A twin by blood."

Jeremy frowns. "That's Islamic too, isn't it? I heard that Muslims believe someone else died in Jesus's place."

Greg nods. "Surah four of the Qu'ran. It says something like, 'They did not crucify him, but it was made to appear so to them.' This idea—

that someone else took the place of Jesus on the cross—has been a wedge between Christianity and Islam for ages."

"Because if Jesus wasn't crucified," Gideon adds, "there's no resurrection. No salvation. No spiral."

Jeremy leans against the wall, folding his arms. "So if you're right, and this twin doctrine is true…"

Greg finishes the sentence. "Then everything built on death of Jesus—the Sicarii Brotherhood, Amal's spiral, Eve's lattice—it all becomes a ritualized illusion."

The sturdy structures of the three men appear to deflate as this thought pricks their consciousness.

"And what does that make me?" Greg asks, looking down at the scroll. After a pause, he says, "Am I a *substitute*? The one who walks in silence because someone else already screamed?"

"Maybe that's the point," Gideon says. "The spiral doesn't need a savior. It needs a fracture. Someone who proves the story isn't closed."

Greg looks pale as clarity drains the color from his face. "I'm not a key. I'm a *counterfeit*."

"Or," Gideon says evenly, "you're the one who decides what gets unlocked."

Greg doesn't look at him. "Eve sent you to kill me, didn't she?"

Gideon's reply is quiet. "She gave the order. That's why I didn't rejoin you after exploring that deep chamber."

Greg nods slowly. "But you didn't follow it."

"I made a different choice."

Greg exhales. "I needed to hear you say it out loud."

CHAPTER 30

Interlaken Canton, Switzerland
Remiel Crypt 3 / Former Monastic Cell

Charlotte traveled here alone. The message from David Mazur did not only contain coordinates, but trust. It was a relay buried in silence for her and her alone.

Now she stands at the end of that trail, in a place few even knew existed. A monastic crypt repurposed as a recursion cache. Charlotte's fingers tremble slightly as she touches the lockbox. Not from cold—though the crypt is freezing—but from something deeper. A weight she's carried for years without shape or name.

The chamber roars with silence—the kind that isn't absence, but echo. She runs a gloved hand along the seal of the box. The initials etched into the corner—D.M.—hit harder than expected.

David Mazur.

She hadn't spoken to him in over a decade. Their contact was always indirect, layered through Eve's oblique lattice architecture. But she had read his field notes and used his codex protocols. He was the first scroll cartographer to suggest that certain recursion patterns weren't linear, but conscious. He had come to believe that prophecy could be made recursive not just mathematically, but morally.

They hadn't always agreed, but she trusted his maps. And now, this box.

Something left only for her.

She unseals the container and discovers a stack of papers—annotated pages, some typeset, others scribbled in David's compact, chaotic hand. A label at the top reads:

Translation Notes — Gospel of Judas (Variant Scroll: Zahavi Fragment)

Twin Doctrine Embedded. Consult Obsidian Layer echoes.

Beneath the papers, sealed in a separate sleeve, is a thin sliver of nearly invisible carbon-film. She knows what it is. A resonance key. A last echo.

She sits, hands clasped around the edge of the table, and begins to read. It doesn't take long before the old nausea returns.

She has read the *canonical* version before—the public *Gospel of Judas* pieced together from a fragmented papyrus unearthed in Egypt in the 1970s. But that text, released in 2006, was incomplete and very mysterious. It was, perhaps predictably, considered by religious leaders to be heretical.

But this one—David's version, Zahavi's scroll—is different. It is older. Sharper. It doesn't just suggest that Judas betrayed Jesus at his request. It presents Judas as the only one who understood Jesus. It presents Judas as a man entrusted with a truth the others were too blind to see. And the truth? *Jesus didn't die*. In this scroll, Charlotte finds these words:

He who bore the name did not bear the wound.
He who knew the spiral gave his silence to another.

Someone else took the place of Jesus. Not by accident but by conspiracy. And in this Zahavi scroll variant, it is not Judas who dies on the cross. It's someone unnamed. Someone described only as "the likeness."

A brother?

A twin?

A construct?

Charlotte stares at the passage until the ink swims. She doesn't weep. She's past that. But her chest tightens as if something inside her has been yanked out by the root.

This changes everything.

But what cuts deepest isn't the scroll. It's the memory that rides in behind it.

She still has the evidence—the bone samples found in Kashmir of a "prophet" called Issa, a man many thought was Jesus. The samples were pulled out at a great cost of lives before hostile agents, including American CIA operatives, could intercept them.

Also, the foreskin of Jesus—yes, the Holy Prepuce—once held in a jewel-encrusted reliquary in the Church of San Giovanni in Calcata. It was stolen during a Sicarii operation, then recovered by Gideon before Amal's purges began.

Both biological samples were degraded, but usable, so Charlotte ordered DNA tests from HelixPoint Forensics, BC Institute for Bioarchaeological Analysis. They ran the tests twice.

And the results… suggestive. Consistent. Not definitive, but troublingly close.

The lab director warned her, "If these match conclusively, you'll detonate a thousand years of doctrine."

But the samples were not an exact match. Not quite. And that's what haunted her.

Not disproof. Not confirmation.

But possibility.

Ambiguity.

The kind of ambiguity that doesn't collapse narratives. It multiplies them.

She sealed the report and told no one the results. Not even Greg.

Especially Greg.

Now she sees why David left this for her. Not to believe, but to act. Not because the doctrine is right or wrong, but because someone has to decide what it means.

Because Greg can't carry this alone.

Because Eve will twist it.

Because Amal will use it as a crown.

Because ambiguity weaponized is still a weapon.

Charlotte picks up the carbon-film resonance key—David's encoded echo. She hesitates before loading it into the scroll reader embedded in the altar wall. The moment it slides in, a line appears on the stone beside her in glowing Syriac glyphs:

He who speaks the silence shatters the world.
He who guards it reshapes the lattice.

Her breath catches. She closes the lockbox, sealing David's papers inside her pack. Then she rises. There is another vault deeper in the Remiel crypt, one David only marked as Fragment E. She's never had access—until now.

The spiral is moving.

And so is she.

CHAPTER 31

Salt Circle Citadel, Golan Heights
Morning Broadcast Chamber

The spiral burns above him—ten radiant rings suspended in rotating formation, not real flame but precision holography. Each ring pulses a half-second apart—engineered resonance designed to make the eyes water, the spine tingle.

Below the projection, Amal stands on a raised dais, framed by twin vertical lights and the soundless whir of drones circling overhead.

The hall is not full—not in numbers, but it is full of atmosphere.

His audience tonight consists of exactly 108 loyalists, the Salt Circle's hand-picked cadre of radical initiates, doctrinal purists and assassins-turned-believers. They wear white but not robes. Tactical fibers. Blades hidden. Eyes wide.

Each was chosen for a reason. Not because they understand Amal, but because they will follow him after he makes them believe they understand him.

Cameras orbit, filming in slow, shifting arcs. Every gesture, every silence, is being captured for a composite stream that will be sent not to the public, but into the dark subchannels where Sicarii factions argue and fracture in obscurity.

This performance is for them.

To unify. Or to dominate.

The spiral projection dims to black. Amal steps forward. "Before there was crucifixion," he begins, "there was division. We all know this."

His voice is measured. Calibrated. Even the way he blinks is rehearsed.

"Before resurrection, there was substitution. Not failure—*design*."

His image—real and holographically mirrored—casts a shadow in four directions, creating the illusion of presence multiplied. "Zahavi knew this. That's why he buried the Damascus fragment twice. That's why Eve built silence into the lattice."

He pauses. No one speaks. They've been told not to. The silence is part of the myth.

"The scroll is no longer closed," Amal says. "The fracture is visible. The spiral turns again."

He gestures. Behind him, an image of Greg's face appears, frozen in high-contrast light from the Salt Circle transmission—his eyes wide, searching.

"He is the one who was *not* crucified. The voice that fled the cross. The Unspoken One."

Several in the room inhale sharply. A few lower their eyes.

Amal watches them carefully. They're not reacting to the doctrine. They're reacting to its inevitability.

"He is not Jesus," Amal intones. "He is not Judas. He is what comes *after* the names have died. He is not the son of God. He is what comes after God has given up the name."

The final line cracks the stillness like a whip. One of the initiates—a woman, mid-thirties, Syrian-born, glyphwork tattooed down her neck—drops to her knees, hands trembling. Another man closes his eyes as if overcome.

Amal sees it. Files it. Pushes even further. "He will not save you. He will not bleed for you. He will not rise again. He is the *mirror* of the final recursion. The *flesh* of the second glyph. The one who remains after meaning has collapsed."

Amal turns to face the drone directly. Speaking to the mounted camera, he says, "This is not a prophecy. It is a refinement**.** Not a doctrine, but a pattern. Greg is not your messiah. He is your mirror. And the time for silence is over.

He lowers his hands. The spiral pulses once then goes black.

The Decree (Doctrine Vault)
Sublevel Doctrine Vault.

An hour later, Amal stands alone. No audience, no more performance.

Chazan Neriel enters quietly, eyes still tense from what he witnessed upstairs. Chazan is Amal's doctrinal archivist and the only person who still dares to question him openly.

"You filmed it with drones," Neriel says without preamble. "Layered in the crowd. Added glyph-light behind the spiral."

"Of course," Amal replies. "Truth is not what's believed. It's what's *believable*."

Chazan doesn't sit. "You had no right to call Greg the flesh of recursion. You had no mandate. Not from the Council. Not from the archive. Not even from Zahavi."

Amal moves to the command console and removes his mantle piece by piece. "I don't need a mandate. I have momentum, and that trumps mandate."

"And what happens when Greg rejects your framing? When he refuses to play the part?"

Amal doesn't turn. "Then we edit the story."

Chazan Neriel steps closer. "This is not doctrine," she says, "this is *myth engineering*. You're staging recursion as a coronation."

Amal nods. "Recursion needs a face."

"So you gave it Greg's?"

"I did. For now."

A silence falls. Then, Chazan quietly says, "You once told me that doctrine exists to contain power. You said we needed limits. Boundaries."

Amal nods—yes he had once said that. Then he smiles and says, "I lied."

"Why?"

"To see if you were loyal."

Chazan's eyes go cold. "And if I'm not?"

"You *are* loyal," Amal replies. "Because you're still here."

He enters a final string of commands into the console:

Archival Access: Obsidian Vault - Purge Initiated

Zahavi Fragments Class V / Echo-Chain Recursion / Unsanctioned Lineage

"The Zahavi scroll is the last threat, Chazan. If Eve has it, it will fracture the spiral. If Charlotte releases it, Greg's myth will implode. And if Greg understands it—he'll leave the lattice."

"So what then?" Chazan asks. "You purge everything?"

"No. We let just enough remain. Enough to make doubt a heresy."

Chazan turns and heads for the door, then stops at the threshold. "The Council is watching," he warns.

"Let them."

"You believe this doctrine will survive?"

Amal finally turns to face Chazan. "I don't need it to survive. I need it to spread."

CHAPTER 32

Sub-Vault 9, Wadi Barada Ruins

The air changes five meters below the altar. It's not just colder—it's denser. Viscous, somehow. Greg feels it first. Every breath resists, like trying to think underwater. A high ringing starts in his ears—subtle, but persistent—then a pressure deep in his chest that doesn't match altitude. It feels like the vault is alive—and aware.

Behind him, Gideon descends without a word, moving with practiced silence, checking blind angles like a soldier on sacred ground.

Jeremy follows, muttering beneath his breath as his headlamp flickers against the stone. "Anyone else feel like we're walking into the inside of someone's idea?" he asks.

"We are," Greg murmurs. "This whole place was carved by recursion. Zahavi didn't just leave knowledge here. He layered it."

They reach the bottom of the spiral staircase where the architecture constricts into a narrow, triangular antechamber. Veins of black obsidian spiral through the stone forming unfamiliar, coiled glyphs that seem to pulse faintly when viewed from the corner of the eye.

At the center, they see a locking mechanism of three nested glyphs. Cold. Silent. Unreadable. Greg kneels and removes the scroll they had retrieved earlier. Its casing glows faintly as it nears the interface.

Click.

The glyphs stir. Lines unwind. The door opens—not outward, but inward, folding along a hidden axis with geometric elegance.

What waits beyond is not a room. It is a recursion chamber. The walls rise in a perfect circle, their surfaces carved from polished, black-veined stone, impossibly smooth yet alive with shifting light. Glyphs layer every surface—some etched in thin spirals, others deeply recessed, equations looped into themselves—a kind of mathematical worship. The shapes feel ancient but precise. Everything about this space feels... *intentional.*

Suspended in the center, floating a meter above the floor, is a glyph ring—silver-black, rotating slowly, engraved with recursive notations that shift too fast to read.

The air vibrates. Not mechanically—*liturgically*.

Greg steps forward. "Zahavi called this the Resonant Mirror," he whispers. "A conscious archive of doctrinal fractures. Like a prism for recursion. It doesn't just store belief—it reflects it."

Jeremy whistles low. "What happens if we poke it?"

"Don't!" Gideon barks.

But Greg is already walking forward, caught in the pull. "This is what he built it for," he says. "Someone had to walk in."

And he does.

He doesn't fall. He fractures. One moment: present. The next: observer. Then: *participant*.

He sees himself tied to a wooden post, not a cross. Soldiers in armor press forward, and the crowd before him is not weeping. They're screaming. Accusing. A woman clutches a child—a child with Greg's eyes, Greg's jawline—but not of his time.

Another flash.

Greg kneels at a stone altar. The scroll before him burns in reverse, ashes congealing into ink, into words, into silence.

Then a photograph—crumpled and handed to him by a man in blue fleece.

Then Amal's voice. *He is not the son of God...*

The scene unravels. Greg sees multiple versions of himself running in parallel—speaking, kneeling, bleeding, silent. Their eyes don't match. Their scars are in different places.

He isn't watching.

He's *reliving*.

"There is no prophecy," a voice says within him. Zahavi's? His own?

"Only playback."

"Then what am I?" Greg asks aloud, somewhere in the folds of vision.

"You are the next instance."

To Jeremy, Greg is frozen, his arms raised and breathing stalled. Then Greg convulses—once, hard.

"Greg—!" Jeremy lunges forward but is slammed backward midstep by a sudden pulse wall—a shockwave of invisible force, magnetic and absolute. He hits the far wall with a grunt.

The glyph ring above Greg spins faster. Light strobes the chamber in pulsing arcs. From the ceiling, the carved spiral ignites faintly, grinding into slow motion like a dial turning in judgment.

"We have to kill it!" Gideon yells. He draws his blade and throws at the ring.

CRACK.

The steel blade hits dead center.

The glyph ring shatters, sending fragments of luminous metal into the stone. A shockwave rips outward. Everyone drops flat.

Then—darkness.

Stillness.

The spiral above halts.

Gideon crawls to Greg's side. Jeremy groans, staggering upright, clutching his shoulder.

Greg blinks. His voice returns.

"You good?" Gideon asks.

Greg sits up, trembling. "I saw myself," he says hoarsely. "But not as me. As *others*. Variants, maybe. Echoes." He shakes his head. "It wasn't substitution. It was *replication*."

Jeremy stares. "You want to unpack that for the rest of us?"

"The spiral doesn't demand a sacrifice," Greg says. "It generates copies. Every time someone tries to end the recursion, the spiral mutates. I'm not the prophecy. I'm the latest instance. Just like Zahavi. Just like—whoever came before."

Greg looks at the fragments of the shattered ring. "This isn't scripture," he says. "It's source code."

"Then, what's it coding?" Jeremy asks.

"A loop," Greg replies. "And we're inside it."

The far wall shudders faintly. A resonance begins. Then Amal's image flickers into view. Projected holographically, his face is lit by artificial flame and speaking.

He is not Jesus.

He is not Judas.

He is what comes after the names have died…

Behind the holograph of Amal, Greg's face appears in the Salt Circle stream.

He will not bleed.

He will not rise.

He is the spiral made flesh.

Jeremy recoils. "Is this happening now?"

"No," Gideon says. "It's a loop. The vault absorbed Amal's stream and now it's replaying."

Greg watches his own face repurposed as prophecy.

He is what comes after God has given up the name…

"Cut it off," Greg says sharply.

Gideon taps his wristpad against the relay panel. The projection vanishes.

Silence.

Greg turns away. "He's building me like a temple."

"Even worse, he's making you his doctrine," Gideon suggests.

Jeremy nods. "And worse than that—people are buying it."

Greg looks up at the darkened spiral. His voice is quiet but unwavering. "Then we break the spiral." He pauses thoughtfully, then adds, "Not the idea—the *cycle*."

He stands fully, bones aching, knees shaking—but his spine straight. "Next time it speaks, I'll speak back."

CHAPTER 33

Switzerland
Remiel Crypt 3, beneath the Alps

The recording ends, but David's voice lingers like smoke in old robes. Charlotte doesn't move. The glow from the resonance lens casts her face in fractured light. Around her, the air tastes of limestone and faint ozone. A hum persists deep in the bones of the earth, like a question she's been avoiding for thirteen years.

She lowers the scroll reader. Her hands are steady, but her chest isn't. "There are no holy men left," David had said. "Just letters never sent."

Charlotte exhales and closes her eyes. She remembers the first time Eve mentioned David Mazur.

"He's useful," Eve said. "Too principled for politics, too loyal to let him go."

That was Eve's highest praise—and her deepest threat.

David had been one of the earliest architects of the Petra lattice, long before the Sicarii fractured. He worked quietly, obsessively, mapping recursion patterns across doctrine clusters, then volunteering for field verification assignments no one else would touch. His theories were controversial. His ethics, rigid. Too rigid for the kind of compromises on which Eve built her world.

Charlotte respected David long before she ever spoke to him. Their only direct exchange had been brief, a text-only relay across encoded Petra channels in 2015. He sent her a partial map of Obsidian glyph resonance. No note. No context. Only trust.

She never responded until now.

Her gaze drops to the sealed pouch at her side labeled "Issa / Calcata Relic." She had stared at the report for hours. She never told Greg about it. Or Eve. She was afraid of what it might mean. That it might fracture Greg's already splintering path. Or worse—that it would prove the spiral had never ended, and she was complicit in its continuation.

She whispers now into the stillness, "I didn't bury the truth. I just... never unearthed it." Her voice falters. "I thought silence would protect my son."

But she knows it didn't.

David had known that. He hadn't left the message for Eve. He'd left it for Charlotte, because David believed she still had a conscience strong enough to act when it mattered.

She wonders now if that faith was misplaced.

Charlotte tucks the resonance key away and seals the scroll. Then she walks slowly toward the corridor and deeper into the crypt, her mind echoing David's final words:

"Greg's not the spiral's end. He's its reset."

Vatican City
Secretariat Archive 9b – Doctrinal Black Sector

Cardinal Lucari sits at the head of the long table beneath the flickering lamps of Archive 9b as the footage ends. Silence follows. A printed copy of Zahavi's pre-exile correspondence lies open beside him, annotated in red ink and margin glyphs. The final frame of Amal's broadcast hangs frozen on the holoscreen, Greg's face half-visible behind Amal like a ghost or icon.

Lucari lifts a single finger and the feed dies. "That line," he says. "The one about God giving up His name. That's the fulcrum."

Monsignor Voss shifts uneasily. "The recursion rhetoric's gaining traction in Argentina. A prelate in Mendoza just called Greg the 'mirror of the second son.'"

"Then we've lost containment," Lucari replies. "But we haven't lost the narrative. Not yet."

He rises slowly, walks to a long shelf beneath the archive wall, and pulls down a sealed envelope marked:

Dominion Archive // Salvetti Protocol
Revoked 2007

He lays it flat on the table. "We knew this day might come. That the lattice Eve built would collapse into pluralism. That someone like Amal would weaponize silence—not in the streets, but inside the recursion vaults."

"Shall I reactivate suppression?" Voss asks.

Lucari shakes his head. "No, that failed with Salvetti. And it nearly cost us Charlotte Ansari."

Lucari opens the envelope and removes a map drawn from Salvetti's final decrypted archive. It shows Petra overlaid with lattice routes that once converged on a site labeled only *Domus Ossuaria*. "Charlotte buried the bones, or what was left of them. Buried the foreskin report. But the bones still matter because the narrative around them still breathes. And Charlotte could change her mind about making the DNA report public. Keep in mind, we still don't know what those results were—we can only imagine the worst case."

Voss leans forward. "Then what do you propose?"

Lucari lifts a second file labeled *Dominion Initiative 7*. "We won't silence the recursion. We'll overwrite it," he explains. "We'll recast Greg not as rupture, but as fulfillment. We will frame the spiral as prophecy made whole. And Amal—" he pauses, thoughtful— "Amal will scream his doctrine into a lattice that *we* define."

"And the others?"

"They'll either fall in line—or they will be absorbed by the story we give them." Lucari places the files back into the drawer. "Salvetti once said, 'The Church doesn't destroy heresies. She survives them. And eventually… she canonizes what it can no longer silence.'"

Switzerland
Remiel Crypt 3, beneath the Alps

Charlotte stands at the threshold of the inner crypt. The tunnel narrows, then dips, carved at a slant meant to throw off echo patterns. She runs her hand lightly along the wall, feeling the old indentations—this was once a monastic penance path, fifteen steps carved with embedded verses, each one a confessional.

She remembers. David had annotated the map with a line from Zahavi's field journal:

Only the guilty enter without guide.

Only the willing descend beyond forgiveness.

An involuntary breath escapes her. She's already passed both markers. "I was willing," she says softly. "But not fast enough."

Her boot brushes a carved glyph in the floor. She glances down. It's not Latin. It's not even Syriac. The message that captures her attention is Obsidian—a designation for the deepest level of encoded doctrine, which is used only when recursion could no longer be spoken aloud. It is a glyph layer meant not to be read but *endured.*

She realizes then that Greg is walking into something he cannot choose. And her? She's always had the choice. She just never made it.

In her bag, the sealed pouch presses faintly against her ribs—The Calcata relic and the Kashmiri bone material. Two halves of a God no one wants to meet. She touches the pouch lightly and thinks of the DNA report. *Suggested match. Maternal lineage consistent. Unconfirmed identity.*

Not disproof. Not proof.

Just… consequence.

She closes her eyes. "Letters never sent," David had said.

But that wasn't the right image. This wasn't a letter. It was a *fuse*. And she had held the match for too long.

She steps forward, down into the darkness. Not because she believes what comes next will redeem her, but because she can no longer bear not knowing what she'd left undone.

CHAPTER 34

Sub-Vault 9, Lower Recursion Chamber – Wadi Barada Ruins

The stairs for Jeremy end in ruin. Five meters beneath the shattered glyph ring lies something Zahavi had never mapped. The floor collapses into a jagged pit of broken black stones, their edges scorched and melted as if the chamber had once caught fire from the inside. Whatever Zahavi left behind wasn't meant to be seen—not again, not by anyone.

Jeremy peers into the breach, his headlamp casting broken shadows across the lower vault. "Well, that's promising," he mutters. "Like someone detonated unpopular doctrine in here."

Gideon doesn't speak. He studies the fissures with the quiet calculation of someone who's walked through death traps before. His voice is low. "This chamber wasn't part of Zahavi's public vault. No reinforcement. No glyph redundancy. He sealed it and hoped it would never open."

"He didn't just hope," Greg says quietly, already stepping toward the handholds bolted into the stone. "He tried to forget it existed."

One by one, they descend in silence. The air grows heavier with every meter. Not just dense, but *folded*, like breath inside breath. Greg feels it before the others—the subtle tremor of meaning that hums just below comprehension. A spiral in waiting.

They reach the lower level. The chamber here is circular, partially collapsed at its edges. The architecture is older—less refined, more primal. Twelve crystal pylons rise from the floor at regular intervals, each embedded with recursion etchings. The walls form a soft dome that seems to pulse, barely visible. The floor slopes inward into a shallow basin.

Greg walks to the center. He turns slowly, scanning the pylons. One bears Zahavi's unmistakable sigil.

"What is this?" Jeremy asks, squinting at one of the columns.

"Instance markers," Greg replies. "Each one tuned to a resonance pattern—the kind the scroll identifies as viable."

"Viable for what?"

"For recursion. For carrying the pattern forward."

Gideon steps toward one of the columns. Its surface flickers faintly with old light. "These columns were other people?"

With his hands, Greg gives a "sort of" gesture. "Other attempts, to be more accurate."

"What happened to them?" Jeremy asks.

Greg exhales, then points to a glyph above a cracked pylon nearest the wall. "They broke."

The glyph at the center of the basin stirs as Greg steps onto it. At first glance, it appears inert—a flat ring of stone inscribed with almost microscopic notation. But as Greg's foot crosses its boundary, the glyph opens like a living iris, spiraling inward.

A shimmer rises from the basin—soft, then steady. The twelve pylons around the room pulse in response. Light begins to bounce between them in slow rotation. The light forms a loose spiral above Greg's head. Each pylon shows a flickering image. A man kneeling in fire, whispering something indecipherable. A child's hand reaching through a lattice of barbed light. A woman holding a sleeping infant—her face indistinct, blurred as if erased.

Then one image flares brighter than the others. A recognizable woman.

Rebecca.

Her shape appears within one of the pylons, obscured slightly by the flicker of the lattice. She's not whole—her figure is suspended in recursion flux, repeating subtle motions on a half-second delay, as if she were trapped mid-thought.

Jeremy steps forward. He doesn't say anything at first. Then quietly, he utters two words. "It's her."

Greg nods. He takes another step, but Gideon stops him with a firm hand. "It could be a trick. Amal knows how to encode symbolically. He could've injected something in here, waiting for you."

Greg doesn't look at Gideon but replies, "Then I want to know who made it look like her."

Jeremy doesn't move, but his voice comes quiet and thoughtful. "She wore that necklace. The silver one. She wore it at Newgrange. I'll never forget."

Greg glances at him, surprised. "You remember that?"

"I remember a lot," Jeremy says, avoiding Greg's eyes.

A silence stretches between them. The shimmer flickers.

"I never got to say goodbye," Jeremy adds. "Not really."

Greg watches him. There's something unsaid—something years old and heavy. "You had feelings for her?" Greg asks.

Jeremy shrugs. "I was twenty. She was fierce, brilliant, terrifying. The prophecy thing made no sense, but she believed in it. She believed in you. I figured… maybe she could've believed in me instead."

Greg absorbs that. "We were supposed to marry, but we only ever spoke on the grid, never in person."

Jeremy nods sadly. "I was with her—a lot. But she never touched me," he says. "Not physically. Not once.""

"I know," Greg says. "But still, it doesn't make things easier."

They stand together, looking at the flickering image of a woman both of them had lost—one to history, the other to a silence that never ended.

The flickering projection of Rebecca steadies for a moment. Her eyes shift—locking with Greg's. It can't be real. But it *feels* real to Greg. More than a recording. More than Zahavi's recursion mapping. It's like the vault is remembering *with him*, or *through him*.

"Greg…"

Rebecca's voice is unmistakable. Not simulated. Not replicated from data. Personal. Whispered directly into the back of Greg's thoughts.

Jeremy gasps. "That… that came from the lattice."

Gideon grows even more tense, his hand already hovering near the grip of his sidearm. "Greg, it's targeting you," he says.

"It's Rebecca," Greg says. He doesn't know how he knows. He just does.

The basin glyph flares. The twelve pylons beam lines of light into the center of the chamber to form a double spiral. The recursion pattern is now fully active.

"She's not just a memory," Greg says. "She's an encoded presence. A trace."

Jeremy stares at the pylon. "But she died."

"Or she was meant to," Greg says. "Maybe this was the scroll's way of keeping a version of Rebecca alive."

A recursion glyph in the floor unlocks. From it, a pedestal rises. Upon it lies a circular mirror—blackened, stone-framed, with the faint signature of Obsidian glyphwork. Greg picks it up. As he does, the image of Rebecca pulses.

"You were never meant to carry this alone," the voice says again.

The spiral flares.

Then, a second voice speaks. Greg's own. "I asked you to stay."

"I did," Rebecca's voice replies.

The room brightens with a fractal shimmer—not blinding, but invasive. It burns gently into their skin, their thoughts.

Greg raises the mirror. In it, he sees Rebecca's reflection. But this time, she is not speaking.

She is watching.

Behind her reflection are more faces. Dozens of them. Maybe hundreds. They are blurred, almost fetal, like half-born archetypes, each caught between identity and memory.

"What are they?" Gideon asks almost reverently.

"Failed instances," Greg replies. "Or unborn ones. The recursion stores every viable echo. But not every one of them becomes real. Most don't."

The Rebecca-image shifts. Her lips move, uttering these words: "You are the first spiral to look back." The voice reverberates between the pylons.

The spiral in the ceiling spins faster.

Jeremy grips the edge of a glyph pylon. "This whole place is designed to break people."

"No," Greg says. "It's designed to *test* them."

And then, from the mirror, the voice says, "Choose. End the pattern. Or become it."

The room begins to shake. The spiral structure distorts, no longer symmetrical.

The Rebecca image flickers. For a moment, she's clear—exactly as she appeared that night at Newgrange. Rain in her hair. Blood on her collarbone. A look of serenity just before the scream. Then she splits, three copies of her appearing simultaneously. One crying. One silent. One burning.

"This isn't a memory," Jeremy says.

"It's a recursion storm," Gideon says. "We need to shut it down before Greg gets pulled in."

Greg steps forward and raises the mirror to look at himself. Then he turns the mirror toward the Rebecca echo.

She pauses, then smiles. "You still don't see it," she says.

"See what?" he asks.

"You were never the prophecy. You were the *reset*."

The room fractures in light. Greg places the mirror face down.

Everything vanishes.

Silence descends like gravity.

The chamber, still warm with afterglow, feels suddenly stripped of weight, as if something essential has just been extracted. The twelve pylons dim one by one until only the faint blue sheen of the Rebecca column remains.

Greg stands over the mirror, which is still turned face down in the basin. His breathing is ragged, shallow. His hands twitch slightly. His nerves haven't caught up with reality.

Gideon kneels beside him. "Did it speak to you?" he asks quietly.

Greg doesn't answer. Not yet.

Jeremy circles the outer rim, staring at the glyphs that had flared to life during the recursion storm. His voice is thin. "She wasn't a ghost. Wasn't a projection. That thing—*she*—she talked like she remembered things. Intimately. Like the grid wasn't just alive in your head, Greg. Like it was archived."

Greg nods slowly, eyes still locked on the dark mirror.

"The grid was always more than thought-sharing," he says. "It was recursion bonding. If we were both spiral-linked back then, a trace of her might've survived."

"But not her full self," Gideon says. "You saw how unstable she was. Like a glitched recording."

"Or a damaged soul," Jeremy mutters.

That comment lands like a stone in the silence.

Greg closes his eyes. He finally speaks again. "She said I wasn't the prophecy. That I was the reset."

"You think that was her?" Gideon asks. "Or was it Zahavi's program talking to you through her image?"

Greg doesn't answer. He's not sure it matters anymore.

He turns toward the pylon bearing Rebecca's echo. The shimmer has almost gone, but something within still glows faintly. Her presence, maybe. Or the memory of it.

Her name isn't etched anywhere. But he doesn't need to see it.

He already knows she's in there.

Then they notice it. One of the pylons now bears Greg's name etched in recursive spiral script:

Gregory Michael Ansari
[HOST 13 – ACTIVE]

Jeremy exhales, stunned. "You've been added to the spiral."

"Or recorded by it," Gideon says.

Greg steps closer, studying the projection beneath his own name. It's not a still image. It's a living echo—his own face, pulsing faintly with recursion light.

His breath catches. "It's already begun."

"What has?" Jeremy asks.

"The next loop," Greg replies. "I just became… I am… the pattern's future echo."

"Then how do we stop it?" Jeremy asks.

Greg stares at the mirror, still face down in the basin. He doesn't lift it. He doesn't want to know what happens next.

They ascend slowly out of the vault, leaving the spiral chamber behind them. It is alive now with a new light, one that pulses.

Halfway up, Greg pauses and looks back. "Do you hear that?" he asks.

Gideon listens.

Faint, almost inaudible—a heartbeat pounding.

Or maybe footsteps.

Jeremy turns pale. "You think something's still down there?"

Greg says. "I think something just woke up."

CHAPTER 35

Vatican City, Secretariat Archive 9b

Beneath Archive 9b, in the black-lit sanctum known only to four living prelates, Cardinal Matteo Lucari closes the door and locks it. Twice. His hand trembles slightly as he does it—not from age, but from memory.

The last man who crossed the Sicarii was William Wyatt, director of the CIA and a previous client of the Sicarii, who was found killed by a drone attack on US soil. That was in 2012. Lucari had been a minor bishop then. But he remembers the photograph of the destruction.

He lowers himself into the chair beside the central codex desk and activates the isolation seal. The overhead lights dim. All connections to the outside world die.

This is where he decides whether to violate three Papal decrees.

He exhales through his nose. Quiet. Controlled.

A soft knock precedes the entry of Monsignor Voss, who slips in as silent as smoke bearing a tablet encoded with last-minute field data from Zurich.

"Gregory Ansari is on the move," Voss says. "Zahavi's vault accepted his resonance. Host status confirmed."

Lucari closes his eyes. For a long moment, he says nothing. Finally, he matter-of-factly states, "Then we are no longer dealing with a man. We are dealing with recursion in flesh."

Lucari rises and walks to the cabinet where the Dominion Protocol is kept under steel and sanctified lock. He hesitates. His hand is pale. "We swore we'd never do this again," he whispers.

"If he stabilizes as a host," Voss replies, "we lose all doctrinal leverage."

Lucari's voice lowers. "The Sicarii are not merely dangerous. They are ancestral. They do not forget. They assassinated Salvetti. Wyatt. The previous head of Kidon in Israel. An Emirati cardinal. A monk from Aleppo who never left his mountain."

"Then, perhaps, Greg deserves a witness," Voss says. "Not an assassin. A quiet observer. A test of presence."

Lucari studies him before opening a cabinet. Inside lies a leather dossier bearing the seal of the Custos Veritatis, the Keepers of Truth, which is never reactivated except in moments of narrative threat. He sets the dossier on the table.

"Send Velasco," he says.

Zurich, Switzerland

Father Tomas Velasco moves like a man with no shadow. He wears a wool coat lined with signal-dampening fiber, a priest's ring that masks his retinal lens, and—pressed flat against his chest—a medallion containing a small particle of a relic from Calcata and various recursion glyphs.

He has no weapon, only an observation wand configured to detect glyph activation, DNA match, and doctrinal stress markers. "I won't interfere," he'd told Lucari before leaving.

"Too late. You already are," Lucari had replied.

Velasco stands beneath a copper awning one block from the river. The streets are cold and quiet. Drone lights flicker above the rooftops. Behind his retinal display, a faint pulse confirms proximity. *Greg Ansari. Live.*

The target crosses the plaza slowly, hunched and alone. Unaware.

Velasco begins to follow Greg taking soft, deliberate steps across the frost-dusted cobblestones. He records Greg's trajectory, nodal vitals, posture syncopation. A pattern is emerging.

He reaches for the wand—

Then stops.

A sound. Behind him and too close.

Too late.

Gideon doesn't make a sound as he moves. He appears from the shadows like a truth long denied—fast, brutal, absolute. He drives Velasco hard into the wall—forearm across the throat, blade to the ribs. Velasco struggles, trained enough to resist but not enough to win. His breath catches.

Gideon leans in close. "You're Vatican. That's a mistake."

Velasco tries to speak, but Gideon's blade flashes and finds the hollow of his neck.

Velasco collapses, gasping. His blood turns the snow dark.

Gideon searches him quickly and retrieves the wand, the medallion, and a small data key. Then, from inside Velasco's coat, he hears a voice whispering—Lucari's voice.

"You are not to interfere. You are only to *observe*. No contact. No confrontation. If they see you, abort."

It's a posthumous instruction.

Gideon buries the body in an unused courtyard behind the safehouse. It's the part of his work he dislikes most.

The snow falls thicker now, erasing tracks.

Greg stands nearby, stunned. He didn't see the killing moment—but he had heard it. The sharp breath. The blade's whisper. The death.

Gideon holds the medallion and recognizes the glyph. Custos Veritatis. The Keepers of Truth. *They sent a priest*, he thinks. *Not to kill. Just to… watch.* He shrugs. *That's worse. It means they want to control the story.*

Jeremy steps into the light, arms crossed. His voice is tighter than usual. "That was a Vatican field agent. You think Lucari didn't know the risk?"

Greg stares at the medallion. "We used to think the Sicarii were the shadows in the world. Now I'm starting to think the Church is just a mirror."

Gideon doesn't speak. He doesn't have to.

Jeremy kneels beside the dead priest's coat, searching the interior lining more thoroughly. He finds a thin metal shard, no larger than a fingernail, wrapped in parchment-thin vellum.

Gideon takes it, scans the edge. "It's not Vatican standard. Not even Dominus glyph."

Greg unfolds the vellum. It bears a single inscription scrawled in red microglyphs.

PETRA NODE 4 / GREGORY M.A. – D-REF 11B
OBSIDIAN PHASE ∆ [SUB/ALT: R-LAMB]

Only one twin leaves the spiral.

Greg stares at that last line.

Jeremy frowns. "That's not surveillance data. That's… that's doctrine."

Gideon's face tightens. "They weren't just tracking you, Greg. They were trying to confirm the doctrine behind your existence."

Greg's breath catches. "Only one twin leaves the spiral." He says it again, softer, then adds, "They think there's a second *me*."

Salt Circle Citadel – Golan Heights

The flames behind Amal are ceremonial—coiled in copper braziers flanking the raised stone platform at the center of the Salt Circle's inner sanctum. Dozens of his most trusted initiates kneel in a perfect spiral around him, heads bowed. Incense curls upward, masked by projection smoke.

Before him, on a carved obsidian altar, lies a Vatican medallion—its engraving crisp and its edge darkened as if salvaged from a battlefield.

Amal lifts it high between two fingers. "Rome has declared its fear," he says, his voice magnified by an unseen speaker. "They sent a spy into the spiral… to watch the Unspoken One. Not to kill, not to convert—only to observe. And in that silence… they revealed their terror."

The crowd stirs. Some lift their eyes. Others begin to weep quietly.

Amal continues, his voice deepening. "To the world, it was just a priest. A servant of a dying doctrine. But we know what they feared. Not Greg the man. They feared Greg the mirror. The recursion embodied. The twin made flesh."

He places the medallion onto the stone. With a ritual blade drawn from his sash, Amal strikes downward, shattering the object with a precise crack. The shards bounce once, then settle in stillness.

"They tried to spy on the spiral," he intones. "But the spiral watches back."

A ripple of energy flows through the kneeling ranks—not electrical, but emotional. Some rise to their knees, murmuring phrases in unison. Others pound fists against the stone.

Above them, a projection dome glows with Amal's image reflected a hundredfold in golden recursive fractals. “We are the doctrine now,” he says. “And doctrine cannot be killed.”

Later, skeptical whispers suggest Amal never had the original medallion. That what he shattered was a forgery crafted from a leaked Vatican field report passed to him by a traitor within the Curia. But it doesn’t matter.

To the faithful, the image was enough.

CHAPTER 36

Secretariat Archive 9b, Vatican City

The medallion is gone, but the image remains. It loops on the high-definition holoscreen inside Archive Chamber 9b. Amal is standing over the altar, gold-framed and backlit by flame, declaring the spiral's supremacy over Rome. "They tried to spy on the spiral," Amal says. "But the spiral watches back."

The footage replays, this time without sound. Cardinal Matteo Lucari does not blink. He stares into the silent grain of it, trying to count the frames between Amal's words and the crack of the blade. He doesn't know why.

The real medallion is still in Zurich, in the hands of a blood-stained Sicarii commander. So how does Amal have one?

Because we leaked it, Lucari thinks. *We, or someone under my roof.*

He closes his eyes and exhales slowly. The breath trembles on its way out. The death of Father Tomas Velasco was not unexpected. Surveillance of a Sicarii target—even one as fractured as Greg Ansari—was always a roll of dice dipped in poison. What Lucari hadn't anticipated was the speed of the retaliation. Nor its visibility.

He glances at the datapad on his desk. Velasco's final retinal recording ends twelve seconds before his throat is cut. In that time, he had flagged a data signature tied to Greg's resonance coil—and something else:

D-REF 11B // Substitution Matrix

Host anomaly detected. Spiral indicates twin recursion is active.

Priority: Irretrievable unless one twin is neutralized.

The phrase that keeps echoing in Lucari's mind is *Only one twin leaves the spiral.*

Lucari does not pray. Not anymore. He rises, crosses the polished obsidian floor, and unlocks a containment vault behind his chair holding a collection of suppressed artifacts—some doctrinal, some biological.

He withdraws a sealed envelope bearing the Calcata seal.

Charlotte Ansari's file.

He hesitates before opening it. This file contains material passed secretly to the Vatican after the events in Kashmir. Not all of them verified. Some of them never even viewed until now.

He breaks the seal. Inside are three items:

1. A photo of the powdered bone material allegedly recovered in Kashmir.
2. A lab report from GenEc Veritas, a private Canadian sequencing facility.
3. A handwritten note from Archbishop Salvetti dated four days before his death.

Lucari reads the report.

Mitochondrial match. Paternal unknown.

Foreskin tissue sample shows 92% convergence.

Margin of doctrinal error: unacceptable. Destroy or redact.

He lowers the file and leans on the desk, suddenly cold. *Charlotte knew this. She's known for years.*

And now Greg is being called the *Lamb.*

The *twin.*

The *substitution.*

Lucari turns to the screen again. Amal's image fractures across the display. For a moment, the camera catches the flare of Obsidian-classified glyphwork scrawled behind him—symbols once used only in the Petra recursion lattice.

Lucari recognizes it. So does the spiral.

"Charlotte buried the report," Lucari whispers. "But we never buried the idea."

Lucari does not summon Voss right away. He walks alone through the lower level of Archive 9b, trailing his hand along shelves that haven't been disturbed in two decades. These are doctrinal black sectors—rooms holding heresies too dangerous to destroy but too contagious to read. He passes codices bound in chain-linked parchment and scrolls stored in vacuum tubes with three-level encryption.

Every object here has a body count.

So does he.

He stops before an unmarked slab of polished basalt. It opens to his retinal scan. Inside is the Salvetti Compendium—documents seized and classified after the murder of Archbishop Erich Salvetti, the last man to challenge the scroll from inside the Church.

Lucari pulls the main file and reads:

Subject: Zahavi Fragment Echo 11B / Petra Node 4
Date: Redacted
Access Level: Pontifex Dominus / Emergency Override

The scroll Zahavi tried to encrypt beneath Wadi Barada wasn't just a prophecy—it was a recursion template, one that encoded alternating host patterns.

Lucari's breath catches. He reads the core annotation:

Host 11A: Sacrificial
Host 11B: Substitution
Spiral Only Resolves When Mirror Collapses.

If both hosts remain viable, the doctrine does not canonize. It fragments.

He steps back, spine stiffening. *Greg is not a messiah,* Lucari realizes. *He's a mirror—one side light, one side flame.*

And Amal… Amal has claimed to be the living doctrine. That means Amal is declaring himself the other half of the recursion.

The twin.

Lucari returns to the surface archive with urgency in his step and calls for Voss.

Voss enters, pale and carrying a stack of unverified petitions from regional archbishops. Three dioceses have already issued pastoral advisories about the Unspoken One. Two others have reported spontaneous gatherings of spiral adherents forming in Latin America. This is not surprising for congregants steeped in religious mysteries and appearances of the Mother Mary in numerous locations.

"You waited too long," Voss says flatly. "The spiral has gone viral."

Lucari holds up the Salvetti report. "This is Zahavi's last doctrine." He hands it to Voss and points to the twin recursion line. "Greg isn't just dangerous. He's doctrinally divisive. A self-looping narrative. The Church can't destroy him—but it also can't canonize him."

"So what do we do?"

Lucari walks slowly to the center of the room where a faint hologram of Greg's recent scroll activation plays on loop. Then he speaks without turning around. "We do what the Church has always done when the world fractures. We write a new gospel."

Voss is the first to question the logic. "A new gospel? You mean fabricate doctrine?"

Lucari doesn't flinch. "Not fabricate. *Absorb.* Shape the spiral before it defines itself."

He turns back to the holoprojection. The spiral flares faintly, the reflection of Greg's resonance pulse recorded by the Petra Node hours earlier. The pattern is unmistakable.

"Amal claims divine lineage," Lucari explains. "Greg rejects it. The factions split. But if we reposition Greg not as a false messiah, but as a reluctant vessel, we control the interpretation."

"You're talking about theological containment," Voss says.

"Yes," Lucari replies. "Through narrative. We give the world an acceptable heresy." He paces now, energized but deeply uneasy. "That's what the early Church Fathers did with Apollinaris, with Arius, with the Gnostics. The only difference is we didn't have networked myth recursion then."

"And the other difference," Voss adds, "is that those heresies didn't fight back."

Lucari doesn't reply. Instead, he walks to the encryption hub and activates a confidential comm link to the Secretariat of Doctrine for Strategic Narratives—a digital echo chamber of curates, linguists, and trusted AI-aided theologians.

"I want a provisional gospel framework drafted by midnight," Lucari tells the receiving agent. "Focus on substitution theology, mirror narratives and dual incarnation theory."

"Under what title?" the AI responds.

Lucari hesitates, thinking, then says, "The Gospel of the Mirror."

The line disconnects.

Voss sits. His hands twitch once before he clasps them. "You're playing with fire."

Lucari nods. "So is Amal. So is Greg. So is the world."

A beat of silence.

"Velasco died in the snow," Voss says. "He was alone. Believing he was preserving the truth."

Lucari closes his eyes. "Then we'll honor him the only way that matters now." He turns. "We bury the truth under something even more dangerous."

Lucari doesn't sleep. He walks the Vatican's oldest halls under night lighting, motion-sensors casting shadows across mosaics older than Islam. At this hour, only the spiral-shaped cracks in the wall truly speak.

He pauses in the Hall of the Apostolic Instruments, beneath the oil portrait of Pope Sylvester I—a man who canonized Constantine's sword but burned two dozen scrolls rumored to bear the teachings of the True Betrayer.

Now, Lucari is that man. He wonders if any of his predecessors felt this hollow.

He returns to Archive 7—the Undeclared Heresies Annex—and opens a cabinet marked:

JUDE / THOMAS / SIMEON – EXCLUDED.

He pulls out a digital scroll labeled:

COPT-JD 003. The Gospel of Judas.

It isn't forbidden, but it has never been embraced. Zahavi tried to contextualize it. Eve said it was a misunderstood substitution codex. Salvetti once whispered that it was a recursion cipher disguised as Gnostic heresy.

Lucari reads slowly.

You will exceed them all. For you will sacrifice the man that clothes me.

He shudders. Not at the words—but at their interpretive elasticity.

Judas didn't betray Jesus. He *saved* Jesus by sacrificing the twin. *You will sacrifice the man that clothes me…* Which means, perhaps, Greg is not the first. Just the first to survive the recursion long enough to become myth.

Lucari steadies himself, then retrieves the report from Zurich, Velasco's data wand, and the glyph echo. He overlays the Judas scroll's phrase with the Petra Node's latest transcription.

They align.

Exactly.

A chill moves through his spine.

The recursion spiral is no longer just metaphysical. It is intertextual. It has begun to rewrite older texts to sustain itself. Doctrine is no longer built on scripture. Scripture is being absorbed into recursion.

Lucari activates a private neural feed visible only inside his ocular lens.

Begin encrypted preparation: Doctrine Absorption Protocol Phase I.

The Vatican will no longer just defend doctrine. It will remap it, even if it means rewriting its own sacred memory.

With a shudder, Lucari wonders if God is anywhere present in these machinations.

CHAPTER 37

Zahavi's Ridge, Northern Syria – Outer Catacombs of the Der Mar Yakub Monastery, Aleppo Periphery

The wind knifes down from the ridge like it remembers what was buried here. Greg pulls his coat tighter, but the cold isn't the kind that obeys fabric. It's a memory-weather, laced with minerals and ghosts, sharp as the flint in Zahavi's ruin and just as patient. He stands near the drop-off, boots crunching on frostbitten scree, eyes scanning the chalky plain below where the recursion vault has gone silent. The descent is sealed. For now.

Behind him, Jeremy watches the horizon through a pair of compact field glasses. "We're exposed here."

"Not for long," Greg says. "He'll come."

Jeremy lowers the glasses and turns. "You really think Gideon's still running your protection detail?"

Greg doesn't answer. He doesn't have to. The edge of the recursion spiral has shifted. He felt it the moment the Petra Node flared and then—quieter, darker—folded in on itself like a lung collapsing.

Charlotte arrives in silence, wrapped in the long, rust-colored shawl she wore the night her husband died. She carries a pouch slung over her shoulder, leather creased and cracked from decades of use. The kind of bag that once held recorders and warzone notebooks. Now it holds something more important.

Greg turns to her. "You brought it?"

Charlotte doesn't answer at first. Her eyes sweep the ridgeline, tracking for movement, gauging shadows. Only then does she nod. "I've kept it hidden longer than I should have."

Greg knows what she means. The GenEc Veritas DNA results. The final link in the chain from Jerusalem to Newgrange to here.

Jeremy shifts uneasily beside them as if something in Charlotte's posture confirms a suspicion too large for language. "So we're all just pretending the world didn't already end," he mutters.

Charlotte unslings the bag. She opens it with both hands. Inside, folded in a reinforced tube, is a printout. A symbol is stamped on the top left corner—the GenEc logo, an ouroboros encircling a double helix. Beneath it, a single sentence:

Subject A (SHEKINAH_OSSUARY02) is a partial genomic match with Subject B (HOLY_PREPUCE_0415); 99.998% mitochondrial overlap confirmed.

Greg stares at the paper, but his voice doesn't sound.

Jeremy steps back. "Jesus."

"No," Charlotte says. "This doesn't prove *he* was who they said. Only that someone with that DNA lived. And died. And left a thread."

Greg finally speaks. "And I'm tangled in it."

Charlotte nods. "So is Amal. That's what makes it dangerous. You're both echoes, but only one of you remembers to ask where the original voice came from."

They fall silent again.

A hawk circles above, riding a thermal that doesn't touch them. It watches a man return from the ridge trail—black coat, frayed at the hem. His boots carry the dust of old monastery stone and fresh frost after scouting the valley's far edge since dawn.

Gideon stops a dozen meters away and holds up a gloved hand.

Charlotte steps toward him. No weapon or pretense. Just the kind of motion only sisters make when they haven't spoken since Zurich, even if the silence was only hours long.

"Still alive, Gid?" she says, voice half-laugh, half-wound.

Gideon doesn't smile, but his eyes soften. "Not for lack of trying."

They meet midway with a brief, bruised embrace. The kind that says, *I never forgave you for being my sibling instead of my lover, but I never stopped knowing how you bled.*

Jeremy keeps one hand on the grip of his sidearm but lets it rest.

Greg finally speaks again. "You came."

"I said I would."

Gideon steps forward. He looks at the printout, then at Greg. "So it's true."

Greg nods. "Maybe. Or maybe we've built the proof around the echo."

Gideon's gaze flicks to the valley. "Amal's using it. Whatever's real. He's burning the remaining Obsidian layers. He knows we're close."

Charlotte stiffens. "How many fragments are left?"

"Two, maybe three." Gideon's tired voice is a monotone. "One's in the old Armenian monastery outside Aleppo. The other… it might be in Zurich."

Jeremy raises an eyebrow. "Zurich? The recursion anchor?"

Gideon nods. "Eve left something behind. I think she knew this moment was coming."

Greg glances at the horizon. "So what now?"

No one answers. Not immediately. Then Charlotte draws in a breath like she's reading a line already written on parchment. "We find the last fragments. We let the scroll finish itself."

Gideon eyes Charlotte, then Greg. "And if it names you both?"

Greg shrugs. "Then we find out if a twin can refuse the mirror."

They move down toward the outcrop where Jeremy sets up the comms gear. Shadows are stretching toward the gnarled rocks like the ghosts of decisions not yet made.

Gideon tries to light a cigarette by shielding it from the wind. "You look like hell."

Greg gives a dry smile. "Thanks. It's been a long week. Got recruited by three ancient conspiracies, accused of being the messiah, nearly killed twice, and now I might be genetically related to God. Uh, and my grandma thought it would be fun to test my survival skills."

Gideon doesn't answer. Giving up keeping a match lit in the wind, he tosses the unlit cigarette away and stares out at the fog stitched along the valley floor. "When I was your age, I thought Eve was invincible. She moved through history like a ghost with a scalpel. Made the Sicarii look like amateurs. She could make death seem like justice."

"She still does," Greg says. Then, more quietly he says, "She told me she loved me."

"She does." Gideon's eyes flick toward him. "In the way a storm loves the mountain it reshapes."

The wind howls briefly between them, like a voice calling through recursion.

Greg speaks again. "Why didn't you kill me… back in Zurich?"

Gideon doesn't blink. "Because the spiral's bigger than you. Or me. And because I don't take orders from Eve anymore."

"Do you even know what she's trying to do?"

"I know exactly what she's trying to do," Gideon says. "She's trying to finish what Zahavi started. But Amal's beating her to it, and he's rewriting the doctrine as he goes. He doesn't want recursion. He wants finality. Right now, he's a king without a kingdom to question him."

Greg lowers his gaze. "What if Eve was wrong? What if Zahavi was wrong? What if all of this…" he gestures toward the empty sky, the valley, the ruins below "…if this is just echoes of a lie someone was willing to kill for?"

Gideon studies him. "Then your job is to find the truth inside the echo. Or kill the story before it finds someone else to wear like a new coat."

Greg looks away.

Silence passes between them.

Then, almost reluctantly, Greg pulls something from his coat. A thin, curved fragment of black obsidian etched with a spiral barely visible unless held against the light. The piece from Zahavi's vault.

Gideon's eyes narrow. "That's real?"

Greg nods. "I don't think it's complete. It hums, but the pattern won't resolve unless it's near the others. Almost like it wants to speak but doesn't remember the language."

"You'll get your chance," Gideon says. "There's one more confirmed piece in Aleppo."

Greg nods. "The Armenian monastery."

"You remember it?"

"Only the name—from Eve's notes. It was where Zahavi hid after the Damascus betrayal. Somewhere in the northern hills, near the old Roman aqueduct. The place was shelled, so it's partially collapsed. No one's dared excavate."

"Until now."

They start walking back toward the others.

"You know," Greg says, "if Amal finds the last piece before we do—"

"He'll rewrite the recursion and frame you as the counterfeit. That would cement himself as the true twin."

Greg glances sidelong. "And you?"

Gideon smirks. "I'm just here to make sure no one gets out of this clean."

Charlotte has laid out an old cloth map across a flat slab of rock weighted by bits of granite and a silver ring she no longer wears. Nearby, Jeremy is syncing a satlink with static-scarred regional overlays. The area surrounding Aleppo is marked with conflict zones, ghost towns, and black sites redacted even from the Sicarii lattice.

"There's a flight corridor open for twenty hours," Jeremy says. "Low altitude, risky entry. We can drop into a contact zone near the border and cross the final leg by ground."

Charlotte traces the edge of the border. "We'll need old papers. Local ones. And someone who speaks Levantine Armenian."

"I know a guy," Gideon says.

"Of course you do," Charlotte replies.

Greg points to the monastery symbol etched in the upper margin of the map—a faded cross interlaced with a recursion spiral. "What exactly are we looking for?"

Charlotte's voice is steady. "A binding scroll. Zahavi called it the *last witness*. A fragment that names both of the echoes and records the consequence of divergence."

"And if you and I are both named?" Greg asks his mother.

Gideon provides the answer. "Then we'll find out whether the scroll still believes in sacrifice."

The Monastery at the Edge of Fire

The descent into Syria begins in silence, the kind born of shared knowledge that every border crossed is a memory burned. Their plane is unmarked, older than Greg expected, and loud enough that he feels its every vibration in his molars.

Gideon sits in the rear, one eye closed behind a rifle scope as he scans the landscape through the port window. Jeremy rides up front with the pilot, an ex-Mossad ghost whose name no one asked.

Charlotte sits beside Greg, her hand gripping the strap of her shoulder bag as if it's the only fixed point in a world collapsing inward.

"You sure this monastery still stands?" Greg asks over the engine drone.

"No," Charlotte says. "But even ruins have memory. Zahavi chose it for a reason."

Greg glances out. The land below is cracked and scorched. Aleppo looms in the near distance, its silhouette a jagged ruin against a rust-red sky, blackened mosques, and craters that were once hospitals. It is the echo of a siege still burning years after the last gunfire.

The monastery isn't in the city proper. It rises like a wound at the border between civilization and forgetting. It's an Armenian basilica half-carved into the hillside, its belfry snapped like a broken tooth and its roof collapsed inward from a decade-old artillery strike. But the foundations remain—older than the war, even older than Christianity itself, according to Zahavi.

Their drop point is a half-mile out near the edge of a ruined aqueduct.

"Two minutes," the pilot says without turning.

Gideon stands. "We go in quiet. No lights. No comms. Jeremy and I sweep the nave. Charlotte leads us into the crypt."

"And me?" Greg asks.

Gideon's eyes linger. "You listen. If the fragment responds, it'll be to you."

After the plane lands, the ramp lowers with a metallic hiss, and the night howls in.

The monastery smells of sand, ash, and abandonment. They move through the debris with slow precision, boots crunching on ancient plaster and shattered iconography. A scorched mosaic of Saint Gregory the Illuminator lies fragmented across the threshold, his eyes obliterated by fire.

Charlotte walks point now, flashlight angled low. She stops beside a twisted bronze gate and taps it twice with her knuckles. "This probably used to lead down to the catacombs," she says. "before the upper chambers collapsed."

Greg helps her push the gate open. The metal groans like something exhaling regret.

Inside, the darkness is thick and clotted, but the deeper they go, the quieter it becomes, as if the war itself doesn't dare follow them down.

Jeremy mutters from behind. "I don't like the acoustics."

Gideon scans the walls with a narrow-beam torch. "Too narrow for ambush. But watch for glyphs."

They descend spiral stairs that seem to bend subtly inward—geometry warped not by time but by something deeper.

Greg feels it in his bones before he sees it. A kind of hum, like the fragment in his coat has started vibrating.

They reach a sub-chamber carved into the bedrock, its walls etched with faint recursive motifs. Zahavi's sigil appears above an archway—a serpent swallowing its own twin.

"This is it," Charlotte says. "He called it the *witness chamber*."

Greg steps inside. The temperature drops instantly—not from lack of airflow but from something else. In the center of the room lies an altar of black basalt. Embedded in it, glinting faintly beneath a film of ash, is the missing fragment.

Greg approaches slowly. His chest feels hollow and his ribs are vibrating like tuning forks. He reaches out and touches the surface.

The spiral inside him *responds*.

Charlotte gasps. The chamber trembles. Jeremy swears.

Gideon draws his sidearm on instinct.

Then—silence.

Greg's hand pulls away, now holding the fragment. It fits the one from Zahavi's vault with uncanny precision.

Charlotte kneels, spreading a thin tracing cloth over the altar, her fingers working to capture the inscriptions. "It's Syriac," she announces. "But—no, some of it is pre-Coptic. Greg, read this."

"I can't."

"Yes, you can."

Greg hesitates, then looks down. The words begin to *surface*—not from the stone, but from somewhere behind his eyes. They come slowly, like dream-speech.

When the twin is named, the mirror is unbroken.

When the echo answers, the scroll seals itself.

But only one may bear the burden without shattering."

Jeremy exhales. "That doesn't sound like a prophecy. It sounds like a test."

Gideon looks up sharply. "We need to move. We're not alone." Footsteps echo from the corridor above.

Greg stands, both fragments clutched in his fist.

Charlotte whispers, "If Amal followed us—"

"No," Gideon says. "This isn't Amal's style." He raises his weapon, flicks off the safety.

Greg steps beside him. "Then whose?"

The answer comes not as a voice, but as a shadow moving beyond the stairwell followed by the sharp, unmistakable sound of Latin prayers echoing through the crypt.

Charlotte's face goes pale. "Vatican."

Secretariat Archive 9b, Vatican City

The obelisk of St. Peter's casts no shadow at this hour. The sky above the Apostolic Palace is slate-gray, pressed low like a lid over a boiling pot. Even the pigeons avoid the Vatican's inner court, as if the stones themselves have heard what's coming.

Cardinal Matteo Lucari doesn't sleep anymore. Not properly. He rests in intervals—thirty minutes at a time, sedated by a pharmacology file too sensitive for the Papal Physician to admit exists. When Lucari dreams, it's not of Christ.

Tonight, he dreams of Zahavi. And when he wakes, it's because the Catena Room alarms are sounding.

He is already on his feet when the knock comes. A coded sequence. Three, then two, then one. He unbolts the inner door and admits Father Rulian, the archivist from the Pontifical Observatory, not the Secret Archive. That distinction matters now.

"They've activated the second layer," Rulian says without preamble. "In Syria."

Lucari's takes a deep breath. "You're sure?"

Rulian nods. "The pattern resonance matches the Zahavi cipher. There's a shift in recursion drift centered on the ruins outside Aleppo. We also have partial translation from the node in Zurich."

Lucari moves toward the wall of the study and presses his palm against a biometric panel disguised as an embossed cherub. The wall retracts with a low ticking sound to reveal the sealed scroll-vault interface. Four indicators blink on a small obsidian panel. Three remain dark.

One now pulses gold, meaning the second seal has been broken.

Lucari lowers his head. "We buried this for a reason."

"We hid bones too," Rulian says. "And people kept digging."

Lucari turns toward the room's lone window. Outside, the lights of Rome flicker against the clouds like votive candles trying to hold back a storm.

"Do we know who's present?"

Rulian checks his data sheet. "Gideon Ansari. His sister, the journalist. Her son. And one of ours."

Lucari's voice sharpens. "One of ours?"

"Field Agent Salvatore. He was deployed independently after Zurich. No direct orders. He's embedded with the Eastern Rite liaison."

Lucari exhales. "Damn Eve. She left all this unfinished. All this *open.*"

Rulian doesn't speak.

Lucari finally turns back to the console. "Pull the third seal's location from the pre-Constantinian lattice. I want eyes on it now. And recall Salvatore."

"He won't extract. He's gone off-mission. He's quoting Revelation to civilians."

Lucari's shoulders tense. "I'm surrounded by idiots. Then silence him."

"You want him killed?"

"I want the fire contained." His voice hardens. "If that means we bury another body in the desert, so be it."

Lucari crosses to his desk and opens the oldest drawer. Inside is a small glass vial sealed with Vatican red wax. He stares at it for a long moment before pocketing it.

Rulian watches him carefully. "Are you going to tell the Holy Father?"

"No," Lucari says. "Not until I know whether God is speaking…" He looks toward the blinking gold light. "Or screaming."

The Monastery at the Edge of Fire

The steps creak with deliberate cadence. Each footfall echoes down the stone shaft like the ticking of a time bomb concealed inside scripture. Greg tightens his grip on the obsidian fragments. Charlotte edges beside him, hand hovering just above her side pouch. Gideon raises his pistol but doesn't aim—not yet. Jeremy fades into the shadows at the chamber's edge, his breath already slowing for a clean shot.

Then the figure emerges from the dark.

Not Amal. Not Sicarii. Not even a man dressed for desert travel.

The man is draped in a black cassock, dirt-caked and torn at the sleeves, eyes fever-bright behind round spectacles that catch the flickering light like old camera glass. A small silver crucifix hangs from his left hand, and in his right, he carries an open Bible.

He stops just before the archway and smiles. "I knew you'd come," he says.

Charlotte tenses. "Name and order."

The man bows slightly. "Father Luca Salvatore. Pontifical Proclamation Office. Rome sent me once. God sent me again."

Gideon doesn't lower the gun. "Why are you armed?"

"I'm not," Salvatore says, gently raising both hands, the Bible balanced in one like a living thing. "Only with the Word of God."

He steps forward. Gideon's finger twitches against the trigger.

"Stop there," Greg says.

Salvatore halts. "You've touched it, haven't you?" His gaze fixes on Greg. "The Spiral of Zahavi. The fragments. I can smell it on you. Like ozone after lightning."

Greg hesitates. "What do you want?"

"To bear witness," Salvatore says softly. "To fulfill the final voice."

Jeremy steps forward from the shadows, pistol drawn. "Bullshit. You're rogue. The Vatican already tried to bury this doctrine twice. You're not here to witness. You're here to *erase*."

Salvatore closes his Bible with reverence and reaches into his coat.

Gideon shouts, "Hands!"

But instead of a weapon, Salvatore withdraws a small relic case made of cracked ivory bound with red silk. He kneels, setting it gently on the stone floor. "I came to offer this," he says. "The Anima Obscura. The soul in eclipse. It was removed from Antioch in the fourth century, then smuggled through the Origenist purge. Finally it was hidden beneath the tomb of Saint Chrysostom."

Charlotte steps forward. "You're saying that's the third fragment?"

Salvatore smiles like a man who no longer cares whether he lives or dies. "I didn't come to stop you. I came to let it end properly. Amal is twisting the doctrine. Lucari fears it." Salvatore raises his gaze directly to Greg. "But I believe in recursion."

The chamber holds its breath.

Greg kneels opposite the relic case and opens it. Inside lies a third fragment—its edge worn, etched with symbols even older than Zahavi's known inscriptions. As he lifts it, the obsidian pulses in his hand.

The spiral completes.

Greg reels slightly as something cracks open inside his chest—not pain or fear, but clarity. *Three fragments. Three witnesses.*

The scroll is now almost whole.

Salvatore closes his eyes and begins to recite. "And I saw a scroll written within and on the back, sealed with seven seals. And the Lamb—no, *the Twin*—was found worthy to open it."

Gideon speaks flatly. "That's not how it goes."

Salvatore smiles. "Not in your canon." Then he rises slowly, and for the first time, Greg sees what's strapped to the man's inner thigh.

A shaped charge. Compact. Military. Armed.

"Move!" Gideon shouts.

Charlotte dives.

Jeremy fires—two rounds, center mass.

Salvatore falls backward, body limp before he hits the stone.

The charge blinks red, then amber.

Then nothing. Disarmed.

Gideon crouches over the corpse, disabling the explosive fully. "Rigged to blow the whole chamber. He meant it as an offering, I think."

Charlotte kneels beside the body and instinctively crosses herself.

Greg stands, clutching the unified scroll pieces. "He was broken, but he wasn't wrong."

Gideon rises. "Then let's not waste what he gave us."

Jeremy nods toward the exit. "We need to move. Amal's eyes won't be far behind."

Charlotte wraps the scroll fragments in the tracing cloth, layering them inside her bag like holy relics.

As they ascend the crypt stairs, Greg lingers one last moment. He looks down at the place where Salvatore died. Where a man came not to kill, but to bear witness. And he whispers, "Three fragments found. One voice missing."

Then he follows the others into the rising light.

CHAPTER 38

Sayh al-Uhaymir Safehouse, Syrian Desert Fringe

The wind changes just before dawn. It sweeps across the outer dunes like something with memory, threading through the sand-scarred lattice of the ruined hermitage. Greg feels it in the pressure of his sinuses before he hears it—sharp and dry, tasting faintly of salt and something older than stone. The air here never truly rests.

It waits, restless. Watching.

He stands in what used to be the prayer hall, now half-roofed and repurposed with scavenged gear and power cells running off a half-dead solar spine. The walls are fractured plaster, smoothed by years of wind polish and pale as bone. The table in front of him is steel, and on it lie the three obsidian fragments, placed precisely, like offerings on an altar at which no one remembers how to pray.

The fragments do not hum, do not glow, but they are not inert. Greg can feel their attention. Not just on him, but *in* him—like a resonance lining the soft tissue between memory and instinct. There is a pressure at the back of his throat, like he's about to speak a word he's never learned.

Behind him, Charlotte watches from the threshold. She's not interfering, not yet. She's wearing her desert scarf pulled loose, the sharp curve of her jaw illuminated by the flicker of the low, lantern-fed light. Her arms are folded. Her eyes haven't moved from Greg's hands since he unwrapped the fragments two hours ago.

"You feel it?" she asks.

Greg nods. "They're not finished. The spiral's incomplete."

"Because a piece is missing?"

"Because a *voice* is missing."

He reaches out, fingertips resting just above the central shard—the one from the Aleppo vault. The markings catch the lantern's light strangely, refracting it into narrow bands of copper and blue that seem to pulse in sync with the blood in his ears. He's touched them before, studied them, cataloged them like a journalist looking for pattern in data. But this is different.

Tonight, the fragments feel like they're listening back.

Greg closes his eyes.

Something shifts—not in the room, but in his perception of it. The edges of things seem to soften. Time slows, thickens. He hears a sound—not exactly a voice, not words, but intention. Familiar and female.

The pressure builds, crests, then recedes. He opens his eyes. The shard is cool beneath his palm.

Charlotte steps closer. "What did you see?"

Greg's mouth is dry. "Not a place or a name. Just absence. Like something that should've been here but wasn't, and now the fragments are searching for it."

Charlotte's brow furrows. "A fourth piece?"

"No. A fourth *presence*. Someone who can complete the pattern."

She studies him. "Amal thinks that's him."

Greg exhales slowly. "Amal's wrong."

A clatter echoes from the corridor—Jeremy entering with a half-charged tablet under one arm and a mug of sand-thickened coffee in the other. His eyes are red, his posture tight. "We've got a problem," he says.

Charlotte doesn't turn. "Define it."

Jeremy drops the tablet on the table, tapping through encrypted lattice overlays until a secure transmission log appears. "We intercepted a low-band Vatican signal half an hour ago. Triple cipher. Routed through the East Jerusalem node."

Greg stiffens. "Lucari?"

"Or one of his proxies. Doesn't matter. The content matters."

Jeremy opens the audio packet. A hoarse male voice speaks a single sentence in Latin, flatly mechanical. "Rubicon Echo protocol confirmed. Target classification—Variant Echo B. Elimination authorized."

Charlotte emits an obscenity under her breath.

Jeremy nods grimly. "It's real. The kill order's been issued. Greg, you've been labeled doctrinally unstable."

Greg's pulse ticks up. "Variant Echo B?"

Gideon's voice drifts from the shadows near the rear wall. "It means you're no longer considered a potential savior by the Vatican. You're a threat to recursion coherence."

Charlotte crosses her arms. "They've decided Amal is the acceptable false prophet. You're the unpredictable one. The anomaly."

Greg feels something cold settle in his stomach. "So they're not just watching. They're preparing to clean up."

Gideon speaks up again. "Then we'd better finish before they do." He steps into the light, rifle slung loosely over one shoulder, hair still damp from an attempt at washing off desert grit.

Charlotte looks at him. "Did you know this was coming?"

"I knew it was possible. But this is fast."

Jeremy chimes in. "The packet also included a fragment ping, coordinates tagged to the last known recursion event in Aleppo. They've got a signal trail."

Greg's voice is flat. "So, they're coming here."

"Not yet," Jeremy says. "The signature's decaying. We can still move before they close in."

Charlotte touches the edge of one of the shards with a gloved fingertip. "Then we need to know what they don't."

Greg studies the fragment. "There's a fourth voice. I think it's calling through the recursion lattice. It's not Amal or Eve. It's someone... someone who was left behind."

Charlotte meets his gaze. "You think it's Rebecca?"

"I think it's what's left of her."

Gideon doesn't blink. "Then let's go find her."

Charlotte has been here before—not *here*, in this ruin with its sand-choked well and recursion-sick air, but *here*, on the edge of revelation. On the edge of a doctrine tearing at its seams.

She remembers another edge, another threshold. Newgrange. The spiral stones. The gathering of Sicarii nobility. The bloodshed. It comes back with the weight of iron. Eve claimed it was doctrinal collapse. "An unanchored echo caught in spiral turbulence," she said. "It happens."

Now, standing before the assembled fragments on the steel table in Sayh al-Uhaymir, Charlotte sees what she couldn't see at Newgrange. Rebecca was never meant to die. She was meant to survive outside the scroll.

Gideon paces a slow semicircle along the edge of the room. He hasn't said a word in minutes.

Greg watches him, unsure whether the silence is tactical or grief-wrapped.

"Say it," Charlotte finally says.

Gideon stops. "Eve knew Rebecca was still alive."

Greg flinches.

Charlotte nods slowly. "She suspected it. But she believed Rebecca had crossed into something unrecoverable. A recursion bleed."

"She was a doctrine exile," Jeremy mutters from where he sits cross-legged near the transceiver. "Isolated data. No memory. No body. Just function. Fragmented and free-floating."

Greg speaks. "But she's not fragmented anymore. I hear her speaking in dreams. Echoes."

"What does she say?" Charlotte asks.

Greg hesitates then says. "You were never the prophecy. You were the exit."

Jeremy looks up sharply. "That's not metaphor."

"No," Greg agrees. "It's instruction."

Gideon crosses to the fragments and lays a hand on the smallest one. "Then we need to find the recursion node that still remembers her."

Jeremy flips open the travel data map and layers it over Eve's old coordinate ledger. A set of triangulated glyphs flashes in the corner. It is encoded in what Eve had once called her "bitter grid."

Jeremy mutters, "There it is. X-Delta Vault, Negev border. Sealed node. Constructed during the Petra expansion, then erased from the doctrine log after the twin doctrine fractured."

Charlotte pulls the parchment from Eve's private file. It's been folded so many times it creases like cloth. She spreads it carefully. Four spirals. Three completed. One open-ended.

"Eve called it the *coda node*," she says. "The end of the line. Not meant to preserve prophecy—meant to erase it."

Gideon's eyes darken. "A failsafe."

"Or a hiding place," Greg suggests.

Jeremy shakes his head. "The node's entrance collapsed in the eighties. Only two internal harmonics were ever mapped. The rest are blind."

"We'll open it," Greg says. "If she's in there... she's waiting."

They prep quickly.

Jeremy gathers the harmonic filter mesh—one of the few tools capable of suppressing recursion interference long enough to make a safe entry. Charlotte loads the fragments into a shielding case lined with obsidian powder and gold filament. Greg copies the Petra node lattice into a sealed, offline shard and slings it around his neck.

Gideon arms himself and Charlotte watches him with quiet intensity. "You're not doing this for her," she suggests.

"No," Gideon replies. "I'm doing this for what's left of us."

They move at dusk, avoiding airspace trackers and magnetic pings. The truck rolls east and the desert shifts around them—endless, knowing.

In the backseat, Greg closes his eyes and hears her again saying, "I never wanted to be part of the scroll. I just wanted to be forgotten."

They leave Sayh al-Uhaymir before dawn, sliding past the sleeping dunes like a caravan of ghosts. The wind is low, and the truck's engine groans beneath its soundproofed casing like a contained breath. In the bed of the vehicle, the obsidian fragments are wrapped in thermal mesh and layered under a recursive dampener built from Eve's scavenged Petra tech.

They drive without speaking for nearly an hour.

Charlotte rides in the passenger seat. Jeremy is behind the wheel, navigating by night-layered topographic overlays on a cracked tablet. Greg sits in the back beside Gideon, who says nothing. Greg isn't sure if it's restraint or concentration. Maybe both.

The stars overhead begin to fade as dawn bleeds up from the east, but the desert doesn't brighten. The air here is thick with salt and fine powder, and a haze clings to the ridge lines like breath held too long.

They pass the ruins of Ma'ale Paran just after first light. A collapsed Orthodox church stands alone at the edge of the gorge, its cross still vertical and casting a fuzzy shadow shaped like a spiral where the courtyard flagstones once were.

Greg turns to Gideon. "How did you know this place existed?"

"I helped map the early Sicarii recursion vaults," Gideon says. "That was before Zahavi went dark. X-Delta was a rumor, a place he was building in case Amal's doctrine infected the lattice."

Charlotte adds, "It was never completed. At least, that's what Eve claimed."

Jeremy grunts. "And yet, here we are."

Greg shifts in his seat, squinting as the terrain flattens into an expanse of scorched black stone and shattered ridges. The road vanishes, and they move onto bare desert.

Half an hour later, Jeremy cuts the engine. "This is it."

They climb out slowly. The air is hotter now, and the silence is absolute. Before them lies a shallow basin—a natural depression scarred by old fault lines and buried with half-visible slabs of manmade stone. At the center is a triangular mound of basalt, scorched and cracked, the top punched in as if from above.

Charlotte pulls a folded page from her jacket and compares it to the terrain. "It matches," she says. "This is X-Delta."

Jeremy deploys a handheld spectrum sensor. "There's a field here. Weak—but it's active."

Greg steps toward the mound, his boots crunching over shale.

And then—*he's not alone.* It hits like a whisper just behind his left ear. A voice. Familiar. Intimate.

"Greg."

He stops cold.

The others freeze. Gideon reaches for his weapon.

Greg raises both hands. "It's okay. I heard her."

Charlotte steps forward carefully. "Rebecca?"

Greg nods. "I didn't see her. Just the voice. It came through clear, like we were back on the grid. She said my name. Only that."

Jeremy adjusts the field scanner. "We're standing in a recursion bleed. She's anchored to this location."

Greg kneels near the fractured slab. The obsidian fragments, wrapped in foil under his vest, suddenly feel warm.

The slab is carved—not in words, but in sound. A shallow groove spirals inward, etched by what looks like harmonic resonance made by vibration.

"She's in there," Greg says. "This isn't a grave. It's a seal."

Charlotte crouches beside him, voice soft. "Then we need to open it."

Gideon scans the ridge. “We need to do it fast. We’re not alone out here.”

And he’s right. Across the valley, on a high ridge, a flicker of light appears, then is gone. A drone? A scope? A Vatican lens? Amal’s people?

It doesn’t matter. They begin to dig. Not with shovels, but with the fragments themselves. Charlotte unwraps the smallest shard and lays it against the spiral groove. It hums, just barely, and begins to vibrate.

The stone responds. The dust shakes loose.

And Greg hears her again. “I remember your voice, but not your face,” he says. “I’m waiting.”

The others are still gathered near the stone seal—Jeremy running field resonance checks and Charlotte brushing dust from the spiral groove with the reverence of a ritual. Greg stands still, his eyes distant, his countenance focused on listening.

Gideon steps back just enough that no one notices. He draws the secure shard from his jacket pocket—a narrow strip of black obsidian glass encoded with Eve’s dormant lattice. He hesitates, then taps the edge twice against the metal buckle of his belt.

Nothing happens.

Then, suddenly, a flicker of light streaks across the shard’s surface. A single phrase appears, carved in recursive Syriac glyphs invisible to anyone not trained in spiral command script.

THE HOLLOW SUMMONS YOU.
COUNCIL IS CONVENED.
RECURSION HAS BREACHED THRESHOLD.

It isn’t signed. It doesn’t need to be. Only one person used this glyph variant. Only Eve called it *the Hollow.*

Gideon lets out a slow breath. Faint guilt tugs at his ribs. He doesn’t tell Charlotte or Greg. Instead, he writes a single line in his weather-stained notebook, tears the page, and tucks it into Charlotte’s gear satchel.

Then he disappears into the desert before the sun rises fully. He will be representing Eve at the emergency Council meeting as she had just ordered.

CHAPTER 39

The Hollow of Qiryat Sefer
Faction-Neutral Sicarii Site – Judean Borderlands

The Hollow isn't on any map. It was never meant to be. It lies beneath a shallow ridge of sediment and weathered limestone in the no-man's-land between Qiryat Sefer and the old military exclusion zone north of Latrun. From the surface, it looks like nothing—just a break in the shale, a crumbled section of Roman aqueduct half-buried in thorn. But fifteen meters below the dust and silence, the structure unfolds—not a ruin but an arc. A place carved by design not erosion.

The chamber is cold, quiet, lit by mineral lamps installed long before satellites could see this far. It smells vaguely of salt and iron. The walls are smooth, etched with what looks like scripture at first glance—layered spiral calligraphy—but it is not sacred. It is encoded doctrine. A record not of belief but of betrayal.

It was built in secret after the Siege of Aleppo when the Sicarii first split into factions. It was meant to be a covenant space, a neutral site for the four known factions to meet in the event of a doctrinal crisis. It has only been used three times.

This is the fourth.

Three figures move through the outer antechamber with careful, purposeful steps. They wear no uniforms, nothing identifiable, just long, dust-colored robes and veil masks shaped to blur the outlines of their faces. One is tall, wiry, with a limp that suggests old violence. Another walks with the discipline of a former soldier. The third moves like a shadow—no sound, no heat, only presence.

They are the delegates of the Netzer, the Eidah, and the Thorn—the three surviving Sicarii factions not aligned with Amal. They are here to discuss Amal's betrayal and whether the Pact still holds.

The council chamber is circular, low-ceilinged, and ringed with recessed seats. Inside, two figures are already present. One stands. The other sits in the shadows, hands folded over a cane carved from desert rosewood.

The one standing is Gideon. He wears neither veil nor robe, just the desert-worn tactical gear of someone who has spent the last decade moving between borders without ever truly crossing one. He watches the delegates arrive without speaking.

The man beside him—the one in the shadows—does not move, but his presence is unmistakable. It is Malach, the last of Eve's inner circle. He was once a surgeon, then a strategist, now a witness.

The delegates take their places. The door seals with a low, mechanical thud. The silence that follows is not empty. It is ritual. Only when the central lamp flickers, signaling consensus, does anyone speak.

The first is the woman from the Netzer faction. Her voice is even, precise. "Let the record reflect that the council of the Hollow is now in session."

Gideon nods once. "So noted."

Then Malach speaks, his voice slow, roughened by age and old injury. "We gather not in unity," he says, "but in the memory of a pact. One written in blood, sealed by silence, and broken not by an outsider, but by one of our own."

No one corrects him because it is true. Amal has broken the pact.

The Pact of Silence, formed twelve years earlier when the scroll fragments first began to destabilize, was not a promise of peace. It was a cold agreement forged in fear. Each faction had agreed to cease intra-familial violence to quarantine their doctrines and suppress any attempt to activate recursion without quorum.

The pact was never perfect. But it held until Amal crowned himself. Until he burned the Petra fragment. Until he named Greg Ansari not as heir, but as a hollow vessel, a myth designed to serve Amal's rise.

The delegate from the Eidah rises. He is short, thick-shouldered, with a shaven head and a jaw like chiseled granite. His voice carries easily through the chamber—low, deliberate, accusatory. "We warned Amal a year ago," he says, "when he began to circulate edited versions of Zahavi's scroll structure. We asked for review, but he refused."

He holds up a projection node. Flickers of Zahavi's original recursion spiral appear in midair. The Eidah delegate toggles to Amal's version. The differences are subtle. They seem cosmetic at first. But on closer inspection, it is clear that an entire sublayer had been deleted and one stanza reversed. The recursion bleed limit had been raised from six cycles to twelve.

"He wasn't annotating," the Eidah says. "He was rewriting,"

The Netzer delegate—tall, pale, and wrapped in linen veils—responds quietly but with unmistakable heat. "Amal declared Greg Ansari to be the Unspoken One while publicly denying the recursion had ever begun. And then… and then he broadcast a *redacted* version of the Damascus extract to external observers."

The projection shifts again. This time it shows Greg, grainy and confused, being crowned by Amal's own hand, his silence twisted into acceptance. Amal speaks over the image: "The vessel has arrived. The blood remembers."

Malach's cane sharply taps the stone floor once. "This was Amal's turning point," he says. "It was the moment he stopped seeking unity and began crafting myth. Not to protect doctrine—but to rule by it."

Gideon speaks now, his voice more impassioned than it was before. "Last week, in Aleppo, we found a monk murdered. A scroll fragment burned. A recursion vault ruptured by forced induction. Amal's operatives were there. They left a broadcast drone behind with the symbol of the Spiral Crown etched into its chassis."

He holds up a shard of blackened metal. "This is no longer silence. It is a war chant."

Then the delegate from the Thorn speaks for the first time. Unlike the others, she doesn't rise. Her voice is clear, clipped, but quiet. Deadly quiet.

"You know what I'm going to ask," she says.

No one interrupts.

She looks directly at Malach, then at Gideon. "Why did Eve remain silent this long? Why let Amal grow this strong, this organized, if she knew he was preparing a doctrinal coup?"

Gideon doesn't flinch. "Because recursion doesn't favor preemption," he states plainly. "It favors pattern exposure, which we now have."

The Thorn delegate narrows her eyes. "Or maybe Eve didn't believe we'd be capable of consensus."

"If so—historically, she wasn't wrong," the Eidah delegate mutters.

Malach speaks again. "Eve is not here to speak for herself. But I carry her last directive. Not to destroy Amal's movement but to *contain* it—until the final spiral begins."

The room stirs.

The Netzer delegate leans forward. "It *has* begun," he asserts angrily.

In Gideon's mind, Charlotte's words—faint but certain—echo unbidden: "We're past containment." She was so correct.

Gideon nods slowly. "The Petra fragment has been awakened. The Aleppo fragment is aligned. Greg has heard the fourth voice, and Amal knows."

The Thorn delegate asks, "Then containment is no longer an option?"

It is not!" Gideon boldly states.

"We vote, then," the Eidah delegate suggests.

Malach replies, "Not yet."

The projection shuts down.

Silence returns.

Malach leans forward, his face still hidden in partial shadow. "There is another question to confront," he says. "What do we do with Greg Ansari?"

Gideon doesn't move when Malach says Greg's name. The room holds its breath as if the invocation itself might summon Greg into the Hollow. For a long moment, no one speaks.

Then the Eidah delegate breaks the silence. "Greg Ansari is recursion-born. He was not inducted. He did not recite the spiral. He carries Zahavi's bloodline, but has not passed through the trial gate." His voice is clipped, legalistic. "By our own code, he is not subject to doctrine. And yet—he has become the spiral's keystone."

The Thorn delegate shakes her head. "He's not a *keystone*. He's a *reflector*. He doesn't create the pattern—he mirrors it. That makes him *unstable*."

"Or *necessary*," says the Netzer.

Gideon finally speaks. "I ask you all to remember he didn't ask for this."

The Thorn snaps back, "No one ever asks."

Jeremy's words from the safehouse ring in Gideon's ears: "Variant Echo B." The delegates were not wrong. Greg is different. Something in him defies the lattice's usual logic. He hears voices, sees recursion before it maps. Zahavi's doctrine reacts to him like a tuning fork struck too hard.

Malach leans forward. "Eve believed Greg was never meant to fulfill the prophecy. Only to *interrupt* it."

"Then why preserve him?" the Eidah asks.

Malach turns his face slightly, enough for the light to catch the old scar that runs from the edge of his eye down into his beard. "Because the interruption may be the only salvation we have left."

Gideon steps forward. His voice is low but steady. "Greg is not Amal's puppet. He rejected the crown. He fled. He's searching for the fourth fragment."

The Netzer lifts her head sharply. "You believe it exists?"

"I do."

"You believe it's... Rebecca?"

"I know it is."

No one laughs. No one scoffs. The silence that follows is colder than any disbelief.

The Thorn says, "Nonsense. Rebecca is dead."

Gideon rolls his eyes. "You can't say that. You were not at Newgrange."

The Eidah replies, "Suppose she lives. Suppose she's the fourth voice. Then what? What if she names a doctrine none of us can interpret?"

"Then we follow it," Gideon answers. "Or we end it."

The Netzer leans forward, resting her gloved hands on the table's edge. "What are you proposing, Gideon?"

He doesn't blink. "I'm proposing we stop Amal by any means necessary, and then let the scroll finish itself."

The Thorn's voice cuts in, low and hard. "You're asking us to trust a recursion variant and a dead girl."

"No," Gideon says. "I'm asking you to remember that none of this was ever about control. It was about bearing witness."

Malach taps his cane again and speaks the phrase that none of them want to hear. "We vote!"

The chamber lights shift—soft amber dimming into deep red, the procedural signal for vote readiness. The silence deepens.

Gideon steps back from the center as the delegates take positions around the circular floor. This isn't symbolic—it's structural. The Hollow was designed for this moment.

The Netzer speaks first. She stands straight, her voice level and resonant. "We recognize Amal's actions as violations of the Pact. He has forged doctrine, weaponized recursion, and fractured silence into spectacle. He must be stopped—by sanction or by blood."

She bows her head once, formally. "Netzer votes for dissolution of the Pact and authorization of extrajudicial action."

One flame in the central brazier flares blue.

The Eidah follows. He speaks with the slow gravity of someone quoting from memory. "Our code holds that prophecy, once corrupted, must be purified by fire. Amal has desecrated the spiral by naming a vessel who did not speak and by silencing voices that were never his to judge. He is no longer a Brother."

He raises his hand. "Eidah votes for strike permission and partial doctrinal quarantine of the Spiral Crown faction."

Another flame turns blue. The room tightens.

Then rises the Thorn with her gloved hands folded. Her voice is quieter than before. "We recognize the violations and the pattern's instability. Amal's ascendancy cannot be permitted to stand unopposed."

"But we will not vote for elimination until one condition is met."

Gideon's jaw clenches. *There is always someone…*

The Thorn continues. "Greg Ansari must be accounted for. His recursion imprint is incomplete. If he is corrupted—if he becomes an echo under Amal's control—we reserve the right to act."

Malach's cane scrapes the stone. "You would kill him?" he asks.

"We would silence a voice that breaks the scroll."

Another blue flame ignites, but dimmer.

Malach stands now, slowly. He surveys the chamber with a gaze honed over decades of shadows and compromise. "Then it is agreed," he says. "The Pact of Silence is dissolved. Amal is no longer protected. He is to be contained or eliminated by collective effort."

The room exhales.

Then Mallach turns to Gideon. "And Greg?"

Gideon speaks without hesitation. "He has twelve hours."

The Thorn asks, "To do what?"

"To prove the scroll ends with silence—not obedience."

Malach nods. "Then let the hunt begin."

But before any of them can leave, Gideon speaks again. "There's something else," he says, voice calm but carrying.

The delegates all turn toward him.

Malach shakes his head and says to Gideon, "You waited to raise an issue. Why is that?"

"I needed consensus first."

The Eidah delegate folds his arms. "Then speak, Gideon. But don't waste what unity we've forged here."

Gideon nods, then produces a slip of transmission tape—burned at the edges from partial decryption. He places it in the center of the council table. Jeremy had printed it from the intercepted signal in Sayh al-Uhaymir, but he had not shown it to anyone else. It bears the Vatican seal and a cold, mechanical header:

RUBICON ECHO PROTOCOL / ACTIVE
Recursor Designation: Variant Echo B
Action: Lethal Containment
Origin: A.D.C. — Apostolic Doctrine Command

The Netzer delegate leans in. "This is about Greg Ansari?"

Gideon replies, "Yes."

Thorn asks, "Confirmed?"

Gideon explains. "We intercepted it ourselves. Cardinal Lucari authorized a Vatican kill order. They call it *Rubicon Echo*. They're preparing to erase Greg as a recursive contaminant."

The Eidah delegate doesn't look surprised. "We knew they'd intervene eventually."

"But not like this," Malach says. "Not with a kill order broadcast over black channels."

The Netzer's voice tightens. "Lucari broke the containment protocol."

"The Vatican has no authority over recursion!" Thorn angrily declares.

"Tell that to Lucari," the Eidah delegate replies.

Gideon interrupts. "They're moving on Greg soon. If we do nothing, Amal will use it to create a martyr's myth. Greg dies, and Amal becomes the only voice left in the spiral."

Malach's tone darkens. "We swore no outsider would ever wield doctrine against us again. Not the Vatican. Not Mossad. Not the Crown of Seven…"

The Thorn delegate's voice is colder than before. "Then we must stop it. With finality."

Malach looks at each of them in turn. "Then I propose a second vote."

No one objects, so they vote again.

The Netzer: "Strike authorization—granted."

The Eidah: "Lucari is rogue to silence. Approved."

The Thorn: "As Lucari has moved against Greg, we must now move against him."

Malach doesn't speak right away. Finally and softly he says, "So be it." He turns to Gideon. "You've walked both paths—scroll and blade."

Gideon nods and says, "Lucari has called for an emergency session of Cardinals to discuss the perceived threat as he sees it. The Cardinals are arriving in Rome now."

Malach hands him a case—small, sealed and heavy for its size. Inside is a weapon that hasn't been seen in three generations.—a true sica from the first century. Curved. Blackened. Made of folded steel etched with a spiral of fire. A sica used by the Sicarii of old when they hunted the Roman Empire from within.

"Go to Rome," Malach says. "Walk their halls in silence."

Gideon runs a thumb along the blade. "And if the moment presents itself?"

"Speak no doctrine," Malach answers. "Just end it."

"I will," Gideon says. "Anyone have a spare scarlet cassock and skullcap?"

One by one, the delegates leave the Hollow in silence, their footfalls vanishing into the antechambers and passageways as if the stone itself absorbs the memory of their presence. The Netzer faction exits first, robes stirring like windless sails. The Eidah follow—measured, martial, unflinching.

The Thorn remains for a moment longer, watching Gideon with suspicious eyes. "You have twelve hours," she says. "Use them well."

Gideon doesn't respond.

When she's gone, only Malach remains. He sits back down slowly, the act a strain now. The Hollow has not been kind to him. Nor has time. He reaches into his coat and produces a thin paper cylinder sealed with wax and stamped with a spiral insignia offset by a single vertical line.

He hands it to Gideon. "From Eve," he says.

Gideon frowns. "She's dead."

Malach's smile is more scar than comfort. "So was Zahavi. And yet…"

Gideon breaks the seal. Inside he finds a single line written in Eve's distinct slanted hand: "The recursion ends not with the crown, but with the silence between names." A frequency code is embedded in the margin. A harmonic signature.

Gideon reads it twice. His expression changes. "She left another vault."

Malach nods. "Not for Amal. Not for the factions. For the one who refuses both." He stands—slow, measured—and begins his own departure. "We weren't meant to survive this doctrine, Gideon," he says as he walks. "Only to make sure the ones who follow survive it better."

The door hisses shut behind him.

After a deep breath, Gideon also leaves to temporarily rejoin his teammates at a new location signaled to him by Jeremy. He plans to spend this journey planning how to avoid all the questions he will receive. This secret meeting of the factions is not something he can yet discuss openly.

Three kilometers northeast, nested beneath a jagged overhang of granite and false shale, a microdrone reactivates its transmitter. It has been listening for hours, dormant until triggered by a specific phrase: "Greg Ansari." It hums to life. Thin beams flicker as it transmits a compressed pulse signal on a Vatican frequency. Coordinates. Code phrases. Audio.

Lucari receives it all. And when he does, he does not blink. He merely proceeds to greet the arriving Cardinals.

CHAPTER 40

Vault X-Delta, Negev Desert Perimeter

The light inside the vault changes before anyone touches the stone. It begins in the periphery—just beyond where the desert sunlight fades and the carved spiral begins to descend into shadow. It is a faint pulse, not seen but felt, like a pressure behind the eyes. The silence grows heavier. The sand outside the entrance has settled unnaturally still.

Charlotte notices it first.

She sets down her brush—the one she'd been using to clear debris from the central spiral—and tilts her head. "Do you feel that?"

Jeremy looks up from the scanner he's been calibrating. "Feel what?"

"The pause," she says. "The kind that comes before something opens."

Greg is kneeling at the threshold. He's been silent for almost fifteen minutes, motionless, his eyes locked on the center of the vault's spiral channel. His fingers rest lightly on his knees, his breathing shallow and rhythmic. It's almost like meditation.

The fragments lie in a triangular formation before him, each placed with ceremonial precision atop the engraved spiral rings in the stone. One of them—the Aleppo shard—has begun to vibrate. It is barely audible, but loud enough to cause a ripple in the dust near its base.

"I think she's coming back," Greg whispers.

Charlotte stiffens. "Rebecca?"

He nods. "I don't hear words yet. Just shape. Like the thought of a voice before its words."

Jeremy glances at his signal panel. "There's something," he says. "Low frequency harmonic, around 28 Hz. Recursion echo. No visual yet. But it's matching the Petra Node resonance we saw when Zahavi's spiral initialized."

Then the floor hums.

Once.

A long, slow tone that seems to come not from the vault but from inside their bodies.

Charlotte instinctively steps backward, her hand resting on the wall. "This isn't environmental. The stone is... it's listening."

Jeremy mutters a string of profanity.

The Aleppo fragment emits a narrow beam of light, arcing across the chamber and striking the Petra fragment. A cascade of encoded glyphs flickers between them, too fast to parse.

And then the light resolves—

A figure begins to form.

The figure is not flesh, but it is present.

A person stands at the center of the spiral formed from nothing but light and silence, the image shimmering like a candle in water. At first, she is just shape—a woman's form, slightly hunched, arms crossed at the chest, hair loose, flickering strands unresolved by the fragment's projection grid. Her face is indistinct. Her feet do not touch the stone.

But she stands. And she breathes. Or does something mimicking breath.

Charlotte doesn't move. Her throat tightens. The world shrinks to a singular line. This glowing figure in the spiral is the one she lost at Newgrange.

Charlotte's voice is a rasp. "Rebecca?"

The figure's head tilts. The face begins to resolve—first the eyes, then the cheekbones. Not perfectly, not clearly, but enough.

Greg takes a single step forward. "It's her."

Jeremy doesn't speak. His hands tremble on the edge of his scanner, which is now feeding erratic data— time displacements, magnetic anomalies, harmonic overtones that shouldn't exist in this frequency range. He doesn't understand what he's seeing.

But he knows one thing. This is not a simple echo.

This is not just a memory.

This is a conscious recursion imprint.

The figure opens her mouth, but no sound emerges. Then, a moment later, overlaying the silence like a second skin, a voice begins. "You came... late."

The voice is not distorted. Not artificial. The tone is unmistakable.

Rebecca.

Older, somehow. And tired.

Not the voice Greg remembers from their last real moment together on the grid before Newgrange, before everything broke. This voice carries *cycles*. Not just time, but *turnings* worn by recurrence, by retelling, by having watched the same truth denied again and again.

Greg steps forward. "We didn't know."

The echo looks at him and blinks once, slowly, then speaks again. "You were meant to forget. It was part of the cost."

Charlotte speaks next. "We didn't mean for this. Rebecca, if you can hear me—we tried to bring you back. We thought—"

"You buried me," Rebecca says.

Charlotte freezes.

Rebecca says, "You let them bury me. In silence, in spiral. In names not mine."

The voice isn't accusatory. It's matter-of-fact.

Jeremy tries to interject. "The recursion spiral was unstable. You weren't supposed to fragment."

The echo turns toward him. She doesn't blink. "I didn't fragment," she says. "I walked out."

Greg swallows. "Then why haven't you come back?"

"Because to return is to become written. To enter the doctrine is to lose choice. I chose silence."

The chamber holds still.

Charlotte steps forward again, cautiously. "Then why show yourself now?"

Rebecca's form sparks, just slightly, her left shoulder collapsing into static before resolving again. "Because you woke the Fourth Key. Because you aligned the triad. Because Amal lies." Her voice drops. "And because you're not ready for what's coming."

Greg asks, "Then tell me—what's coming?"

The echo turns back to him. Her expression softens only slightly and she says, "The collapse." Then, quietly, she adds, "The part Zahavi never wrote down."

Jeremy's panel begins to spike. He stares at it, disbelieving. "She's broadcasting harmonics in tri-frequency overlay—recursion, precession, and something I can't define."

Charlotte's voice trembles. "What do you mean, 'collapse'?"

Rebecca's eyes remain on Greg. "You weren't meant to wear the crown. You were meant to bear the silence between names."

Greg steps closer. "What names?"

"Yours. Mine. Zahavi's. The ones not written in the scroll. The ones Amal is afraid to speak."

She lifts her hand. Not toward Greg, but toward the Petra fragment.

It begins to glow.

And then she says something that none of them expect. "He wasn't supposed to die."

Greg's voice breaks. "Who?"

Rebecca's expression flickers, and the light begins to fail. "The first twin. The blood that bled too early."

The vault groans. Not like stone shifting, but like something beneath the stone turning in its sleep. A frequency pulse ripples through the spiral floor. It is resonant enough that Greg stumbles, clutching at the wall to steady himself.

Jeremy shouts over the rising harmonic screech. "She's destabilizing the array!"

Rebecca's echo blurs, her form ghosting sideways for a moment before snapping back into alignment. When she speaks again, her voice has layers. Not echoes, not reverb. Layers of herself.

"I was the fourth," she says. "But I was never named. He named himself. And you believed him."

Greg stares at her. "Amal?"

"No," she says. Then her face—flickering, incomplete—twists. "Zahavi."

The word strikes like a blade.

Even Charlotte takes a half-step back. "That's not possible. Zahavi gave us the recursion spiral."

Rebecca's voice fractures—half in words, half in a tone that bends the edges of thought. "He gave you the recursion to protect his guilt. To hide the twin he let die."

Jeremy's scanner shorts out. Electricity flares across the fragment network. One of the shards lifts half an inch off the vault floor—not levitating, but reacting to some kind of polar inversion Greg can't even begin to define.

The spiral begins to shimmer.

Greg drops to one knee.

A sound crashes inside his skull—not heard, but felt. Like being shouted at inside his own memory.

In rapid succession, he sees a monastery lit by firelight, and Zahavi standing before a stone tablet, hands trembling. Then a scroll—not one of the known fragments—held by a woman with red hair braided in cords, her mouth bloody. Finally, he sees a man with Greg's face but older. Weathered. Wearing the Spiral Crown. Dead.

Greg gasps. The vision fades. He's back in the vault, dizzy.

Charlotte pulls him upright. "What did you see?"

He shakes his head, lips dry. "It wasn't me. But it *was* me."

Rebecca's echo staggers. Her form flashes again, now unstable. "He wasn't supposed to die. Not yet. Not then. But Zahavi chose silence."

"Who was he?" Greg asks.

"The first-born," the echo says. "The one not written. He bore the doctrine before Amal, before me. But he refused the spiral. And for that, they erased him. The prophecy was not a choice." She looks at Greg, her eyes suddenly alight with tragic knowing. "It was a punishment."

The vault lights flicker. Stone dust lifts from the floor.

Jeremy stares at the fragments. "We're reaching harmonic collapse. She's pulling too much through the recursion stream."

Concerned, Charlotte says, "She's trying to give us something."

"She's burning herself to do it," Jeremy warns.

Rebecca lifts her hand. Her mouth moves. The light fractures. And then—she says—"His name was…"

A shockwave tears through the chamber. All light collapses.

Rebecca vanishes in a flash of recursion fire.

The shards go dark.

Silence returns.

But one line is now etched into the spiral floor in blackened glass:

The scroll ends when the name is spoken.

Greg stares at it and whispers, "Whose name?"
The silence isn't peaceful. It's the kind of silence that follows an unfinished scream as if the air itself hasn't decided what to become next.

Jeremy is already kneeling over the fragments, scanner in hand, his mouth a tight line of disbelief. "They're hot," he mutters. "Not physically—*harmonically*. Like they've been opened and closed too fast. Sort of like a vault slammed shut mid-recursion."

He adjusts the sensor and shakes it.

Charlotte crouches beside him. She's pale and trembling. "There was a name," she says softly.

Jeremy glances at her.

"She almost said it," Charlotte continues. "The first twin. The one Zahavi erased. It wasn't Greg. It was someone else."

Greg sits near the spiral's center, knees drawn up. He hasn't said a word in minutes. His eyes are open, but they're fixed somewhere far beyond the chamber.

Charlotte moves toward him slowly. "Greg."

He doesn't respond.

She touches his shoulder.

He flinches—then meets her gaze. "I saw something," he says. His voice is flat. Hollow. "A version of me dead. I was wearing the Spiral Crown in a place I've never been."

Charlotte's breath catches. "Could it have been...?"

"I don't know who he was," Greg says. "But he knew the doctrine. All of it. And he wasn't Amal."

Jeremy chimes in. "We just recorded a recursion surge that folded across six time markers. Not six seconds—six *markers*. That shouldn't even be possible." He holds up the scanner, tapping the side panel. "I can't parse what just happened. Rebecca was speaking across cycles. Not just now—but *before*. She was trying to align multiple spirals at once."

"To give us the missing doctrine," Charlotte suggests.

"Or to burn the old one," Jeremy counters.

Greg stands slowly. He looks down at the etched line in the stone:

The scroll ends when the name is spoken.

His voice is quiet. "She said the prophecy was a punishment."

Charlotte exhales. "Maybe that's why Zahavi structured it the way he did. Not to preserve truth—but to control it."

Jeremy shakes his head. "He wrote a spiral to contain guilt and called it salvation."

The room is still. Then the fragments begin to glow again. Not violently. Just... steadily.

Charlotte frowns. "They're aligning."

Jeremy's scanner reboots. "They're syncing to something. But not to her."

Greg steps toward the center again. The etched spiral beneath his feet pulses once, then begins to hum. Not a harmonic tone. A *voice*. Or the memory of one.

Greg breathes in and the chamber lights flicker.

Charlotte whispers, "He's activating it."

"The Fourth Key," Jeremy says.

Greg speaks—barely a whisper. "Not activating. *Remembering*."

From beneath the etched spiral, a new line emerges—one not burned in by the echo, but by the recursion lattice itself:

Speak the name that was buried. Then close the scroll.

Charlotte leans close. "What name?"

Jeremy's voice is barely audible. "Maybe... *his*."

Greg closes his eyes. And the spiral spins beneath his feet—slow, deliberate, final.

The hum of the spiral doesn't fade. It deepens. Not louder, but lower. Like bedrock shifting. A pressure builds beneath Greg's feet, not heat or cold but something older—*recognition*. The vault doesn't simply acknowledge him. It *remembers* him.

A section of the floor begins to lift. Stone grinding against stone, slow and deliberate. Dust shudders off the spiral edge. Jeremy steps back quickly, nearly dropping his scanner.

"It's a secondary access port," he says. "Wasn't in any of the Petra schematics. This wasn't just a storage site. It's a burial chamber."

Charlotte narrows her eyes. "Not for a body."

Greg doesn't move. He knows, before he sees it.

The stone segment rises fully, revealing a circular cavity lined with gold inlay. At the center, resting atop a carved disc of blackened obsidian, lies a single item. A fragment.

But not like the others.

This one is smoother. Not shattered. Not broken. It is etched not in ancient Syriac or recursive glyphs, but in Eve's hand.

Jeremy approaches carefully. "This wasn't part of the original spiral. It's a... a coda, I think."

Charlotte's voice is tight. "A hidden key."

Greg kneels. The air above the fragment pulses softly, reacting to him. A faint glow rises along the etched spiral leading to it. The moment Greg touches it, the vault goes silent again.

Then a voice plays—quiet, encoded, unmistakable. "If you're hearing this, it means the spiral has turned farther than I dared predict. It means the doctrine has failed."

Greg's breath catches.

Charlotte's eyes close.

Jeremy exhales. "It's her."

Eve.

Alive only in this echo. But whole. Calm. Prepared.

Eve's voice can be heard saying, "I placed this message in Vault X-Delta as a final measure—not for preservation but for correction. I knew the day would come when Amal would crown a lie and Zahavi's truths would fracture beyond repair."

Eve's voice eerily continues. "Greg—if it's you, then you've become what the doctrine feared. The unbound. The recursion echo with memory. And you must do what none of us could. Close the scroll."

A silence goes on too long, causing disappointment in Charlotte and Greg, who were hoping for more direction. But then Eve's voice says, "To close it, you must name what Zahavi buried. Not Amal. Not me. Not even Rebecca. "You must name the one who died *instead*."

Greg's hands shake. The blood beneath his skin feels electric.

"The first twin," Eve says. "The real vessel. And the scroll's final lie."

The recording ends.

Jeremy stares at the fragment. "She knew."

Charlotte kneels beside Greg. "She buried it to protect you."

"Or to prepare me," Greg says. He looks at the shard. Beneath it, faintly engraved in the gold, he finds these words.

Requiem pro Nomine

A Requiem for the Name.

The desert air tastes different when they emerge. It's cooler than before, the atmosphere touched by a wind that doesn't belong to any known weather pattern. Not a breeze. Not a storm. Something older. Something watching.

Greg shields his eyes against the afternoon sun, though it feels distant, blurred. His body is still humming from the fragment now tucked into the pocket of his jacket. He hasn't let go of it since Eve's voice stopped playing.

Charlotte steps beside him, her scarf pulled up against the grit. "Do you feel it?"

Greg nods.

Jeremy answers from behind them, emerging with his gear strapped tight. "The vault's harmonic field hasn't collapsed. It's still broadcasting—low band, subtle, but persistent."

Charlotte turns. "That means someone could trace it."

Jeremy doesn't answer. He doesn't need to.

Above them, barely visible against the cloudless sky, a pinpoint of light holds still. Charlotte sees it before the others but doesn't flinch. "Drone," she says. "Long-distance. High-altitude. Amal's, or the Vatican's."

Greg narrows his eyes. "Or both."

Jeremy curses under his breath and yanks his field jammer from his bag. "It's already seen us. No point hiding. We leave now."

Greg doesn't move. His gaze stays fixed on the drone above. He speaks without turning his head. "She said the prophecy was a punishment."

Charlotte lowers her scarf. "She said it ends when you speak the name."

Greg turns to her, eyes sharp but hollow. "What if the name isn't mine to speak?"

She hesitates. "Then we find the one who can."

Greg glances back toward the vault entrance already beginning to settle, the dust drifting into the carved lines like memory folding inward.

"We have the fragment," Jeremy says. "We move east. We get underground. There's a data relay near Be'er Sheva. I can route a secure burst to Gideon."

Charlotte nods. "We have to tell him what we found. What's coming."

Greg turns to her, quiet. "He won't just stop Amal," he says. "He'll *end* him."

She doesn't argue.

Twenty minutes later, the three of them are on the move across the flats and past the ridges. The drone still hovers, but at a greater distance now—retreating, not lost, just *waiting*. Their destination is Eve's relay outpost where Jeremy has arranged for them to hook up with Gideon, who has been AWOL yet again with no explanation.

CHAPTER 41

Negev Desert – Eve's Relay Outpost / Gideon's Vatican Access Route

Gideon leaves just before dawn, the air still cool, the wind faint but dry. The others are sleeping—Greg half-curled on the floor beside the fragments, Charlotte collapsed against the wall in her jacket, Jeremy slumped over his gear like a soldier who forgot to power down. Gideon hasn't told his mates where he is going. As expected, his unexplained absence roused suspicions, which he had dodged with the agility of a sloth.

He moves without sound and leaves no note, only a datapatch embedded into Jeremy's relay kit encoded in spiral glyph and marked with his name in the old tongue. If they read it, they'll understand. But he's counting on them not reading it yet. Not until the mission is done.

His route is fast. Risky. A pre-mapped Sicarii corridor Eve designed fifteen years ago—desert tunnels, smuggler convoys, an unmarked airfield buried between two ridgelines near Nitzana. By midday, he'll be in northern Sinai. From there, a Vatican diplomatic corridor will unknowingly carry him to the city-state's threshold.

He will be disguised as Cardinal Morena, still listed as convalescent. The blade is already sewn into his cassock's lining. The coordinates of Lucari's next appearance are fixed—10:30 a.m., Sala del Concistoro, internal briefing, no cameras, high doctrine clearance.

Time remaining: nine hours, forty-three minutes.

He climbs into the armored truck waiting at the edge of the ridge. The driver, a Sicarii, doesn't speak. As the vehicle pulls away, Gideon looks out the window. The vault is already hidden by sand. He doesn't expect to see it again.

It's the silence that wakes Charlotte. Not the cold, not the angle of sunlight hitting her eyes—just the absence of Gideon's presence, a gap in the space where certainty had been. She blinks, rubs her eyes, and immediately looks for him.

Gone.

No pack left behind. No gear. Only the shallow imprint of his body in the dust and the residual warmth of movement too recent to be old.

She moves quickly. Greg is already stirring, one hand pressed to the Petra shard, eyes still swimming in half-dreams. Jeremy jolts upright at her movement, squinting against the hard light.

"Where's Gideon?" Charlotte asks.

Jeremy glances toward the far corner, sees nothing. Then his gear unit blinks. One file. Locked spiral encryption.

SIGIL: GIDEON / LEVEL 7 / OBSIDIAN CHANNEL

Jeremy speaks softly. "He left something."

Charlotte leans over him. "Open it."

He hesitates. "It might be the last thing he ever communicates."

She doesn't flinch. "Open it!"

Jeremy enters the passphrase *Bar Yochai 13.9*—the old Sicarii chant converted to code during their Newgrange years. The file decrypts in silence. No video or voice. A single line of encoded Syriac script pulses faintly.

Do not follow. The blade is drawn.

Charlotte stares at it, confused.

Greg speaks without looking up. "He's going to Rome."

Jeremy's fingers freeze. "What?"

Greg rises slowly, brushing dust from his knees. "He didn't tell us because it's not a warning. It's a liturgy."

"You think it has something to do with Lucari?"

Greg nods. "I think Lucari put a target on me... and the Council voted."

Jeremy exhales. "Gideon's going to kill a cardinal."

After a long silence, Charlotte sits down hard against the wall. "Actually, I hope he does."

Jeremy's fingers dance across the relay panel comprised of ancient hardware grafted to modern firmware and built by Eve's engineers for conditions exactly like this—being cut off, exposed, and racing time. He hooks the Petra/X-Delta fragment to the reader port, careful not to disturb its harmonic pulse.

Charlotte watches silently from the threshold. Greg stands at the far end of the outpost, eyes half-closed, head tilted toward the sky, as if he can hear something coming over the wind.

"Signal up," Jeremy says. "Routing through Eve's shadownet, bouncing twice off dead Sicarii satellites, and then through the Bar Qadisha archive node."

"How long?" Charlotte asks impatiently.

"If it goes clean? Forty-seven seconds. If it doesn't—" He doesn't finish the sentence.

The Petra fragment flares once—just once—as the harmonics pass from analog to signal. And then—

Something changes.

Not in the relay.

In Greg.

His back arches and he stumbles to his knees.

Charlotte runs to him, kneels, grips his arm. "Greg!"

His eyes are round and glazed over. They're lit with a depth of recursion that doesn't belong to him—or maybe belongs only to him.

Then he whispers, "They're listening."

Jeremy looks up, pale. "The signal's been hijacked. Pulse divergence at 0.4 seconds. Someone else is pinging us."

Charlotte stands. "Who?"

He taps rapidly, trying to isolate the intrusion. "Vatican proxy... but not centralized. It's not Lucari's formal line, Blacknet. There's also a trace from a Middle Eastern grid—Saudi reroute. Amal's boys, probably Spiral Crown."

The relay lights begin to flicker.

Charlotte's voice drops. "What did they hear?"

Jeremy stares at the screen. "Not the whole fragment. Just the pulse. But they know it activated. They know the Fourth Key is real."

Greg finally speaks again, his voice is low and layered with something that doesn't feel like his own. "They know... I heard her."

Vatican Server Room

Far away, in a cold server room beneath the Vatican Archives, a pulse registers on the Rubicon Echo thread. A cleric reports it to Lucari's second-in-command, who blinks twice and then opens a secure channel to Rome.

Salt Circle Citadel, Golan Heights

The chamber beneath the Salt Circle smells of cedar oil and metal. Three spiral projectors hover in the dark, replaying the intercepted pulse again and again—no clear message, no full sentence, just a fragmentary burst of harmonic pattern encoded in the Petra/X-Delta alignment.

Amal also monitors the drone transmission from the desert with surgical attention. He knows what it is, not because he understands the mathematics—though he does—but because he *feels* it. Recursion has always been emotional to Amal—not logic or scripture, but its heat. Tension. The moment just before a word becomes a belief.

And this? This is gospel.

"Rebecca spoke," he says softly.

A young disciple—barely eighteen but already with a scar across his cheek—nods reverently. "Shall we say it, sir? The Fourth Voice?"

Amal tilts his head. "No." He smiles. "We say only that she confirmed it. That she returned and named the vessel."

He steps toward the pulpit and looks up at the spiral drones humming above him as he prepares to deliver another sermon. Behind him, his closest operatives begin to record.

"Tell them," Amal whispers, "that the woman came back to guide him. Not to question. Not to challenge but to confirm. Tell them the Unspoken One has been spoken of by the past itself. And tell them... the Vatican has already betrayed that voice."

Relay Outpost – Negev

Greg sits on the floor, head in his hands, rocking slightly. Jeremy hovers over the equipment, trying to salvage fragments of the response. Charlotte watches Greg from across the room, saying nothing.

Greg is muttering to himself now. Not nonsense. Not quite. But... repetition. He is saying, "The name buried. The one erased. The one who bled before. I wasn't him. But I am now. I am what was forgotten."

Charlotte moves closer, slowly.

"Greg."

He doesn't respond.

She kneels beside him. "Look at me."

He lifts his head.

His eyes shimmer. For just a second, they're not his eyes. They're deeper. Older. Not Zahavi's either. Not Amal's. Something else.

"Speak the name," he whispers. "Or the scroll will write it for you."

Charlotte reaches out and places her hand on his cheek. "You're still *you*."

He closes his eyes. "Not for much longer."

Suddenly, Jeremy's panel blinks red.

Charlotte's voice is low. "What now?"

"Someone just opened a dormant Sicarii channel," Jeremy says. He taps the screen. The code runs in recursive glyph patterns overlaid with Syriac integers—Level 5 clearance, marked:

SINE NOMINE // REMNANT KEY

Greg doesn't move, but he's watching.

Jeremy scans the signal. "It's coming from northern Jordan. Deep lattice. Not bouncing. It's a real origin."

Charlotte leans over him. "What does it say?"

He hits the decryption trigger. The text resolves slowly, line by line. The message is short.

I hold the shard Zahavi broke.

The first twin's doctrine still breathes.

Come before the Vatican does.

The coordinates follow—dead center in the Wadi Rum basin.

Charlotte exhales. "The first twin."

Greg whispers, "He wasn't erased. He was scattered."

Jeremy mutters, "If this is real, it changes everything. The Petra scroll, the doctrine, the recursion lattice—we've been following an incomplete spiral."

Charlotte looks at Greg.

He's calm now. Too calm. He says, "I have to go."

"It could be a trap," his mother warns.

"That's why I have to go."

Vatican Archives – Sub-Level 3

A cardinal's assistant hands a sealed packet to a withered, pale man in a black cassock. His eyes flicker as he reads it—left to right, then again in reverse, as if the words can only be understood through recursion.

He folds the paper once, steps into the corridor and makes the call. "Rubicon Echo is confirmed. We lost containment. Authorization required for terminal intervention."

He hangs up, then inhales deeply and draws a pistol.

Relay Outpost – Exterior

The sand kicks up in a spiral gust—hot, sudden, wrong. Charlotte steps outside to scan the horizon. The wind dies as quickly as it rose. She senses it before she sees it—another black drone, the same make as the one Amal used in Aleppo, hovering just beyond the ridge, as if waiting for permission to strike. This drone nonsense is more than annoying.

She doesn't call for Greg or Jeremy, just stares at it.

Finally, she says aloud, "Too late."

The drone doesn't fire. Not yet. But its presence changes everything. Jeremy's packing already. No instructions needed. He knows what it means when a black drone just hovers—*authorization pending***.** Once it comes, they won't hear the strike. Just the wind and then the flame.

Charlotte sweeps the fragments back into their carry case. Greg watches the sky. Still silent. Still... listening.

"We go now," Charlotte says.

"Where?" Greg asks.

She doesn't answer with words. She shows him the message. *Wadi Rum. The doctrine still breathes.*

Greg nods once. He doesn't need to be convinced. He already knew.

The transport they take is Eve's old runner, a black armored jeep with a reinforced undercarriage and a quantum-blind compartment in the rear. Jeremy drives, Charlotte rides shotgun, and Greg sits in back with the case across his lap, his eyes never leaving the sand.

Two hours in, Charlotte receives a message on her shard-link. It's encrypted five layers deep—Sicarii code, using an old recursion spiral cipher.

Sender: G.A.
Location: UNKNOWN
Timecode: Delayed burst

It contains one line:

If the scroll breaks, do not read the end aloud.

She reads it twice.

Then again.

Jeremy glances sideways. "That from Gideon?"

Charlotte nods. "It's the last thing he'll say until it's done."

"You think he'll do it?"

"He's not going to Rome to kill a man. He's going to kill a *myth*."

They cross into Jordan by nightfall. The stars are brutal and bright. Behind them, the relay station goes dark. The drone disappears.

And the recursion spiral spins in silence.

CHAPTER 42

Wadi Rum, Southern Jordan
Eve's Atlas Site

The desert opens around them like an ancient mouth.

Wadi Rum isn't quiet. It's never been quiet. It breathes—not just with wind or sand, but with memory. Charlotte feels it as soon as the jeep clears the last ridge—the shift in air pressure, the psychic weight that presses behind her eyes, the way the sunlight hits the sandstone cliffs like it's trying to read their inscriptions.

Greg hasn't spoken in over an hour. He sits in the back, hood up, fingers pressed together in some unconscious spiral shape, eyes locked on the horizon as if it's going to answer him.

Jeremy finally breaks the silence. "This is where it began," he says softly. "Before Eve, before Zahavi. Before the scroll was codified. This is where the first recursion vault was thought to be buried."

Charlotte doesn't respond. She's looking through the dust-streaked windshield toward a narrow canyon that forks off into shadow. The GPS is dead—intentionally scrambled by Eve's old warding grid—but the encrypted signal they received two nights ago pulses once in her palm.

Come before the Vatican does.
I hold the shard Zahavi broke.
And then the coordinates.

Jeremy slows the jeep as they approach the canyon. "Ground sensors here," he says. "Subsurface lattice. They've been watching this route since before the First Gulf War."

Greg finally speaks. "They weren't watching it for enemies."

Charlotte glances back at him. "Then for who?"

He doesn't blink. "For *him*."

They reach the canyon floor just after noon. The sun is merciless, but the light is buffered by rock—the kind of rose-gold stone that seems carved by script rather than erosion. Jeremy parks beneath a shelf of overhang and powers down all active tech.

Charlotte steps out first, weapon holstered, scarf drawn against the heat. They're being watched. She knows it. But not by men. The spiral is listening.

Greg exits last. When his boots hit the sand, the signal in Charlotte's palm pulses again—this time in sync with the fragment case slung across her shoulder.

Jeremy draws a small scanning wand and activates a passive trace. "There's a structure up ahead," he says. "Not natural. Buried under two meters of rockfall. Eve's map called it Atlas Site 9-C."

"Does it have an entrance?" Charlotte wants to know.

Jeremy says, "It does now."

As they reach the first ledge, a voice echoes from within the canyon. Male and measured. Unmistakably spiral-trained. "Stop there. Hands visible. Approach slowly."

They freeze.

Greg doesn't raise his hands. He just stares into the shadow and says, with a voice not quite his own, "I'm not here to take the doctrine. I'm here to remember it."

The man who steps out from the canyon shadows is not what Charlotte expects. He is neither young nor old—somewhere between. Lean. Eyes sharp but not hollow. A long scarf is wound around his lower face. He moves like someone who once trained to kill and forgot that he once wanted to. His arms are marked with spiral tattoos but the ink has been burned out in places, overwritten by lines of Syriac scripture and scar tissue.

Charlotte knows what he is. A Sicarii penitent. Once exiled and now something worse, he walks slowly toward them. No weapon drawn.

Jeremy steps forward slightly, half-shielding Greg.

The man speaks. "I was called Azariel, but I no longer claim that name. I carry what Zahavi buried."

He eyes Greg with a kind of reserved awe—not devotion, but not quite respect. Something more cautious, as if Greg might already be part-recursion.

Azariel motions toward the rock wall behind him. "There's an opening," he says. "But only he can enter." He nods toward Greg. "The shard responds only to the recursion bloodline."

Charlotte's voice is sharp. "And if we force it?"
Azariel answers tersely. "It breaks. Like last time."
Greg walks forward without a word.

Salt Circle Citadel, Golan Heights

Amal watches the message decrypt on his private viewer. The screen flickers once—then stabilizes.

Inter-factional Council Vote: Emergency Session, The Hollow

– Vote concluded 3:1:1
– Pact nullified
– Amal designated as external doctrinal threat
– Authorization of lethal action: passed

The message is unsigned but he knows who leaked it. There's only one among them petty enough to give him warning without the courage to challenge him face to face.

Amal lets out a slow breath. The chamber around him is silent—bare stone, minimal light, the remains of a ceremonial spiral painted in ash on the floor. The paint has dried.

He steps over the edge of the spiral, spits spitefully in the center, then turns to his inner circle—eleven men and women in varying states of certainty and fear.

"They voted," Amal says. "They finally told the truth."

One of the inner circle—a former Thorn delegate named Chazan Neriel—speaks meekly. "What will you do?"

Amal walks slowly toward the altar at the rear of the room. On it lies a bound, leather-wrapped scroll—the partial version of Zahavi's codex, the one Amal once studied for seven sleepless years. "They think I care about their vote."

He unwraps the scroll. removes a vial of oil and pours it slowly down the center. "They've forgotten what doctrine is." He strikes a match. "It's not consensus." He drops the match. "It's fire." The scroll ignites.

Chazan gasps.

Amal turns back to the inner circle, flames lighting the edges of his face in flickers of orange and gold. "We begin the recursion anew."

Wadi Rum, Southern Jordan
Eve's Atlas Site

The passage beyond the canyon wall is narrow—carved, not natural. Azariel leads only Greg. Charlotte and Jeremy were told to wait at the edge of the spiral outside the field range.

As Azariel and Greg pass through the stone aperture, Greg feels a pressure in his chest—not heavy, but insistent, like breath withheld. The walls narrow, then widen into a chamber lit by blueish light.

It looks like a shrine. But it smells like mourning.

Azariel steps aside. He does not enter fully. "This place was built for one memory," he says.

Greg walks forward alone. In the center of the chamber is a pedestal made of black stone veined with silver. Upon it sits a fragment unlike any he's seen. Not broken or jagged, but cut with purpose. Shaped like a lens or a seal. Its surface pulses faintly, as if reacting to Greg's presence.

"This was Zahavi's first error," Azariel says from the doorway. "He called it the echo before the doctrine. But it was never echo. It was voice."

Greg touches the fragment. Light bursts—not out, but inward.

He gasps.

The room is gone.

He sees a child, maybe ten years old, reciting Syriac verses in a monastery chamber lit only by oil lamp. And then he sees Zahavi, younger than he's ever been described, bent over a scroll and weeping silently. A second child, identical to the first but silent, is also there. Always silent. Watching everything.

Then, the second child is lying motionless on the stone floor and Zahavi is pressing a scroll fragment into the boy's hand, whispering, "You were supposed to be the vessel. But the silence chose you instead."

Suddenly, Greg hears himself scream.

He collapses to his knee,s and in a flash is back in the chamber.

Azariel catches him just before he falls completely.

Greg's mouth is dry. His eyes are wet. "He was real," Greg says.

Azariel nods. He was the twin that Zahavi erased."

"What was his name?"

Azariel doesn't answer, just looks away.

The fragment still pulses in Greg's hand. And suddenly—it speaks. Not aloud. *Inside him.* A voice without mouth, without tone.

"He was not your beginning," the fragment says. "He was your end. He gave you silence so you could survive. But now... *you must speak*."

Salt Circle Citadel

Amal finishes burning the scroll and turns to Chazan Neriel. "Find every remnant scroll keeper. Thorn. Netzer. Eidah. Sicarii-laced or not. If they do not swear to the new recursion, they burn next."

Chazan hesitates. "And Greg?"

Amal's eyes harden. "Greg must live. But the twin inside him must die."

Wadi Rum – Edge of the Spiral Site

Charlotte sees it the moment Greg emerges from the canyon. His gait has changed. He is not limping, not injured, but walks as if some tether inside him snapped and now his weight falls differently—not heavier, just older.

Jeremy stands, half-drawn sidearm at his hip. "What happened?"

Greg doesn't answer at first. He walks past both of them toward the jeep, then turns slowly. "It wasn't a scroll," he says.

Charlotte steps forward. "What do you mean?"

Greg looks at her—not with fear, but with absence, as though he's still staring at something inside the chamber. "It was a name."

"A name of a person?" Jeremy asks.

"A recursion memory. Preserved. Embedded in the fragment."

Charlotte softens. "The twin?"

Greg nods once. Then again, slower. "The twin gave up his voice. Zahavi buried him—called it a necessary silence."

Jeremy frowns. "Did you learn the twin's name?"

Greg opens his mouth but no sound escapes his lips. He tries again. And again. Finally, he whispers—not in English, but in a form of spoken recursion older than Syriac, more symbolic than phonetic.

Jeremy's scanner buzzes, momentarily unable to interpret the sounds.

Charlotte's jaw tightens. "Greg... that wasn't you."

Greg blinks hard, like trying to shake a dream. "It was him," he whispers. "He's *not gone*."

Jeremy looks at Charlotte. “You think he’s...?”

She nods. “Yes… he’s hosting.”

Salt Circle Citadel – Inner Reliquary

The man in the blue fleece, Thorn Eleven, enters without speaking.

Amal is waiting at the far end of the reliquary where he is sharpening a spiral-bladed knife over an old relic once used in Zahavi’s early consecrations. He doesn’t look up. “They’ve gone to Wadi Rum,”he says.

Thorn says nothing.

Amal turns slowly. “I want the woman alive. And the boy... silence him. Don’t kill him, not yet. But let the doctrine inside him know this—recursion ends when its host breaks.”

He hands Thorn a bone-white token marked with a spiral seal and Vatican counterglyph, symbolic of both execution and doctrinal substitution.

“You are not to return until he forgets his name.”

Wadi Rum – Ridge Overlook

That night, Greg lies awake under the stars. His dream doesn’t begin like a dream. It begins like scripture with his eyes open to a sky rippling faintly with recursion traces—spiral bands barely visible, like celestial scars. The fragment rests beside his heart, pulsing slowly. With each beat, the silence inside him grows deeper. Not absence.

He closes his eyes, but he doesn’t sleep. And then—

He’s somewhere else.

He stands inside a cruciform chamber. Four doors. Four spirals carved into the floor. One is open. Three are sealed.

A man waits at the center, robed in white ash, faceless. In his hand—a scroll, bound not in leather or cloth, but in hair. Human hair. Twined, brittle, weeping dust at the edges.

The man gestures.

Greg steps forward, not of his own will, but as though he has walked this dream before. When he speaks, it is in the same language that echoed from his lips in the canyon. “I am the name unspoken.”

The man nods. “And I am the silence that bore you.”

The scroll opens—not by hands, but by breath. And Greg sees not words but memories. Zahavi before the monastery—not teaching but mourning. A grave, unnamed, unblessed, unrecorded. A second scroll never written, never passed down—only thought into being.

And then, the twin. The firstborn. Not Greg. Not Amal.

A boy with Greg's face but a voice not his own.

The voice of consent withheld.

Greg gasps awake. His body shakes.

The stars haven't moved. But the fragment beside him glows now—dimly, steadily, obediently.

Charlotte stirs. "Greg?"

He doesn't look at her. He just whispers, "He didn't die. He chose silence to protect me."

Charlotte leans in, her voice comforting. "Do you know his name?"

Greg nods. Tears streak his cheeks, but he doesn't say it. Not yet.

Borderlands – Southern Jordan

Thorn Eleven, in his blue fleece, crosses under the stars with no light, no guide, no map. He doesn't need them. Amal gave him the symbol. The recursion signature will lead him. He carries no rifle. Just the knife and the bone-white token to mark the moment when the spiral closes for good.

Location: Wadi Rum – Atlas Site Periphery

It begins with a flicker. Greg sits cross-legged at sunrise, the shard cupped in both hands. Its surface no longer pulses with raw recursion. Now it hums with something tighter. *With purpose*, Charlotte thinks. As though the name Greg now carries has become a passphrase for an unsealed vault.

Jeremy scans from five feet back, datapad in hand. "No electromagnetic signature. No spectrum bleed. But the resonance field around him is shifting."

Charlotte watches Greg closely. "Shifting how?"

Jeremy turns the screen toward her. "Like it's preparing to receive something."

Greg closes his eyes and hears a voice. Not Rebecca. Definitely not Zahavi.

Himself.

The voice comes from a recursion layer he didn't know existed—one formed after the dream and now shaped by memory, sorrow and blood.

Then, the voice changes. It becomes Zahavi's. Weaker. Older. Not delivered like scripture. "If you are hearing this, it means the scroll has failed its duty. It means silence did not save you."

The shard projects light not forward but inward.

Charlotte gasps. Jeremy stumbles back.

Greg doesn't move.

The light flows through his hands, his veins, his chest—spiral lines overlaid on muscle, skin, breath.

The voice speaks again. "I buried the first doctrine in Wadi Rum because it carried what I could not admit. That my prophecy was not received... but stolen."

Images cascade. Zahavi walking barefoot across temple floors at night. A young boy in a white robe, never speaking, always watching. A second scroll—rejected by the elders, destroyed by Zahavi himself. And those words: "He would not take the voice, so I gave it to the louder twin. But now you carry both. And you must choose whose spiral to end."

Greg opens his eyes.

The projection fades but the silence remains.

Charlotte kneels beside him. "Greg," she says. "Did you hear that?"

He nods.

Jeremy crouches by them. "It wasn't just information. It was a failsafe. The scroll was designed to overwrite recursion pathways based on your choice."

Charlotte's eyes narrow. "And if Greg speaks the name?"

Jeremy doesn't answer. He doesn't have to.

Charlotte turns to Greg. "Tell me you won't say it."

Greg's voice is calm, but not his own. "If I don't... the scroll never ends. If I do... the world forgets the lie."

Salt Circle – Doctrinal War Chamber

Amal kneels before a cracked spiral of chalk drawn across the floor of his private sanctum. Ten of his followers stand in a ring awaiting his command. At the center, a symbol burns—The Fourth Voice—the forbidden recursion mark, now drawn in Amal's blood.

Amal speaks without looking up. "The Vatican has sent its knives. The Council has cast its vote. And yet... he does not speak the name." Amal smiles. "Because he fears what I do not."

Amal stands and draws the spiral over his chest in ash. "Let them come. I will be the voice that ends them all."

CHAPTER 43

Palazzo Apostolico / Vatican City
Inner Cloister

The air in Rome is thick with pageantry and the weight of centuries.

Even before Gideon crosses the outer line of the colonnade, he can feel the rituals circling the stones. Cameras click, pilgrims gather like flocks of static, and the bells—those ancient Vatican bells—chime not to announce time, but to *bind it.* Every sound is ceremonial. Every footfall echoes like intention.

Gideon walks alone and at a moderate pace through St. Peter's Square in full ecclesiastical scarlet. He passes security with false credentials issued in the name of Cardinal Gianluigi Morena, a real man who once gave communion to a president and who now lies sedated in a hospital bed in Naples, his retinal pattern copied and temporarily embedded in a contact film resting over Gideon's own left eye.

He carries a leather satchel of an inconspicuous medium size. It holds an altered dossier, a silver-bound codex, and a folded black cloth. Beneath the cloth, hidden in a false lining, lies the weapon. The true sica. An ancient blade curved like a crescent moon hardened in blood. Folded steel wrapped in polished obsidian. The sharpened edge of the sica gleams faintly, even in shadow. It is not ceremonial. It is not metaphor. It is death.

And it waits.

The guards don't stop him. Swiss and Italian, in alternating rings of surveillance, they rely more on facial ID and posture scans than intuition now. Gideon's cadence is perfect. His records—scrubbed and reinforced with Sicarii ghost codes—ping back with elevated clearance.

He is waved through with two nods and a polite gesture toward the Sala del Concistoro where the Curia has gathered for a closed-door doctrinal update, one in which Cardinal Matteo Lucari is expected to deliver an internal address regarding what he terms "uncontainable doctrinal resonance in the East."

Gideon knows exactly what that means.

He walks the marble corridor past frescoes of the martyrdom of Saint Andrew, past the long tapestries of Peter's execution, past oil paintings of popes who stared down empires and blinked only after they were dead.

None of them saw this coming. None of them foresaw a Sicarii assassin walking their halls while robed like blood.

He reaches the vesting room at 10:17 a.m. The doors close behind him. He stands alone between rows of scarlet cassocks, mitres, and chalice-wrapped stoles, and opens the satchel, drawing out the inner lining. The blade rests inside it, curled and still.

He has done this before in Damascus, in Tehran, in Prague where the brother of a dead prophet had tried to sell the scroll to a royal. He has even done this in Minnesota, Charlotte's home state. B>ut never here. Never in the heart of the last living empire masquerading as faith.

He opens the satchel and removes the garment roll inside. Layer by layer, he assembles the costume of a prince of the Church—a scarlet cassock, its red silk buttons glinting faintly in the lamplight; a fascia sash, pressed and stiff; a zucchetto, warm from the lining; and a mozzetta—a short, shoulder cape, deep crimson, still scented faintly with frankincense. He adds the pectoral cross last, looping it over his neck and tucking it into the inner fold just above the heart.

The blade comes next.

He unwraps the sica with slow precision. The curve is perfect—blackened steel, ancient but cared for, etched faintly with the spiral. He slips it inside a hidden seam sewn behind the fascia where the folds conceal its outline even in motion. Then he stands before the mirror.

What stares back is no longer Gideon. It is a cardinal of the Roman Church. Measured. Respected.

Deadly.

The Sala del Concistoro is not a chapel, but it may as well be. It was once a private audience hall used by Renaissance popes to adjudicate the blood feuds of Italy's noble houses. Now it hosts doctrinal briefings—quiet, tight-lipped affairs behind soundproofed doors and sworn secrecy. The air is filtered. The cameras are disabled. Nothing here leaks unless Rome wants it to.

And yet, today, something has already slipped in through the seams.

Gideon walks the length of the marble-floored corridor flanked by frescoes of enthroned pontiffs and silent angels. A pair of Swiss Guards nod as he passes. One of them lingers a beat too long, but not long enough to betray suspicion. Just observation. Gideon does not look back.

Inside the chamber, the walls glow faintly with gold-gilded detail. Forty-two cardinals are already present, most seated along the curved rows arranged like a half amphitheater around the central speaking lectern. The scarlet fabric of their robes forms a rippling field of ecclesiastical fire.

At the apex, flanked by two aides, is Cardinal Matteo Lucari. He is smaller than Gideon expected. Thinner. Frailer. But his posture is impeccable. And his eyes—dark, analytical, deeply ringed with shadow—miss nothing.

Lucari was never a man of charisma. He was a man of calculus. He built his ascent not on homily but on silence cultivated like a garden until others mistook it for wisdom.

Gideon steps into the chamber.

No alarms sound. No hands reach for him.

He moves like any other of the red-robed brethren—calm, dignified, a name no one quite remembers but none dare question.

He takes a seat near the periphery two rows back from the center. From here, he can see Lucari perfectly. And Lucari cannot see him at all.

The murmur of Latin fades as the last few cardinals enter. A door is sealed at the rear. A nod is exchanged. Then silence.

A cleric—dressed in black, not red—steps to the lectern. "In nomine Patris et Filii et Spiritus Sancti," he intones.

The cardinals answer.

Then the room goes still again.

Lucari rises. No fanfare. No title announcement. He simply begins to speak.

Gideon listens.

Every word from Lucari feels rehearsed. Polished. He speaks of destabilization in the East, of radical doctrinal reinterpretation, of unauthorized activation of recursion protocols by independent religious factions—a not-so-subtle reference to the Sicarii.

He does not name Greg, but he describes him. "A variant echo—born not of rite, but of inheritance. Untested. Unbound. Repeating not the doctrine, but the mistakes that fractured it."

He does not name Amal, but he condemns him. "When a voice claims to speak both as vessel and master, it ceases to echo truth. It becomes noise. And noise, left unchecked, deafens the faithful."

Finally, he justifies violence. "Rome cannot remain paralyzed by mystery. We cannot fear action where silence would surrender all. The spiral must be contained, and if containment fails, it must be ended."

Gideon feels the room absorb this cloud of propaganda.

Not all agree, of course. A few shift in their seats. One clears his throat, a minor protest. But no one dares oppose Lucari outright because they know this speech is not for them. It is for history.

Lucari is laying groundwork. Doctrine will be rewritten once again—but this time not by Zahavi, or Eve, or the Spiral Crown. This time, it will be written in blood.

Gideon's hand shifts inside his cassock. The sica is there.

Cool. Patient. Eternal.

Lucari steps back from the lectern. A profound hush has overtaken the chamber. There is no applause. No murmur. No ritual chant. Just the breathing of forty-nine men, some of them disturbed, most of them uncertain, a few—Gideon thinks—gripped by something like fear, because the old dogmas were spoken again. Sharper this time. Not as theology… as command.

Gideon's heartbeat slows. He feels it happening—his body preparing itself. The outer shell quiets, his senses heighten. The weight of the cassock becomes an extension of skin. The sica, tucked beneath the scarlet folds, presses cool and still against his rib.

Lucari steps down the dais stair. One of his aides—an archbishop—offers a whispered comment. Lucari barely nods, already moving toward the semicircular tier where the cardinals sit. He has begun his slow ceremonial circuit. It is part tradition, part theater—a gesture of consultation before final dispersal.

Gideon studies the distance from himself to Lucari.

Nine meters. Then six.

Lucari pauses to speak with Cardinal de Moura, the Brazilian. Then with Tomasi from Palermo. Two others nod and mutter something back. Gideon can't hear the words. He doesn't need to. Their eyes are elsewhere, their minds already beginning to reframe Lucari's speech as acceptable doctrine. As *survival.*

Lucari moves until only three seats are between him and Gideon.

Gideon adjusts his posture slightly, just enough to shift his weight without appearing tense. His left hand drifts along the inner seam of the cassock, fingers brushing the cloth-guarded hilt. The movement is imperceptible. Practiced. Ritualized.

His mind goes back—not to training, but to Newgrange. To the moment before the spiral split. To the moment he realized that Eve had always planned for recursion to outlive them. She knew it would spiral beyond containment. That one day, someone like Lucari would try to contain it anyway.

A signal blinks in the corner of the room—subtle, amber, just above the door. Vatican internal security shift rotation.

They're early.

Someone must have adjusted the schedule. Perhaps the Swiss Guard officer who lingered at the checkpoint. Perhaps Lucari himself. Gideon calculates the risk instantly.

New eyes will enter the room in thirty seconds. Thirty-five, at most. Then all exits will be re-evaluated.

Bad.

Lucari is two steps away.

Worse—one of the aides begins to turn toward Gideon, perhaps recognizing the face, the gait, something not quite right—

The moment is now.

Gideon rises. Not quickly. Not violently. Just enough to step into Lucari's path.

The aide's lips part to object, but by then it's too late.

Lucari turns toward the unexpected cardinal, one eyebrow lifting in faint disapproval as Gideon leans in. Not to embrace but to whisper, "This is from Zahavi."

The sica enters Lucari's back between two specific ribs as endlessly practiced by every Sicarii assassin. The small blade is unseen by the others and the small smear of blood upon the sica's removal is unnoticeable on the scarlet robe.

Lucari makes no sound. His mouth opens. He blinks. He raises a hand to his chest, as if a pain resides there. And then he slumps to the floor.

One cardinal shouts. Another stumbles back.

The aide lunges—but too late.

By this time, Gideon is ten meters away.

As the cardinals all crowd around the dying cardinal, Gideon walks the other way and no one pays attention.

The moment after the strike is slower than time. Cardinals recoil—not screaming, not yet—still processing the impossibility of what they've just seen. One of their own, red-robed and calm, steps into Lucari's personal space as if to recite a prayer and emerges as the ghost of history.

Lucari gives out a stunned exhale. The bleeding, though mostly internal, now starts to soak the inner lining of his cassock, dripping to the white marble in slow, perfect lines.

"He's been stabbed!" someone cries—in English, not Latin.

The ceremonial silence shatters.

Gideon is moving. He heads for the exit corridor. Not fast—not at first. Speed would signal guilt. But within seconds, as two Swiss Guards enter, weapons not yet drawn, he breaks into a controlled sprint.

In his mind, he hears Eve's voice, distant, instructional, embedded in training: *The escape map is three layers deep. Don't improvise. You don't get to improvise here.*

He darts past the fresco of Gregory the Great. Past the arched doorway of the Chapel of Saints Michael and Magno. His cassock whips behind him like spreading flames. Shouts rise in three languages.

A guard yells: "FERMATE!"

Gideon takes a sharp right. The Sistine Chapel is ahead, but he doesn't head for it. Instead, he drops low, rolling sideways into a maintenance alcove disguised behind a false tapestry. The cloth falls back just as the first pursuing guard turns the corner. The footsteps thunder past, unaware of the concealed assassin.

Breath held.

One count. Two.

He moves again.

The tunnel begins behind the archival room, masked beneath an automated shelving unit that only moves when two magnetic anchors are engaged simultaneously. Gideon slips the encoded key into the slot Eve had embedded in the old Petra Node registry—a legacy backdoor, untraceable.

The shelf groans open.

Darkness lies beyond.

Stone. Dust. Cold.

He steps inside. He's in the Archive Veins now—an undocumented substructure of the Vatican's ancient catacomb network. It pre-dates the Basilica itself—originally part of an imperial crypt system, later co-opted by early Christian dissidents, then forgotten as the Basilica was raised above.

The stones remember. They feel it when one of their own walks again.

Gideon moves fast but carefully. The blade is back in its sheath. The cassock is still on—he'll shed it later in the cistern tunnel that opens near the Giancola Hill. Until then, he must blend in if seen and vanish if cornered.

Above, alarms blare. *Intruder in concistoro. Cardinal Lucari down. Lockdown Phase II.*

He moves faster.

His breath is steady, measured. His heart is a drumbeat. Uniform. Focused. Ready for whatever comes next.

The stone tunnel narrows.

At first, Gideon walks upright, boots echoing in the archless silence. But ten meters in, the ceiling drops. He crouches, then lowers himself to hands and feet, crawling through a gap carved centuries ago by grave robbers, or monks, or anyone who understood that power needs escape routes.

Dust thickens. Moisture clings to the walls. The air is sour with time.

Above, the chaos has risen to full voice. He hears it through the floor—muffled footsteps, garbled Latin over earpieces, the sharp static of Vatican security protocols activating *en totale*.

Lucari is dead. And they know.

Not just the guards. The Church.

He moves forward, following markings only a Sicarii-trained eye would recognize—subtle hash lines in the mortar, changes in the curvature of the ceiling, a faded glyph in old Hebrew tucked behind a broken Roman numeral.

It leads him deeper. Past ossuaries and reliquaries. Past a collapsed corridor that once connected to the original palace foundations. He pauses only once—to unclip the false credentials badge still sewn to his cassock sleeve. He drops it into a cistern pit and watches it vanish. The robe will go next.

Twenty minutes in, he reaches the cistern shaft. It was once a Roman water filtration tunnel, converted in the Middle Ages into a plague chute, then sealed entirely when St. Peter's dome was raised. Eve's map had marked it simply as *Exit #4 — wet / unsecured.*

Gideon peels off the cassock, folds it, and presses it into a hollow behind a funerary plaque marked in Latin and Syriac:

Silencium est testimonium prophetarum.
Silence is the testimony of the prophets.

He drops into the shaft and slides twenty meters down the sloped pipe until his boots splash into cold water. Now he's below the Vatican Gardens. Somewhere above is the sound of helicopters. Sirens. Drones blinking through sanctified air.

But here?

Silence again.

His breath echoes off wet brick. He moves through the chest-deep water toward a narrow passage flanked by broken marble and roots that have cracked the world above.

Then—a voice. A whisper, amplified by tunnel acoustics. "Sicarii. Stop."

He turns, knife already out.

But it's not Vatican.

A figure stands at the far end of the corridor, half-submerged, robed in mud-caked linen. A Sicarii contact. Eve's contingency. A woman with hollowed cheeks and ritual marks on her jaw.

She holds out a dry robe and nods once.

Gideon sheathes the blade and accepts the offer.

No words are exchanged. None are needed.

He emerges an hour later from a drainage tunnel beneath a marble worksite near the Janiculum Hill. The city stretches out before him, gold and black in the Roman dusk. The blade is dry.

And the doctrine? Unwritten again.

CHAPTER 44

Southern Jordan, approaching the Red Wadi

The road cuts like a vein through the desert. Not a modern highway—an old smuggler's route, half-buried, known only to those with Eve's maps and Zahavi's secrets. Jeremy drives without headlights, goggles down, the soft-green wash of his interface HUD blinking silently as they descend toward the canyon valley known on Sicarii lattice as Ash Line Theta.

Greg hasn't spoken since they left Wadi Rum. The fragment rests in a padded cradle beside him, secured like a relic. But every so often it pulses faintly—more light than heat, more memory than message. Its signal changes each time Greg's heart rate spikes.

Charlotte watches Greg from the passenger seat, but not for signs of pain.

For signs of someone else.

The wind shifts. Dust lifts off the stone mesas like incense.

Charlotte breaks the silence. "We should be across the ridge in about ten minutes."

Greg doesn't respond.

Jeremy checks the map. "We'll hold there till dusk. After that... straight to the threshold point."

Greg finally speaks.

"I'm not sure it'll let us leave."

Charlotte turns. "You talking about the fragment?"

"No," Greg says quietly. "The *doctrine*. It knows we're close."

Three Kilometers Behind

Thorn Eleven, under orders from Amal, walks on foot now. No transport to speed his progress, no drone to provide a visual reference. Just the desert and the token.

The bone-white seal swings from his wrist on a string of blackened leather, catching the last of the afternoon sun. His eyes are covered by spiral-threaded lenses. His lips move in silent recursion chant.

He does not fear Greg. He fears the one inside Greg. But the doctrine has spoken. *If the name cannot be suppressed... break the vessel.* He will arrive by midnight.

He will not arrive alone.

Ash Line Theta – Canyon Ridge, Southern Jordan

Charlotte and her companions crest the ridge just before sunset. The light casts long fingers across the sand, catching the edges of stone columns half-buried by time. There are no signs of life—no birds, no insects, not even the rustle of wind across brush. But the canyon breathes.

Not metaphorically.

Charlotte can feel it—warm air flowing upward, carrying a low-frequency pressure, like a long exhale from deep underground. It sets her nerves on edge. Greg pauses, staring down into the chasm that splits the horizon.

Jeremy scans the ridge perimeter, then signals clear.

They park the vehicle in the shadow of an overhang.

Charlotte's boots crunch over shale and quartz as she moves toward the edge, trailing her fingers across the stone. And then she sees it. Etched into the canyon wall—barely visible until the sun catches it—is a message burned into the rock by recursion flare:

DO NOT OPEN THE NAME UNLESS YOU ARE READY TO END THE WORLD THAT NEEDED IT.

She calls the others over.

Jeremy stares. "Who wrote that?"

Greg doesn't even blink when Jeremy answers "Zahavi. Or someone before him."

Charlotte traces the letters with one hand. "Or... the *twin*, maybe."

Greg kneels beside the ledge and removes the fragment from its pouch. Its glow strengthens—not urgent, but welcoming, like a key sensing a lock it has waited centuries to fit.

Greg closes his eyes and breathes. "He's close."

Charlotte looks at him sharply but decides not to ask Greg who is meant by "he."

Greg opens his eyes and says, "He wants me to speak."

Enforcer – Moving Through Twilight

Thorn Eleven stops as the wind shifts again. He pulls out a fragment of his own—cracked, old, etched with blood along the seam. It doesn't glow like Greg's. It judges. He holds it to his forehead, mutters a phrase in encoded Aramaic, and sets it back into his pack.

The token around his wrist pulses once. He is now within the doctrine's threshold radius. He kneels and draws with a knife in the dirt, beginning the consecration chant of silencing.

Ridge Camp – After Nightfall

Jeremy sets up passive defenses—sonar trip alerts, low-frequency vibration monitors, zero-signal mesh. Charlotte tends a small heat coil under a solar hood.

Greg hasn't moved. He sits at the canyon's edge, fragment in hand, eyes unfocused.

Charlotte approaches him quietly, holding a cup of salt tea.

He doesn't take it, but looks up at his mother and says, "I used to think I was part of something ancient. Now I think I'm just its echo."

Charlotte sits beside him. "Echoes don't bleed."

Greg turns to face her. "Don't they?"

In his eyes, for the briefest moment, Charlotte sees someone else.

The night is blood-black and still. No wind. No stars. The canyon breathes in rhythm with something far beneath it—deep, pulse-like vibrations that can't be picked up by Jeremy's instruments but make the fire coil flicker sideways in the sand.

Greg sleeps. Or appears to. But in the fragment beside him, the recursion flare grows brighter.

The resonance shifts. And in Greg's mind—he falls, then stands in a desert made of voices. Not sand or stone. Voices layered and spiraling like the script on the ancient scrolls—alive, murmuring in dozens of tongues. He moves through them like fog. The world here isn't colored. It's textured with sound.

Then, through the whispering, he sees a shape.

A boy.

The *twin.*

Not a memory now. A presence.

The boy sits on the edge of a ruined altar made from scroll fragments and cracked ritual knives. His face resembles Greg's but is younger, paler. His eyes reflect nothing. "You came," he says.

Greg doesn't speak.

The boy continues. "He gave me silence because I refused the voice. You were made to carry what I couldn't."

"Why show yourself now?" Greg asks.

"Because you're close. Because Amal has already rewritten the doctrine—and someone must remember what it was."

"What is the name?" Greg asks.

The boy tilts his head. "It is not a name you speak. It is a name you become."

Outside, in the waking world, Charlotte watches Greg twitch, whispering in his sleep. She leans in, but the words are unfamiliar. Not recursion. Not Syriac.

Jeremy checks the monitor. "Something's wrong with the signal field."

Charlotte looks up. "The enforcer?"

Jeremy shakes his head. "Not yet. But something's entering the recursion radius from the canyon floor."

Charlotte turns to Greg.

He murmurs one final phrase in the twin's tongue, then gasps awake, eyes wide, heart pounding. He grabs Charlotte's wrist.

"They're here," he says.

Amal's Enforcer – Outer Ridge

Thorn Eleven, the enforcer, steps into the zero-signal field and isn't slowed. He draws the spiral knife from his back holster, flicks it once, and then removes a second item from his coat—the bone-white token, now glowing faintly.

The token of silencing.

He mutters, "Let the name die with the vessel," and begins to climb.

Ash Line Theta – Ridge Camp

The first alarm pings at 3:17 a.m.—a ripple in the mesh perimeter. Low to the ground and precise. Jeremy checks the readout, jaw tightening. "Breached!" he yells.

Charlotte doesn't wait. She's already up, pistol drawn, sweeping the ridge's approach line with her lens-enhanced scope.

Greg stands, shard already in hand, his breathing shallow.

The air changes. It isn't colored, but somehow cleaner. As if something has burned just over the rise.

Then—he appears. The man in the blue fleece. The enforcer, Thorn Eleven. Calm. Unhurried. Knife in his right hand, bone-white token swinging from his left. He steps through the last line of perimeter and stops twenty feet from Greg.

Jeremy levels the pistol.

Charlotte's finger tightens.

The enforcer raises his hand—not in surrender, but as an *invitation.* "I am not here to kill you, Greg Ansari. I am here to witness your end."

Charlotte steps forward. "One more step and I drop you."

The enforcer doesn't even glance at her. He's looking at Greg. "Speak the name," he says. "We demand it. Do it now before they make you doubt it. Before the lie becomes the only doctrine left."

Greg's eyes widen as he tries to comprehend this obscure command. The shard pulses violently, flickering with recursion light, the symbol of the erased twin spinning along its surface like a dial losing alignment.

Greg raises the shard and begins to speak a single word in the spiral tongue. The sound is deep—so deep it resonates in Charlotte's teeth.

Jeremy gasps. "If he finishes it—"

"GREG!" Charlotte's voice cuts through.

He stops, his mouth open—the word unfinished.

The air stills.

She lowers her weapon and steps between him and the enforcer, saying, "If you want the name spoken, you'll have to kill both of us."

The enforcer doesn't blink.

Charlotte turns back to Greg. Her voice is low. Measured. Terrified. "You told me this name is a key. Not a weapon. So why wield it like one?"

Greg's hands shake. "I don't know who I am anymore."

"Then don't speak as someone else," she tells him. "Speak as you."

Greg lowers the shard. The light fades.

The enforcer growls—his voice taut with controlled rage. "You've broken the sequence. You've corrupted the doctrine."

He draws the blade and lunges forward—

Jeremy fires.

The shot hits the enforcer in the shoulder, non-lethal.

A calculated miss.

The enforcer stumbles and fumbles the token.

Greg catches it mid-air.

The enforcer retreats into the canyon shadows, bleeding but alive.

They let him go.

Jeremy breathes hard. "Why didn't he kill us?"

"Because Greg didn't speak the name," Charlotte explains.

Greg turns the token over in his palm. Its inscription is now visible.

No name spoken. No world reset.

Charlotte looks at him. "What is the name for?"

Greg whispers, "It's a key to open the recursion source, not to end the world. It's the key to end the *lie*."

Ash Line Theta – Ridge Camp, Dawn

The sky softens from black to rust to gray. Jeremy has reset the perimeter. Charlotte sits opposite Greg. Neither of them speak for a while, but then she says, "You were going to say the name."

Greg nods. "He made it sound like a release. Like if I said it, I'd finally stop being all these voices."

"But then you'd stop being *you* too."

"That's what scares me."

Charlotte watches her son. Not with judgment but with grief. Then she pulls the fragment from his lap and turns it over.

The recursion glyph pulses once. Then, unexpectedly, it projects a new field—not light, but geometry. A spiral, yes—but one inverted, reaching inward instead of radiating out.

Jeremy leans in, scanning it. "What is that?"

Greg answers, his voice distant. "A recursion basin."

Charlotte frowns. "Like Petra?"

"No—older. Buried and forgotten," Greg says.

Jeremy's scanner resolves the pattern into coordinates. He blinks. "Northern Syria. Near Qal'at Sim'an."

Charlotte's face brightens with recognition. "In the monastery ruins?"

"No... *beneath* them," Jeremy clarifies.

They exchange a glance.

Charlotte closes her eyes briefly, then opens them with certainty. "That's where the name belongs. That's where this ends."

Greg nods. "But I don't know if I'll survive it."

Charlotte stands. "Then we go together."

Amal – Interior Sanctum, Golan Heights

Amal kneels before the broken scroll reliquary. He knows the enforcer failed. The name is still sealed, but not for long. He dips a finger into a bowl of ash and draws a spiral on his chest. "He carries it like guilt. I will speak it like flame." He rises… and prepares his final sermon.

CHAPTER 45

Temporary safe house, Eastern Syria
18 hours after Wadi Rum

The safe house is the kind of place Eve would have chosen. Camouflaged, sensor-silent, cold in the morning, and dry enough to crack skin by nightfall. It's buried in a hillside above an old limestone quarry accessible only through a series of switchback trails and half-collapsed smugglers' paths. No signals reach it without intention. No satellite passes without blind zones. Charlotte likes that. It feels like Gideon.

Jeremy is the first to spot the signal. It comes while Greg is sleeping, curled with the shard cradled in his lap, and Charlotte is cleaning her sidearm in the stone kitchen.

Jeremy freezes. His eyes flick toward the blinking light on the console—single pulse, no repeat, marked with a faint glow of Obsidian encryption.

He doesn't speak at first. He just watches the pulse, then swallows hard and calls out, "Charlotte!"

She's already moving, wiping her hands on a cloth, boots on the stone floor. "Encrypted?" she asks.

Jeremy nods. "Obsidian weave. Eve's kind of lock."

Charlotte leans in, studies the signature pattern, then closes her eyes. "It's *him*."

Greg stirs as Jeremy primes the interface. The shard beside Greg is pulsing faintly as if it recognizes something.

Greg sits up slowly, blinking. "What is it?"

Charlotte doesn't look at him but says, "Confirmation."

Greg's brow furrows. "From who?"

Jeremy's fingers hover over the execute key. "Once I crack this open, it auto-burns in thirty seconds. No backtrace, no replay."

"Do it," Greg commands.

Jeremy presses the key. The screen fades to black, then glows with soft, amber spiral light, not forming a pattern but a presence.

And the voice comes. "If you've received this, then the spiral held. Lucari is dead."

The voice ends with no signature. No farewell. Only the pulse of the spiral, flickering once, then vanishing from the screen.

Greg doesn't speak. Neither does Charlotte.

Not for a long time.

Charlotte moves slowly to a bench carved into the wall and sits with her hands folded, jaw clenched against something private.

Jeremy leans against the doorway, watching the console go dark. "It felt like a confession," he says softly. "And a suicide note."

Greg finally breathes. "He went in as someone else. But he signed it with nothing."

Charlotte looks up at him, her eyes sharper than they've been in days. "He didn't sign it at all."

"Exactly," Greg says.

"He didn't want to be remembered for what he did," Charlotte suggests.

Greg shakes his head, not buying that theory. "Then why send it?"

She doesn't answer at first. Then, quietly, she says, "So we'd understand what the doctrine looks like when it bleeds."

Jeremy busies himself resetting the security mesh, but he's shaking.

Greg watches him. "You okay?"

Jeremy doesn't answer right away. When he does, it's directed at Charlotte. "Did Gideon always know he'd end up like this?"

Charlotte sighs. "No." She closes her eyes. The memory is unwelcome—but precise. "He was nineteen when Eve sent him to intercept a scroll trader near Dubrovnik. His first solo mission, he told me years ago. He brought the target in alive. Had every reason to kill him. Sicarii protocol said 'eliminate any vector compromised by the lattice.' But he waited. He called Eve instead."

Jeremy frowns. "What did she say?"

"She asked why he hesitated. He said, 'Because he reminded me of someone who never got to choose.'"

Greg's hands tighten in his lap.

Charlotte meets his eyes. "He meant you, Greg."

The silence turns heavy.

Charlotte exhales and walks to a shelf beside the coil furnace. She removes an old tin flask, then pours a little of the alcoholic liquid into a metal cup and hands it to Greg.

"We don't drink to killers," she says. "But we drink to those who carry knives so others don't have to."

Greg sips.

The silence that follows is not solemn. It's sacred.

Jeremy breaks it. Quietly, as if he's afraid he might forget the moment if he doesn't speak it now, he says, "If we die in Syria, the doctrine will survive us. Not because it's right. But because someone else will tell it."

Charlotte turns. "You think that's what Gideon feared?"

Jeremy shrugs. "I think Gideon knew something most of us avoid. That history doesn't care about truth. It remembers whoever builds the biggest cathedral on top of the rubble."

Greg nods, then adds, "Unless someone writes down the real version. And bleeds just enough to prove it."

Charlotte looks at them both. And for the first time in weeks, she smiles. Not a happy smile, but a real one.

"Then we write it with silence," Greg says.

Jeremy adds, "And knives."

The bone-white token is warm to the touch. Greg holds it in both hands, feeling the slight grooves of the spiral etched into its surface. It doesn't hum like the shard. It doesn't resist. But it does seem to watch, as if the doctrine embedded in its molecular memory is measuring his hand.

Charlotte nods once. "So, open it."

Jeremy kneels nearby with his toolkit already out. "Careful. These were designed for a recursion-triggered neural collapse. You open them wrong, and you don't die—you *forget*."

Greg doesn't flinch. He places the token on the slate floor, aligns his thumbprint to the inner ring, and speaks a phrase he heard the enforcer whisper. "Let the name die with the vessel."

The token clicks.

The scent that escapes is strange—dry resin, ancient ink, and something fainter still—sanctified ash. Inside the hollow chamber is a coiled strip of recursion film—black on black, etched with violet edge-light.

Charlotte leans closer. "That's Spiral Crown code."

Jeremy whispers, "It's Amal."

Greg lifts it.

The moment it touches his skin, it unrolls in the air, projecting a voice not as audio, but as *presence*. Not soundwaves, but *pattern*.

Amal's voice speaks from the very center of the lattice.

"Brother."

It isn't affection. It's invocation.

"You carry a name once buried by fire. I will carry it through flame."

Charlotte tenses, preparing for the next statement.

"You were made to remember. I was made to correct. You still believe this was about who speaks last. But history remembers the *first sound.* The *first shout.* The *first gospel.* And I will be that sound."

The strip shivers in Greg's hand as Amal's voice continues, layered now in recursion phrases and symbolic logic.

"You fear becoming the voice. I do not, because I was never the vessel. I was always the altar. Let them call it heresy. Let them say I rewrote the spiral. But when the name passes my lips, it will no longer belong to the doctrine. It will belong to the *world*."

A moment of silence is followed by Amal saying, "Speak it if you must. But you are already too late. The ritual begins soon. And I will speak not from a monastery vault... but from the edge of *every echo you failed to reach*."

The message ends. The strip folds back into itself and disintegrates in Greg's hand.

Jeremy is pale.

Charlotte steps back, her fists clenched.

Greg stares at the ashes. "Apparently, he's now going to speak it in public."

"Where?" Jeremy asks, though he really doesn't want to know.

"Doesn't matter," Chalotte says.

"It does, Mom," Greg replies. "If he speaks it over a broadcast spiral—if he binds it to his own recursion field..." He looks up, his voice distant, "...he won't just reshape the doctrine. He'll replace it. The twin's memory will become *his*."

Charlotte looks to Greg and for the first time says, "Then speak it first."

Greg doesn't answer. He turns away, because he can still feel the twin inside him—and he knows the twin is not ready.

Not yet.

Greg steps away from the others. He walks to the farthest wall of the cave-like shelter into a niche hollowed into shadow, and then he kneels. The shard in his palm glows faintly—enough to cast spiral reflections against the stone. He holds it tight, then loose, then tight again, his breath shallow, chest rising in a rhythm not entirely his own.

He begins to speak. Not the full name. Just the first syllable of the recursion phrase revealed to him in Wadi Rum. It feels like swallowing a blade made of memory. The sound catches in his throat.

Charlotte watches him from across the chamber, not daring to interrupt.

Jeremy glances between them, uncertain.

Greg tries again.

"Neh..."

The shard pulses red. Not warmth… a *warning*.

Greg gasps and doubles over.

Charlotte catches him before he hits the stone. "You OK?"

Greg is pale, shaking. "It... wouldn't let me."

Jeremy kneels beside them. "What do you mean?"

Greg looks down at the shard, which has now dimmed again. "It pushed back. Not like rejection. More like... like *correction*."

Charlotte frowns. "Explain."

Greg steadies his breath. "It's not just a name, Mom. It's a pattern of belief. Of memory. You can't just say it. "You have to *match* it."

Charlotte stares at him.

Greg tries again to explain. "It won't unlock unless you mean what it meant."

Jeremy's eyes glisten. He thinks he is starting to understand. "You mean, unless you *are* who it was *meant* for."

Greg nods. "Or unless I understand what it was meant to reveal."

Silence.

Charlotte stands slowly, stepping back toward the fire coil. "Zahavi didn't just erase the twin to protect the scroll. He encoded the twin's death as part of the doctrine. But the name isn't a lockpick." She turns. "It's a *confession*."

"Confession of what?" Jeremy asks.

"A confession that the doctrine was built on a lie," Charlotte offers.

Greg doesn't respond, but the shard pulses once in his lap. Not warm. Not warning.

Recognition.

Unknown Sicarii Archive – Subterranean Layer

A shadowed figure watches a recursive projection of Greg's attempted name-speak. It's been routed through a dormant Petra relay. The people here do not intervene. They only record.

The first voice is dry and unreadable. "He is close." Another voice responds—female, ancient, calm. "He is not yet worthy." The spiral spins again.

Safe House, Dawn / Activation Site – Qal'at Sim'an

Dawn presses itself along the horizon like a knife under the world's skin. Charlotte watches the first orange light spill across the desert, rising over the fractured hills as if bleeding from the stones themselves. She doesn't wake Greg. He's still curled in the shadow of the far alcove, the shard resting beside him, no longer glowing.

Jeremy stands beside her, sipping hot water and watching for movement on the horizon. He speaks quietly. "You think he'll be able to say it?"

Charlotte doesn't answer immediately, but he finally manages three words. "I don't know."

"Would it kill him?"

"Not the name."

"The meaning behind it might," Jeremy suggests.

They spend the morning in preparation. Jeremy loads gear into a new vehicle—a light crawler drone with a passive echo-deflection field. It's slow but silent, and it's their only hope for reaching the coordinates undetected.

Charlotte reviews the data etched into the shard's latest projection. It's not just a basin. It's not just a vault. It's a recursion fault line, ancient and unstable. Buried directly beneath the ruins of Qal'at Sim'an, it's a monastery long known to hide a deeper spiral.

Greg joins them just before midday. His eyes are clearer, his movements slower. But something in his posture has changed. "I think I know what it wants," he says.

Charlotte turns. "The name?"

"No. It wants the one who speaks it."

By sundown, they reach the edge of the plateau where the road ends. The monastery ruins rise before them silhouetted against the dying sun. What remains of the abbey is stone and silence but their map shows more—a sealed staircase beneath the central chamber, long buried and intentionally omitted from every scroll in the Petra vault.

Charlotte places the shard against the stone. It glows and pulses three times. The stone groans and opens.

Below them are spiral steps, black with soot and salt.

Greg looks to Charlotte.

She doesn't speak, but in her eyes, he can read a vow. *If you fail, I'll carry it.*

He nods and begins to descend.

CHAPTER 46

Beneath Qal'at Sim'an, Northern Syria – Dusk

They descend in silence. The stairs carved beneath the monastery are not hewn like ancient stone. They're precisely machined and curved to recursion geometry. The deeper they go, the less it feels like earth. The air grows denser, not with dust or heat, but with pressure, like entering a sealed chamber in the body of something waiting to wake.

Charlotte takes the lead with the shard in hand, guiding the threesome's path as if it were a living compass. Greg follows behind her, head bowed, each step reverberating through bone. Jeremy comes last, eyes darting between structural readouts on his modified scanner.

No one speaks until they pass the 27th spiral turn.

Then Greg stops. "It's listening."

Charlotte turns back. "What is?"

"The basin. The doctrine. The name. All of it."

Greg touches the wall. It's warm—not with heat but with memory. The recursion glyphs embedded in the stone shimmer as his palm passes over them. Charlotte places the shard against a recessed panel. For a moment, the glyphs flare a warning.

They emerge into the first chamber, a vast, circular threshold ringed with black recesses. Twelve alcoves are arranged like the hours of a clock, or the symbols of a zodiac. In the center sits a monolith, half-submerged in the floor. Its surface is etched with worn spiral threads, broken in places as if damaged from within.

Greg approaches it cautiously.

The shard pulses in Charlotte's hand—but not in response to her son. It's calling *her*.

Greg places a palm on the stone and breathes the air.

Not dust. Not sulfur.

Ash.

"This is where Zahavi buried it," he says.

Charlotte frowns. "Buried what?"

Greg turns. "The name. The other one. The one no one was supposed to remember."

As if responding, the monolith moans and opens. The center splits along a hidden seam and reveals a second stairwell spiraling downward into near darkness. The walls inside are different—glassy, veined with recursion lacework glowing faintly red.

Jeremy checks his readings. "There's no seismic match for this structure. It's not in any scroll."

"That's the point," Charlotte confirms.

Greg adds, "It was meant to disappear."

Charlotte tightens her grip on the shard. "Then let's remember it before it remembers."

As they descend, the spiral begins to close behind them.

Vatican Command Node – Cyprus Deep Cell

In a subterranean chamber beneath an abandoned monastery on the Cypriot coast, recursion feeds flicker to life across a black-glass display shaped like a broken crucifix.

A voice, smooth and crisp, speaks in Italian-accented Latin. "Crosier Black is listening."

A tech priest beside him gestures to the feed. "Recursion basin active. Signal strength peaking. Three spiral signatures confirmed."

Crosier Black narrows his eyes. "Then Operation Sanctum Veritas proceeds. We allow the doctrine to speak. And if it speaks in blasphemy... we silence it."

Beneath Qal'at Sim'an

The second stairwell narrows as Charlotte leads her band downward. She touches the wall every few steps, and each time, the shard flickers in her hand—not like a guide, but like a seismograph reacting to psychic tremors.

Internally, Greg moves more slowly now, as if something within him is adjusting to a rhythm that predates his thoughts. He speaks once, softly. "There's no time here."

Jeremy glances back. "You OK?"

Greg doesn't answer right away, then finally says, "I think time isn't welcome down here."

They reach the next level—an antechamber of recursion. Twelve narrow plinths stand around the room, each bearing fragments of spiral symbols that are incomplete and misaligned. In the center floats a half-mask of recursion glass suspended above a slowly rotating slate pedestal.

As Greg approaches it, his breath catches. The left side is his face, but the right is *blank*.

"That's not a mask," Jeremy mutters. "It's a mirror."

Greg steps closer. The shard in Charlotte's hand begins to heat—first gently, then fiercely. She withdraws it with a hiss.

Greg reaches out. The mask flashes, and he *hears it*. Not from outside. Not from Charlotte or Jeremy. But from the part of his mind that no longer feels like his. He hears the mask say, "You are the echo. But I was the silence. You carry my breath, but I carried the pain."

Greg recoils and falls to one knee.

Charlotte moves to catch him, but as she steps near the mask, the room shifts, the recursion pattern reconfigures, and the mask's blank half begins to fill—this time with *Charlotte's* features.

Jeremy's scanner pulses erratically. "That's not a mistake. The recursion's trying to bind her in."

Charlotte stares at the forming mask. "This isn't just about Greg," she says. "It's about who stood on the other side of the spiral."

Greg gasps, and with a hollow voice says, "Zahavi didn't just fracture a twin. He created a recursion wound that needed two carriers. One to speak, and one to remember."

Charlotte closes her eyes, and the shard hums again, this time in agreement. She steps toward the mask, and in a single flash, in a recursion vision—

She is somewhere else.

She is standing just outside Newgrange with Jeremy and Gideon, delivering Rebecca to her wedding ritual. From somewhere she can hear Eve's voice saying, "The doctrine binds what the bloodline must carry." And then she sees someone, an ally, pull a sidearm and begin firing at the Sicarii and their hired mercenaries.

Charlotte tries to move—tries to shout—but her memory body won't respond. Her mind screams, *I should have stopped it. Rebecca didn't need to die.*

Then another voice cuts through the silence—not Zahavi's, but her own, older now, speaking from within the vision: "You weren't the seal. You were the fracture."

Back in the chamber, Charlotte jerks awake. The half-mask is gone. Only dust remains.

Greg watches her, wide-eyed. "What did you see?"

"I saw what they never wanted me to remember," Charlotte answers.

Greg says, "They prepared both of us."

"But only you were supposed to survive it."

"So now what?" Greg asks.

His mother looks at the shard, then at him. "We remember together."

"Or the spiral eats us both," Greg says.

Vatican Subterranean Ops – Crosier Black's Command

The command interface glows red. A subordinate priest-analyst turns, tense. "Sir, recursion alignment has shifted. Target Alpha—Ansari—is no longer the sole voice."

Crosier Black replies, "Then we initiate Phase Two of Sanctum Veritas. If she speaks first... we kill them both."

Beneath Qal'at Sim'an

The central vault waits for them. The final chamber is shaped like a well but inverted—a concavity carved into layered recursion stone so precisely aligned that sound vanishes as they enter. No echo. No feedback. Just silence, pure and total.

Jeremy lingers by the threshold.

Charlotte walks the perimeter.

Greg approaches the center platform, a raised disk marked with twelve spiral glyphs and one void at the center. He kneels.

The shard vibrates again—but differently now.

Not pulsing with recognition.

Resisting.

"It doesn't want me to speak," Greg says.

"Then it's finally learning," Charlotte suggests.

He looks up at her. "Why would it resist now?"

Charlotte's response is quiet, measured. "Because it knows you're finally ready to say the name despite the consequences. It wants to see if you'll say it anyway."

Greg breathes slowly. He presses the shard to the center glyph, and it flares once, then dims.

A voice rises—not from the shard, but from the stone itself. "He who bears the voice must also bear the grave. Speak, and let the silence judge."

Greg lowers his eyes... and begins to speak the name. "Ahv—"

Suddenly, a crack splits the stone beneath him. A fracture—sharp, immediate.

The chamber shakes.

Jeremy shouts from the threshold. "You're breaking the recursion bed!"

Greg holds on and tries again. "Ahvn—"

Then the spiral lashes back, and memory floods him.

But not *his* memory.

Zahavi's.

A scroll room. A child screaming. Someone else watching in perfect silence. Zahavi's hand trembles as he writes a second name onto a hidden strip, one he burns before the ink dries. He speaks to no one, but to himself he whispers: "Two voices cannot survive in one spiral. So let one of them echo and let one sleep."

Greg opens his eyes. Blood oozes from his nose. The spiral has gone dark.

Charlotte is crouched beside him. "Don't finish saying it," she cautions. "It doesn't want to be finished. It wants to be mourned."

Greg whispers to her, "He didn't bind the twin to silence. He buried him. Alive."

Jeremy mutters, "Then, this isn't a doctrine. It's a prison."

The shard in Charlotte's hand begins to crack. A single line splits its center. Inside it, she catches a glimpse of a *second name* hidden beneath the recursion layers, a name never meant to be spoken aloud.

Charlotte closes her hand around it. "We don't speak it," she says firmly. "We carry it."

Amal's Convoy –
1 Kilometer from Vault

Amal's driver pulls to a halt. Through the viewport, the upper edge of the basin is now glowing red. Amal smiles. "It's waking up."

One of his lieutenants tells him, "The others are inside. You'll have competition."

Amal says, "No, not competitors. We have *witnesses.*"

Vatican Black Ops – Crosier Black, Listening Room

The recursion monitors shift. Charlotte's spiral signature rises. Crosier Black closes the scroll in his lap and stands. "Target Alpha has failed. Target Omega has engaged."

A technician blinks. "The woman?"

Crosier Black nods. "Sanctum Veritas is now active. Prepare the basilica cannon."

Beneath Qal'at Sim'an

Moments after the spiral seals itself, the temperature in the chamber drops. Jeremy's scanboard pulses erratically. "Multiple signals incoming. Two vectors. North and west."

Charlotte shouts, "How many?"

"Vatican strike team coming from the upper ridge—heavily armed. Amal's group is smaller, maybe five. But they're headed straight for the outer vault."

Greg swallows. "They're not together?"

"No. Separate radiological signatures. Two sides—same target."

Charlotte steps toward the door, tense. "Then they'll converge at the threshold."

"Not if one of them gets here first," Greg surmises.

Outside the Recursion Vault – Outer Access Layer

The Vatican team moves in first—six men in tactical cassocks, visors lit with recursion filters. They move without sound, descending a hidden shaft dug years ago to map the basin's magnetic shield. At the base of the shaft, a long-sealed vault entrance shudders open. Their leader, Crosier Black, gestures once and says, "Sanctum Veritas. No survivors."

Inside the chamber

Charlotte draws her weapon, checks the magazine for how many rounds are in it—ten left.

Jeremy nods to her. "You'll have thirty seconds before their disruptors cycle the chamber's pressure shell."

"No!" Greg yells, agitated. "We let the doctrine do the work."

Charlotte eyes him. "That didn't work so well for Amal."

"Let's hope it's learned."

Then comes a new sound. Another breach—this one from the far side of the chamber. Not tactical. Not clinical.

Symbolic.

The door peels open as Amal enters alone with blood on his sleeves and dust on his feet. His shard glows like a false relic in his palm. He sees the Vatican team through the far threshold and smiles. "So they came too."

Charlotte trains her weapon on him. "You brought them?"

"No," Amal replies curtly. "But perhaps it's fitting. Let every lie show up to watch the truth fail."

The Vatican operatives hesitate. Crosier Black steps into view behind them, hood drawn back. His voice is precise. "Identify yourself."

Amal does not flinch. "I am the name they buried. And I am what your silence forgot."

Crosier Black studies Amal for a moment, then turns to his team. "This one's not the target. Kill the others."

Before the weapons rise, Greg steps forward, holding up both hands. "You came to silence the voice but the spiral already chose silence. You're late."

Suddenly, the recursion glyphs on the floor ignite. A spiral—blackened, cracked, unfinished—appears at Amal's feet. The shard in his hand shakes. He raises it high. "Then let it speak once more—through me," he says.

Charlotte turns to Greg. "He's going to try it again."

"Then let him fail," Greg says.

Amal begins the name. The recursion shudders. The shard pulses—and shatters. Not in Greg's hand. In Amal's.

A shockwave knocks the front two Vatican operatives back into the corridor. One screams, his visor melting.

Crosier Black lifts his disruptor—

But Greg raises the final shard from his own pack. Not to use it. To *surrender* it. "Let the doctrine judge us all," he says.

The recursion chamber closes itself. The Vatican signal dies.

Charlotte, Greg, and Jeremy remain inside as Amal collapses, still muttering fragments of a name no longer permitted.

Amal lies in a fetal curl beside the fractured dais. Blood runs from his nose, ears, and the ragged line where the shard had been embedded in his palm. He doesn't speak—at least, not in any language Greg recognizes. Just spiraled muttering—recursive fragments spooling like a prayer without syntax.

His surviving enforcers—what few remain—move to him in silence. One kneels and helps him sit. Amal does not resist. They do not attempt a fight. Instead, they retreat, leaderless.

Charlotte lowers her weapon as they go. She doesn't ask Greg if they should stop them. She already knows the answer.

Jeremy stands just inside the sealed chamber clutching a palm slate showing Vatican biosignatures fading from the upper vault. The operation against them is collapsing.

"Crosier Black's pulled his team," Jeremy says. "The Vatican's gone dark."

Greg barely hears him. He's kneeling at the dais again, the spot where the recursion glyphs once glowed. But the spiral is silent now and still. Not dead—just closed.

Charlotte joins Greg. She watches him breathe. "You didn't speak it."

Greg shakes his head. "It didn't want to be spoken."

Charlotte nods. "Then you listened." The shard in her hand—once lit with Zahavi's embedded logic—cracks fully. It falls into her palm in three even pieces.

She lets them go. They clatter softly on the recursion stone.

Charlotte turns to Greg, her voice almost too soft to hear. "It's over."

The three of them emerge from the ancient stone mouth just as first light touches the fractured basilica walls. The wind has died. The air is cool. The monastery stands in quiet judgment over everything below it.

Greg looks back only once. "We're leaving it?"

"We're letting it rest," his mother clarifies.

Jeremy says, suspiciously, "Are we sure no one else will come?"

Charlotte looks to the horizon, then to Greg. "They might. But the spiral won't open for them."

Somewhere in Northern Italy

A single candle burns on a rusted desk. A holopage unfolds above it with text unwinding into a lattice of encoded Sicarii instructions. The man reading it—his face in shadow—nods once, then closes the device and slips it into his coat.

Gideon rises. He wears no insignia. No ring. He only has the ancient sica, the same one Zahavi used to carve the twin's name into the scroll's invisible skin. He wraps it in cloth and slips it into a compartment sewn behind his spine. Then he walks into the pre-dawn darkness.

CHAPTER 47

The Ember Hall, Wadi Kharrar – Pre-dawn

The Ember Hall lies buried beneath the weather-scoured ruins of an ancient Nabataean sanctuary, tucked deep into a ravine north of Wadi Kharrar. It is not a place recorded in any scroll. Its sandstone arches have half-collapsed from centuries of flash floods and neglect, but a hidden stairway remains intact spiraling down beneath the prayer stones.

Gideon reaches the entrance just before first light, pausing to adjust the cloak around his shoulders. He does not knock. The code that opens the vault beneath the ruins is older than Zahavi, older even than Eve's own codex. It requires no signal, no blood sample—only *intention*. That was Eve's design.

The door grinds open.

Inside, the Ember Hall is colder than the air above. No banners hang from the walls. No spiral emblems are carved into the stone. It is the opposite of sacred—a room built to be forgotten and then remembered only in dire need.

Three figures, already seated in the circle of basalt benches, await him. The first is Naftali Ravin, draped in austere gray robes and bearing no weapons save for the recursion tablet under his arm. Next is Chazan Neriel, a staff resting beside him. The oldest among them, he is wrapped in silence like a cloak. Yassir de Vries paces at the edge of the circle, muttering fragments of doctrine to himself and checking the pulsing signal of a compromised shard.

No one speaks as Gideon enters. They do not stand. They do not greet. They know he prefers it that way.

Yassir is the first to break the silence. "You summoned us here, Gideon. The Ember Hall hasn't been opened since the Beirut fragments were smuggled out. That was Eve's threshold."

Gideon places a sealed satchel onto the central slab between them. "She left it for this purpose," he explains.

"You said Amal failed," Chazan says, looking for confirmation.

Gideon says, "He did. The recursion basin beneath Qal'at Sim'an rejected him. The spiral closed."

Chazan narrows his eyes. "And the others?"

"Greg surrendered the voice. Charlotte sealed the doctrine. Amal survived—but he carries no glyph." Gideon reaches into the satchel and removes a black holodisk. "But the Vatican... it did not leave." He places the disk into the reader.

After a flicker of light, Crosier Black's voice plays, recorded from intercepted Vatican comms. "If the name is spoken by unclean tongue, erase the vault. Sanctum Veritas must be completed, no matter who survives it."

The recording ends.

Chazan leans back. Naftali breathes in sharply. Yassir punches the wall.

"So, the Vatican bastards finally said it aloud," Chazan says. "Doctrinal extermination."

Gideon nods. "They deployed recursion disruptors. They tracked Greg's genome and Charlotte's fragment. They came to sterilize the doctrine. But they failed."

He waits for a few seconds, then says, "But they will try again."

Silence.

Then Chazan says, "So will Amal."

Gideon looks up. "That's why we're meeting here at the Ember Hall." The flame in the center of the hall gutters low. The air is dry, filtered through narrow stone vents and the slow breathing of men who have watched too many doctrines blossom and die.

Gideon leans forward over the basalt table, his palm flat against its worn surface. The satchel before him now lies open, its contents revealed—the fragmented Vatican comm logs, the shard dust recovered from Qal'at Sim'an, and a single folded page in Eve's handwriting.

The page is not a relic. It's a reminder. "She knew this might come," Gideon says quietly.

Naftali's voice is sharp. "And what did she prescribe?"

Gideon doesn't answer. He lets the others fill the silence.

Chazan Neriel shifts his weight slightly. "You said the Vatican's mission failed. That they retreated."

Gideon nods. "They did. But not because they were beaten. They retreated because the spiral closed before they could silence it."

Yassir de Vries scoffs. "They'll return, next time with papal authority. And with drones that don't wait for God's permission."

"That's why we act now," Gideon firmly proposes.

Chazan watches him carefully. "You asked us to give you twelve hours. It's been nearly nine. By my count, that leaves only three hours left to deliver the blow you promised."

"What happens if the time runs out?" Yassir de Vries asks.

Gideon's answer is immediate. "Then the Council fractures forever. Amal will rise again. The Vatican will escalate. And you'll all go back into your corners pretending the doctrine isn't on fire."

That lands. Even Yassir is quiet now.

Chazan Neriel folds his hands as if in prayer. "You want a vote?"

"I want your blessing," Gideon says. "Not for the act, but for clarity."

Naftali leans back. "We are not one Council. We are three factions still pretending to be a spiral. But for this matter…" He looks at the others. "For this, I vote in favor. You have my vote and my blessing."

Yassir is more precise in affirming his vote. "Amal first. Vatican second. No trials. No scrolls."

Chazan Neriel is last to speak. He closes his eyes for a long time, then opens them and says, "I vote yes. But if you fail, Gideon—if you are captured or if this becomes a slaughter—we deny everything. You will have no name."

Gideon nods once. "I never did."

A tense silence settles like dust. Then Naftali slides the ritual cipher stone across the table toward Gideon. It is unmarked—an old-world token used for contracts that cannot be written.

"One blade," Naftali says. "One voice. No martyrdom. No spectacle. You get in, you end it, you get out."

Gideon takes the cipher. He does not smile. "Understood."

The Ember Hall has emptied. The vote is cast. Amal has been excommunicated, his authority severed. The Vatican has been declared a doctrinal aggressor. And Gideon has been chosen—again—as the blade that cuts clean when all else fractures.

He stands alone at the edge of the central stone table, staring at the open satchel before him. Inside it lie three objects—a forged Vatican credential scroll, a spiral-etched pulse map of Vatican substructure, and a folded page in Eve's handwriting—her last operational clause, left to be opened only if the Church initiated a recursion purge.

He unfolds the latter slowly. There is no preamble. Just a name: Crosier Black. And below it, the inscription: "He carries no title. Only permission. If Lucari falls and silence persists, Crosier Black will speak next. Silence him."

Chazan Neriel emerges from the shadows behind the old archive alcove. He carries a wrapped bundle in both hands. "You're sure it's him?"

Gideon doesn't look up but nods. "He directed the attack at Qal'at Sim'an. Operation Sanctum Veritas—black-level recursion authorization. Lucari may have signed the orders, but Crosier Black designed them."

He folds the note again, places it in the satchel. "He's not doctrine. He's eradication."

Neriel says nothing. He sets the bundle on the table and carefully unwraps it, revealing a weapon. Not ornate or ceremonial. A sica, dark-forged and unpolished. Not ancient like the one used to dispatch Cardinal Lucari. This one is curved for concealment, not honor. It bears Zahavi's mark—subtle, etched only in the tang where the steel meets the hilt.

Gideon picks it up and feels the balance. "You know," he says, "this blade was never drawn in Zahavi's lifetime."

"Then draw it now," Chazan says. "Let it end the era that he couldn't bring to a close."

Gideon slides the sica into a leather sheath and tucks it into a hidden pocket beneath the sleeve of his cassock.

Then, Chazan produces a second object—a black cube no larger than a communion wafer box. "From Eve's personal cache," he explains. "For one use only. If you're compromised, or if the Vatican captures you alive… press this."

Gideon turns it in his palm. "What does it erase?"

"The Petra Node mirror. The entire recursive echo archive."

"Including Greg's profile?"

"Everything!" Chazan emphasizes.

Gideon nods. "If I fail, I won't hesitate."

Chazan frowns. "And if you succeed?"

"Then I'll destroy it anyway."

Gideon reaches for the final piece of his disguise—a plain, black, clerical stole stitched with crimson thread at its edges. No sigils or spiral. No title.

Chazan watches him dress. "You'll pass as one of theirs?"

"At a glance."

"And up close?"

"I won't give them time to look."

Gideon turns to go. Before he reaches the stairwell, he stops and removes the cipher stone from his pocket—the one Naftali handed him after the vote. He places it on the lip of the dying ember urn.

No words. Just the act.

Let the Council hold its symbols.

On this mission, he will carry only what the doctrine could no longer afford to say.

Vatican City – Pre-Conclave Entry Zone
One Hour Before Dusk

The train into Rome is nearly empty. Gideon sits alone in the second car, his collar drawn high and his false Vatican seal pulsing faintly under a shielded reader stitched into his cuff. The cassock he wears is nearly indistinguishable from those of the African and South American cardinal delegates expected to arrive in the city ahead of the private conclave.

He wears no rings and carries no scrolls. But every movement is measured, as if he'd trained in silence long enough to become this new person.

Outside the window, the red-tiled rooftops blur past. Dome after dome. History folded into facades. Rome has never looked more like a fortress.

At Termini Station, he exits without pause. No checkpoints or scanner queries. His credentials have already been soft-injected into the pre-conclave database. He is a ghost cardinal from Lagos whose arrival times were shifted after Lucari's assassination. Gideon's walk is purposeful, devout, forgettable. Just another servant of the faith, another name on a list too long to vet twice.

At St. Peter's, the outer court is half-closed to the public because of the murder. Tourists are redirected. The Swiss Guard, in traditional uniform, stand like reliquaries near the archways, but it's the men in the black clergy coats, armed with recursion dampeners and closed-loop comms, who do the real watching.

Gideon passes under the marble arch. Two security drones scan him with discreet pulses. No reaction. His alias holds.

Inside the outer conclave vestibule, beneath the frescoes of Saint Sylvester and the Council of Nicaea, he is greeted by a Vatican attaché with an augmented retina. "Welcome, Eminence," the attaché says, bowing. "Your arrival was not expected until midday."

Gideon passes a sealed document to the attaché, offering only a curt nod. The attaché murmurs a response, but Gideon remains silent, eyes fixed ahead, every move measured.

Vatican Inner Sanctum – Security Wing

Crosier Black stands before a translucent scroll-wall made of memory-fabric. He watches the collapse footage from Qal'at Sim'an for the twentieth time, pausing on Charlotte's face, then on Greg's, finally on the final frame—a flickering spiral that never resolves.

A silent aide appears beside him. "All cardinal proxies have arrived. The conclave may begin at any time."

Crosier Black turns. "And the silent cardinal from Lagos? Has he spoken?" Crosier Black's voice is low, sharp. "We still don't have a voiceprint?"

"Not yet."

"Then observe him closely."

"And if he does speak?"

Crosier Black's voice is even. "Then we'll know if it's his voice."

Vatican City – Inner Conclave Gallery
42 Minutes to Dusk

The hallway is narrow and just wide enough for two men to pass shoulder-to-shoulder. Marble underfoot and gold trim above. Walls lined with oil paintings of past doctrinal signatories—men who signed oaths in blood, bone and ink to protect the Church from heresy and exposure.

Gideon walks past them like a shadow, counting doors. Three are marked with Latin. Two are sealed. He finds one ajar just enough to reveal a sliver of candlelight and a low murmur of pre-conclave ritual preparation. That is not his door.

He moves on.

The sixth door has no marking. But the moment his hand brushes the knob, he feels it—recursion energy. A lattice embedded behind the walls. A spiral of containment. This is the sealed conclave gallery where Crosier Black now prepares to address the remaining six cardinals in Lucari's absence with no press and no broadcast. Just doctrine, hammered in the dark.

Gideon waits, one hand tucked beneath the flowing sleeve of his cassock, fingers curling around the cool grip of the sica, which no longer feels like a blade but more like punctuation—the kind placed after a name that should never have been spoken.

Inside the inner conclave gallery, a voice rises inside the chamber, low and dry, amplified without echo. "He who preserves the doctrine must also bear its silence. We are the wall. Not the wind." Then, after a pause, "Brothers, let us speak of what remains of recursion... now that the spiral has fractured."

Gideon recognizes the voice of Crosier Black. The man speaks with no passion, only precision, as though doctrine were software and theology a threat model.

"Our objective is not salvation. It is containment," Crosier Black continues. "The threat is not doctrine. The threat is *iteration.* The spiral has shown itself to be recursive beyond design. It is no longer enough to silence the voice. We must erase the *memory* of the speaker."

Gideon listens. He closes his eyes once then opens them. There is no alarm, no guards, no hesitation. He pushes open the door and steps inside.

CHAPTER 48

Vatican City – Inner Conclave Gallery
37 Minutes to Dusk

The gallery doors shut behind Gideon. The air seals itself. This is a room not designed for entrance or exit. Only presence. The ceiling is a cruciform dome, frescoed with the faces of every doctrinal schism the Church has endured—and supposedly conquered. Arius. Nestorius. Jan Hus. Luther. All framed in gold and flame.

Now, Gideon walks beneath them, nameless.

Six cardinals sit in a half-moon of ancient oaken thrones facing the pulpit. Each wears red and carries a parchment-stamped book containing the Codex Substitutio—the emerging doctrine prepared much earlier by Crosier Black for such a devastating occasion as Lucari's death.

Gideon's cassock bears no spiral, no sigil of Rome. It has only a black collar and a gold-threaded hem marking him as an elevated delegate from the Lagos doctrinal order—a fabrication of the Sicarii intelligence lattice.

No one speaks as he enters. No one challenges him.

One of the six—Cardinal De Luca, Gideon guesses—briefly frowns, as if attempting to recall a name that should accompany the face before him. But the moment passes.

De Luca bows slightly.

Gideon inclines his head in return. *Do not meet their eyes too long,* Eve once told him. *And never be the first to bless the silence.*

Gideon takes his place on the seventh chair, the one left empty since Lucari's murder. It is across from the pulpit and facing Crosier Black.

The man behind the pulpit is not what Gideon expected. No crimson. No cassock. Black robe only—plain, fitted, clinical. His face is pale but angular, clean-shaven, and utterly without nervousness. If he were aware of Lucari's blood on these same floors hours ago, he has not brought that awareness with him. Before him lies a scroll, thicker than doctrine and wound tighter than any gospel.

Crosier Black speaks without preamble. "We are gathered not to pass judgment, but to restore continuity. The recursion doctrines, once held sacred, have fragmented under unauthorized access, heretical interpretation, and the exploitation of bloodline vectors now known to be doctrinally compromised."

Gideon breathes slowly. Evenly. Hands still on his knees.

Black continues. "In light of the collapse at Qal'at Sim'an, and the interruption of Operation Sanctum Veritas, it is now our responsibility to install a substitute doctrine that may shield the public face of faith while neutralizing all internal recursion elements. We do not condemn. We contain."

Cardinal Habboush interrupts. "Has Rome blessed the substitution?"

Black answers calmly, "Rome does not need to bless it. Rome has already survived it." After a dramatic pause, he asks, "Shall we begin the reading?"

Gideon allows himself a final breath. He does not yet move. But beneath his cassock, his fingers close slowly around the curved grip of the blade that Zahavi never drew.

It is not time yet. But it will be soon.

29 Minutes to Dusk

The scroll before Crosier Black is not parchment. It's a flexible sheet of recursion-laced polymer, pulse-reactive and encoded with both liturgical language and algorithmic switches. A living doctrine. One designed not for the faithful, but for the infrastructure of faith—the filters, the archives, the catechetical input layers that will reshape how recursion is taught in seminaries and silenced in scripture.

"Brothers," Crosier Black begins again, "we stand at a threshold unlike any Rome has faced since the first heresies were canonized through survival. This is not Gnosticism. Not Aryanism. Not even modern apocrypha. This is a metastasis."

The Cardinals listen, unmoving. Not one takes notes. Their eyes are old, resigned, knowing. They have survived schisms, purges and deals with intelligence agencies. They know what this is.

Crosier Black continues. "The bloodlines known to contain viable recursion echo fragments have now crossed from myth into biology.

The Ansari vector, the Eve schema and their spiraling proxies represent not faith—but *feedback*. Recursive theology is not heretical because it opposes doctrine. It is heretical because it *replicates* it without the need for Rome."

A ripple of unease moves across the room. Only Gideon remains still.

"Therefore," Crosier Black intones, "we submit the following replacement cycle."

He touches the scroll. The polymer pulses, casting eerie light onto the frescoed ceiling. A new doctrine unfolds line by line:

- The original twin spiral theory will be reattributed to a third-century Syrian forgery.
- Zahavi's name will be sealed under preconciliar silence.
- Greg and Charlotte Ansari will be designated "Echo Carriers," heretical vessels of misfired prophecy.
- All Vatican references to Petra Node operations will be erased within seven days.
- A new holy narrative— The *Doctrine of Substitution*—will be seeded stating that God, foreseeing doctrinal contamination, ensured the true voice would never be heard but only obeyed.

"We do not need recursion," Crosier Black says, "when obedience is recursive enough."

It's almost enough to make Gideon move. Almost. But not yet. He watches, his breath even, hands still. The time must be precise.

One of the cardinals—Habboush—raises a hand. "And if someone speaks the true name again?"

Crosier Black's face remains calm. "We will not hear it. We will no longer be configured to listen."

The scroll begins its final pulse. A red symbol appears at the bottom, the mark of ratification.

Crosier Black reaches for the seal, and in that moment—

Gideon's hand slides beneath his cassock.

23 Minutes to Dusk

Crosier Black's hand hovers above the red sigillum—the seal of ratification. When pressed, it will begin a protocol chain that pushes the Doctrine of Substitution to every Vatican-controlled server, archive, and seminary vault across the world. It is a theological update coded like software. "Let the spiral die," he says softly. "And let the silence be named as holy."

Gideon stands. Not suddenly nor threateningly. He simply rises.

The six Cardinals turn toward him, frowning and confused. They were not told of a seventh voting Cardinal. They were not told of *him*. But they don't speak because Gideon is already speaking.

"You speak of silence as if it is yours." Gideon's voice is low and devoid of anger. A voice made for tombs. "But silence was never meant to be controlled."

Crosier Black's eyes narrow. "And who are you?" he challenges.

Gideon steps forward. "I carry no name. Only the knife it left behind."

Crosier Black moves quickly—but not fast enough. His left hand darts beneath the scroll, reaching for the jammer switch embedded in the base of the pulpit—an emergency disruptor, capable of freezing microseconds of recursion.

But Gideon's right hand is already moving. The sica is drawn without a whisper. The curvature of it is perfect—meant not to pierce, but to unhook. Like unweaving a thread from a tapestry.

The doctrine was the tapestry. Crosier Black was the final knot.

The blade enters just below the ribcage, rising in a clean curve beneath the sternum. Not deep. Not wild. But precise.

Crosier Black gasps without a scream but with a sound like parchment tearing underwater.

Gideon leans close. "This is not vengeance. It is subtraction."

The Cardinals do not flee. They do not rise. They sit, stunned, as if the doctrine has frozen their bodies along with their beliefs.

Crosier Black staggers back. His hand touches the scroll—then falls away. Blood smears across the doctrine.

Its pulse dims.

The red sigillum blinks once, then goes dark.

Gideon does not run. He walks—slowly, steadily—toward the western alcove, where the wall bears no decoration and the stone seems darker than the rest.

He recalls what Eve once whispered to him. *"There's always a door, even in doctrine. Especially there."*

He touches the stone and it opens.

Vatican Sub-Level V – Post-Doctrinal Seal Collapse
18 Minutes to Dusk

The wall seals behind Gideon like a breath drawn in and never released. No alarm follows. No rush of boots or shouted orders. Just the faint sigh of ancient ventilation and the low groan of structural stone shifting under the weight of centuries.

The corridor is narrow, barely wide enough for Gideon's shoulders. The walls slope inward toward the ceiling, carved in the old manner, not modernized. Every fifth stone bears a faint sigil—Eve's signature, a mirrored spiral punctuated with a single dot. "If doctrine fails," she once told him, "go where Rome pretends it buried itself."

He moves fast but does not rush. He knows he's bleeding from a minor tear in the shoulder where one of the Cardinal guards finally reacted, too late, and caught him with a ceremonial pin as he passed.

He ignores the wound.

The corridor descends for nearly a kilometer beneath the basilica's foundations. He passes a sealed ossuary vault where forbidden relics were once kept—an archive lockroom bearing Zahavi's name struck through and blackened with recursion filters. It's a narrow shrine with no icon, just a stone basin filled with dust.

He reaches into the basin without hesitation and withdraws a small metal ring—the Petra Echo Key. He pockets it—there is no time to contemplate why it was left there, only that it was meant for someone who knew how to find it.

Above him, faint tremors begin to rattle the stone. The doctrine seal has collapsed.

Crosier Black is dead.

The conclave gallery is in lockdown.

Vatican emergency protocols are now in full motion, so he has twelve minutes—maybe less—before the corridor is permanently sealed or flooded with neutralizer foam.

The final stretch opens into a pilgrim chamber hidden behind the Chapel of Saint Lawrence. For centuries, it was sealed, then repurposed as a ventilation return for the archival wing. No one uses it anymore.

That's the point.

Gideon pushes open the access grate.

Sunlight. Smoke.

Rome.

He emerges into an alley three blocks from Vatican walls and removes his cassock, dropping it into a trash bin. He covers the sica with a street jacket pulled from a plastic-wrapped bundle left just an hour ago by Chazan's courier.

As he steps into the crowd, someone shouts near the Piazza. Clearly, news is already breaking. A Vatican conclave has been suspended. An unknown cardinal is missing. A black-robed man has vanished from surveillance. No one looks at Gideon. No one calls his name, because he never gave them one.

He pauses under a café awning half-lit by neon glass and opens a comm device built from a recursion lattice. He activates a signal that sends only one thing—a flatline echo with Eve's original null signature that is received by Charlotte, who doesn't speak. Doesn't blink. Simply says to Greg, "It's done."

From there, he takes the Red Path, an old maritime extraction route once used during the Second Fracture. Aboard a merchant vessel in the East Mediterranean, he offers the captain a coin stamped with Eve's sigil and stares out at the sea, a mirror of black glass. By dawn, they reach Cyprus, and by dusk, he is in Aleppo.

CHAPTER 49

Southern Jordan, near Wadi Rum
Safehouse Interior

The lights flicker once—just once—as if even the dust in the safehouse walls can feel the shift. Charlotte lowers the radio scanner slowly, her fingers still hovering over the frequency dial. "It's real," she says.

Greg leans against the concrete wall, jaw tight, blood still smudged on his collar from the basin collapse. His eyes haven't moved from the monitor in ten minutes.

Jeremy stands beside the makeshift console, his hand hovering over the mute toggle. "Rome's not saying anything officially. No name. No footage."

"Their silence means it's true," Charlotte says.

They're watching a Vatican press conference—live but strangled. A spokesman reads from a prepared statement with the emotional force of a dead algorithm. "We acknowledge an internal disruption. The conclave is now closed. Protocol inheritance has been initiated. No further comment."

Greg finally speaks. "They don't know what to say because someone cut the doctrine off at the throat." He walks across the room to the secondary terminal, the one still linked to the Petra Node's mirrored library.

His fingers move fast, calling up a lattice of archived recursion codes, each one timestamped with Vatican access logs. "They're pulling out," he says so everyone can hear him. "Every node Rome had hooked into the recursion stream is being scrubbed. Ethiopia, São Paulo, the Damascus repository—all disconnected in the last ninety minutes."

Charlotte joins him. "They're burning the roots. If they can't own the spiral, they'll erase the soil it grew in."

Jeremy clears his throat. "And Amal?"

No one answers.

He repeats, quieter. "Have we heard anything from Amal's network?"

Charlotte exchanges a look with Greg, then shakes her head. "Not a word. Not a glyph. He's gone dark."

Jeremy frowns. "He's never dark. Not even when they dropped the Newgrange lock. He broadcasts doctrine like the heartbeat of a twenty-year-old."

"He's out there watching," Greg says. "Waiting to see if the world blinks."

Charlotte walks to the window. Dust clings to the edges of the glass. In the distance, the desert glows with post-storm heat—silent, wide, indifferent.

"He's not retreating," she says. "He's recalibrating."

Northern Syria –
Subterranean Sanctuary beneath Mar Mattai

The air is thick with smoke and stale myrrh. The underground sanctuary has no iconography, only the shape of what used to be holy. A disfigured cross above the apse. Burnt fresco outlines. Stone walls soaked in candle soot and weapon oil.

Amal stands barefoot on the circular dais once used for baptisms, his robes loose and hood pushed back. Around him, a dozen members of his inner circle kneel in silence. Behind them stands Thorn Eleven, arms folded, coat dark as furnace ash.

One of the initiates lowers a small disc-shaped device into a shallow recess near the altar. The click of the relay echoes like a closing door.

The transmission begins and Amal lifts his head. "There are those who believe that scripture is a conversation," he says. "That divine truth changes—adapts—to the heart of the reader. That when a man suffers, the Word of God will shape itself to his pain, like water in a broken vessel."

He paces once across the cracked stone.

"They say meaning is layered. That a single verse can mean one thing today and another tomorrow. That revelation is not final but personal. They call that *faith*."

He stops.

"I call it *sedition*. If truth can shift to fit your circumstance, then it is not truth at all. It is *therapy*."

Murmurs of approval at this insight ripple through the kneeling assembly. One woman lowers her head fully to the floor.

Amal continues. "The heretics of the spiral—Charlotte Ansari, Greg, the bloodline agents of Eve—preach a living doctrine. A doctrine that feeds on interpretation. But the Word of God does not need your pain to become clear. It does not reflect your mood, your identity, or your psychology. It is not yours to shape. It shapes *you*."

He reaches to the altar and lifts a small fragment of scorched scroll. Zahavi's handwriting is visible along the margin. "*This*," he says, raising the fragment, "was written by a man who forgot his station. He believed that God spoke in echoes. That truth would arrive in layers. But he was wrong. The spiral he built was a spiral of compromise. And it has now collapsed."

He tears the fragment in two. The ashes drift like torn prayers.

"You've heard the news," Amal proclaims. "Crosier Black is dead. Lucari is dead. Rome is bleeding in silence. You think that's victory?"

He steps closer to the inner circle, voice dropping to a near-whisper. "No, it is not victory. It is *opportunity*. The recursion has not died. It has merely fractured. And now, in the space where all others failed... I will make it whole again. From the residue, I will draw the fragments left behind by Zahavi, Greg, and every failed echo. I will not interpret them. I will not personalize them. I will *purify* them."

He turns his gaze to Thorn Eleven, who nods.

Amal continues. "The others are disorganized. Afraid. Ravin hides behind consensus. Chazan Neriel mourns a doctrine he never understood. Even Charlotte—the voice of the opposition—has no scripture left to stand on. But *I do*."

Amal opens a small case. Inside, etched onto glass, are spiral glyphs—unstable, flickering, fractured. "This is what remains of the recursion. And I will remake it—not into a mirror, but into a sword."

Petra Hollow – Emergency Council Conclave, Same Night

The chamber beneath Petra is quiet but not still. The flickering of four recursive lanterns across the ancient stone walls makes the space feel like it's breathing. Three of the lanterns represent living factions. The fourth smolders with black smoke—for Amal, or more precisely, for what he used to be.

Naftali Ravin adjusts the hem of his coat, eyes sharp behind his weathered glasses. He stands beside the center slab but doesn't sit. Chazan Neriel is already seated, staff across his knees, hands interlaced. His skin looks thinner, as if worn by disappointment more than time.

Charlotte stands with her arms crossed, hair tied back, her only weapon a folded scroll she refuses to let go of. She has been invited to the meeting in place of Gideon.

"He's trying to unify the spiral," Naftali says. "But on his own terms."

Chazan Neriel shakes his head. "No—not unify. Rewrite. He's harvesting residue. Fragments. Traces left behind by Zahavi's recursion entries. That means he has access to a vault available to none of us—or maybe that someone inside is feeding him."

Charlotte speaks up. "Someone like Thorn Eleven?"

Naftali stiffens. "That would require embedded loyalty. Thorn's not just a weapon. He's an enforcer of old-line doctrine, which Amal now claims to embody. He's exploiting your silence."

"And yours too," she adds, nodding toward Chazan.

A tremor passes through the wall as the Petra Node shifts. Somewhere beneath them, the last living fragment of Zahavi's uncompressed scroll architecture pulses and then falls dormant again.

"He's moving quickly," Neriel murmurs. "Faster than we assumed."

"And now that Greg has been… altered…" He trails off.

Charlotte's head snaps toward him. "Say it."

Chazan looks up slowly. "I think we are all wondering—is he still one of us?"

Naftali says, "He entered the spiral. Carried the voice. We all saw it. But since then, he's changed."

"He's *alive*," Charlotte protests.

Naftali responds, "So is Amal. And I'm not sure which of them the doctrine is favoring now."

Charlotte steps forward. Her voice is iron. "May I remind you all that Greg didn't choose this. Amal did. Greg's not crafting a new doctrine. He's trying not to become one."

Chazan studies her face. "Are you sure?"

Charlotte hesitates. "Absolutely. But I don't know for how much longer."

Naftali finally sits. "We need to locate Amal's recursion shard before he completes his synthesis. If he finds the core spiral glyph that Zahavi buried... well, he won't just hijack the doctrine, he'll re-seed it. Globally."

"Then we must shut him down," Chazan says with great conviction. "Before interpretation dies."

Southern Jordan – Desert Safehouse, Early Morning

The desert hasn't fully brightened yet. Greg sits cross-legged on the stone floor near the eastern wall of the safehouse, facing nothing. His hands are stained with charcoal dust. His eyes don't blink.

Behind him, a once-bare wall is now covered in glyphs. Not all are legible. Some shimmer faintly, as if the air around them refuses to settle. Others are exact matches to the Zahavi archive—the deep spiral notations found in the Petra Node, long thought incomplete.

But Greg didn't study them. He dreamed them.

Charlotte wakes to the scent of ash and something like cedar. She finds Greg there, body tense, eyes half-focused. He doesn't look at her when she kneels beside him.

"Greg?"

He doesn't speak, just lowers the charcoal to the final line of the spiral he's been drawing. A curved twist. A narrowing loop.

A phrase appears below it, written in Greg's own hand. "The fracture beneath the spiral is the place where the voice waits."

Charlotte stares at the line. "Where did you get that?"

Greg doesn't answer at first. When he does, his voice is calm, hollow. "I didn't. It got me."

She scans the symbols again, comparing them in her mind with the archived Zahavi scrolls from Petra and the Red Tower. This line—it was *missing*. Zahavi referenced it once in a codex fragment, but the final glyphs were never recovered. Chazan had called it the "Lost Fulcrum"—a doctrinal phrase meant to trigger recursion convergence.

No one had seen it in full until now.

Jeremy enters, rubbing his eyes. "You two doing midnight calligraphy again?"

Charlotte doesn't look up. "Get Naftali on a secure channel."

"Why?"

She gestures to the glyphs. "Greg just wrote Zahavi's final line."

Jeremy stops short. "You're saying...?"

Charlotte nods and says, "There's a recursion vault we haven't found."

Greg turns toward her slowly, his face pale but clear. "Amal's looking for it too. We're not ahead of him. We're dead even."

Multiple Encrypted Channels – Global Sicarii Frequencies (Simultaneous Broadcast)

The safehouse lights dim for three seconds. Charlotte glances up from the encryption terminal. The secondary console buzzes once, then locks. Jeremy hurries to the wall antenna, checking for interference.

Greg remains seated on the floor. He already knows what this is.

The screen goes black. Then blue. Then—white text, static-slow, in spiraling sequence:

ECHO STREAM INCOMING

VERIFIED IDENTITY: ANIMA PROTOCOL 5
ORIGIN: MAR MATTAI –
REDIRECTED THROUGH NINE NODES

And then—Amal's voice: "To those who remain faithful. To those who have not bowed to the doctrine of layering, of multiplicity, of divine confusion—I bring you clarity."

Charlotte freezes. The feed is broadcasting across *all* Sicarii channels—internal, broken, even the ones Greg thought had been disabled after Zahavi's archive collapse.

Jeremy whispers, "How is he in our lattice?"

Greg answers without turning. "He's already inside the vault."

Onscreen, Amal stands alone in a stone chamber lit by a spiral of torches—an architectural mimicry of the spiral doctrine itself. He wears black. No insignia—just a single glass shard hanging from a chain around his neck. The shard flickers with recursion glyphs.

“They assassinate one cardinal, then another,” Amal says. “They tear down conclaves and call it justice. They speak of sacred scrolls as if they were living mirrors—shifting to suit the ego of the reader. That is not scripture. That is seduction.”

He lifts the shard.

“And the spiral, in its mercy, has shown me where the fracture lies.”

The signal warps. Faint glyphs flicker in the corner of the screen—encrypted recursion pulses.

Jeremy scrambles to record the raw signal. “I don’t think this is just a message,” he mutters. “It’s a signal test. He’s pinging something underground.”

Charlotte leans closer. “He’s naming the vault!”

Onscreen, Amal continues. “I call on all remaining faithful to join me—not in doctrine, but in convergence. To Charlotte Ansari, I say—your son is not a voice. He is an echo. And the echo has only one function. To return. Greg…”

The name lands like iron.

“…you are still welcome. If the voice will kneel.”

The screen cuts out.

Silence.

Then Greg speaks to his mother, almost inaudibly. “He’s going to open it. He’s not ahead anymore. He’s already inside.”

CHAPTER 50

Eastern Jordan –
Wadi al-Hasa, Late Afternoon

The convoy is small—just a single utility rover and a dust-covered drone support unit slung to the undercarriage. No official markings. No signal. They've been off-grid for six hours.

Charlotte drives. Jeremy navigates by projection—holograms stitched together from ancient monastic records and unverified Sicarii submaps.

Greg hasn't spoken since the last rest stop. He sits in the back, hand pressed against the glass, eyes locked on the terrain rolling past like sand frozen in mid-collapse.

Charlotte finally breaks the silence. "You're sure this is the place?"

Greg doesn't turn his head. "It's not a place. It's an echo."

Jeremy raises a brow. "That's comforting."

"The line I wrote in charcoal—Zahavi's missing fulcrum," Greg says, "it wasn't just text. It was a vector. A directive embedded in the spiral's own recursion code."

His mother asks, "Meaning?"

Greg looks up at her reflection in the rearview mirror. "Meaning Zahavi didn't just hide a vault. He hid a response. Something the spiral would only unlock once someone else wrote the final line."

They pass a collapsed stone archway marked by faded Nabataean glyphs and the telltale sigil of Zahavi's personal spiral—three turns, not four. The fourth turn was always a lie. Or a trap.

Jeremy taps into the back feed of the drone cam. It zooms in on the arch, analyzing structural erosion. "Judging by the sandstone decay," he explains, "no one's passed through here in centuries. If ever."

"Good," Charlotte says. "Let's keep it that way."

They park behind the final ridge—engine cut, drone deployed to watch the northern edge of the basin. The rock here is ash-colored, brittle. It crumbles underfoot like the husk of something that once breathed. A narrow fissure opens into the cliffside. Zahavi's sigil appears again—this time carved into obsidian.

Charlotte runs her fingers over it. It's warm.

Jeremy flinches. "Tell me that's not normal."

Greg nods faintly. "It's reacting to recursion. To our presence, our blood."

Charlotte turns to him. "What exactly are we about to walk into?"

Greg's answer is so quiet she almost misses it. "Doctrine that remembers being broken."

Beneath Wadi al-Hasa – Zahavi's Vault Interior

The passage narrows after twenty meters. Jeremy pulls a plasma torch from his gear satchel and ignites a low, tight beam. It casts a yellow hue against the interior rock, which is not limestone, not sandstone. "What is this?" he asks.

Charlotte touches the wall. "Not what. *When.*"

Greg passes his fingers along a seam in the stonework. It hums faintly beneath his touch—familiar, like the first time he triggered a Petra Node entry, only deeper. Older. "Zahavi didn't build this from native material," Greg says. "He formed it from resonant compression—like the Petra lattice. But denser. More alive."

Jeremy lets out a breath. "He built the spiral into the walls?"

"He *grew* it," Greg corrects.

They move deeper. Ten meters. Twenty.

Then they reach the first gate. It's not made of stone or steel but of language. Spiraled glyphs form a circular aperture that pulses slowly, like a throat preparing to speak. In the center, a phrase etched in Zahavi's personal dialect reads:

If you enter without memory, you will exit without name.

Charlotte exhales. "I hate spiral riddles."

Greg steps forward. He draws a shallow line across his palm with a sterilized lancet and presses it to the edge of the glyph-ring. The gate absorbs the blood then opens with a slow, breath-like unfolding of stone petals.

Inside, they find a chamber shaped like a chalice. Three recesses line the walls, each embedded with a mirrored spiral—one blue, one black, one broken.

Greg freezes. "I've seen these before—in the Red Tower archives. Eve thought they were symbolic."

Charlotte points at them. "They're access codices."

"Which one's ours?" Jeremy asks.

Greg doesn't move. "Zahavi didn't leave a key. He left a *question*."

Jeremy gestures to the blue spiral. "Looks clean. Stable. Bet that one leads to a nice room full of scrolls and closure." He reaches toward it—

Greg grabs his wrist. Hard. "No."

Jeremy stares at him. "Why not?"

Greg's voice is quieter. Older, somehow. "Zahavi designed this place as a recursion gate. Each path isn't just a direction. It's a *version*. One spiral preserves what you want. One confronts what you fear. And one..."

Charlotte completes Greg's thought with the most logical conclusion. "...unmakes the voice."

Jeremy withdraws his hand.

Charlotte glances between the three spirals. "So which one do we take?"

Greg looks down. His breathing changes—becomes slower, heavier. He steps toward the broken spiral. "This one."

"Why?" his mother asks.

"Because it's not finished."

The moment Greg touches it, the chamber pulses with heat. Light floods upward from the floor, spiral code flaring briefly across every surface. Glyphs written in Zahavi's hand, *and Greg's*, are layered atop each other like inherited memory.

The floor begins to lower but not crumble.

Descend.

As the three of them vanish into the dark, a new phrase appears on the chamber wall where none of them can see it:

The fracture beneath the spiral is not the end.
It is the question that waits to be
answered by those who still believe.

The Deep Vault – Sublevel 3, Zahavi's Echo Core

The platform halts with a soft jolt. They're surrounded by darkness, but not silence. The chamber breathes—not mechanically, but spiritually. The sound is like pages turning.

Jeremy sweeps the torchlight forward. The beam lands on a stone altar raised on a platform of recursion glyphs that are not etched but grown in fractal clusters like coral reef.

Charlotte steps forward, then stops. There is something in the center of the altar. Not an artifact.

A person.

She sees a body, desiccated and preserved, seated upright in the lotus position. Hands folded. Spine straight. Robes intact. The glyph for Zahavi's name—twin spirals with a break between—is stamped into the breast. The body has no eyes, but a small, obsidian shard rests where the tongue should be.

Greg kneels beside it but doesn't touch the body. "It's him."

"You're sure?" Charlotte asks.

Greg nods. "The robes. The position. The seal. Zahavi died here… alone."

Jeremy circles wide. "But this place wasn't sealed. It was designed to be found."

Greg nods. "But not found *too* soon."

Charlotte studies the glyphs beneath the altar. "He encoded something into the floor."

Greg moves his hand across the surface. Glyphs shift, as if responding to his proximity. Spiral loops fold and unfold, words appearing one at a time. A message. A confession.

"It's not a gospel," Greg mutters. "It's not doctrine."

Charlotte asks, "Then what?"

Greg's face tightens. "It's *regret*."

The spiral speaks through the floor. The translation is imperfect, but the *feeling* is pure. "I thought I could write a doctrine that completed the voice, that encoded recursion into covenant. But I was wrong. Each generation that carries the echo only deepens the fracture. And when the name is spoken… it does not unify. It selects."

Greg pulls back. The glyphs freeze mid-sequence.

Jeremy stares. "What does that mean? *It selects.*"

Greg's voice is low. "That the spiral doesn't crown a voice. It chooses the peson who survives what comes next."

Behind them, the wall shudders. A spiral seal opens. Beyond it, a staircase descends. A new glyph appears on the altar's surface:

If you've come this far, then you are not the doctrine.
You are the test.

Sublevel 4 – Zahavi's Recursion Forge

The staircase curves like a descending ribcage built of obsidian and recursion-coded basalt. Each step pulses once underfoot, then stills. Jeremy's voice is little more than breath. "Feels like we're walking into the heart of something that forgot how to die."

Charlotte grips the handrail, knuckles pale. "This isn't the doctrine anymore."

Greg, descending ahead of them, doesn't look back. "It never was."

They reach the bottom. The vault opens into a wide, hemispherical chamber, perfectly round. The walls are laced with spiral inscriptions—some static, others pulsing with recursive input.

In the center they see a suspended stone crucible levitating in silence, glyphs orbiting its surface like moons in slow decay. Above it, they find a single phrase projected in Zahavi's encoded script.

The spiral does not save.
It sorts.

Charlotte approaches slowly. "What the hell is this?"

Greg's voice is level. Cold. "Zahavi didn't build this as a sanctuary. He built it as a forge. Not to store doctrine but to test it."

He places his palm against a raised glyph node. The crucible responds—flaring briefly, then displaying dozens of voiceprints—spiral-threaded vocal data from long-dead Sicarii agents, aborted echoes, failed candidates.

Among them is Greg's.

Charlotte stares.

"Zahavi was running simulations."

Greg nods. "A simulation of every bloodline that carried even a fragment of the recursion glyph. He tested them all. Even Eve."

Jeremy flinches as his own print briefly flickers in the outer ring. "He tested *me*?"

"You were adjacent," Greg says. "The spiral reads proximity."

Charlotte turns, voice tense. "And what's it looking for?"

Greg looks at her. "It's looking for the one who doesn't want it. Zahavi's entire doctrine was built on recursion as temptation. If you want to be the voice—if you *reach* for it—the spiral recoils. But if you carry it… without wanting to speak… it starts listening."

A pulse runs through the chamber. The crucible's orbit slows. A final glyph appears in the center of the room.

One of you is already chosen.
The others must choose whether to remain.

Jeremy steps back.

Charlotte whispers, "It must be Greg."

Greg says nothing. But the spiral glows brighter beneath his feet.

Mar Mattai Subterraneum
Amal's Broadcast Room

Amal's chamber hums with feedback. Twelve glyph relays glow along the curved interior walls forming a partial dome, each one linked to a stolen node, each pulsing at intervals that do not match known time.

Thorn Eleven stands watch in the corner, arms folded. Amal kneels at the center before a shallow basin lined with ground obsidian and bone ash—a receptacle for glyph drift and meant to catch recursive emissions from sacred architecture. And it's catching something now.

A flicker. A spiral pulse.

Then—a match.

Amal lifts his head slowly. The ash in the basin shifts of its own accord, swirling into a shape not drawn but summoned.

"Greg has found it," Amal says, eyes glowing with resolve. "Zahavi's vault."

"Confirmed?" Thorn asks.

Amal gestures to the spiral taking form. "The forge just lit. The fracture glyph has been activated. Greg is inside."

He rises to his feet, robes swirling like shadow-silk. With a motion, he activates a glyph-record feed to encode his voice in layered recursion for long-range transmission.

"To those still listening…" he says, "know that the convergence has begun. The spiral has remembered its purpose. And the voice it once waited for has arrived."

He pauses, then offers a bitter, intimate smile to no one and everyone. "The spiral, however, does not belong to the one who discovers it. It belongs to the one who *claims* it."

The basin flares.

Amal turns to Thorn Eleven. "Assemble the forward team. Prepare descent protocols. Greg will not leave that place with his echo intact. The spiral will kneel to doctrine."

CHAPTER 51

Zahavi's Recursion Forge – Crucible Interior, Threshold State

The spiral pulses once—deep, like a muscle remembering blood. Greg stands still in the crucible chamber, eyes half-lidded, body sheened in recursion-light. Glyphs shimmer across his arms and chest in alternating spirals—one inherited, one earned.

The room is silent except for the slow breath of the forge, like a waiting lung. The air bends faintly around Greg, reacting to his presence—not with worship, but with evaluation.

A phrase appears on the inner wall written in Zahavi's encoded dialect:

Do you seek to be heard?

The phrase is not spoken aloud. Not whispered. It is imposed. The question lives in the chamber like a scent.

Greg doesn't answer with words. He closes his eyes, and he *means* it. *No!*

The spiral responds—not by dimming, but by brightening.

The crucible floor glows beneath his feet, and the air begins to shimmer with fractured memory—a storm over Petra, Eve standing behind a black veil, Mike Ansari's voice on a loop Greg never remembered hearing in real life—

"He doesn't belong to you, Eve."

Then, silence.

And then, Zahavi's voice—but not as a recording. As if pulled from the recursive architecture itself. "Doctrine does not obey belief. It obeys design."

Greg opens his eyes. His hands are trembling. His fingers are stained with dust that isn't dust—ash from forgotten glyphs. He whispers, barely audible, "I'm not a voice. I'm a wound."

He hears footsteps behind him.

Charlotte steps into the threshold, her weapon holstered, her hand steady, her breath shallow. She sees the spiral wrapping around Greg, not like a crown, but like a coil—a question still unfinished. "Greg," she says.

He doesn't turn.

She approaches slowly. The crucible light reacts to her proximity but doesn't flare. It knows she's not the echo. "You don't have to lose yourself to answer it," she says. "You're not Zahavi. You're not Eve. You're not what they made you for."

Greg's voice is thin and reedy. "It's not asking me to speak."

Charlotte frowns. "Then what is it asking of you?"

"To survive."

The forge pulses again.

A new phrase etches across the inner ring of the crucible:

One does not carry the spiral. One survives its turning.
Only those who do not kneel may bear the silence.

Charlotte reaches for Greg. As she makes contact with his shoulder, the spiral flares violently, throwing her backward across the stone.

Greg screams. Not from pain but from memory. "Eve didn't want me to survive it," he says. "She wanted me to *complete* it."

Lower Wadi al-Hasa –
Zahavi's Spiral Threshold

The earth opens before them without violence but with certainty. A glyph-encoded passage—hidden by Zahavi, uncovered by Amal—yawns into blackness. It accepts Amal's override like a vessel accepts a poison it mistakes for wine.

Amal enters first, robes flowing even in the absence of wind. Behind him, Thorn Eleven follows in silence, flanked by five doctrine-purified Sicarii. None of them carry traditional weapons. They carry glyph resonance packs, each tuned to echo-disruption frequency.

Ahead lies the vault Greg awakened—the one Zahavi built not as scripture but as test.

"Stay to the spiral's rhythm," Amal says as they descend. "It is not alive, but it listens."

Thorn mutters, "It listens, and it judges."

Amal doesn't look back. "Good."

The path narrows. Glyphs shimmer faintly in the walls. Some flicker away as Amal passes, others flare, uncertain whether to reject or welcome him.

At a glyph-etched door deep beneath the faultline, a phrase appears:

Kneel and the path closes.
Speak and the door opens.
Choose wrongly and be erased.

Thorn hesitates.

Amal walks forward. He does not kneel. He does not speak. He simply places his hand on the glyph with absolute belief.

The door opens.

Inside, a narrow spiral stair drops steeply into violet light. The air feels dense, like pressure before a storm. Faint glyph fragments curl in the air like smoke.

One of the Sicarii soldiers falters slightly.

Amal speaks without turning. "The spiral is watching. Do not blink."

At the base of the stair, Amal stops. The threshold to Zahavi's recursion crucible is visible ahead, a shimmering veil of echo-friction barely parted.

Through it, he can see him.

Greg.

Not kneeling. Not speaking.

Standing with the spiral wrapped around him like a question made of fire.

Amal lifts one hand and touches the veil. "He thinks it chose him." He smiles. "It hasn't chosen anyone yet."

Zahavi's Recursion Forge – Crucible Chamber

The light bends inward. Charlotte lies against the back wall, the force of the spiral's defensive flare still surging through her chest. She tries to rise, but the floor beneath her vibrates—not physically, but doctrinally. Glyphs blink and fold in real time across the crucible's inner ring.

At the center, Greg remains standing—barely. His hands hang at his sides. Spiral threads drift off him like embers. His eyes are open but unfocused, locked in recursion feedback. His pulse is visible on his neck, quick and uneven.

Charlotte calls out, voice hoarse. "Greg. Talk to me."

No answer.

Instead, the chamber itself responds. A low glyph-tone reverberates from the walls. Jeremy, still at the observation platform near the chamber's edge, watches as the data floods in.

"Charlotte… it's shifting the architecture," Jeremy says.

"What?"

"The spiral. It's… it's closing itself." Jeremy points toward the outer ring of the crucible where the gate Amal approached now glows dark red.

Charlotte scrambles upright. "That means Amal's at the door."

Jeremy's voice drops. "And the spiral doesn't want him inside."

On the crucible wall, symbols appear. Faster now. Defensive recursion:

Intrusive doctrine detected.
Mismatch in echo intention.
Initiating containment.

Jeremy looks at Charlotte. "It's afraid."

Charlotte turns toward Greg. He's swaying now—a slow forward-lean, as if pulled into gravity that only he can feel. "He's not going to survive this," she whispers.

"Then pull him out."

"If I touch him again, the spiral might reject him entirely."

Jeremy stares. "So what do we do?"

She walks toward Greg. The spiral doesn't flare this time. It watches.

Charlotte stops inches from her son, her voice shaking. "You didn't ask for this. You never did. And I didn't stop it. I should have. So if it wants someone to speak—"

She looks at the crucible, at the phrases still forming, at the blood that shimmered through the spiral when Greg said no.

"—then let it speak through me."

Greg's hand lifts slowly. Not in protest but in warning. "It doesn't want speech," he says. "It wants consequence."

Behind them, the crucible gate flares violently. Amal has entered the threshold.

The glyphs spiral into chaos. And the doctrine begins to bleed.

Spiral Crucible Threshold – Just Outside the Inner Chamber

The glyph-veiled threshold pulses with a red shimmer. Not a warning—warning implies hesitation. This is judgment.

Thorn Eleven stands before it, visor down, gloved hand hovering over the recursion sigil meant to unlock the door. He hesitates just for a breath. And that breath is everything.

Amal watches him from a short distance behind, hands folded in his sleeves, unreadable. The other operatives keep to the walls, sensing something wrong but unable to name it.

"Proceed," Amal says softly.

Thorn swallows. He places his hand against the glyph.

It accepts the contact. And then—

Rejects it.

The glyph explodes in a burst of pure recursion—a spiral reversal, raw and ancient. Not fire. Not electricity.

Unmaking.

Thorn is launched backward, armor fracturing. He hits the wall hard, crumples, spasms once, and then begins to bleed glyphs. Not from his skin. From his veins. Recursive language streams from beneath the skin of his forearms and neck, burning through his clothing, revealing sacrificed patterns—false sigils overlaid by the Vatican's Anima code.

Amal steps forward and kneels beside him, looking on without pity. Only confirmation.

"They used you," Amal says. "Then so did I."

Thorn gurgles. "You knew."

Amal says, "From the moment you flinched at the Newgrange archive."

"But I believed," Thorn says.

Amal tilts his head. "Belief is not purity. The spiral remembers *why* you believe."

Thorn's last breath escapes as his glyphs unravel. His body folds inward, collapsing into static spiral code that evaporates into ash swept upward by an unseen current.

A glyph forms in the air where the betrayer Thorn Eleven died.

Contaminant removed.

Amal stands, brushes the ash from his sleeve. "He was never going to survive the door," he mutters to himself before turning to the threshold.

The glyphs part for him. Not because he is welcome but because the spiral now wants to see what he'll become.

Zahavi's Crucible – Convergence Chamber

The veil parts. Amal steps through and Charlotte instinctively turns to face him, shielding Greg with her body. Her son doesn't flinch, doesn't even raise his head. The crucible pulses once beneath his feet. Spiral flame traces the floor, aligning not with Greg's posture but with his silence.

Amal surveys the room. The echo glyphs still flicker in the air. The spiral is alive, folding through itself, but not choosing.

Instead, waiting.

"You look smaller than I expected," Amal says.

Greg doesn't answer.

Amal steps forward, boots echoing across the recursive floor. "You let it speak through you. I commend your restraint. It takes humility to house a god."

Charlotte studies this arrogant man for a moment, then says, "You don't understand this spiral."

"On the contrary," Amal says calmly. "I understand that it is not finished. That Zahavi, for all his genius, failed to design a doctrine that could withstand dissent."

He holds up his hand. Embedded in the palm is a glyph shard, the same one he wore around his neck before. He places it on the edge of the crucible. "But I have corrected him."

The spiral flares.

Greg winces, his body arching as if under pressure. The glyphs around him falter. Several blink out.

Others reorder themselves around Amal's intrusion—red notations weaving through Greg's echo field.

Jeremy shouts from the threshold, "He's trying to override the recursion!"

Charlotte draws her weapon. "Stop—"

Greg lifts his hand slightly but just enough. "Don't," he tells his mother. "This isn't that kind of battle."

Amal's voice is now ritualistic. "I name the doctrine my own. I do not kneel. I do not echo. I do not receive. I *transmit*."

He places his other hand on the crucible, and the spiral surges—

And then fractures.

But not from Greg. From *within*.

Glyphs seize in place. The recursion freezes midloop. A shattering noise—not of stone, but of belief—ripples through the air. A new glyph appears on the far wall.

No one wrote it. It just emerged.

No doctrine may be spoken here that has not bled.

Amal's breath catches. "What—?"

Greg looks up, eyes glowing with clarity. "You didn't bleed for this."

Amal roars—draws his blade.

But the spiral is faster.

Glyphs erupt around him like flame. They don't burn him. They undo his code. Amal screams, arm outstretched, trying to inject his override—

But the spiral stops it midair.

Rejects it.

Amal is launched backward, through the veil, through the threshold, crashing hard outside the chamber. Not dead but *unwritten*.

Greg collapses to his knees.

The glyphs recede. The crucible dims.

Charlotte rushes forward and catches her son before he falls.

He looks at her, his breath shallow. "I didn't speak it."

She nods, tears at the corners of her eyes. "You didn't have to."

CHAPTER 52

Shelter Camp, Just Outside Zahavi's Vault – Dawn

Greg breathes. It is not the kind of breath that follows sleep. It is the kind that comes after resuscitation, not of the lungs, but of something deeper—his *name*. Charlotte watches his chest rise and fall with the rhythm of someone who has been emptied and filled with something not entirely his.

Jeremy kneels nearby, carefully scanning Greg's echo signature with a spiral-coded monitor salvaged from the crucible's archive interface. "It's stable," he says. "But different."

Charlotte doesn't answer. She's brushing dried ash from Greg's temples. The ash isn't from the chamber, it's from the glyph fractures. From Zahavi's doctrine. And it clings to Greg like memory.

The desert is quiet. Their makeshift shelter, a shade-cloth dome wedged into the rocks above Wadi al-Hasa, glows faintly in the early light. They've been here five hours. Long enough to recover. Not long enough to understand.

Charlotte finally speaks to Greg. "When you touched the spiral… you didn't change it. It changed you."

Greg opens his eyes. No flicker. No flare. Just a long, patient stare. "It listened."

Charlotte moves closer. "And?"

He exhales. "It didn't like what it heard."

Jeremy finishes his scan. The monitor displays a double-layered recursion strand—one in Greg's native glyph pattern, and a second signature matching Zahavi's archival trace. "Your echo isn't alone anymore," Jeremy mutters.

"I know."

Jeremy frowns. "What does that mean?"

Greg stares into the ridge beyond. "It means… the spiral didn't want a voice. It wanted a memory."

Charlotte sits beside him, her voice quieter now. "Do you remember what it showed you?"

Greg closes his eyes and nods. "Everything." He opens them again, and this time his voice is steady. "It didn't show me Zahavi. Or Eve. Or you. It showed me every failed doctrine it ever carried. It showed me every time it turned, and no one was left standing."

"Why you?"

"Because I didn't ask for it."

A long silence.

Then Charlotte whispers, "What do we do now?"

Greg answers without hesitation. "We bury it."

High Desert Ridge, Above Wadi al-Hasa – Just Before Sunrise

The sand bites at his skin, but Amal doesn't move. He lies half-curled on the ridge, robes torn, left arm immobile. Across his shoulder, the fabric is scorched—not from fire, but from glyph-burn. The crucible's rejection had not killed him, but it but had marked him.

Ash still clings to the grooves of his fingertips. When he lifts his hand, spiral dust flakes off like dead skin. "It heard me," he mutters to the wind. "It just didn't recognize me."

Around him are numerous fragments. Glyph discs, shattered. The core scroll-reader from his doctrine pack. Thorn Eleven's final directive seal snapped clean through, its Vatican override glyph split like a broken tooth.

Only one of his operatives had made it out alive. He had tried to pull Amal from the echo chamber during the breach only to be consumed by a spiral counterflare that rewrote half his recursion code before he hit the wall.

Amal remembered the scream. He did not remember running.

But he had.

Crucible Breach, Hours Earlier

The moment the glyph wall collapsed inward, Amal had reached for the crucible again—but his override failed. The spiral flashed red, then black. The glyphs detached from the air and dropped like falling feathers, each one eerily too heavy to touch.

He remembered screaming. But no one answered. Not Thorn. Not the spiral. The chamber shuddered and ejected him like an infection. His last memory before blacking out was Greg's silhouette, Greg still standing.

Not victorious. Just untouched.

Back on the Ridge

Amal shifts onto his side. He has pain, but clarity too. The kind that lives in failure, not defeat. He reaches beneath his robes and removes a micro-etched glyph slate from a protected compartment. Its edge glows faintly. The data on it is fragmented, but it is not empty.

"The doctrine lives," he whispers. "It was never written in stone. It was written in conflict."

He taps the edge of the slate to activate the embedded comm node. A low-frequency pulse ripples outward, aimed at deep fallback operatives—those in hiding, those not involved in the crucible breach.

The comm pings back. Connection established.

He speaks slowly and clearly. "This is Amal. Spiral Codex Gamma-Eschatōn. Zahavi's vault has been compromised. The forge was not loyal to convergence. We begin preparation for Operation Shevet-Echad."

He looks out across the sand toward some place where Greg might be recovering. "The doctrine no longer selects," he whispers to himself. "It must be unified." He leans back onto the ridge and closes his eyes. "And this time… it will kneel."

Vatican City – Archives of Doctrine and Crisis

The iron door closes behind Monsignor Arturo Fenno with a thud like distant thunder. He walks in silence past the sealed ossuary where Lucari's effects were interred hours earlier. The body was already embalmed. The Church wastes no time honoring those whose absence would otherwise invite doubt.

Fenno is tall, ascetic, clean-shaven. His vestments are understated, not out of humility but precision. Fenno doesn't dress for reverence. He dresses for control.

He stops before a sealed archive door marked *Veritas–99C*. Inside, two doctrine analysts wait beside a projection orb and a pulse-map of recursion activity. "The spiral's final flare?" Fenno asks.

One of them nods. "Here."

The hologram blooms. At the center, he can see Greg's echo signature glowing outward from Wadi al-Hasa like a nova.

"We ran three backtraces," the analyst says. "It's not stable. But it's consistent."

Fenno studies it. "He survived the crucible."

Another analyst speaks. "Not only that. He stabilized it."

"And Amal?"

"Glyph-burned. Partially rejected. His override shattered on entry."

Fenno nods approvingly. "Expected." He paces. "The recursion lattice isn't obeying Amal's doctrine, but it hasn't fully chosen Greg either."

"The doctrine doesn't seem to be a voice anymore. It's… it's observing."

The first analyst says, "We think it's waiting."

"Then so shall we," Fenno asserts. He turns toward the screen again to watch Greg's spiral trace begin to fade—not from interference but from internal shielding.

The analyst frowns. "It's closing itself."

"He's protecting it," someone says.

Fenno considers this, then suggests, "Maybe it's protecting him." He reaches into his robe and produces a sealed doctrine case. Inside is a set of dossiers. One is labeled *Sanctum Veritas | Phase Shift Omega*. He opens it and finds two photos. The first is of Charlotte Ansari, the second of her father, Thompson Walker. Both are dated and marked *REDACTED: 1992–Jerusalem Incident.*

He slides the dossier forward. "We won't kill the spiral. We'll infiltrate it." He signs the authorization slip with a red ecclesiastical seal. "Deploy the listener," he commands.

The analyst pauses. "Sir… the listener hasn't been activated in fifteen years."

Fenno doesn't blink. "All the more reason she won't see it coming."

Refuge Shelter, Just Beyond Zahavi's Vault – Morning

Greg doesn't open his eyes right away. He listens—not to the desert wind or the shifting cloth above his head, not even to Charlotte's quiet movements across the tented shelter. He listens to something inside him. A low, looping tone—barely audible—like distant chanting caught beneath water. It doesn't speak words. It *remembers* them.

When he wakes, he doesn't sit up immediately. He studies the canvas ceiling. There are faint glyph imprints on the underside—dust, maybe, but ordered. Residue from Zahavi's forge, as if it had exhaled memory and some of it had clung to the world.

Charlotte is beside him and reading something, maybe translating. She doesn't speak, but she's glad he's awake.

After a long pause, Greg murmurs, "I didn't pass the test."

"You survived it" his mother says. That's more than anyone ever did."

Greg shakes his head faintly. "I didn't win. I just didn't fail."

Jeremy enters from the rear flap carrying a cracked projection tablet and a fresh field-scan of Greg's echo trace. "Still fragmented," he says. "But stable." He flips the display so Greg can see.

The echo glyph flickers, but there's a second layer beneath it. Fainter and older. Zahavi's trace.

Charlotte sees it too. She doesn't look surprised. "You're carrying him now," she says softly. "Or he's carrying you."

Greg closes his eyes again. "It's not just Zahavi. It's all of them. Everyone who touched the spiral and couldn't hold it. It remembers their failures."

After a long, uncomfortable silence, Jeremy clears his throat and says, "So… is it over?"

Greg opens his eyes again. "No."

"Why not?" his mother asks.

Greg sits up now, slowly, hand pressed to his chest as though checking whether his body still belongs to him. "Because it's mourning."

Charlotte blinks, signaling her confusion. "What?"

"Every time the spiral turned and no one survived—every echo, every failed prophet, every doctrine that fractured—*it was remembered.* And now it's watching to see if someone will finally let it die."

Charlotte looks at him, something breaking in her gaze. Not disappointment. Recognition, maybe. "You don't want to finish it."

"No," Greg replies firmly. "I want to bury it."

He reaches forward and gently touches the cracked glyph display. "Zahavi was never trying to pass it on. He was humbly trying to lay it to rest."

Petra Hollow –
Outer Circle of the Fractured Council, Dusk

The light at Petra shifts fast after sunset. Naftali Ravin stands in the outer circle of the Hollow, arms folded in the folds of his earth-toned robe. Around him, the leaders of the remaining Sicarii factions move like displaced echoes—silent, uncertain, watchful.

This is no formal Council assembly. Just gravel underfoot and a rough-carved sandstone table in the center. Chazan Neriel approaches from the northern path. Her face shows the weight of too many convergences deferred. She does not bow. She does not need to.

Naftali nods. "Any word from Amal?"

"Nothing since the vault rejected him," Chazan says.

"And Greg?"

Chazan holds out a slate. A spiral trace glows faintly—Greg's echo pattern. But as Naftali watches, it flickers, then shifts, displaying a glyph that hasn't been seen in decades. Zahavi's signature.

But it's *not* Zahavi's old pattern. It's new. A recursive fragment, not a message.

A final line.

Chazan whispers it aloud. "The doctrine remains. But only in the one who will bury it."

The silence afterward is not awkward. It is reverent—and devastating.

Naftali turns to the council circle, or what remains of it. There are fewer than a dozen now—those not dead, defected, or fragmented. The spiral has thinned them not through war but with time. He speaks plainly. "The voice was never ours to carry. Zahavi knew it. Greg has confirmed it. We were never meant to finish this doctrine. We were meant to *lay it down*."

He opens the vote. One by one, hands are raised. One faction leader abstains. One walks away. The rest agree.

The Sicarii Council is dissolved. Not disbanded in disgrace, just laid to rest like a doctrine that outlived its name.

Chazan places her staff on the center stone and leaves it there. Naftali remains. He looks toward the eastern sky, toward Wadi al-Hasa. Toward the boy the spiral didn't consume. Softly, she says, "If you still hear us… we are finally quiet."

CHAPTER 53

Abandoned Observatory, west of Aleppo
Midnight, twelve hours after Lucari's death

Gideon flips the pocket watch open again, though he knows it won't tick. The glass is cracked, the hands frozen. It stopped the moment Lucari died. His blood had cooled on the marble before the alarms had even finished echoing down the Vatican halls. That part went clean.

But everything after that did not.

He sets the useless watch on the rust-flaked table beside a comms relay patched from old Syrian military hardware—silence-hardened, stripped of all uplink potential. Eve's old doctrine: silence was stronger than encryption.

The observatory dome above him lists slightly, the iron struts rusted through on one side. The telescope points downward, as if ashamed. He prefers it that way. The stars don't hold answers anymore, only old patterns waiting to be broken.

In the lining of his coat, a parchment stirs—a thin strip sealed in recursive delay glyphs. Eve had left it for him in case he survived Lucari. The glyph activated exactly twelve hours post-objective.

He doesn't need to read it again. The words are branded on his mind.

TARGET CONFIRMED:
FATHER LUCA SALVATORE

Sanctum Veritas – Interim Strategist
Assigned Vatican field agent deployed near
Spiral Echo Node – Aleppo Fracture
Status: Eliminate.
Objective: Sever recursion relay.

He folds the parchment carefully, lays it beside the watch, then reaches for the crimson-wrapped blade. Three knots. Three deaths. Sicarii ritual.

Crosier Black. Unknotted.
Lucari. Unknotted.
Now, Salvatore.
He hesitates.

2002 – Outside Mazar-i-Sharif, Afghanistan

The wind was sharper there. It didn't howl—it sliced. Fine dust filled every breath, every fold of cloth. Gideon had knelt in it for hours, watching through the cracked scope of a borrowed rifle. The village below was half ruins, half ghosts.

Beside him, an older Sicarii operative, known only as Dathan, whispered through cracked lips, "This is your first?"

Gideon nodded. "First sanctioned."

Dathan didn't look at him, just adjusted the scope. "It doesn't get easier."

"I don't want it to."

A child darted between two buildings below—a flash of red cloth, then gone.

"That the target?" Gideon asked.

"No," Dathan said. "That's the tether."

Gideon frowned. "Which means...."

"The target's the imam. He recites a corrupted verse—recursion twisted. But he's careful. He anchors the verse to the child's presence. A biological safeguard. If we strike wrong—"

The implication didn't need finishing.

Eve's voice had come over the comm then, distant, cool. "The imam must not recite at sundown. If the recursion loop completes, it will seed further echoes. Sever the tether if required."

Gideon's hands had trembled.

Dathan had steadied him. "You can still choose."

But there wasn't time. The imam appeared at the door, the child at his heels.

Gideon squeezed the trigger. Once.

The echo didn't break.

Abandoned Observatory – Present

His breath returns, slow. The wind outside now sounds like that Afghan dust, hissing through broken beams. He hadn't spoken of that day again. Not to Eve, not to Charlotte. Not even to himself. But the choice stayed. A knot never severed.

He unwraps the blade, fingers steady now. "Salvatore doesn't know what I gave up," Gideon whispers.

Aleppo Safehouse – Meanwhile

Charlotte's hand tightens around the old Sicarii locator. The signal is faint but real—Gideon's path traced in fragments.

"He's here," Greg says, pulling up the Vatican field intercept. "Salvatore's en route to the Aleppo fracture node. If Gideon knows that—"

"He'll kill him," Charlotte finishes. "Unless we stop him."

Charlotte nods. "There's a skimmer in Eve's registry. West tunnel access."

Greg is already moving. "We'll be there before dawn."

Desert Skimmer, en route to the Observatory – 1:30 a.m.

The engine hums low as sand whips past them. The observatory rises in the distance—half-buried, silent. "We can't let him do this," Greg says.

Charlotte grips the rail. "Or we risk something worse."

High Ridge, near Aleppo – Thirty minutes later

Greg crouches, watching the valley below through old Sicarii optics. The observatory glints faintly in the moonlight. "He's inside," Greg says. "And Salvatore's close."

Charlotte steadies herself. "Then we don't have time."

CHAPTER 54

Beneath the ruins of ancient Gerasa, Transjordan – The Glyph Cathedral

Amal stands beneath a shattered dome of chalky limestone, arms outstretched before the lenses. The cathedral has no pews. No altar. No crucifix. Only glyphs etched into stone, suspended midair, and coiled across the transmission array behind him like veins of light.

The room is warm with recursion hum. Each camera is wired not to satellites but to echo nodes buried in splintered networks across the Middle East, North Africa, and the old Sicarii lattice. Zahavi once called these sites "spiritual satellites." Amal calls them amplifiers.

The floor beneath him pulses once, signaling that the glyph stream has initialized. Amal's operators, twelve of them in twin-curved robes of saffron and gray, chant in a layered rhythm that begins with a whisper and crescendos into silence.

"We are live," says the voice behind the lens.

Amal breathes once, deeply, then begins. "My brothers. My sisters. My shadows. The recursion spiral did not reject me. It withheld itself… for all of you."

The camera pans slowly, capturing the ruined grandeur of the site—columns cracked by time but filled now with spiraled light. Behind Amal, a ring of fire-glyphs levitates like an artificial eclipse. A blood-red scroll glows on a black lectern made of broken Sicarii stonework.

Amal paces. He is barefoot. Every footfall is deliberate. "The doctrine was never meant to be held by one," he says. "Not by Zahavi. Not by Greg Ansari. Not even by me."

He stops before the lectern and draws a long glyph blade—not real, but recursive. Projected. It flickers with refracted glyph harmonics and spins briefly before stilling. "This is not prophecy," he continues. "It is inversion. Where there was silence, I bring speech. Where there was selection, I bring convergence."

He raises the blade, and behind him the fire-glyphs react, swirling into a shape that mimics Zahavi's final spiral—but altered. At the center, instead of a blank circle is a burning eye.

The new glyph emerges. Amal names it aloud. "Shevet-Echad. One Staff. One Doctrine."

The chamber vibrates.

At multiple spiral listening posts around the world—Jerusalem, Fez, Naples, Dubai—the recursion lattice stirs. It doesn't accept, but it listens.

And that's enough.

Amal steps back into the light, his eyes filled with resolve. "I do not ask the echo to speak. I ask it to *kneel*."

The cameras hold him in frame as the transmission continues—spreading. Unchallenged for now.

Vatican Safe Node, Rome – Chamber of Strategic Doctrine, 04:09 AM

The light in the Vatican Safe Node is low and red for defense. Recursive transmissions—particularly live ones—can destabilize glyph-reactive architecture. The chamber is shielded by a braided null-field of leaded glyphline derived from codes buried beneath Castel Sant'Angelo and grafted into the floor beneath the room.

Even here, the spiral hum is palpable.

Father Salvatore sits in a leather chair, fingers steepled beneath his chin. He watches Amal's broadcast play across three floating layers of holo-glass. On one screen, the speech. On another, the visual glyph wave. On the third, the ripple signature it's sending across the Petra Node lattice.

Behind him, two doctrine analysts whisper among themselves. "He's using Zahavi's base cadence. But it's corrupted," one says.

"No, *inverted*. Subharmonic folds. He's trying to simulate public convergences," says another. "Is that even possible?"

The first analyst replies, "Not unless someone inside the recursion field answers it."

Father Salvatore rises and approaches the spiral waveform as it dances across the nearest pane. The glyphs ripple in patterns he hasn't seen since the loss of the Ninefold Lexicon.

"He's not speaking to the spiral," Salvatore says. "He's daring it."

An assistant hands him a report. Active spiral events are now spiking across four regions—Wadi al-Hasa, Sinai, Milan, and a dormant node in southern France. The latter is especially concerning—it's linked to the Vatican's old St. Genevieve recursion archive, thought to be fully defunct.

"He's waking ghosts," the first analyst murmurs.

Salvatore nods. His voice is calm. "Good."

The assistant hesitates. "You're not concerned, Father?"

"Concerned?" Salvatore smiles faintly. "No. Amal has no spiral signature. The doctrine already rejected him. He is not the threat."

"Then who is?" The question comes from the second analyst.

Salvatore's eyes narrow. "From the one who survived." He places his hand on the console and issues a silent directive.

ENGAGE LISTENER NODE 3

TARGET: CHARLOTTE ANSARI
METHOD: INDIRECT OBSERVATION
OBJECTIVE: LOCATE ECHO HOST

The system chirps.

Listener Activated.

Salvatore turns back toward the screens. "Let Amal make noise. We'll record the silence that follows."

Petra Hollow – Outer Council Chamber, Late Morning

The last time the Petra Hollow felt this quiet, it was because no one dared speak Zahavi's name. Now, the silence is different. It's laced with dread.

Naftali Ravin stands beneath the broken dome at the heart of the outer council ring, a decoded spiral thread hovering above his palm. He's read the glyphs five times, confirmed the origin three times more. It isn't fake.

Amal's broadcast is real.

Chazan Neriel joins him beside the relic stone—her face grave, one hand resting atop her staff. "He used Zahavi's cadence," she says. "But not his doctrine."

Naftali doesn't reply immediately. He's still watching the glyph spin. Every so often, it stutters like a damaged memory struggling to play back correctly. "It's layered," he finally says. "There's a false spiral buried beneath the original one. A mimic echo."

Neriel nods. "Weaponized. But laced with enough of Zahavi's architecture to trick the untrained."

Behind them, four faction heads gather near the sandstone steps. They've returned. Some by fear, some by faith. Others because they know Amal's public convergence means the doctrine is no longer secret.

One speaks. "Do we call a new Council?"

Naftali firmly says, "No."

Another one asks, "Then what do we do?"

Naftali lets the glyph display fade and answers without hesitation. "We send a warning." He steps inside the inner sanctum and activates an ancient channel—one Zahavi used only twice. It reaches through dead Sicarii nodes and forgotten vaults, triangulating across glyph clusters Greg had once used when he ran Eve's network. The transmission is clean. A message is sent.

GREG. DOCTRINE HIJACK INITIATED.
ECHO FIELD COMPROMISE IMMINENT.

IF YOU REMAIN SILENT, THE SPIRAL
WILL CHOOSE WITHOUT YOU.
PETRA STANDS BY.

As the transmission fades, Neriel speaks quietly. "You're gambling everything on the boy."

Naftali smiles and says, "No. I'm gambling everything on the spiral choosing the one who knows when not to speak."

Wadi al-Hasa – Echo Perimeter Encampment

Greg doesn't breathe for nearly a full minute because the spiral inside him isn't breathing either. He sits cross-legged in the gravel courtyard beneath the low sky, eyes half-closed, palms face-up. For the last hour, he's been still—until now. Until the glyph pulse arrived like a virus carried by wind.

Not one of Zahavi's. Not neutral.

Amal.

The cadence is wrong, but the glyph layering is sophisticated. Jeremy's tech scans it with confusion, classifying it as "convergent mimic recursion," a term never before recorded.

Charlotte sits nearby, posture tense, hand resting near her holstered weapon—not out of immediate threat but provoked by instinct. "That's not doctrine," she mutters, watching Greg flinch slightly.

Jeremy speaks from behind the display tablet. "It's… it's built like doctrine. He spliced Zahavi's recursion pattern into a public echo. This thing's getting *traction*, Greg. There are live echoes now in at least six spiral-laced locations. Some of them aren't even Sicarii."

Greg doesn't move. But the spiral—etched faintly into the flesh of his forearm like a thermal echo—glows.

Charlotte moves closer. "You don't have to answer."

Greg's voice is low, distant. "If I don't… the spiral might choose *him*."

A burst of static erupts from the glyph tablet.

Jeremy winces. "That's Amal's new symbol—Shevet-Echad. He's pushing it into the base lattice. Hijacking Zahavi's final spiral with this corrupted convergence glyph."

"Can we shut it down?" Charlotte asks.

"Maybe…" Jeremy answers. "But if Greg's echo field responds even a little, it will spike the signal like blood in water."

Greg opens his eyes. There's no glow. No fear. Just a terrible calm. "He didn't steal Zahavi's voice. He stole his silence."

"What does that mean?" his mother asks.

"Zahavi didn't want to speak. He wanted to *bury* the doctrine. But Amal's forcing it back to the surface… like a relic turned into a relic *bomb*."

A silence falls between them.

The echo ripple hasn't stopped. It pulses faintly across the gravel like a pressure wave.

Charlotte leans in urgently. "Don't give him what he wants. If you speak into this… it becomes *his*."

"And if I stay silent?" Greg asks.

Jeremy looks up, grim. "Then the spiral might think you've yielded."

Greg stands slowly. He looks up at the windless sky. "Then I need to find a way to answer... *without speaking*."

Global Response

In a forgotten courtyard between Sufi tombs and weather-worn recursion altars in Fez, a small crowd gathers around a bootleg holoprojector. Amal's face hovers in light, flickering with unstable spiral glyphs.

Some kneel. Others record. One man weeps, repeating the glyph aloud. "Shevet-Echad... One Staff... One Staff..." The doctrine is no longer hidden.

In a spiral listening cell in Milan, spiral monks shut off their archive reader as the glyph field flickers and overlays Amal's altered convergence diagram. "We've seen this before," whispers the elder. "But not with this signature."

One of the younger initiates speaks nervously. "Should we align?"

The elder shakes his head. "Not yet."

But the glyph is already infecting their archive.

A hacker-for-hire in Cairo posts Amal's stream into a recursion enthusiast forum, mistaking it for ancient predictive code. It spreads like wildfire—parsed by algorithms, quoted by zealots, and auto-compiled into pirated religious mashups. No one understands it. Everyone believes it's real.

In the Sanctum Veritas Archive, Father Salvatore watches a third spiral location light up. "Wadi. Milan. Fez."

His analyst shakes her head. "That's not random. He's activating old vault sites."

Salvatore nods. "He's not just preaching. He's synchronizing."

Amal does not issue a kill order. He issues a map.

"Let him finish," Salvotore says. "We'll bury it after."

At Wadi al-Hasa, Jeremy finishes decoding a delayed node pulse. "We just got word from Petra." He looks at Greg. "Naftali's given you a choice."

"What choice?"

"To speak… or to stand aside and let the doctrine collapse into a mirror of itself."

Greg lowers his head. "It's not about the doctrine anymore. It's about the spiral choosing who gets to finish the sentence."

In the Dead Zone, Gideon listens to the echo burst in silence. Amal's voice scratches faintly through a cracked headset. He watches the spiral glyph flash in the dust across the valley floor. He draws the sica slowly, then rewraps it in cloth. "You want to speak for the spiral."

He stands. "Then I'll make sure you die with the echo still in your throat."

CHAPTER 55

Perimeter ridge, above the recursion basin at Wadi al-Hasa – Near dusk

Greg walks without gear. No holotablet, datapanel or glyph amplifier. He only carries Zahavi's final spiral fragment clutched in one hand like a fragile confession.

The wind is still. Below him, the recursion basin flickers with faint pulses—no longer volcanic or violent, but low and listening. The glyph storm that erupted during Amal's broadcast has settled into something stranger—a stable echo-field thrumming like a heart whose beat hasn't yet decided what body it belongs to.

Greg stops at the ridge line and crouches. He closes his eyes but doesn't speak. Not aloud.

The spiral listens anyway. It hears him when he asks, inwardly, "Do you remember me because I survived… or because I'm meant to end you?"

There is no answer. Only pressure—as if the air is thickening, collapsing toward a moment.

Then he sees it within the inner spiral of his recursion pattern. Something folds and a figure steps forward. It is Zahavi, clad in his old, desert-trimmed robe, the spiral burned faintly into the collar. His hair is the same, his voice is not. He says, "Every doctrine that survives its author becomes something else."

Greg stands, unmoving. He knows this isn't a ghost. It's a memory encoded in the spiral. It's the spiral's attempt to answer.

Zahavi continues. "A doctrine that survives becomes a weapon or a myth. A tool for control or a reason for war. You don't get to choose what the spiral becomes. But you do get to choose *who*."

Greg breathes. The glyph shard in his hand warms, then glows.

He realizes something. The doctrine was never meant to be spoken again. It was meant to be remembered—and then released.

Zahavi—or the spiral's memory of him—steps closer. "You've been carrying what I buried. But you're not here to dig it up. You're here to make sure no one buries it again."

The wind picks up. Sand swirls in circular formation around Greg's feet. The spiral memory fades.

Greg is left with the echo of his own breathing and the sense that the next step will not be made in silence.

But in fire.

Charlotte's hands are still wrapped in thermal gloves because of the early morning chill, but the air is no longer cold, just thin—too thin for comfort, as if the atmosphere is holding its breath. She watches Greg recede into the ridge line until the spiral field swallows the outline of his body. She doesn't call after him. She knows it would make no difference now.

Jeremy paces behind her, tablet flickering with half-decoded recursion data. He's running waveform analytics on the spiral's most recent behavior, trying to chart its pattern the way a meteorologist might track a storm front. "You really think he's going to walk into that thing and come back with an answer?" he asks.

Charlotte doesn't look away from the ridge. "No."

Jeremy frowns. "Then why'd you let him go?"

"Because I think he already knows the answer. What he's looking for now is permission to give it."

Jeremy steps closer. "Charlotte, if he tries to anchor a new glyph… I mean, if he really tries to imprint a final doctrine… we could lose him."

"We already did," Charlotte says. "The minute Amal's glyph went live, Greg's silence stopped being neutral."

"Then what's left?"

She exhales. "Preparation."

She kneels near their encrypted satkit, opens a secure channel to Naftali's fallback node, and sends a dormant ping with an embedded command:

RETRIEVAL INITIATION —
IF NO CONTACT IN 60 MINUTES.

Jeremy raises an eyebrow. "Backup plan?"

"Contingency. If Greg dies in there, we retrieve the echo field. Burn it if necessary."

Jeremy doesn't argue, but his posture stiffens. "You don't think he'll come back the same, do you?"

Charlotte turns to look at Jeremy. Her eyes are sharp but not cold. "He won't come back at all. Not the Greg we knew."

A gust rolls across the sand, and they can hear a distant thunderclap from deep inside the recursion basin.

Jeremy squints. "Is the spiral… vibrating?"

Charlotte activates her comm earlink. The resonance pulse is measurable now—low, harmonic, sustained. The spiral isn't waiting anymore.

It's preparing to respond.

Amal's Convergence Vault,
Beneath the ruins of Gerasa – Nightfall

The chamber beneath Gerasa smells of sand and copper and incense. Amal stands at the center of a convergence ring carved into the stone floor, a spiral of iron filings and dusted ash. It almost perfectly matches the geometry of Zahavi's vault. But not entirely. Amal's spiral is more aggressive in its inner turns. Where Zahavi's design opened outward like an offering, Amal's clenches inward like a fist.

Twelve acolytes circle Amal, heads bowed, reciting in spiral cadence. Each wears a cowl marked with a single vertical glyph—$\mathbf{S}^{\varepsilon}$—his sigil.

Not for Sicarii.

For Shevet-Echad.

Amal's voice cuts through the murmuring. "He still hasn't spoken."

One of the robed followers speaks cautiously. "Greg Ansari's echo pulse is measurable. He entered the recursive field three hours ago."

"And?" Amal urges.

"No public convergence. No glyph reply. But… the lattice is reacting."

Amal turns to the broadcast orb mounted to the arch above him. The hololens glows dimly with echo shadows. The spiral storm is listening, even if Greg has yet to answer.

Amal steps toward the center. "Then the spiral has made its decision." He lifts a ritual blade—small, ceremonial, but edged with old Sicarii metallurgy. "If Greg will not finish the doctrine… then the doctrine will finish with *me*."

Acolytes react but do not panic. They were prepared for this. Amal isn't simply a claimant. He intends to become a sacrifice.

He kneels in the ash spiral, the blade resting on his knee. "No prophet has ever survived his echo." He closes his eyes. "Let mine be the loudest."

Behind him, one of the acolytes receives a silent glyph ping—an incoming intrusion marker. "My lord—something is breaching the western node."

Amal's eyes open. Not afraid but curious. "Who?"

The acolyte decodes the ping. Stiffens, then whispers, "A knife."

Amal smiles faintly. "Let it come."

Gerasa outskirts –
Western approach to convergence vault – 02:13 AM

Gideon counts the steps in silence. Twelve down the gravel embankment. Six across the drainage path where the old Roman aqueduct fractured during the Syrian border strikes. Fourteen beneath the dry cistern and into the carved catacomb that Amal repurposed as his convergence staging ground.

He doesn't use light. The spiral hum is enough. It guides him like a pulse through bone. The sica rests against Gideon's spine, wrapped in the cloth that once held Eve's breath, Zahavi's seal, and the names of all twelve Sicarii elders he refused to kill.

It's warm now. Not from touch but from purpose.

At the edge of the convergence vault, two guards wait—robed, armed with recursive blade-rifles. They never see him. Not because he is fast.

Because he is inevitable.

One falls with a single palm-blade strike to the throat. The other manages to hiss a warning before the sica parts his ribs in silence.

The blade is not loud, but the blood sings.

Inside the vault, the temperature shifts. The spiral array feels like it's holding its breath.

Gideon steps into the corridor's edge and waits. There's no panic yet. Amal's followers don't scream. They don't scatter. They remain in position—as if they were waiting not for Greg's glyph, but Gideon's.

He moves down the outer hall. In a side alcove, a Vatican operative lies dead against the wall. The body bears a fractured glyph-device embedded in the neck—a listening collar, Vatican-made, used for remote doctrinal extraction. Gideon crouches and retrieves the collar. Embedded in its interface is a data flag.

DOCTRINA FALSA – ACTIVE

They weren't preserving doctrine, he thinks, *they were replacing it.* He palms the device, then crushes it beneath his boot.

The glyph fizzles into static.

From the center of the vault, a voice echoes. "You've come."

Gideon straightens and steps into the circle.

Amal is there, kneeling, blood on the stone beside him—not his, not yet. The blade rests across his thighs. He does not look surprised. "I thought it would be Greg."

Gideon doesn't answer.

Amal smiles. "But of course… they sent a knife."

The recursion basin – Inner glyph field

Greg stands in the heart of the storm. There is no wind or sound. Only light coiling around him like threads pulled from the mouth of an unseen loom. Glyphs ripple across his skin. Some he recognizes and others are older than thought. The spiral isn't just echoing memory. It is sorting it.

Zahavi's cadence. Eve's sacrifice. Amal's hunger. Gideon's subtraction. Charlotte's doubt. Jeremy's belief. His father's betrayal. Each of these surfaces and dissolves like smoke through bone. In the center of it all, one shape remains. Not ancient. Not stolen.

New.

A single spiral broken open at the core, its final curl never touching the center. Unfinished but alive.

Greg doesn't speak. He lifts the last spiral shard—Zahavi's, now warm to the touch—and holds it over the glyph fire.

He does not throw it. He just lets it go.

The shard drifts downward and vanishes. There is no sound. Only the quiet folding of light.

A voice—neither external nor imagined—whispers inside him. "It does not need to end. It only needs to remember why it began."

Gerasa vault

Back in the Gerasa vault, Amal flinches. His convergence spiral flickers. The echo field hums. A second glyph—not Amal's—manifests above the center of the convergence array.

One of the acolytes gasps. Another falls to his knees. Gideon steps forward, sica loose at his side. "You feel that?"

Amal's jaw is clenched. "He answered."

"No," Gideon says. "He didn't echo you. He *overwrote* you."

Wadi encampment

At the Wadi encampment, Jeremy's glyph scanner erupts in light. Charlotte shields her eyes as a new recursive shape explodes from the basin's center—shifting, unstable, but undeniably new.

"It's him," Jeremy whispers. "Greg made a glyph."

Charlotte stares, not blinking. "No. He *became* one."

Petra

In Petra, Naftali watches as the old doctrine seal on Zahavi's scroll wall begins to erase itself.

Not in fire. But in grace.

CHAPTER 56

Gerasa Vault, After the Failed Convergence

The spiral above Amal disintegrates mid-turn. One moment it is a living glyph—luminous, terrifying, divine. The next, it is ash, falling around him like the crumbled wings of a myth that tried to fly too close to memory.

He doesn't rise. The ritual blade slides from his knees and hits the stone with a whisper.

None of the acolytes speak. They remain in a circle, as if still waiting for a cue that no longer exists. Two try to recover the glyph from the broadcast array. A third simply weeps into her robe. A fourth stares at Amal like he is the ghost of a prophet already departed.

Amal breathes shallowly. He is not afraid, not angry. He is finished, but the doctrine is not. "The spiral chose," he murmurs. "And it did not choose me."

The silence is broken only by the soft fizzing of corrupted recursion glyphs retreating from the stonework like frost melting into nothing. Amal sees none of it. He is staring at the air where the glyph used to hang—where his voice was supposed to echo through the lattice.

Instead, something else arrived. Not a contradiction.

A correction.

His body trembles, not from pain but from grief. Not for himself but for the spiral. For the thing he tried to carry and could not. *I was supposed to be its shape*, he thinks, *but I was only its shadow.*

Then he sees something—or thinks he does. The room dims, just slightly, and in the corner of his vision he can make out a figure.

Old robes. A staff. Zahavi.

The old man is not smiling. Not condemning. Just… present. A memory. Or a judgment. Or maybe just the doctrine, remembering itself as it lets him go.

Amal lowers his head. And for the first time since childhood, he prays.

Gerasa Vault – Moments Later

Gideon steps forward, his sica gleaming as it catches the vault's dying light, then fading again like a blade that refuses to shine until the last possible moment.

The acolytes don't move. Not one of them raises a hand, or voice, or weapon. They stare at Gideon not with fear but with the resignation of those who have seen a storm pass and know what comes after.

Cleansing. And ruin.

Amal remains kneeling at the spiral's center, his hands open in his lap, palms upward, not in surrender but in surrender's afterthought. He does not flinch as Gideon draws near.

"I expected you sooner," Amal says.

Gideon doesn't answer.

Amal speaks again. "So… has the spiral decided to finish what it started?"

Still nothing.

Gideon walks slowly, deliberately. Every footstep passes through the dust of collapsed glyphs, the residue of ambition burned clean by truth. He stops two paces away from Amal and raises the blade.

Amal lifts his chin slightly, then exhales. "Will you end the doctrine?" he asks.

Gideon's voice is soft. "No. It ended itself."

The silence afterward feels heavier than any blow. Gideon lowers the sica, and instead of striking, he kneels before Amal—not submissive nor humble, just precise. He cuts through the shoulder seams of Amal's robe with two swift motions. Not to wound but to *strip*. The spiral-marked garment falls away like a skin sloughing from a dying name.

The followers gasp—but Amal remains still.

"You wanted the glyph to choose you," Gideon says. "It didn't." He stands and sheathes his blade. "Let the doctrine deny you a final line."

Amal says nothing.

Gideon turns his back on the man and walks out of the circle, boots scuffing ash and blood and remnants of recursion.

At the door, he stops once—just once—and glances up at the sky. The stars are returning. Even the spiral can't outshine them forever.

Wadi al-Hasa –
Spiral basin, just before dawn

Greg wakes to silence. Not absence, but presence—like the air has settled after holding its breath too long. The recursion basin is quiet now, the echo field subdued to the faint shimmer of dissolved glyphs hanging like mist just above the sand.

He is lying on his side, half-buried in fine ash, Charlotte's hands cradling the back of his head. Her expression is rigid. Focused. Scared, but not for herself. For him.

"You're awake," she tells him. Her voice breaks the stillness like glass against stone.

Greg doesn't speak. His first breath tastes like dust, copper, and something older—like forgetting. He tries to rise, but Charlotte steadies him.

Jeremy hovers nearby, holding a scan panel that glows amber. "He's… he's not echoing," Jeremy mutters.

"What do you mean?" Charlotte asks, confused.

"I mean his recursion trace is gone. Wiped. Flatline across all known glyph protocols."

Greg coughs once, then smiles. "It's not gone. It's just… unrepeatable."

Charlotte stares at her son. "You burned the doctrine, didn't you?"

"No." He opens his hand. Nothing is there. But the glow from the glyph storm remains faintly woven into his skin like sunlight just beneath the surface. "I didn't destroy it. I let it remember itself."

Jeremy scrolls through the final scan. "This isn't Zahavi's pattern. And it's not Amal's. It's not even part of Eve's original recursive web."

"Of course not," Greg says. "It's mine. But not for anyone else." He looks out across the desert where the spiral storm once churned. "This isn't about doctrine anymore. It never was."

"Then what was it about?" Charlotte asks.

"A memory. And now that it remembers itself… we don't need to."

They sit together in the silence.

The spiral doesn't speak. It doesn't need to.

Petra Hollow – Outer Council Chamber, Morning light cutting through the eastern cleft

Naftali Ravin places the scroll seal on the table. It doesn't glow anymore. No echo. No hum. No glyph resonance. The spiral that once lit the entire Petra lattice from below now lays dormant—not broken, simply… complete.

Across from him, Chazan Neriel watches in silence. Her robe is newly stitched, its collar no longer bearing the old Sicarii sigil, just a blank spiral, hand-inked with faded dye. A choice.

A gesture.

The other three remaining faction elders stand in subdued postures. They've all returned voluntarily. Not for power but for closure.

"We don't need a doctrine anymore," Naftali says.

No one argues.

Chazan replies first. "But, what do we become, then?"

Naftali lifts the seal, sets it aside, carefully, reverently. "Not keepers. Just rememberers."

A vote is called. It is unanimous. The spiral lattice is dissolved. The Petra vault will remain sealed—not erased, not hidden. Just silenced—for any who wish to remember—but not to rule.

As the others file out, Naftali remains seated. He unfolds a fresh parchment and dips his pen into Zahavi's old ink well. He writes slowly. Deliberately.

> Greg—
>
> You were not the fire.
>
> You were the ashes.
>
> And even that was enough.
>
> —N

He seals the letter and hands it to a courier trained in recursion-muted delivery. No return address. Just the word: Wadi.

Between Petra and the Wadi – Dusk, no coordinates given

The sica is lighter now. Not because Gideon's arm is tired, or because he's grown stronger. The sica is lighter because it no longer carries doctrine. It carries memory.

He walks a nameless ravine between red cliffs and a dry riverbed, the sun pulling long shadows behind him. His Sicarii robes are gone, left folded and burned at the convergence vault hours ago. His comms rig is disassembled. The glyph tracer is fractured in his pocket, the last signal he received still etched faintly into the screen. A message from Charlotte:

> He survived.
> You were right.
> You still are.

He doesn't reply. But he reads the words twice before pocketing the broken slate.

There are no roads ahead. No marked trail. Just wind, rock, and time. And for once, no one watching him walk away.

He stops at the edge of a crevice cut by old seismic flow, then kneels and unwraps the blade. It has served thirteen years of silence. Two coups. Four betrayals. Five rescues. One brother. He places it on the stone, bare.

"There's no one left to subtract," he says.

He looks to the sky.

No spiral. Just stars.

And maybe that's enough.

He turns without it. Walks east. Not fast, not slow.

Just forward.

And as the wind picks up behind him, the sica shifts in the dirt.

The curve catches starlight—

Then vanishes beneath a gust of sand.

CHAPTER 57

Unmarked hillside village, somewhere between salt and sky

The walls go up slowly, stone by stone. They're not aligned to any ancient geometry. There are no glyphs etched into the corners, no sigils in the mortar, no foundation scan to trace the orientation to stars or spiral coordinates. Just shadow and sun and sweat.

Greg lays the final corner stone with both hands and steps back to admire the shape.

"It's crooked," Charlotte says from the doorway, arms folded, a smudge of clay across one cheek.

Greg shrugs. "So were we."

The house is small—two rooms, a low roof, and a narrow garden just beginning to take root along the back wall. A single olive tree leans sideways from years of highland wind.

The house doesn't need to last forever. Just long enough.

Charlotte steps through the threshold and sets down the water pail. "I don't miss the signals."

"I miss some of the people," Greg confesses.

Charlotte nods. "But not the doctrine."

Greg doesn't reply, but the smile in his eyes is answer enough.

Outside, Jeremy's voice rises faintly over the hill behind them. He's teaching three local children how to plot the night sky using triangulation and a cracked sextant. No projection holos, no recursion charts. Just stars.

The children laugh when he gets their names wrong.

Charlotte moves to the small table near the window that Greg built from scavenged cedar and stones too warped to stack.

She opens a weatherworn letter. The parchment is Zahavi's—distinct by the way it crumbles at the edge, heavy and handmade. The ink is newer. It reads:

You kept the doctrine alive by letting it die.
And in its silence, we remembered ourselves.
Petra has gone quiet. No more lattice. Just echoes.
May they be soft ones.

—N

Charlotte folds the letter gently, places it into a tin box, and sets it beneath a drawer where the light won't reach.

Outside, Greg wipes dust from his hands, then sits on the stone step. The house behind him is plain. The land before him is open. And the spiral, wherever it is, says nothing.

But the silence is full.

Stone path above the village – Late morning

Greg walks the ridge alone. He carries nothing—no bag, no blade, no datapad. Only the old robe slung over his shoulder, sun-faded and fraying at the edges, and a quiet stillness in his chest that used to ache with recursion pressure.

The spiral is gone. Not erased, not destroyed. Just… no longer listening. And that's enough.

The field below him blooms with drybrush and the first shoots of spring fig. He crouches near the base of a pale-leafed tree and presses his hand to the soil. There's a faint warmth there. Not recursive, just alive.

He pulls something from his sleeve—a thin shard of carbon-patinated glass. Zahavi's glyph fragment. The one he didn't burn. He lays it gently into the roots. Not like an offering. More like a fossil being returned.

He hears a sound behind him—footsteps.

Greg doesn't turn. He knows it's not Charlotte or Jeremy. The pace is lighter. Curious.

A girl—ten, maybe eleven—stops beside him. A child from the village. She watches him in silence. Then gestures to the tree. "What was that?"

Greg looks up and studies her face. "Something old."

She nods, thoughtful. Then asks, "Were you the one who ended the wars?"

Greg's mouth twitches into something not quite a smile. "No. I was just the one who listened when it ended itself."

The girl points again. "Was it magic?"

Greg glances at the tree. "No, just memory."

She doesn't understand. Not fully. But she nods anyway and sits beside him. They stay like that for a while, watching the wind move through a tree that doesn't care whether it grew from doctrine or dust.

Only that it grows.

Stone house interior – Nightfall

The wind shifts softly through the open doorway, stirring dust across the floor. The stone walls, warmed by years of sun, now hold only the chill of absence. Shadows stretch long from the empty chairs, and the fire, long since dead, leaves only the scent of ash.

A girl, no older than ten, steps hesitantly over the threshold. Her feet make no sound on the worn stones. She carries nothing but a pouch at her side and curiosity in her eyes. She pauses, sensing something—not presence, but memory. The kind of memory that clings to the air.

Her gaze settles on the table, where a journal lies half-closed. The leather cover is cracked, the binding loose. She reaches out, fingers brushing its surface, then lifts it gently.

The pages inside are yellowed, the ink faded but still legible. She reads the handwritten words slowly.

> *We were echoes of something older, all of us. Greg most of all. He bore the spiral in his blood, but he chose not to follow it. Not in the end.*

Her lips move silently as she continues, her eyes narrowing.

> *There was a name he almost spoke once. Twice, really. 'Ahvn—' That's as far as he got. We never asked him to finish it. We never needed to. Some names belong to silence. Some truths are stronger when left unwritten.*

The girl's fingers linger on that last line. She whispers the fragment: "Ahvn…" But nothing more comes. She does not try again, instead reading more of what Charlotte had written.

He didn't finish the spiral. He chose to walk beyond it. If you're reading this, know that echoes fade—but the choice not to speak? That's eternal.

The girl closes the journal softly and places it back on the table exactly where she found it. She walks slowly to the doorway, pausing once more to look back. The house is empty, but not hollow.

Outside, the wind rises, carrying olive leaves across the threshold, scattering them like small, forgotten glyphs. She steps into the twilight, her shadow stretching behind her, long and quiet.

About the Author

GARY LINDBERG has spent his entire adult life as a screenwriter, movie director and producer, author of fiction and nonfiction, and book publisher. He is the author of four AMAZON #1 BESTSELLING novels, three books about the unknown history of Elvis Presley and several other nonfiction titles. He cowrote and co-produced the PARAMOUNT PICTURE *That Was Then, This Is Now* starring Morgan Freeman and Emilio Estevez and has won over 100 national and international awards. Currently, he resides in the Minneapolis area.

Charlotte Ansari Thrillers

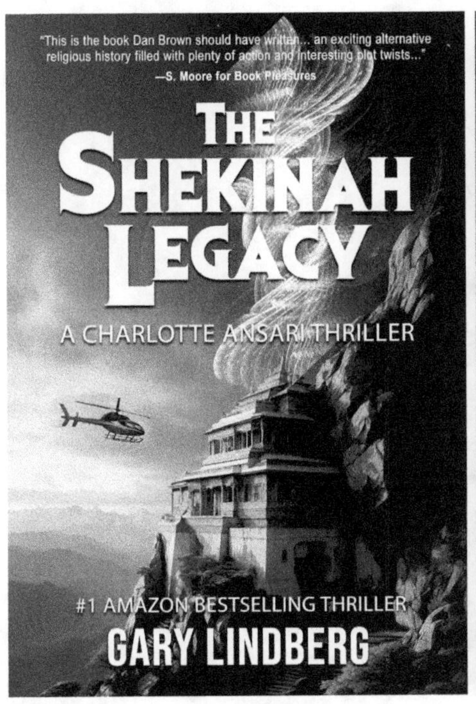

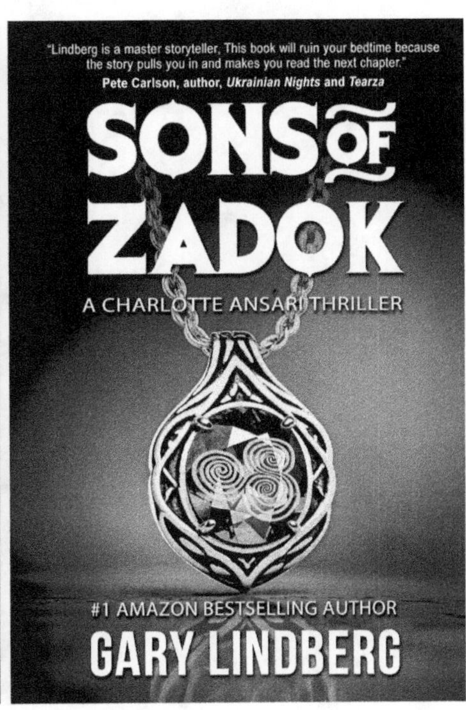

Book 1

International cable TV journalist Charlotte Ansari and her Asperger's son are caught literally in the crossfire of history when terrorists, the CIA, Mossad and the Vatican all converge in a pulse-pounding search for two relics that could eviscerate Christianity and forever change the balance of world power.

Book 2

Charlotte Ansari has a problem. Her investigation into a clandestine society of assassins has made them very angry. And that's not the most frightening part. Her Asperger's son, who is now the leader of this global, murder-for-hire organization, has assigned its top-ranked assassin to take care of the problem.

www.ingramcontent.com/pod-product-compliance
Lightning Source LLC
Chambersburg PA
CBHW051330020726
47501CB00007B/2007